THE SAXON TAPESTRY

From the library of

Mary Ann Reece Feb '92

THE
SAXON
TAPESTRY

SILE RICE

Arcade Publishing • *New York*

Little, Brown and Company

For Alfred Lynch

First U.S. Edition 1992

This is a work of fiction. Many of the
events and figures in the book are drawn
from historical research, but they have been
fictionalized for the purposes of the novel.

First published in Great Britain by Hodder & Stoughton Limited

Library of Congress Cataloging-in-Publication Data
Rice, Sile.
    The Saxon tapestry / Sile Rice. — 1st U.S. ed.
        p.   cm.
    "First published in Great Britain by Hodder & Stoughton, Ltd." —
T.p. verso.
    ISBN 1-55970-158-7
    1. Hereward, fl. 1071 — Fiction. 2. Great Britain — History —
William I, 1066–1087 — Fiction. 3. Great Britain — History — Edward,
the Confessor, 1042–1066 — Fiction. I. Title.
PR6068.I226S29 1992
823'.914 — dc20   91-16617

Published in the United States by Arcade Publishing, Inc., New
York, a Little, Brown company

10 9 8 7 6 5 4 3 2 1

MV NY

Printed in the United States of America

I sing a true song!

House of King Edward (The Confessor)

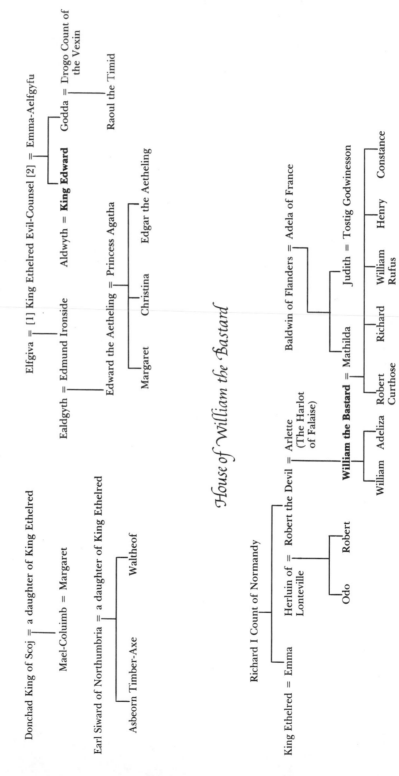

Elfgiva = [1] King Ethelred Evil-Counsel [2] = Emma-Aelfgyfu

Aldwyth = **King Edward**

Godda = Drogo Count of the Vexin

Raoul the Timid

Ealdgyth = Edmund Ironside

Edward the Aetheling = Princess Agatha

Margaret   Christina   Edgar the Aetheling

Donchad King of Scoj = a daughter of King Ethelred

Mael-Coluimb = Margaret

Earl Siward of Northumbria = a daughter of King Ethelred

Asbeorn Timber-Axe   Waltheof

House of William the Bastard

Baldwin of Flanders = Adela of France

William the Bastard = Mathilda

Robert Curthose   Richard   William Rufus   Henry   Constance

Judith = Tostig Godwinesson

Richard I Count of Normandy

Herluin of Lonteville = Robert the Devil = Arlette (The Harlot of Falaise)

Odo   Robert

William   Adeliza

King Ethelred = Emma

House of Leofric

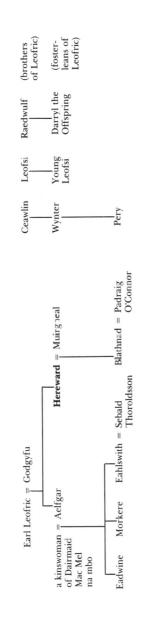

House of Godwine

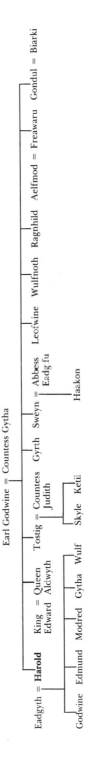

My narrative is a work of many threads,
liberal with jewels. The shuttle ever
moving, giving voice. Listen, O listen
to the word-play of the loom. Hearken
to the syllables of birds...

The Crying of the Waters

Swan Mere was once the Place of Gulls.

A thousand years ago they came, those birds, a motley, tatter-coated, clamant; goose and plover, mallard and blue hawk, filling the walls of heaven with their wet, creaking, whimpering wings, like thunder in the dawn. Following the salt-trails from the stormy Wash and the wide, drowned waters of Cowbit and Earith.

And in the morning times, early, when the moorhens wandered, the lonesomeness and the ancientness of it all would have been yours to feel. Through the love-song of the bittern and the curlew's lament you would have heard the wind in the tall reed-ronds and the rank wilderness of cut-throat sedge, and the tossing white showers of meadowsweet, rippling the slad all lashy. The wind would keen far, far out upon the brown face of the glittering floods. And it was the saddest sound. It never gave over its blowing, not for a day nor for an hour. It never let you be. And while it blew there was always unquiet in the air and a troubling of the waters, yet withal a peace, older, deeper, that was not the peace of God.

When England belonged to the Saxons, Swan Mere, mist begirt and vast against a vaster sky, was part of the lands of Earl Leofric. At the Hall of Little-Bethlehem-of-the-Rushes that stood at the end of the world, east of the sun and west of the moon, where the Earl dwelt with his household, the birds would have flocked in their multitudes, dipping and rolling as they swept in across Heart-Break Fen by way of Powt Hole and Whaplode Fleet.

And so, chance-time, was Hereward wont to see them when he came back from fishing with Wynter, son of Ceawlin, and Darryl the Offspring and Young Leofsi at his side, carrying the grigs and shouldering their shiny glaives. The Middle Hidage of Old England this was, where the tribes of the Gyrwe and the Wigesta and the

9

Wideringas forged the shire of Mercia. Call it what you will. But folk in those parts called it Leofric Country then.

Hereward's father was Earl at that time and had much to his lordship. The kingdom of Lindsey and the walled city of Chester were his. The five burghs of the Danelagh and the Holy Isle of Ely. And some say the Forests of Charnwood and Rockingham and Sherwood. Many fisheries and mills had he also, as well as basket-weirs and hackle-weirs, the fowling-places and the hunting-grounds thereof, and the swine pastures and the host of cornfields where the cow-mumble and the love-lies-bleeding and the gold-of-pleasure abounded and the wind whickered in fairy-knots and hen's-nosefuls among the sheafs at the boon-work.

These he had held through the reigns of four kings and they had been held by his father before him as ealdorman under the rule of Ethelred Evil-Counsel or the Unraed. There had been Leofrics there ever since there was anybody, descended of the royal blood of the Tomsaetan, the Bracelet-Chiefs of the Dove. And the Hall of Little-Bethlehem-of-the-Rushes was ancient too, built of timber – crucks of it cut from the primeval Brunnesweald and talking black bog-oak dug up from the lost forests sunk deep under the Fen – with god-nails in the pillars by the high-seat, carved all over poppies, older even than time when Hereward was a lad.

Outside the hall yard there was a hedge woven of whitethorn and a hurdle-gate. And past the haysel shed and the byres and the priest cottage lay the fen meadows and Mere Witch-Water, and beyond it all, the marshes.

But it was on Witch-Water, hazy with purple willow and circled thrice by tall, rosy-pink flowering rushes as in a charm, that everything always seemed much louder, as if breaking in upon it from another world. The hollow echo of the bells of Croyland Abbey – home of the sacred ravens and swallows of St Guthlac – over by the Welland Stream, rang out across the flat with a music liken to no other bells in England. And even your own voice, no matter how softly you spoke, would go big-sounded as a shout in the great, abiding quiet.

Aye, there was something to be felt at Little-Bethlehem-of-the-Rushes. Mostly it was in the evenings after cock-shut when the skerries used to knock against the old causeway that crossed Witch-Water sounding as footsteps and the Tiddy Ones chaffered in cowslip tongues. When the lych-fowl churred and the frogs croaked and the fish broke water to jump out on the mere. And with no one going there hardly ever save for the few lads that were friends to Hereward and perhaps a wandering minstrel once a year, the loneliness would settle like the elves' cap-of-darkness about the place and it made for dreaming then.

And indeed, you might have thought it was all a dream, for you could never see anything clear out there. Chance-time, you might see the heavens, all three of them, stretching one beyond the other, fallen then and lying beneath the furthest deeps, and the bogland moon and clusters of stars would be in it too, floating among the glozed, fragrant lilies; and the reeds would be spears against it all, sliding thin and sharp, rustling in the wind of night. And out on the marsh a flight of ducks would go across the red of the setting sun.

Here Begins the Saxon Tapestry

The Changeling

ereward was born in the first year of King Harold Hare-Foot's reign. He was the second son of the mighty Earl Leofric and the roomy-hearted Countess Godgyfu. And as they were troubled times a strong name which spoke of both ancestor glory and peace was bestowed upon him, a name which meant Guardian of the Army.

But it was ill-fortune that gave him birth in the Witching-Month of May with eyes that were different colours – one blue, the other grey – and a mark on his face, a puckered-up scar it was, the length of Old Skrat's claw. And quick to grow among the hut dwellers and fen-slodgers were the tales that he was cursed in the sight of God. Bogle-shotten. His soul elf-kept. They would shake their heads and mutter of dark things and there was not one of them who would not rather have walked ten miles out of their way in any direction save Widdershins, than cross his path.

Times, combing his thick hair, rejoicing in its likeness to shorn wheat, Countess Godgyfu would say, 'How broad you are for a nine-years boy!' But other times, when she vainly tried to rid his face of the mark, 'O, the cruelty of it! The wrong! Why, you are not my son! You are the one the Nixies left!'

Though used to that cry, cutting a stick or watching the coots mate, Hereward could not but sorrow over it. Yet he had his voices. Not just those of his birds in their little wooden cages, lost or lame, found blown from their nests or with wings and legs broken by snares on the marsh, which he tended and fed. Kept a sick otter and her kittens up there in a wicker ped, he had, that previous winter, and could whistle like them. And an injured whooper swan. All in the small poke of a place that he called his cot beneath the brown sedge thatch. These were voices of a different sort. Voices that whispered through the slats; in the knot-holes of the wall and between frame and shutter.

15

'What do they say, bor?' Young Leofsi would ask, the book bound by bluebell slime open on his crunched up knees, the soft rush candle burning. And though each small thing that happened at Little-Bethlehem-of-the-Rushes was written down – Young Leofsi being the only one at the time who could script properly, decorating his letters with twisted vines and animal heads no bigger than a thumbnail and painted with the pinks and purples from the fruit and flowers of the turnsole plant – as can be imagined it would take a great many years to fill.

'It isn't words. Just sounds,' said Hereward.

'Like Byggvir the Ear-Chatterer?' whispered Young Leofsi.

'Or goblin noises?' And he shivered.

'Nay,' said Hereward softly, ''tis like the wind amongst the paigles . . .'

The Kindred Tree

The folk of Leofric, though hardy, were never abundant. Sparsely they flourished, their generations notched on a hazel wand, their roots deep in the black, peat earth, their moods and wants and longings governed by the wax and wane of the giant yellow moon.

Earl Leofric was the eldest of four brothers. His sons begotten were two. His brothers had a son each, three in all, and they became in turn Leofric's foster-leans. The Welsh wars had carried off Ceawlin, Wynter's father, at the battle of Rhyd y Groes, while the father of Young Leofsi had died on a pilgrimage to the Holy Land. But it was the father of Darryl the Offspring who had been put to the horn long ago for his wicked ways, outlawed, that is, and whither he'd gone or if he were dead in his sins nobody knew.

The Earl had his foster-leans to Little-Bethlehem-of-the-Rushes often, lodging them there, though their homes lay far flung at Wyntering and Cherry Hurn and Keale-Haven, and he would continue to succour them until they came of an age to inherit their own hide of land. Land was precious – bequeathed and will-given. Land was loved, even so inhospitable and grey-sad a place as the marshes. Times, the King had urged Leofric to leave them and to stay at the court of the Palace of Westminster, and Countess Godgyfu would lief have gone. But the Earl would not. Not even the King could make him budge. 'I'll be laid in my grave first,' he'd said, deep and low like he always spoke. Stubborn men ever they were, the men of Leofric.

So news from the Uplands, which is what fen folk call the rest of England, was slow and scarce, and they relied upon the seasons and holy days to chapter their lives. Like the bells of Croyland Abbey ringing on the church feasts such as Christmas when the cake was baked in honour of the Three Wise Men and at Passion-Tide and All

17

Souls and the Exaltation of the Holy Rood. And it was on such a holy time, the Long Friday or Good Friday in the year after King Edward was crowned at Winchester, that Hereward's older brother Aelfgar was outlawed.

As was the custom then the altars of all churches had been washed and draped in black and the bells tolled in mourning for Christ's death. Hereward and Wynter and Darryl and Young Leofsi should by rights have been at church-school since Matins, but instead they had spent the morning dyeing and painting the eggs for egg rolling on Pasch Monday. Then they had gleaned for fairy loaf shells and for pearls which abounded in the muddy reaches. It took hours of searching and discarding and cleaning in the pools to get but a few; competed for, coveted and hoarded. And what to do with them? Why, the very chapel was pearl-encrusted both inside and out, wondrous to behold, from the oak shingle roof to the ground. And the altar itself was carved of lumps of solid shell, hard as rocks. In those parts many were the pouches and purses, knife-sheaths and comb-boxes worked in a pigeon's neck of coloured pearls. And there were always the shells to listen to with their murmur of sea and old sorrows.

'A knob for yours!' said Young Leofsi, propped on his elbows in the goose-grass, blue eyes dreaming.

And Wynter, picking up a pearl of rare violet hue between thumb and forefinger, said, 'Nay, this is for my thane-right. Choose how.' Fair and open-faced and solitary was Wynter, never in a hurry to be heard nor slow to do a kindness.

'You've got to have a kitchen and a bell-house and a helmet and a coat of mail also,' said Darryl, lying on his back amid the goblin's-gloves and fairy-cheese, idly swatting midges. Dark curls he had that hung to his shoulders and lashes that swept his cheekbones. His eyes were light, not really blue nor yet really green. He was wearing a posy of violets in his jerkin, then, and his eyes were of that colour, changeable with flecks of amber in them. Goodly to gaze at, or at least so thought Hereward, more than usually conscious of his own lacking. Head kept down, a habit with him, that gave him a secretive, closed-in-unto-himself look, he made festoon beads with his pearls. Strings of them. Good with his hands, threading them holed on twine, he wove solidly, skilful at plaiting and knotting in the old Norse way.

Thus the sky candle was dim, nearing Vespers, when horsemen were to be seen crossing the causeway from the direction of Bourne-by-Holy-Brook and through Strawberry Wood. Hereward recognised his father on his steed Hrimfaxi to be foremost among them with Aelfgar

18

at his side. They both had their hearth-troops with them, following behind, and had ridden the long journey thence from the Folk-Moot in London Town.

Lord of the Kindred Tree

tuffing the pearls in their scrips, the boys hastened up.

'Got something for us?'

'What tidings?'

'O, give us a ride!'

But reining his horse, the Earl cut them short. 'Has school finished early that ye should be here? And you,' he said to Hereward, 'you look as if you've been dragged t'ru a brush faggot!'

In his cloak of ram fleece fastened with huge ouches of gold and deep red garnets, Leofric looked the man he was. His features were gradely, dourly handsome. It was in the set of his head, the generous, masterful mouth, the strong dark brows over wide-spaced, clear grey eyes. Jutish grey. Broad Saxon cheekbones, skin Saxon fair. And many was the sprig of parsley – the male herb of virility – he had been given to wear in his belt.

Hereward answered him, 'We have been preparing for the Lord's Day.' And he wiped his hands on his jerkin.

'No shywanicking?'

'Nay, father.'

The Earl looked round on them, all four of them, and said, 'At Mass you begged pardon for your many failings?'

'Humbly.' Darryl it was who spoke up sweetly on an ousel note. No ha-and-hacker with him.

'And what of the Rood?'

'We crept to it and kissed it,' chanted they together.

Ordinarily the Earl was quick to see it. Often he'd already met with Ywar the Churchwarden of Peterborough sent by Prior Brand to discover the whereabouts of the reluctant pupils. The taking of dog's-leave brought chastisement, the threat of the bamming stick. But he only said, 'Well, you mind you have.'

All seemed in a solemn mood. Aelfgar, though fine in a double mantle of blue wool lined with yellow silk, was chary of words. Likewise the hearth-troops, those fearless hus-carls, always ones to roister and chaff, sat their mounts glum-faced.

Puzzling, Hereward said, 'May we wend along of you, father?'

'You may not. You'll bide here till I say so.'

'Just to the gate.'

'Give over pestering and do as I tell thee. You're to stay put, understand?' The Earl did not speak loudly. No man could recollect ever having heard him shout. He didn't have to. Meaning weighted the words he uttered like August-ripe apples on a bough. 'And wash your clogs. There's mud on 'em.'

Thus did the horses pass by, hooves clopping and harness clinking, and Darryl let out a low whistle. 'I'm flummoxed,' said he to no one in particular.

Then they washed their clogs for indeed they were muddy.

'It will be dark in above a quarter hour,' said Wynter. Hereward looked up at the Paschal moon risen over the mere. 'We will go back – see what's for supper.'

Just then a white rabbit hopped across the grass, and white rabbits being witch-souls as all folk know, Young Leofsi crossed himself. 'But bor,' said he, 'what of your father? He said we were not to.'

'We can but look in at the door, can we not?'

'Not empty handed!'

So they plucked daffodils enough that each had an armful of nodding gold.

'Now make haste!' said Hereward.

'Why?' said Darryl, eyes a-dance like mayflies.

'Something after us?'

'Ah! All the dead men out the bogs!'

Place of the Kindred Tree

When they reached the house within it was low and dim, cavernous as the Hall of Utgard-Loki, where the elves rode the sunbeams through the keyholes, the gnarled, knotted, crabbed, crooked walls, tapestry-clad, glowed all of the shades of alkanet and nettles, woad and ragwort. Its floor was strewn with a burthen of sweet grass and the immense cross-roof beams, wherein deep lived the home-sprites, were decked with shields. The trestle table was set for the meal: platters of herrings and eel pies, hazel bread made with young milky nuts and flower butter and beastings pudding and wassail-bowls of mead and apple-wine. Amidst tallow candles the first forget-me-nots trailed from a jug, minding of a child's blue eye in the dusk.

The hus-carls stood ranged in a half circle, Earl Leofric's and Aelfgar's both. Among the Earl's troop were men who had fought alongside him at Ashingdon and later during the Welsh wars and whose fathers had served the old ealdorman, Leofric's father, in the days before the coming of the Danes. Their Marshal was Rudgang Wolf-Cloak, a stern-faced warrior, proud in his scars, with long moustaches and a torque of gold about his neck.

Countess Godgyfu sat by the hearth where the peat fire burned, for once unaccompanied by her bower-maidens. A small, slender, blossom-bosomed woman like one of the Norns, she wore two tunics over her kirtle, the second more richly embroidered than the first, a rhyme of snapdragon colours and pinned with gilt brooches. Keys, silver spoons and a ball of rock-crystal hung from her girdle. Of her blonde tresses only a glimpse was shown, covered withal by a head-rail of fine linen. She looked fragile but she wasn't. Queen of the Fens, they called her, and the lands and counsel-power she held and the respect she commanded were equal to no other save than to Godwine's Gytha, Countess of the West Saxons.

22

Nearby the two chaplains of the household were in attendance, staff-bearing Sigeferth, a stout, white haired old man, house-father since Leofric's boyhood, and Lilla the underchaplain, foster-son to the Earl.

Earl Leofric, having shed his cloak, was standing before the window paned of emerald glass that looked out over Witch-Water. Then he broke his word-hoard. 'Judgement has been given by the Moot so it will do no good to rake over cold ashes. Ah, but I'm thinking that you could have had no more sense than a May gosling, lad. To let yourself be goaded by the Wessex men!'

Aelfgar had answered a charge of unlawful slaying and been found guilty. The dead man – a captain in Bjorn Estrithsson's troop – had been killed during a quarrel at the King's hunting lodge in Sweet-Fern-Oak Forest. Bjorn Estrithsson was nephew to Earl Godwine and thus old rivalries and grudges had been stirred afresh.

But Aelfgar was unrepentant. He swore by all the saints of Ely and smote the sword on his thigh. He was strong-docked, as was the Earl, though the taller and more lissom of the two. 'And be thought a Nithing? What I did I'd do again – aye, and be damned! Bjorn Estrithsson! Why, he doesn't even have an earldom as yet though he be the King's fair-weather favourite!'

Countess Godgyfu said, 'But will the man's kinfolk not settle for his price?' She appealed to Leofric. The complexion of an autumn crocus was hers. 'You could pay enough for a King's wergeld.' She had a soft speech, like grass growing.

'They'd lief have revenge, lass,' the Earl answered her. 'A blood feud.'

'So he is to go? To bear the Wolf's-Head? An outlaw?' Still very soft she spoke. Sharp ears were needed to hear her then. 'Leofric, he is our son!'

Hereward called from the doorway, 'Man! O, man! They cannot do such!'

Aelfgar turned and so did the Earl. Hereward cast down his daffodils and ran to Aelfgar, catching hold of the great gold buckle of his belt. 'Tell us it isn't true!'

The other boys crowded the step, and Darryl, his arms full of daffodils, making his skin the colour of day-old cream, said, 'My father was a Wolf's-Head and never came home.'

Earl Leofric stood watching them, his eyes upon Hereward especially. Then he called him by name. Everything went quiet; even the lazy bird-caws ceased in the thatch. Hereward turned.

23

The Earl said, 'You disobeyed me.'

'I wanted to see what was happening, father.'

If Hereward had expected anger it was not forthcoming. Earl Leofric sounded very tired as he said, 'So now you know.'

Tears spilled onto Hereward's cheek. 'Father,' he whispered, 'O, father, do not let them send him away.'

'Do you think I want it so, lad?'

'But you could stop them. You are the Hidage Chief.'

'That isn't such a grand thing, Hereward.'

Hereward looked up at Earl Leofric. Around his neck he wore the chain of the Folk-Founder and a crucifix. On his forefinger the Ring of Oaths. 'But they would listen to you.'

Earl Leofric shook his head. There was much grey in the dark mane of his hair. 'You do not understand, child,' he said.

Despair welled up in Hereward's soul. He saw Sigeferth counting his prayer-beads, wood opals as big as almond nuts, drawing them forth with trembling fingers.

Only Lilla gave comfort. An arm about Hereward's shoulders, he whispered, 'Be still, lad. God abides.'

Aelfgar made ready to take his leave. Countess Godgyfu clung to him and covered his face with kisses, like at the parting of lovers.

'Whither goest?'

'Baile Atha Cliath. Dairmaid's court.'

He bade farewell then to Sigeferth and to Lilla, his boon-companion of early days. There was much sorrowing among the house-folk, for Aelfgar, no matter what his wrongdoings, was dear to them all. Lastly he went to Earl Leofric, holding out both hands. 'I have been a poor son to ye,' he said.

Whereat Leofric took his hands in his own and, robbed of words, pulled him close and fell upon his neck.

Said Aelfgar to him softly, ''Tis said even Iscariot was child to someone.'

And in a moment he had passed from the hall with his troop. Hereward would have run to follow him had not the Earl bidden him nay. The door was closed clang-shut on its iron hinges and the candles lit. When grace had been said the young kinsmen of Leofric took their places at the trestle in silence, Hereward's being close to his father's platter. The hus-carls filled the long benches, and the wassail-bowls of glass with gouts of amber and blue and green marvellously blown in the sides like tears were given from hand to hand.

Countess Godgyfu sat next to Earl Leofric on the richly wrought

24

box settle that was the high-seat, accepting the fish that he boned for her and the bread he cut so carefully with his knife, sharing his own great jewelled cup. But every now and then she would glance up, hearkening to the preparations being made in the yard. The tramp of the stable-keeper, a snatch of song, the jingle of horse-brass. And yonder the calling of the birds coming home to roost out on the marsh. The hollow 'Broomp – roomp' of the bittern down on Witch-Water.

Once, Earl Leofric said to Hereward, 'Why do you not eat, lad? 'Tis good bread and will make Our Lady cry to waste it.'

And it was so with Wynter and Darryl and Young Leofsi.

'What ails ye?'

They answered him not. But Hereward ventured, 'Can I leave the table, father?'

'Why for?'

'To be with Aelfgar.'

'Nay.'

'But father . . .'

Earl Leofric put aside his knife and said, 'Hereward, sit and be still. There's no changing things.' The Earl was never to know, leastways not for a long while after, just how much Hereward feared him, and when he did it was to sadden him greatly, weighing heavy upon his heart. But then, that day, he had lost one son and all he could see was that the other, a queer, foolish boy, shrank from him. Weary of his own thoughts and the silence, he said at length, 'You may talk if you want.'

No one did. Only Darryl whispered softly to Young Leofsi, 'I wonder if he means we can talk about cousin Aelfgar? My father left by night just like him. All unhouseled. But he was never spoken of any more.'

Farewell in the Witch-Hours

elfgar waited by the causeway with his hearth-troop till it was late. And it was there that Hereward and his kinsmen came upon them, stealing down through the fen fields.

Hereward clung to his brother for a long time. 'I shall miss ye sorely,' he whispered.

'And I shall miss you.'

'But you'll have your adventure.'

Aelfgar lifted Hereward's face. 'Adventure? Nay, lad. This is in deadly earnest. East Anglia, my earldom, is forfeit and the King has given the hidage of the Gewissae to Harold Godwinesson. My life is forfeit also for any man can cut me down and claim my geld.'

One of the hus-carls stroked the horn handled seax at his waist. 'No man touches you while we live,' and his look was hard upon Aelfgar.

The other men echoed, 'Aye. Aye . . .'

Aelfgar mounted his horse, but hardly was he in the saddle when there came a shout of his name and Lilla the under-chaplain hurried down towards them. He was breathless, his robe of coarse black burel sodden from running through the knee-high grass, his prayer-beads tangled with the chain of his bog-oak crucifix.

'I was afraid I had missed you!'

'Did father send you?'

'Nay. I come myself. In love.'

Lilla, the son of a freed theow, had been raised in the household of Earl Siward Digre of Northumbria for the first fifteen years of his life and had been as a brother to Siward's eldest son Asbeorn Timber-Axe. Thus it had befallen one winter time – the season of the Twelfth Night Fires – when Leofric had been visiting Siward, that he had taken a liking to Lilla, seeing a rare intelligence in the boy, and on his return to Little-Bethlehem-of-the-Rushes Lilla had travelled with him. He had left the north with great sadness on the understanding he was to be trained for the priesthood. Earl Leofric had always treated him like his own son, for he had once cherished hopes that Aelfgar would enter the church, a mass-priest for the altar of Ely, or follow in the footsteps of his great-uncle, Prior Brand of Peterborough, or Ulfketyl the Good, Abbot of Croyland. But as ever he was doomed to disappointment.

The night wind blew like a chorus of little bells. Aelfgar said, 'Have you something to preach to me, Lilla?'

'You know I've never preached to you.'

Aelfgar smiled. 'Aye,' he said, 'I know. That is why I've always liked ye. You do not act like a priest.'

'But I am a priest nevertheless,' Lilla answered him. 'And my duty is towards all men. Towards you, Aelfgar.' He came nearer, his hood back-thrown, taking hold of the bridle-ring. 'Have you been to confession?'

Against Lilla's jewel-blue eyes speaking up from the shadows, Aelfgar dropped his gaze. 'Nay.'

'But lad, if aught were to happen to you – you would be unshriven.'

'Nothing is going to happen to me, Lilla. I'll return to ye again.'

'I will light a candle this night and pray for thee.'

'For a sinner, Lilla?'

'For a friend.'

And thus it was with a sprig of wild ash, the holy tree, in his bridle given him by Young Leofsi and watched by Wynter and Darryl, that Aelfgar rode across the causeway at the head of his loyal band. The bells of Croyland were silent at last and the only sound was of hoofbeats on wood echoing as those upon Gjallarbru. And Hereward, his cheek mopped dry, waved until they were lost to sight in the dark.

The Buttercup Fields
of the Moon

Wynter and Darryl and Young Leofsi stayed the night at Little-Bethlehem-of-the-Rushes for the will o' the wisp had lit his corpse-candles and was dancing his deathly dance on the bogs. 'A little old hoppity man that came straight at me!' so one of the serving-folk would have it. To which Earl Leofric never said yea or nay but took care to put the great bar across the door himself on such nights.

Hereward led the other three up the steep-winding stairs beneath the eaves where the sparrows slept snug as mice – and the elves were wont to leave small bunches of flowers in times of sorrow – to his own place, his cot betwixt thatch and floor, where from the horn-paned window – no more than hand-broad – you could see all worlds. Like Odin's seat.

Below, Witch-Water was a sea fashioned of stars. Owls hung on silver strings. All manner of wonders were in the moon; at first look the Thickmost Shoe, perhaps even the stolen children, a field of buttercups all yellow.

Long Friday was finished so Darryl reached in his bag and brought out a pie in which was the meat of hens and pork with yolks of egg and breadcrumbs and pepper. He broke it up and they each had a lump.

'When we are men will we be your hus-carls?' said Young Leofsi.

'Nay,' Hereward answered him. 'It won't be the same for us. Aelfgar was brought up at the court. Trained to be King Harthacnut's cup-bearer. Father would like me to go into the church.' He spoke with deep sadness.

Darryl upturned his face in the moonlight. 'To be under the rod?'

Hereward nodded. Of late Lilla had been giving him extra lessons.

He could repeat the Rosary and sing the Benedicite and Magnificat and Paternoster thrice, and on Countess Godgyfu's insistence he wore the red spinel prayer-beads round his neck and was made to fast on Wednesdays and Fridays until the ninth hour.

'Bugger that,' said Wynter. 'I'd rather grow my apples.'

Early next morning, just past the hour of Matins and Lauds, they were summoned to the house-place and upon the table there was piled armour and weaponry. Earl Leofric, seeing their jaws drop, said, 'Aelfgar left his war-hoard in my keeping. He'd want you to have the pick of it.'

Coming forward, Hereward said, 'I did not know that Aelfgar had so much that was beautiful.' And he picked up a round shield by its iron handle, polished so brightly as to be a mirror. It glowed about the black bog-timber walls and its weight taxed his arm.

Watching them, Wynter and Darryl and Young Leofsi, crooning, marvelling, testing spear-tips and bow-strings, Earl Leofric said, 'Much of what you see was made by King Edward's own weapon-smith in London. That belt now, it has four pounds of silver upon it. Too heavy for you as yet.'

'But will Aelfgar not want them when he returns home, father?' said Hereward, seizing upon a sword, its hilt cunningly mounted in bronze.

The Earl replied, 'Nay. He'll no doubt bring back a Viking's haul from Baile Atha Cliath ere he returns.'

'How many years must he be an outlaw?'

'Eight years.'

'But that is so long a time.'

'Ah, I know.'

'Does the King truly love him no more, then? Is that why he allowed it to happen thus?'

'The King loves no man. Nay, not even Godwine's kinsman, and that lad will find it so to his sorrow.'

Thus it was with full arms that Wynter and Darryl and Young Leofsi bade farewell by the causeway that evening. Sitting on the old crooked stile Hereward watched them pole their skerries away across the mere and was conscious of an ache in his heart. He picked up a handful of stones and flung them at the willows, trying to knock down the hanging yellow goslins. A duck was arse-upwards among the frog-bit and lily-pads. Water-rail and mallards and little come-backs flitted like brown ghosts through the rushes.

*   *   *

29

'And what will you do with your weapons, lad?' Rudgang Wolf-Cloak the Marshal asked of Hereward. 'Will you fight frost giants and Hell-monsters?'

'There's no such thing,' said Hereward. 'Lilla says so.'

'Isn't there now? And I suppose you do not believe that the souls of the dead dwell in thyme bushes or that Odin's shuck prowls the fen banks of a May morning?'

Hereward looked up at Rudgang. He was a big, broad shouldered man, half-Norse by birth and his hirsute throat and arms were tattooed and he wore many bracelets and rings. 'Ah, I believe it,' Hereward whispered, 'but 'tis against the teachings. And my father – he doesn't hold with that sort of talk.'

And at that Rudgang had brushed a lock of hair from Hereward's forehead. 'Do not you be too sure about your father,' he said.

The Ballad of the Wounding-Wand

mong Aelfgar's war-gear was an age-bitten sword with a three-cornered wooden hilt much splintered. Bigger than the others, it had seen hard fighting for its blade, rune-cut and thick as a man's arm, was blunt and sadly in need of cleaning. Earl Leofric seemed to covet it highly, though why Hereward was at a loss to understand.

But one morning the Earl said, 'I would you'd take this sword to Aethelmaer the blacksmith over at Bambweare yonder. Find out from him how long it would be to mend.'

Hereward came back with the answer, 'Friday sennight.'

'Good. You'll fetch it when it's ready.'

And so when the sennight was up, Hereward took a skerrie and sailed forth to the forge at Bambweare. He liked going there and sharing the company of Aethelmaer the young smithy. Bambweare was a settlement partly built on poles on a large island of black peat and cuckoo-haunted grey sallow. Lying north to Ogre-Spring-Marsh and bounded by the meres Jewel-Water and Matlade-Flottons and Wash Ballock, it was near the site of an older village long since gone, but whose church bells were still to be heard ringing beneath the deeps, mingling with the whimbrel song and the wind.

Hereward always strained his ears as he neared the isle, though the only bells were those of the sheep and goat flocks grazing on the firm fen. And the forge would loom up from the early mist full of clang and thunder then. And 'How do!' or 'Morn!' or 'Watcher, bor!' would be Aethelmaer's greeting, and welcoming the smell of woodsmoke and leather and maybe a jugged hare or a chunk of sage and apple pudding.

'It's docky time. D'you fancy a dollop?'

Inside the forge it was dark as the World beneath the worlds. The roof, shingled with holy-stones, was supported by four huge traves of timber, each carved with the legend of the dragon's slaying. Leaning

31

on a plough-share with the tools of the smith's trade hanging from the beams overhead, Hereward watched Aethelmaer beat a spade-shoe into being with great strokes. He was rare-strong and his yard-span shoulders, beloved of the maids from Cowmouth to the Dibbin, streamed with sweat. As well as being weapon-smith to Earl Leofric, Aethelmaer was also the champion wrestler of the shire and had promised one day to share his skill with Hereward.

But then Hereward's mind was full only of the words that Aethelmaer, whose tongue was not easily loosed, used to describe the old sword: 'By'rlakin, bor, the One-Eyed himself would have been proud to own such. A wounding-wand! Like as not forged with powerful spells by the light elves! Ah! Pattern-welded. Rods of iron and steel twisted together and worked and hammered, then folded and hammered again. And quenched. It will never break, not even in the thick of battle. That is why your father prizes it, for 'tis the worth of a dozen others.'

'But it was so blunt, bor,' Hereward said. 'I reckon I could've ridden bare-arsed to Ely on it.'

At which Aethelmaer winked and grinned. 'Ah, well, you could carve a flea's eye with it now, see?'

Honed and polished it seemed to have coiling snakes in it and twigs and sheafs of corn. And the runes standing up as bold as the day they were wrought. Also the wooden hilt had been replaced with one of iron and set with a lump of magical amethyst stone.

Hereward was reluctant to go home and when he could put it off no longer, he dragged his feet and said, 'Would you teach me to be a blacksmith, Aethelmaer?'

'You, my dear?'

'I'd be willing.'

'I've no doubt.'

Aethelmaer was raking the glowing embers, work done for the day. By this time the birds were coming hither to roost in their many thousands, wheeling above the grass-grown humps of the settlement. The reed-ronds echoed to their sweet, searing, plaintive cries. Wings blotted out the maturing sun. And the chorus of the fen nightingales was to be heard from the banks of every mere. Aethelmaer came to stand in the doorway then, stooping beneath the shingle, shoulder against the jamb. He said, 'Your father no doubt has other plans for thee.'

'To be a chanter-boy. To be learned.'

'They do say as learning is a fine thing.'

Hereward laid the sword carefully in the back of the skerrie. He

32

cast off from the bank then. 'Ah, but I'd as lief be dead or face the Yeth-Hounds, so I would, Aethelmaer,' he said, 'than be mewed up in a church for the rest of my days.'

At the Hall of Little-Bethlehem-of-the-Rushes the candles were lit and the shutters stood open beneath the hanging thatch. Flittermice danced in moonbeams. Countess Godgyfu asked of Hereward, 'What kept you?'

'I was talking with Aethelmaer, mother.'

She'd eyes like great damp pansies. 'Your shirt is torn.'

''Tis no matter.'

Bidden, a bower-maid brought forth the Countess's sewing casket, and selecting a spool of thread Godgyfu stitched his shirt using a needle of fine bone.

'You are careless,' she said, breaking the thread with her teeth. 'Folk would mistake you for a henwife's brat!'

Hereward said, 'With my face as it is folk know who I am.'

The mark showed clear in the candle glow. Shotten from cheek to jaw. Countess Godgyfu laid her fingers across it as though to wipe it away. But it was useless as giving him silver-water to drink. Then she whispered, 'Go now, take the sword to your father.'

Earl Leofric was in his chamber and he looked up from the parchment on his table, laying aside his pen, when Hereward entered. 'You have missed Vespers.'

'I am sorry, father.'

The chamber was wedge-shaped and at the narrow end where the Earl sat the roof almost sloped to touch the floor. Two great hounds sprawled before the fire. In one corner stood a chest guarded with nine locks wherein was kept the Earl's own war-gear. An iron lamp burned steadily, its cake of beeswax beset with moths. The tapestries that hung there were of the soft yellows of apple and pear bark and the warm brown of walnut hulls.

Sitting back in his chair Earl Leofric held out his hands to receive the sword. 'Did you find it heavy to bear?'

'Nay.'

The Earl turned the sword over. In the lamplight a garden of tiny purple crystal flowers was in that chunk of amethyst. 'Aethelmaer's done a good job. 'Tis a joy to behold again.' Leofric gripped the hilt. He had much dark hair on the backs of his hands. ''Twas said that the kings of Strathclyde and Scotland knew this to their cost. And my great grandfather won his renown by King Aethelstan's side on the field of Brunanburgh. For I mind he told me of the story – Him an old

33

warrior done with battle – how when the day was ended this sword was so blood-covered that there was scarce an inch of iron to be seen.'

Hereward realised then the full wonder of the burden he had carried back and forth. 'Brunanburgh? And you gave it to Aelfgar?'

'Aye,' said the Earl, 'when he was a lad. See these runes? They are victory runes.' Wotan called Woden. Tiwaz – Tiw – Tig. Gods of war and of the sky. Leofric's thick, countryman's thumbnail traced the legend. Freyr – god of sunshine, rain and crops. Plenty-Giver – his gold-bristled boar ran rampant the full length of the blade.

'O, but why did not Aelfgar take it with him?'

'He had no need of it. It weighs mightily in the wearing. He chose the seax of the southern men in preference.'

'Aethelmaer said it would never fail in battle.'

'And in that he was right. It served my kinsman well.'

'What will you do with it, father?'

'I thought happen you would like it,' Earl Leofric said, 'though you are somewhat young.'

'I am strong, father.'

'Aye, you are that.'

Hereward came forward, his jerkin ungirt, his hair tangled upon his broadening shoulders. He did indeed look older than his years. Also he'd begun to spraddle his legs slightly as he walked and it pleased the earl that it was so. 'I would treasure it, father,' he said softly.

Earl Leofric held it out to him. 'Very well. Take it. It's yours.'

And it was with a reverence that Hereward grasped the sword by the hilt in both hands. 'I do not have to give it back – even to Aelfgar himself should he ask for it?'

Earl Leofric shook his head. 'But remember one thing. Never let it get the better of ye, lad. Always be its master.'

Hereward named the sword Brain-Biter and while he was not slow to show off before his admiring kinsmen, he was loath to let anyone handle it saving himself, though he found it hard to raise even shoulder-high and nigh on impossible to lift above his head.

'You'll grow soon enough!' said Rudgang Wolf-Cloak.

But it was on a day in summer that a waking dream came upon him without the sweet speech of his voices. Sitting on the bank he saw the lands of his fore-elders – those ancient star warriors of the Tomsaetan – belonging to him by name-right as they had always belonged to his heart. The rushes were blowing in threnody and he saw a man he knew to be himself. A man grown. Iron-hard. Gold-clad. But the bee-skeps were forsaken and the roof-trees snapped and everywhere was dark as when the wolf swallows the sun. And he knelt, that man he was to be, and dipped sword Brain-Biter in the mere, washing clots of blood from the blade.

The Weather of Rainbows

O f all the aforesaid happenings Hereward had Young Leofsi make a careful rendering in the book, save for the dream, which like the word-hoard of his voices, he told to no man. And thus the pages stood empty the while for it was full summer and the Mead-Month and there was no writing done. Then to Little-Bethlehem-of-the-Rushes came a minstrel, Hwita Clatter-Clogs, carrying tidings.

Earl Leofric had been in London with his hus-carls holding the town loyal for King Edward while the fleet lay at Sandwich under the command of Earl Godwine and his sons Earl Sweyn and Earl Harold, awaiting attack from the forces of Magnus of Norway, brother to the Battle-Master Harald Sigurdsson, the Haardrada.

'He is safe? He is well?' Countess Godgyfu begged news of Leofric.

'No man ever looked better, lady,' answered Hwita Clatter-Clogs.

But by the autumn the danger had passed and the court was busied with other preparations and Countess Godgyfu had travelled to London to be with Earl Leofric.

'Why,' said Hwita Clatter-Clogs, as he sat again in the Hall of Little-Bethlehem-of-the-Rushes and supped of a dish of buttered herrings, 'the King is to wed Godwine's eldest daughter – the Lady Aldwyth.' The whole household gathered to listen.

'So the great Earl Godwine is pleased and the lady is pale.' Hwita smacked his lips and drank the black beer they plied him with, then he winked. 'But I've heard it said that the King's not a marrying man.'

And when Young Leofsi did pick up the pen once more to write of the honey-gathering two years had passed and it was the Mead-Month again.

In the space of that time Hereward saw Wynter and Darryl and Young Leofsi grow taller than himself, owing their good looks to the

Leofricsson strain in their blood. The village girls had already begun to cast smiles their way often – but for Hereward no such smiles were forthcoming.

'Why do the lasses not like me, mother?' he asked one day.

Countess Godgyfu was spinning like Skulda by the Well of Urd. She wore a collar of turquoise and shells and glass. She looked up at her son. 'What can I answer thee, Hereward?'

'I am not ill-looking, am I?'

'Nay.'

'Nor hunch-backed nor club-footed nor knap-kneed?'

'Nay, but you are eye-smitten. And 'tis believed that no woman would give her maiden-head to such as thee.'

His heart burdened, Hereward took a skerrie and crossed the mere to Wyntering. But before he reached there he met Wor-Will-Be-So, the cunning man and blood-charmer who lived on the tiny isle of Harts Booze.

'Seal of the day!' called Wor-Will-Be-So.

Hereward waved in answer and Wor-Will-Be-So came down through the yellow loosestrife and meadowsweet, a bent and ancient man with the water wisdom of an otter. He always whistled the same tune. Hereward had once asked him what it was and he'd said that it had been the battle song of the men who had fought by Edmund Ironside against the Danes on the field of Ashingdon.

Wor pulled the skerrie to the bank. Hereward jumped off dry-shod and said, 'Is Wynter home?'

'Aye, and the other lads with him. Bagging honey.'

At Wyntering, Hereward walked through the old orchard where Wynter had already begun to clear the dead wood and shore up the trees and plant anew with pear and mulberry and quince and apple, helped by his father's labouring men. Lucky hagstones were slung from the branches as from the cowshed and thatch as protection, and red rose bushes grew among the apple trees to make sure of a crop of scarlet fruit.

Nearer to the house the bee-skeps, numbering a dozen or more, were clustered in the shade of a mighty cloud of whispering poplars, and the honey yield was heavy and fragrant.

'An amber and half a sestier,' said Young Leofsi.

Hereward picked up a slab of honeycomb. It smelt of lavender. 'What'll you do with it all?'

Wynter said, 'I am of a mind to take some to Oundle market or to the Cherry Fair at Peterborough. Should fetch a good price.'

'The maids are pretty in Oundle and Peterborough,' said Darryl.

'That's all you ever think of.' Young Leofsi licked his sticky thumbs.

'Old randy arse!' said Wynter.

Hereward took off his trousers to be as the others in nothing but a shirt of homespun. He sat down and sucked his honeycomb. Praise be he didn't have to attend church-school any more, for he had proved so troublesome and so indifferent to all that was taught to him that Earl Leofric had decided reluctantly against having him trained for the priesthood and allowed him his freedom.

After they'd finished bagging the honey they drank deeply of a jug of sweet mead and drowsed until Darryl got to his feet and said, 'I'm as drunk as David's sow. I'm going to have a piss.'

'Me too,' said Wynter. 'Up the apple trees. Does 'em good.'

Hereward fumbled for his cock, his head muzzy, his bladder full. The others had theirs out ready and waiting.

'Now soak the buggers!' said Wynter.

Hereward's flow spurted quick. He spread his legs, rocking back on his heels, and made water long and vigorously, aiming for the knobbly branches lowermost. He sighed. It was quiet there, with no sound except their splashing. He felt the sun on his face and on his bare buttocks. It was possible to dream. To be someone and yet no one. To be a flower husk in the wind.

Thus when the Earl arrived back at the Hall of Little-Bethlehem-of-the-Rushes in July, the Mead-Month, he asked where Hereward was.

Countess Godgyfu replied, 'He has been gone these past three days.'

'Whither to?'

'Wyntering.'

Earl Leofric leaned on the sill, gazing out across Witch-Water. Honeysuckle rioted there, its deep, curled-cream and orange-buff flowers scenting the air. 'He always did like that place better than his own home.'

The Earl had washed the dust of the ride from him and wore both fresh tunic and trousers and a belt having many rich clasps and mounts. 'I sometimes wonder if I did right by that lad,' he said softly.

'How do you mean?' Godgyfu whispered.

'In letting him forego the church.'

Church teaching meant much to Earl Leofric, an education he had never had, his boyhood and youth given up in the struggle against the Great Army of the Danes. But Godgyfu, a daughter of Dudda the thane of Coventry, had tasted books. And in the early days of her marriage to Leofric, as a bride of fourteen summers, she had helped her grave and gentle lord to both read and write.

Plaiting her hair then with blue and white eye-beads of glass, Godgyfu said, 'Abbot Ulfketyl could do nothing with him at Croyland and it was the same when he was sent to Peterborough. You know how wilful he can be.'

'Aye, I do . . .'

In his mind's eye Leofric saw himself in the humble, prayer-cleansed chamber of his uncle Prior Brand, one of the noblest of God's thanes, as he partook of his single Lenten meal, a little bread, one hen's egg and a cup of milk and water.

'The lad is not meant for this life, kinsman, believe me. He is no child of the cloister.'

'Never to be found for All Saints and Matins nor for Tierce or the Mass of the Day,' Ywar the Churchwarden had chimed in, 'but first in at the dinner table.'

'He has been beaten for error and laxness as would any other boy be,' the Prior had said, 'but the Lord wants only willing servants and not prisoners in His House.'

With a sigh, Leofric came then to kneel at Godgyfu's feet. He'd brought the scent of wood-ruff to her bower, longed for those many months. He took her hands in his. 'The burden falls to ye when I'm away.'

'I manage well enough.'

Hanging upon her answer, the Earl said softly, 'But for the lad.'

'There are times . . .'

'He vexes ye?'

'I never know where he is or what he does.'

'You don't want him to mouze in the house all the day.'

'Nay, but . . .'

'He's just a bit different. I mind my father telling me of an old woman flung from London bridge into the river for pin-sticking, they said. She was just a bit different also, like as not.'

'He should have gone to court. He is heir to Mercia and may one day be the Earl.'

But Leofric, as ever, was adamant over not taking Hereward to court. 'The life there would do him more harm than good. It would be too much for him. I think he is a kind-hearted lad for all he makes a show of wildness. Nay, Godgyfu, sending him thither is not the answer.

39

Why, you have only to see Godwine's eldest, Sweyn. A Wolf's-Head twice now, in four years. Lastly for the murder of his own cousin Bjorn Estrithsson and before that for raping the Abbess of Leominster and getting her with child.'

'If rape it was,' said the Countess, at which Leofric, sitting back on his heels, grunted and half-smiled. The attractions of Earl Sweyn of the Hwicce were such that few could credit he would ever have to force a woman. But he had, or so the story went, and a sister of the Holy Mother Church, which made it a grievous sin, an ugly stride towards the pit, and King Edward would brook no more.

'Ah, he'll ride the gallows one of these days,' the Earl finished darkly, 'and no mistake.'

Godgyfu said, 'But what of Hereward? What of his taking a wife? You know as well as I do that no damsel, not even a theow's daughter, would have him in these parts.' Leofric answered sadly and without much hope, 'Mayhap there'll be some woman somewhere might look kindly upon him . . .'

But if the Earl had worries over his youngest son, the approaching autumn was to bring news of Aelfgar. He had allied himself with Gruffyd ap Rhydderch, Prince of Deheubarth, and they had brought an Irish-Viking fleet and raided up the Severn, over the Wye and into the Forest of Dean where Bishop Ealdred and the local fyrd had challenged them, but had been defeated at Worcester.

Aelfgar was then the father of three children by his marriage with an Irish princess and kinswoman of King Dairmaid Mac Mael na mbo. And he might have been stashing away a gold-hoard for them after he and Gruffyd ap Rhydderch shared out their booty and retreated to the mountains, leaving a trail of destruction in their wake, after being put to flight by a fresh fyrd-muster led by Earl Harold Godwinesson.

Thus, at odds with his world, and bearing the wrath of the King, Earl Leofric came again unto Godgyfu and sought solace in her arms. And when he'd finished his hungry motion within her, he lay at quiet and slept, his head between her breasts.

'Ah, the unfairness of it all!' Sigeferth the chaplain was wont to lament to Lilla the underchaplain, 'for he is such a very good lord and her ladyship so devout!' And he went on to list the monasteries enriched by Countess Godgyfu, not least of them her own church-minster of Coventry. 'Is it not wrong that such misfortunes should be visited upon them?' And Lilla, lighting the tall blue wax candles in the chapel agreed that it was so.

Dawn was late on the marshes in the autumn, coming as no more than a glimmer on the face of the waters. The wealth of green suddenly turned to brown, and even during St Martin's Little Summer when the weather was wont to turn mild over the rest of the countryside and the gossamer webs of small spiders floated in the calm air, at Little-Bethlehem-of-the-Rushes it was kept chill and sad. And far out only the starlings returned to the reed-ronds at dusk.

Bishy-Barnabee Days

By the time Hereward was fifteen years old not another of his kinsmen could match him for strength. He was not tall, but the breadth of chest and shoulder that he had on him was liken to that of a man twice his age. It was not a graceful strength, as Aelfgar's had been, nor did his voice, very much broken then, have the melodious tones of his brother's. For when Hereward spoke, which was not often, it was deep and husky, and all the while his strange eyes would hold you as he sought to string the words together.

Wynter and Darryl and Young Leofsi had lately had their tithes of land made over to them by the Earl who had cut the sod and handed them the knife. Henceforth their visits to Little-Bethlehem-of-the-Rushes grew scarce. Work was hard and the fields had to be coaxed into giving. But in the Rye-Month of August the weather turned so hot that all labouring had to be abandoned by noon.

Going to Wynter at Wyntering, Hereward often found Darryl and Young Leofsi there also, and the four of them would strip naked and swim in the cool mere water and compare each other's bodies, muscle for muscle, not forgetting to measure their cocks by the length of the dangling male willow goslins.

'You have a bonka one, bor,' said Darryl, eyeing Hereward's enviously.

'Ah, with a cock like that you'd mate with a lass easy as anything,' said Wynter, squinting up against the sun.

Those words answered a lonely echo in Hereward's heart, for of late he'd begun to identify with his penis. Contemplating it, weighing it, shrouded in its wrinkled foreskin, already grown large as a full bulrush spike, and the balls on either side, lumpy between his legs. And times, also of late, he'd felt the muddle and pain of having his cock harden and grow even bigger. Of wanting a woman. To be received into a yielding cunt. Of the urgent need to beat and to thrust

. . . Yet when he was clothed women would see no further than his face; disfigured, elf-shotten. And they would shun him. Aye, even the local harlots who had the custom of blind men and half-wits and cripples were loth to open their doors to the great Leofric's son.

One day he said to Wor-Will-Be-So, 'Can you not make me handsome?'

'O, handsome is it you want to be?' And Wor-Will-Be-So gave a bit of a cackle. He was making a fever-drink of the juice of barberries and stirring all with a wolf's teazle. The hut, in its nook of leaves, walled with clay and woven grass and moss, had no other opening save the hole in the roof and the door which was overgrown with flowers and hidden from mortal gaze like the way to the fairy kingdom, to which only he had the cowslip key. And thus had Wor-Will-Be-So lived, on the tiny isle of Harts Booze, no more than a few perches long, since before anyone could remember. Ah, truly! He was said to have webbed feet and when he'd got his leaping-pole of green ash-wood he was very nimble for all his great age. He wore dried eel skin garters above his knees and carried a hag-stone and a mole's foot in his pocket. He had cures for the face-ache and the ear-ache. He could parry spells and charm warts away at midnight and had remedies for the chin-cough and the pox. And as he stirred the brew he muttered:

> Thrice I smite the Holy Crock,
> With this mell I thrice do knock,
> One for God and one for Wod and
> One for Lok.

Hereward said, 'You work the magic for other folk. Make me handsome.'

'I cannot do that, lad,' Wor-Will-Be-So answered him.

'Why for?'

'I have not the wort-cunning.'

'But on St John's Eve they say as how you collect fern seed and make yourself invisible. Lasses come to you when they don't want to get with child. You can charm hell-weed and devil's-guts from the fields . . .'

'Aye,' Wor-Will-Be-So nodded slowly, 'aye . . .'

'Then, O, why cannot you do something for me?'

Wor-Will-Be-So saw Hereward's rough, unlovely face upturned to him. 'Child,' he said, 'I cannot make wicked folk good nor bring the flower from its bud nor piece together a broken heart. Beauty is not

43

mine to give either. It is something that must come up from inside your own self. Up from your soul.'

At sixteen Hereward already had a bad reputation, mainly because of the superstitious fear folk had of him and misfortunes were attributed to his evil powers, such as the failing of crops and the dying of cattle in the neighbourhood. But despite this he was often to be found at the local sports, and though he was far from welcome, at leaping and wrestling (at which he'd been well taught by Aethelmaer) and the throwing of the hammer he had few equals. And at bandy-matches he played to win and win he did, and was liked no better for it.

Old fenmen, like a clutch of brown gnomes, peeling seasoned willows and weaving hives and grigs and talking over old days would say, 'Don't fight like they used to – save that Leofric boy.'

'The Boggart?'

'Boggart or nay, he's spunky. Got a rare pair o' fists on him. I've seen him fight at the Scything Ales. Three against one. What a troshing he gave the others!'

But when the Reeve Eowa of Candleshoe brought a complaint from the folk of Thrackenholt one warm day before Midsummer's Eve, Countess Godgyfu was obliged to send hither for her youngest son.

Met with uneasy defiance, she said, 'But Hereward – brawling thus in an ale-house!'

'They riled me, mother. I could not abide it.' And that was all he'd say.

So Hereward was chidden and the folk of Thrackenholt placated. But a further blow was when Countess Godgyfu refused him money to go to St Aethelthryth's Fair at Ely.

'If you could but try to mend your ways, Hereward. Think of how proud your father would be of you then.'

'Of me? A changeling?' Hereward replied. 'Nay, mother, you needs must bear him another child, whole and unmarked, then mayhap he'd have pride in his spawn.'

Later he saw Darryl on the far bank. 'Whither goest?'

'To St Aethelthryth's Fair.'

The brackish pools of standing water were massed with showy bog-bean and mauve orchids and the reed-ronds turning to dull gold. Hereward went down to the causeway and leaning on the ropes, called, 'Will you do something for me, bor?'

'Aye, surely!'

'Buy one of St Aethelthryth's Chains and lay it on her tomb.'
'Are you not coming?'
'Nay, lad, not this time.'

Pedlar of Dreams

A t Wyntering they were reaping the cornfields and gathering the mustard, yellow in flower, that had flourished since Wynter had been master there. There had not been a sight like it save for in his father's day. And as Hereward walked the five miles across the causeway towards Wyntering he heard the voices of the labouring men at work in the fields, and a hazy, dreaming light was upon it all, and up above larks soared, making a thin, sweet sound, appearing no more than flecks against the tremendous arc of the sky.

But before Hereward reached there he met old Wor-Will-Be-So. He was sitting outside his hut on a bell-wether fleece weaving osiers. They bade greetings and Wor-Will-Be-So said, 'You have come the slow way this day, bor. A skerrie would have been quicker.'

Hereward shrugged. 'I don't mind walking.'

''Tis hot, but the Jack-go-to-bed-before-noon closed early today so I'll ween it'll rain before nightfall.' Hereward knelt and washed his face in the mere water. Sweat made dark patches beneath his arms and across his broad, cambric-shirted back. 'You'll be splitting out of that soon,' remarked Wor-Will-Be-So.

Hereward knelt up straight, wiping his face. 'But 'twas only stitched for me at Candle-Mass.'

Old Wor cackled. 'The lasses will be wanting to feel those muscles and more besides!'

'There's not much chance of that.'

'Time will tell.'

Hereward's heart beat soft and quick. He sat on the ground at Wor-Will-Be-So's feet and thought of how often he'd entered the village contest of corn-showing – that of weeding the corn-cockle from the Lent grain – and though he usually pulled up the most, his reward was always a piece of cake, never a kiss from one of the maids . . .

'I'd lief have a lover,' he said.

'Then you must be patient. Why, ye're but on the sill of life.'
And Wor-Will-Be-So crooned:

> Tell me, broom wizard, tell me,
> Teach me what to do,
> To make my sweetheart love me,
> Tell me, broom wizard, do.
> Silent tongue and still,
> Shall bring you all your will.

Hereward said, 'You know so much, bor. Is it the second sight?'
'Bless ye, no, lad. 'Tis just biding here by the bank,' said Wor-Will-Be-So, weaving on.

> Peter stands at the toll-gate,
> Begging butter for his cake . . .

And when his hands grew tired of their task, he said, 'Are ye hungry?'
Hereward nodded.
'D'you like pluck pie?' Whereupon old Wor disappeared into the hut where he always had something a-simmer and came out with the pie which he broke in half, and a jug of heather beer. When they had both eaten and drunk and Wor-Will-Be-So had wiped the gravy from his wizened stubbly chin, he fell to whistling softly.
Hereward said, 'That is the battle song of Ashingdon, is it not?'
'It is, bor.'
'It has such a sad, sorrowing sound.'
Old Wor gave a sigh. His fingers, never still, chimbled at a stalk of knot-grass. ''Twas a sad and sorrowing time, lad. Must be all of five and thirty years ago now. Aye, and the pasque flowers blooming the breadth of the field as only they can where Saxon blood has been shed! Your grandfather was killed there. Split to the chin by a Danish axe. Fighting side by side with Edmund Ironside. And your father – breaker of maidens' hearts in his elf-coat of gold rings and sprig of lad's love – lucky to escape with his life. I was younger then, aye, and quick. I was there and I saw it all. Eh, dear heart, what a night that was! October and cold. A black sky. A scalder o' stars. Warriors crying with shame, and others, poor buggers, calling for a priest to shrive them. And King Edmund slain and his Queen and two sons sent into exile. Leaving Cnut the Widow-maker master of the land.'

47

Hereward said, 'O, that I had been there to fight and die by the Ironside!'

Wor-Will-Be-So picked up his weaving again. 'Aye, lad, but what would have been the good?'

'But for a man to die by his lord's side – there is no greater honour.'

'True. True. But maybe living on as your father did needs the greatest courage of all.'

And when Hereward told Wynter of this, Wynter wiped his forehead and said, 'Ah, he do tattle on.'

All the corn was cut and lain upon the carts, save for the one sheaf that was left for Odin's horse, and the black fields were stripped of their glory. In the orchards it was likewise. Cupboards and barrels were crammed with fruit. Hatfuls, barnfuls and bushelfuls. There was even a little heap under the stairs. And going home, his pockets bulging with red-cheeked apples and ripe, squashy, musty, dusty yellow pears, Hereward was sure that the tree-spirits, the apple-men, unpredictable beings to be humoured, woken from their slumber by the beating of sticks in January, watched him from up among the leaves, chuckling and fickle and crafty.

Earl Leofric was due back for the bringing in of the corn, but that year the first swath fell without him. He was kept away by the summoning of the King, and Countess Godgyfu sat often at her stitchery by the window of emerald glass panes that looked out across Witch-Water, and thence to the causeway and Strawberry Wood, waiting to hear news of her lord.

And it was when the winter floods went down and the Virgin Mary's tapers and liriconfancy were seen to flower in the meadow, that Rudgang, Marshal of Earl Leofric's hearth-troop, rode to the Hall of Little-Bethlehem-of-the-Rushes one day, and these were the tidings he brought.

The Word-Hoard of Rudgang Wolf-Cloak

arl Godwine outlawed?' said Countess Godgyfu.

'Aye, and his lady – the whole family fled the country. Some to Flanders, others to Baile Atha Cliath. The Queen to the nuns of Wherwell.'

And Rudgang told her why. The Earl had disobeyed the King's order to punish the folk of Dover after a dispute had arisen between them and the retinue of the King's brother-in-law, Eustace of Boulogne. King Edward had wanted Earl Leofric and Earl Siward Digre to take his part and bear arms against the House of Godwine.

Countess Godgyfu said, 'And what was your lord's answer?'

'Ma'am, my lord, he refused,' replied Rudgang, 'saying that Englishmen had never fought each other and by all that was holy, while he lived, they never would.'

The chroniclers were to call it the Black Year. The Norman favourites, stealthy, clever, eavesdropping men, who had begun to beset the court of the childless King, some of whom he had brought to England with him when he was crowned, were given positions of power where they overbore themselves mightily.

Also King Edward received a visit from William the Bastard, Duke of Normandy, about this time. 'Thither he came unto his kinsman when the snow lay upon the ground,' wrote the cleric. And the King entertained his foreign cousin – a son of Count Robert the Devil and the Harlot of Falaise – with pomp and splendour at both the Wardrobe Palace and the ancient Hall of Southwark.

Rudgang had much to say of the gifts bestowed on the Duke of the Normans: 'Tumbrils and sumpter-mules laden with baggage. Welsh hawks he'd given the Harlot-Son and prize steeds from the pastures of the Hwicce and Sweod-Ora. And the rest of the hangers-on with their jays' voices and weasels' eyes – their tongues in the dust for scraps . . .'

* * *

49

Aelfgar came back that same year to be welcomed in the Hall by his kin, and was pardoned and given part of Harold Godwinesson's southern estates. The other hidages the King gave to his nephew Earl Raoul the Timid of the Vexin, but the shiremen refused to reap Harold's fields for a Norman's gain.

After this events unfolded swiftly. The Godwines had made their return to England with ships, gathering great support from the shires on the way, and were welcomed with open arms by the people of London. For most of the King's Norman favourites their days of power were at an end. And though no holder of sympathy towards the Wessex lords, Rudgang's word-hoard was a grudging one in their praises. With candlelight aglow on his arm-rings, he'd pause to drink mead during the recital, having the listening ear of the Hall. 'The foreigners, knowing all was up with them, fled, aye, with terror in their guts and gold in their belts, stolen from the box in the wise-fool's own bed-chamber and all the gems he'd chosen but the day before for his new crown!' This made Rudgang shake his head and laugh long into his beard. 'Pursued, they were! Out! Out! Down with the outland men! 'Twas said they fought their way through the east gate of the town – churchmen, some of them – bashing at all comers with their maces, and holed up in Essex from whence they took ship for Normandy . . .'

The demands having been met that all their estates be returned to them, the south hidages awarded to Aelfgar were claimed by Harold Godwinesson, and though offered lands elsewhere, Aelfgar refused them with ill grace and set out for the Orkneys thereupon to take hospitality of Thorfinn the Mighty and his Viking warriors. Hereward begged to be let go with his brother but Earl Leofric forbade it. Hereward thought him hard but it was love that bespoke in his actions.

However, the Godwine triumph was not without its penalty. First the Earl was called upon to surrender hostages to the King, one of them being Wulfnoth, the youngest of his sons, who was afterwards sent into Normandy for safe custody. Then news came of the death of Sweyn while on the return journey from Jerusalem where he had lain aside his weapons and vain ornaments and had walked barefoot and clad only in a hair shirt to drink the Jordan's holy waters and beg forgiveness for his sins.

As though all his years of power-building were but so much chaff to the blow, Earl Godwine grieved sorely for his double loss, and it was at the Eastertide feast held in Winchester Palace that a heart weakness came upon him and he collapsed at the King's own table and died three days later.

Harold then succeeded to Wessex. Ruler of the richest shire in England and brother-in-law to the King (for Queen Aldwyth had been reinstated with all honour and in consequence her power was steadily and quietly growing a-pace) he was then surpassed only in influence and ancient right by Leofric. But there was little or no rivalry between them and the country was at peace.

And when the violet candles of Advent were exchanged for the white ones of Christmas and the Yule-log lit and the boar's head roasted, Earl Leofric rode home from Westminster with gifts for all, like he who bears back the Golden Apples.

For Hereward it was a cloak of white bearskin with topaz-laden clasps of cunning workmanship.

'Is it to your liking?' the Earl said in his deep voice.

'It is very fine, father,' Hereward answered him. And when he put it on to the admiration of the gathering it made his shoulders appear almost too broad for his lack of height.

Thus his great bodily strength, as well as the mark that was his bane, made Hereward more noticeable wherever he went in those days. And on one bitter day in January when he happened to be in the town of Bourne-by-Holy-Brook he was to give succour to a theow-man, and so drive the wedge between himself and the folk of his father's shire still deeper.

51

The Month of the Wolf

I t was after Plough Monday, when the doors were opened to let the old year out and the new one in, that a fair was held on the village green of Bourne-by-Holy-Brook with a bonfire and stalls and a straw bear. The plough was dragged through the street and the Plough Stots danced, and there was skating also on the frozen mere, for all fen folk skated in winter, and prizes were given. A round fox-skin hat. A pig. A purse of coins. Crowds came from far and wide and once there they bought generously of bowls of eel-soup and hot brawn and apple dumplings to ward off the bitter chill, for it was said that the wind or fen-blow there was lazy, it didn't bother to go round you, it just went straight through you.

Wynter, slinging his sheep bone skates over his shoulder, said, 'I could do with a mug!' And he smote his hands together. Hereward and Darryl and Young Leofsi were with him and all were agreed save Hereward. He wasn't keen on going into a tavern. There were many, cheek by jowl, tipping, leaning and tilting along the bank and clustered in the market place, with painted signs of the Ivy Bush and the Shoemaker and the Green Man and the Brethren of the Water, and most were the favourite haunts of the fen-slodgers and fowlers, you could see their fen donkeys tethered outside, and they'd be none too happy to share their hearthside with such as he, a bogle-shotten man. He knew the outcome so well. Slodgers and fowlers who seldom took off their clothes and never washed unless they fell into a dyke, who when they'd had a skinful of dumpsie-dearie would dance to the fiddler's music till the sparks flew, who feared not pole-cats nor black ice nor the shakes . . .

The tavern door was low, and with his great bearskin cloak pulled up to hide his face, Hereward stooped beneath the lintel as he entered, to be met by the smell of barley malt and the sight of a peat fire, with

52

a soft red core, and packed benches. But they recognised him within minutes. Didn't wear gold ear-rings to give long sight for nothing. And soon they were digging each other in the ribs and saying, '''Tis the lad with the blight on him!'

'Laws-a-massy-me!'

'Do not let him o'erlook ye!'

'Ah, he'll pisen yer innards!'

'And ye'll shrivel away till ye're no bigger than a hand-worm's hip-bone!'

Geese and ducks and snipe had they on poles. Nets of plover and teal. Supping of 'sparrow pudden' – a dish of shin beef and bacon with a suet crust. Drinking deep of hot-pot. Mole skin gartered legs thrust under the trestle. And none of them willing to hitch up and make room near the fire. How different was the greeting for his father the Earl! A chair by the hearth, a mug of the best humming-beer and a muckle of friendly speech.

Hereward took the seat furthest from the lamplight and fire, trusting the shadows to hide him. Both ale and mead were ordered and brought by a fair, thick-buttocked serving wench who would have been only too glad to flirt if it had not been for Hereward in the corner. She was fearful lest the power of his glance fall upon her, and even Darryl could not persuade her to come any nearer.

Hereward drank his mead, feeling it warm his belly. But a cold wad was in his chest. Why me? he thought, questioning his lot, not for the first time. Have I not bigger shoulders than any of my kinsmen? Does hair not grow upon my body where they are yet smooth? But they had already had their share of wenches, and Darryl, lucky sod, more than his share. He knew, for he'd often heard them swapping the joys of their light-o'-love's body amongst themselves. Lasses eager to be tumbled at Harvest Ales and those who had no objection to 'bundling', that was courting in bed whilst the fields and droves were too muddy. And there was Nutting Day and A-Mayering, when men and maids went into the woods to gather flowers and all of them mother-naked.

Hereward had never been A-Mayering. There was no point. Who'd go into the woods with him? Where was the maid who'd lift up her mouth for his kiss? 'All blokes are the same in the dark,' Wynter had often said. But every mother had told her daughter to beware of the Lord Leofric's son. How he changed into a brute beast at night when the witches flew across the sky on broom sticks and cat's-tails, butter-churns and tree trunks. How he danced with the goblin folk of

53

whom he was a familiar, all moping and mowing. And if ever a woman was ravished by him she would bear the Devil's child . . .

They left the tavern without further mishap, the fenmen having turned their backs and ignored Hereward so long as he chose to sit among them. But the serving wench would not take the money from his hand so Hereward gave it to the tavern keeper, who seemed relieved that he should be going and held out his apron to catch the coins.

Outside snow was falling in thick wet flakes, but it did not dampen the holiday mood of the fairing crowds. Wandering gleemen were there and cloggers, chair-bodgers and pedlars with their packs of thread-boxes, spindle whorls, cowrie-shell amulets and bronze needles. Reed- and sedge-cutters hauled their loads on sledges with marrow bone runners across the knotted ice. An old woman sat with chestnuts in her lap. Fortune tellers rubbed shoulders with cut-purses and stall keepers called their wares. Love cakes and angel-water and firkins of lambswool and pans of gingerbread husbands and wives . . .

Then all in a moment, above the general whoobub, a shout was heard and a man, a thin, tatter-coated figure, came running down the street for all he was worth, a loaf of bread under each arm.

'Thief! Thief! Stop that thief!' The cry was up. Eh, the banging of pots and pans followed him in mockery! A hue and cry with the horn blown, bringing folk from every nook and cranny, every stall and tavern in pursuit. The priest came from his church. The potter from his wheel. The weaver from his shed, and the crowd grown to fifty or more when suddenly the man slipped on a patch of cat's-ice and went down sprawling head over heels amidst yapping dogs and the clanging of washtubs and pails, and the crowd closed in thick as a hedge, mean, beer-tempered, some with holly and thorn flails and ladles and besoms. And children were chanting, 'Flay or redeem! Flay or redeem!'

Among the watchers was Ywar the Churchwarden, in the town upon his master's business. Caught up in the jostle and all but thrown from his mule, he sat rooted to the saddle with all the faint-hearted man's horror of life's ugliness. What would the good Prior Brand have said to see him shirk his Christian duty thus? A-prickle with the nettles of conscience he imagined the Shepherd of Peterborough's look upon him, quizzing his soul: 'And what did you do?'

'There was naught I could do. The crowd was so big.'

And Brand, lighting the green candles for Epiphany, 'Poor Ywar – is your faith not bigger?'

But quicker than it takes to recount all this, a path was already being cleft through the press and where folk were slow to move they

54

were shoved aside by a pair of hefty, fur-clad shoulders. Seeing this, the town priest, wrapped in age, worn with kneeling and work, hurriedly crossed himself.

'God forbode!' said he, rheumy eyes sharpening. ''Tis him! O, the sorrow of his father!'

Hereward got in between the crowd and their quarry, staving off blows. 'Leave him alone, can't you?' he shouted at them. 'He's had enough!'

Why did he do it? Buggered if I'll ever know, thought Darryl, pushing to the forefront closely followed by Wynter. It was the same when bull-baiting was held in the market square on St Mark's Eve and St Bartholomew-Tide, Hereward would fight with the dog-keepers and go freeing the tethered beast, thus bringing down the wrath of ten villages on his head.

Ring-leader of the crowd was a certain Wluncus Moue the baker, nicknamed Snake-in-the-Eye. He had a big head of greasy red hair and a barrel chest and did not take kindly to be crossed by the likes of Hereward. He growled, 'You'd no cause doing that!' And kicked at the remains of the bread and spat. ''T'ain't fit for the crows! Two of my best cob-loaves. Good wheaten. Thieved 'em, he did, and if you aid him you've equal share of the blame! Get out of it now – I'll deal with this my way!'

Hereward did not budge an inch. 'No you won't,' he said, 'ye bloody great lummox! You've had your sport of him. Let him be!'

Wluncus Moue was in such a rage by then that he didn't know which leg to stand on. 'Won't?' he said. 'Won't? Who are you to say that to me? Coming among honest God-fearing folk with your elf-shotten face! Thunder and giblets! What of the mulct?'

'Flay or redeem? I'm redeeming him. So shut your slavering before you bust a gut! I'll pay for what he took,' said Hereward.

But as it was in the tavern the baker would not take anything from his hand. So Hereward threw a silver penny at Wluncus's feet, adding two more for good measure.

'Not so fast!' said Wluncus Moue to Hereward, pocketing the coins, his snake-eye darting back and forth under bushy brows. 'Think yourself very brave, I dare say, ye cursed young boggart. Will ye try a fall about it?'

Wluncus Moue had a reputation as a wrestler and was fond of proving it. So he gave Hereward a lam in the chest then, fit to fell a door. Whereupon Hereward seized Wluncus's hand in a grip, bringing all his strength to bear. It was no pretty sight. They struggled and glared and grunted and bared their teeth. Sweat stood out in great drops. Those nearest swore they heard bone crack and saw blood burst from under the nails of both of their hands, before Hereward at last forced Wluncus Moue down onto one knee.

The crowd shrank back as muck in the wall. 'Did ye ever see the like?' they asked of each other, apple-and-turnip faces closed up with old fear.

Wluncus Moue, burning with shame, nursed his big ham of a hand in which all the joints felt to be mangled. 'God damn you! There's a score to settle. Ah, surely!' And so saying, with many more oaths beside, he barged off through the crowd, scattering folk left and right.

'Looks like a rag-bag,' said Darryl, prodding the man with the toe of his boot.

'What's to do?' said Young Leofsi.

'He's naught to us,' said Darryl.

'All the same – we can't leave him.' This from Wynter.

Hereward squatted down by the man where he crouched in the snow, head buried between thin legs, hands and knees blue with cold and caked with old dirt, his feet tied up with sodden rags, the soles all bloody. 'Can you walk?' he said.

At which the man brought up his head suddenly and looked Hereward full in the face as though to say he'd walk through fire for him. But when he tried to stand he crumpled like a pricked bladder. Hereward caught him and slung him over his shoulder.

'Whither, bor?' said Wynter.

'To Lilla. He'll know what to do.'

So they took the man to the priest's house. A tiny cottage with a crooked roof huddled between ancient apple trees, within it was warm and welcoming. Lilla was chaplain then and had been ever since the death of old Sigeferth. With gentle hands he sought to unfasten the man's coat to see if he had wounds, but the wretch who had said no word betwixt the village and that very door, let out a wail like as if Garm of the Underworld was upon him. He had a thin, sallow face in the lamplight, with a hooked nose and pointed chin, and his hair cut Danish fashion with shaved neck and blinded eyes. He had a beaver-skin bag inside his coat stuffed with all manner of odd things.

Among them Hereward saw some coins that glittered and he said, 'You could have saved yourself a troshing.'

But the man clenched the coins in his bony hands. 'My burial money,' he muttered.

Looking down at the man as he lay snoring on the rushes before

56

the fire, having devoured a bowl of ram's head broth and a whole plum pudding, Lilla said, 'He's no stranger to the lash. His back is a mess of sores.'

'A theow, do you think?' said Young Leofsi.

To which Lilla answered, 'Aye, likely as not.'

A theow was a chattel and had no wergeld. His value was that of eight oxen. He could be bought and sold with other household goods, having nothing of his own save certain rights by custom. Hereward had heard of runaways being stoned to death. Yet the church encouraged their manumitting as acts of charity.

Hereward asked of Lilla then, 'Will ye take care of him?'

And Lilla nodded, straightening up, dimming the lamp, 'I'll take care of him. We once shared a common bond. He can go up in the loft. But what will happen when he's full better?'

'How d'you mean?'

'He will have to go back to his owner.'

'Nay.' Hereward shook his head. 'That he'll not.'

The Saga of Hogni Tricksleeve

hen Countess Godgyfu heard of it, she said, 'There is a penalty for helping theowes.'

'I know.'

'Yet still you did it.'

Across the supper trestle Hereward knew she watched him often, trying to see some semblance of his father in him where there was nothing. He broke a wheat cake and chewed on it slowly. 'Aye,' he said. 'Felt sorry for 'un, that's all.'

Thus Hogni Tricksleeve, as the man was found to be called – 'Why Tricksleeve?'

'Because I'm the best thief in the nine worlds!' – made a sort of company for Hereward at the Hall where he was brought after he recovered. Hereward gave him a tunic of dun wool and trousers of wool also and a new coat and a pair of leather shoes.

'Do they fit you?'

'Aye.'

'What about the tunic?'

Hogni grinned. It was so loose that it hung on him. 'Lots o' room!'

'You're so ganty-gutted!'

'Shrivelled skins often give good advice.'

At first Hogni Tricksleeve was close-mouthed. From whence he came was a mystery. But later, realising Hereward meant to keep him, his tongue began to wag, and they spent many a winter hour together in Hereward's own place under the eaves, made more comfortable with sweet hay and flag iris. Crouching and a-nibbling of his knees, Hogni would recite the old legends word for word until you'd almost have been able to smell the dragon's heart roasting and hear the wheels of Thor's goat-drawn chariot thunder and flash across the heavens.

One dark afternoon, Hereward said, 'Can you read?'

'Some.'

'And write?'

'Aye.' Fear crept into Hogni's eyes. He bit at his thumbnail.

Hereward said, 'Don't worry. I'll not ask any more questions of ye. Your past is your own.'

'Do you still want to keep me? I'll gladly be oath-held to ye. Content with a harvest handful.'

'Nay, no oaths.'

'There's folk who say I'm mad.' Hogni put his finger to his head and snickered. 'A loon. Buttercup mad!' He had a strange sing-song voice. 'One time I was whipped with the hide of a mere-swine to cure me of the crazies.' His grin was sharp and sly. 'Didn't work!'

'Folks are wicked buggers.'

'So you are bitter against the world too?'

Hereward shrugged.

Hogni leaned closer. He rubbed his nose and winked. 'We are alike then – you and me.'

'I suppose.'

'D'you understand the plaint of the wind?'

'Chance-time.'

'You've got a soul.'

'Have I?'

'Aye.'

'How d'you know?'

'I can tell. Most have just emptiness.'

Calling the Butterflies

hrough February, the Month of the Bear, and into March, the Month of the Goddess of Storm, the bad weather continued with blizzards and great drifting. And when the world seemed to have been under snow for an ageless time, at last, one morning, the meres began to crack and the sound carried for miles across the silent fen. The ice slowly started to melt and the crying of the waters came upon it all again and the lands were flooded, tremendous lakes, stretching far, far away.

As the Passion-Tide drew near the fen tracks were open and the Lent lilies were weaving the first gold weft among the grass, when word came that Earl Leofric – as Guardian of the Bread, the Loaf-Lord – would be arriving back for the festival.

Hereward had not seen his mother so happy for weeks as she was then, and deep in his heart he envied his father a love like that.

Thus it was at this time – known as Freyja's Joy – when the earth bursts into flower, baring a white bosom, that Hereward went over to Wyntering for the first visit since the snows, taking Hogni Tricksleeve with him, for Hogni would have come anyhow whether he'd given him leave or nay, having become his shadow during those past months.

Playing a tune on a pipe he'd made from the hollow stem of elderwood, Hogni wandered across the fresh ploughed furrows.

'I did not think you would have him still,' said Wynter, pushing back his sheep-wool cap.

'Who? Hogni?' Hereward smiled. 'I'm used to him.'

'Talk much?'

'When he wants.'

'Make any sense?'

'Chance-time.'

Contemplating Hogni's spindly legs and mop of tow-coloured hair,

Wynter said, 'Well, if he ever wearies you I could do with him to scare off the crows.'

The fields of Wyntering, once called Empty-Purse, Bare-Bones, Pinchgut and Labour-in-Vain, waxed rich and black then, and rooks nested, bringing luck. And when Wynter drove the broad swerve of the cumbrous plough, walking behind the oxen, Hereward trod the wet earth with him, clearing the ruts of stones.

Once, balling the loam in his fist, he said, ''Tis sweet. Kind ooil. What'll you grow?'

'Barley. Over there, millet. Yonder, oats.'

Coaxed by the warmth of the sun butterflies danced, scattering like a handful of petals in the early light.

'You have a thane's wergeld now. That counts for something. Will you be thinking of a morning-gift?'

'A wife, you mean?'

'You must get lonesome.'

'I admit I wouldn't mind settling.'

'I'll wager many a lass has an eye to you.'

Wynter laughed. 'Happen. But it's Darryl who draws them. You've doubtless noticed. Must be his curly hair.'

'He's had lots?' Hereward kept his voice soft but his heart was pounding.

'Spoilt rotten for choice.'

'Will he ever wed, do you think?'

'Not while they fall into his lap like they do.'

'Like bog-berries?'

'Aye.'

'And he's not so big. His cock, I mean.'

'Nay.' Wynter gave thought to that. 'Not near as big as yours.' He halted the oxen and leaned on the plough-beam. 'What's up, lad? Spring in thy blood?'

Hereward shrugged. He watched a bird with a worm in the sappy, fluorescent air, and the oneness with the vernal sod-pulse was almost too much to bear in silence. Chance-time, he wanted to cry out loud, shout until his gut ached, though the godwits and gulls and red-shanks might mock him. But he only answered, 'Spring – winter. Don't make no difference.'

Wynter smote a midge from his neck. He said, 'Want of woman is always worse in the seed-time.'

Hereward laughed, jamming his hands in his belt. 'That's a bloody good jest, that is. No woman would bed with me. They're all afraid,

61

you know that. Even my mother's bower-maids. They run away when they see me as if I were a leper or some idiot man.'

But Wynter, ever kind, said gently, 'Faith, there is much to love in you, lad.'

The Loaf-Lord

O n his way home Hereward met his father on the causeway astride his favourite Hrimfaxi. It was raining then heavens-hard. The Earl wore his ram fleece held by ouches of bronze and silver. Hereward wore no cloak and his jerkin and shirt were already soaked.

'Been with Wynter?' said Earl Leofric.

'Aye.'

'You like it there, do you not?'

Hereward shrugged his shoulders. 'Places are much the same to me.'

Earl Leofric sat back in the saddle, considering his last-born. 'I have heard about you saving the man Tricksleeve.' Hogni was crouching by Hereward's side. 'Is that him?'

'Aye.'

'Wluncus Moue begrudges you still.'

'Sod him!' said Hereward. Then, 'I suppose that churchwarden has been telling tales also. I recollect seeing him that day.'

'Ywar? He's said naught to me.'

'Makes a change.'

'Feeling was running high among the townsfolk, though. It took me a time to talk them round.'

'Sod the lot of 'em!' was Hereward's reply. 'I'm not bothered.'

Earl Leofric said slowly, 'That's all very well, but there is not always such a simple answer.'

Hereward looked down at the boards beneath his feet. Through the slats he saw the mere water. Anything rather than face his father's steady, soul-searching gaze.

'Hereward,' the Earl said, 'times you burden my heart with worry.'

'You think I did wrong?'

'Nay.'

'I redeemed him when he surely would have died. Isn't that what is preached of in the Scriptures? Mercy and forgiving and kindness? I'll pay what's owing – no matter the cost.'

Earl Leofric said, 'Come here, Hereward.'

Hereward was reluctant. He did not come willing. Leofric put out a hand, strong, the Ring of Oaths uppermost. Hereward did as he bade him. The earl drew him near to shelter beneath his cloak, wiping the streaming hair from his eyes, lifting up his face. He said, 'There are things in life that are going to make you angry. Many things. It's a cruel, sad, ugly world. And I can protect you only so far, and make no mistake, I do protect you – for if you had not been mine, both you and that theow-man would have felt the consequences by now on the cucking-stool. He for running away from his master and you for helping him. Aye, you are big and strong and do things for yourself, I know. But you are still my son and my power is your surety. In me you are safe. Only promise me, Hereward, try to be more careful in the future. I ask nothing else in return from you than that.'

All about the reeds shook, massing in the wind, and the grey waters were wed with the sky. Hereward said, 'I promise.'

Earl Leofric took Hereward's wet, clenched fist. 'We'll say no more on the matter. 'Tis done with. Now come back home with me, lad, and dry your clothes, for I have some tidings to tell you.'

Seated by the glowing house-heart, the Earl said, 'King Edward will keep the festival here.' A band of trusted thanes were to accompany him, numbering among them Harold Godwinesson and his brother Gyrth. The King favoured his estates in the south and west, rarely venturing to the Danelagh and never beyond.

'What is he like?' said Hereward.

'The Witling? Vain of his feathers. But there is little of the man beneath them,' said Rudgang, cracking walnuts in his fists. 'He cannot even give his wife a child.'

Hereward had heard tell of Queen Aldwyth's beauty. The rose of Godwine's thorn. And of her brother Harold, tolerant lord of the southern shires, a half-score of years hand-fasted to Eadgyth of the Swan-Neck with whom he had exchanged the *tru-lofa* – the lover's knot. A woman he could never marry, for she had had a husband already, and parted from him.

Feeding Hogni from his platter, Hereward said, 'But does not Harold Godwinesson now hold East Anglia also? The lands that were Aelfgar's?'

'He does,' said Earl Leofric.

'How could you have him here, father?'

'I have stayed many times in his house in London town. He is a good man.'

'Though he be a son of Godwine,' said Rudgang darkly.

At which Leofric bade his old arms-fellow guard his peace. Filling his mead cup, he said, 'Make no judgement until you have met him, lad. I'll be bound that you'll have changed your mind ere the night is over.'

Grigs and Glaives

A s no one had much time for Hereward on ordinary days, so they had still less on the Paschal Sabbath when the King was due. Thus taking Hogni Tricksleeve with him he set out before Matins to go eel catching. He met Wynter on the causeway. He had his own glaive and eel-nets and a sack slung over his shoulder.

'What time must we be back?' Wynter said.

'The Hour of Nones,' said Hereward.

'I'd lief we did not have to.'

'There'd be my father to answer to if we did not.'

'I've heard tell that the King is no warrior,' said Wynter.

Hereward tested the tip of his glaive. 'Rudgang says that he cares for but the raiment he wears.'

'Sounds empty as a wind-egg. It must grieve your father to serve such a man as that.'

Hereward nodded, looking out to where the sun rose above the reeds beyond Guthrym's Gowt. 'My father should serve no man,' he said.

They went to Swan Mere that was called the Place of Gulls. There were two ways to get to it. One was by the Witch's Ladder, the rope and plank causeway. The other was by the fen paths, in some places no more than string thin. The old way trodden by goblin feet. The fairy way. They chose the paths.

Upon reaching Swan Mere the early mist was gone from it and it spread away on all sides; the water, great shining washes, mirror to the sky. And as they beheld the soggy fields of meadowsweet and cowbane, the tiny isles of willow and alder stretching like stepping stones to the far horizon, without warning the birds rose up in a mighty clamant throng, from every corner and dip and hollow and rond, ten score thousand, and the world was filled with the beating of their wings.

You could see more birds in the air and upon that single mere at one time than anywhere else in the fens. Coots clanking, ducks spattering, snipe drumming, peewits wailing. Haunt of the mute swan with its singing wings. Of gaggles of geese and flocks of dunlin and redshanks, and little gadwalls dancing in the shallows.

Out there you lost all sense of being and belonging. The passing hours mattered nothing. Hereward fished for eels in the pools with his broad-bladed glaive, keeping an eye out for their blow holes in the mud, straying away by himself, having not even the sight of Wynter, and with only Hogni Tricksleeve to dog his heels.

Hogni had got his pipe with him, as always, but then he gave full power to his playing as never before. Ecstatic, melancholy, squatting on a grassy hummock, his head flung back in rapture, his thin fingers moving in a weird harmony, he played and played . . .

Once, Hereward said to him, 'You're a rum 'un.' To which Hogni gave a piskie laugh. 'Where did you learn to play?'

'Nowhere. D'you like the tune?'

How many miles to Babylon?
Three score miles and ten,
Can I get there by candlelight?
Aye, and back again,
If your heels are nimble in flight,
You may get there by candlelight.

As the silvery notes died on the wind, Hogni's grin grew wide. 'But I know a better. One that summons a succuba.'

'What's that?'

Hogni looked sly. 'A female demon who obliges ye while ye sleep.'

'You know what? I reckon you're a wizard, Hogni.'

'Me? Ah, no, master. Naught so grand. Happen just a go-between.'

And it was getting late as Hereward cut off the head of the last eel he'd caught for the day, and the sun just about to set and the moon risen, hung in the same boundless sky, when suddenly there came a splashing sound nearby, ripples spreading over the water, and Hereward looked up, narrowing his eyes against the blaze of light, and saw a man on horseback in the shallows.

67

Meeting at Sunset

ereward stared at him, still holding the eel in his hands. He said, 'Who are you?'

The man wore a cloak of heavy crimson wool, its great folds blowing in the wind. He answered, 'I am Harold Godwinesson.'

Hereward had never seen a man as big as him, not even Aethelmaer the blacksmith. He fair took his breath away. He said, 'How did you know I was here?'

'They told me at the house where you might be.' His voice was very deep, hay-meadow vowelled. That of a south-country man.

'Is the King come?'

'Nay, not yet.'

It was custom then for a few men to travel ahead to inspect the larder. To see how many hung hogs you had and cheeses. What ale and butter.

'Don't you know 'tis dangerous to ride over these marshes? There are bogs hereabouts that have no bottom. One foot in and you just go down and down forever. 'Tis death to strangers.'

'I've ridden fen paths before. I stuck to the firm ground. 'Twas safe enough.'

'You were lucky.'

Harold Godwinesson shrugged his truly massive shoulders, watching a flight of geese overhead. 'Is this where you always come to?'

'Chance-time.'

'It's lonesome. Even the rushes seem to cry.'

'What would you know of crying?'

'Not much. But I'd lief see it in the dawn.'

Hereward measured this man, awesome, flaxen of hair and beard, with a rugged, weather-beaten face and said, 'You are not like I thought you'd be.'

'Indeed?'

'Nay, I thought you'd be older.'

Harold smiled at this. His rough features softened and creases came round his blue eyes. 'I am past thirty.'

'And you are so big. How tall are you?'

At the obvious wonder in Hereward's voice, Harold's smile deepened somewhat self-consciously. 'I am six foot and six inches tall, as big as was my brother Sweyn. Only he was much the better looking. Not a great ugly bugger like me.'

Hereward did not think Harold to be ugly. He said, 'I am but five foot and eight inches. I'd take it kindly to be your size.'

Harold leaned forward, stroking his horse's neck. 'You also are different to what I expected, Hereward Leofricsson.'

'I am? Why for?'

'Oh, I thought you would be dressed finely like some of the young men at court – that always make me feel so hulking and awkward. Yet here you are catching eels and not giving a damn for me nor anyone.'

Hereward smiled up at him. A liking stirring in his heart for this man he had thought to hate. 'You must forgive me, Harold Godwinesson,' he said, 'I meet so few folk, my manners are not as they should be.'

Harold smiled also, saying nothing, lifting his head to the sky. His neck, about which hung a crucifix, was thick with muscle, arms heavily bracelet-clasped, his hands holding the reins loosely, looked to be immensely strong, the fingers bare of rings, save one, a gymmal-ring of straw coloured gold. 'You love your marshes greatly.'

'Aye,' Hereward answered.

'What name has this place?'

'Swan Mere.' Hereward dropped the last eel in his sack and for no reason his tongue was quickened. 'But we call it the Place of Gulls. There is an old legend which says all the birds that come here are the souls of the ones that have died, that way, you see, they return year after year. No one touches them. I suppose you might say it was sacred.'

And that was how Wynter came upon them. His kinsman stringing more words together than he had in a month, and the giant stranger bending to hear, the dragon-ring of Wessex a fetter of balas-rubies on his arm.

69

The Worlds in the Kindred Tree

L ittle-Bethlehem-of-the-Rushes was to beckon all to its hearth that night, but first the talk was of the coming succession in Northumbria. Earl Siward Digre of the House of the Bear was no longer young and in the summer of that previous year he had led an army against Macbeth, Mormaer of Moray, who was King in Scotland by right of his wife Gruoch, in order to secure the throne for Mael-Coluimb, King Edward's foster-lean. This he had failed to do, but with Macbeth put to flight, Mael-Coluimb had gained Lothian as well as Cumbria, and Earl Siward much renown. But among the slain had been his eldest son Asbeorn Timber-Axe, leaving his last-born Waltheof but a child of green years. And the likeliest man to hold Northumbria after Siward was Tostig Godwinesson, a favourite of the King. Earl Leofric said, 'Not that I'm saying Tostig hasn't got his virtues. He has. He's able and gifted and generous with alms to the church. But I ask you, is it wise – he being a southern man?'

'I agree, Leofric,' Harold Godwinesson answered. 'But my brother is beloved of the King like a son. He wishes an earldom and his every wish is granted.'

'Even unto the ruin of the country?'

'The King sees no further than Tostig's bright eyes,' said Harold.

Close by, Gyrth Godwinesson sat in his elder brother's shadow as if content to be so. He had the look of a man monk-taught, sparing with ale, and seldom broke his word-hoard. The other few thanes were Godwinesson men and they were silent while their lord spoke and all eyes were upon him.

'Given the chance, if it were not for the Witenagemot, he would grant all the high positions at court and in the church on a whim.'

'And most of them to foreign-born men,' said Leofric dourly.

'Aye,' Harold replied, 'his heart lies in Normandy still.'

70

Rudgang rose in the company and said, 'That Norman capon should give Northumbria to my lord Aelfgar. They would accept him. There would be no trouble if they had a man of their own choice. In the kingdom of Odin a Godwinesson's life would come cheap!'

Harold looked up at the man called Wolf-Cloak, weighing the force of the moment, then he smiled. 'You must have Viking blood in your veins,' he said.

Rudgang met those calm blue eyes squarely. 'My father was Norse. He came hither before Knut the Raven-Feeder held sway.'

'Loyal and brave-hearted. Your lord Aelfgar is a fortunate man to have your love.'

Earl Leofric shook his head. 'Aelfgar, though he be my son, is not the man to rule in the North.' And when Rudgang made to dispute this he held up his hand and said, 'Be silent, bor, you do not have to say such for my sake.'

Seated by Leofric, Countess Godgyfu, her ear-jewels pear-shaped amethysts, said, 'Whom do you suggest to rule in the North, Earl Harold?'

'I have no suggestions, ma'am. Northumbria is no man's to win easy. Northerner or southerner would find the challenge of holding it great.'

'What of yourself, my lord?'

'I have Wessex, ma'am. I want for nothing else.'

The Sabbath Feast

When the King and his hearth-troop finally arrived it seemed all else was thrust out of mind. Countess Godgyfu began the feast by bearing a mead cup wrought of precious gems first to King Edward and then to Earl Harold. It was a great honour and they received it from her graciously. Then platters were brought to the linen-laid table piled with both boiled meat and roast fowl. Venison with marigolds. Pike cooked with puddings in their bellies. Rosemary bread and kept apples, and nuts and honey. And jugs of mead and ale mulled in winter chimney-corners.

The King was not without good features. He had thick white skin easily flushed and masses of fine fair hair, but a habit of stooping robbed him of his natural height, and his smile, affable and open as it was to all men, seldom reached his eyes to warm their chill pale blue. It was said that he washed the feet of the poor on Corpus Christi. That he watched in the chapel and endowed churches. That he was pious as a monk. Yet his delight in richly coloured robes, stiff with embroidery of gold and silver – what Rudgang had called his feathers – did not to Hereward's way of thinking become a monk. Yet at the same time he could not imagine him sweating or making water like a proper man or even having a cock.

Now with Harold Godwinesson it was different. He was warm and earthy, his eyes the blue of cornflowers. Men would feel safe trusting their back to him. There was something of a comfort about those immense shoulders and in that slow turn of speech. The kind of man you'd lief have as a friend. And he would have a charm for women too, they looking at his badly broken nose and his muscles that packed his shirt like pumpkins in a sack and wondering what it would be like to be taken by him. No woman could ever feel that way about the King.

The hum of voices and laughter swelled in the firelit house-place and the mead was jewel-bright and fragrant. By turns men were boastful, men were eloquent. Tempers were mellow, tongues were gilded.

One of Leofric's hounds took an ox bone from the King's hand. 'A fine animal,' said he in thick accents of Norman-French. 'Is the hunting good here?'

'The fishing is better, Sire,' Earl Leofric answered him. And when he went on to describe the teeming meres and lakes and streams the King was mazed. Trying to picture bream and golden rudd, eels by the hundred bushel, pike and eel-pout and prickly barred perch, the nets and barrows groaning with the weight of them. Eager to sample carp with cream and fat tench fried crisp brown.

'And do herons truly sprawl in the tree tops and are there ducks by the score?'

'You cannot count 'em by the score, Sire. There's too many . . .' Plover, duck, snipe, teal, widgeon, crane . . . 'Till your eyes would ache with the looking.'

Whereupon the King had stroked his cup, fingering the bronze gilt mounts and smiled. 'Ere Lent comes I must hold my feast beneath your roof, Leofric!'

Casting the Runes

fter the feast the harp was passed from hand to hand and the old songs sung. Men played dice or set riddles as was their wont. Then, tired of his game, one of the thanes said, 'Can any among us cast the runes?'

And Hogni Tricksleeve came hither, noiseless as a fetch, and said, 'I can.'

Yonder the wind had got up as though someone had whistled for it, bringing rain against the stout shutters. Hereward threw Hogni a warning look but Hogni only smiled and laid a knobbly finger to his lips. From his bag he brought forth a cloak of black skin in which he garbed himself and a handful of red twig-like carvings. Odin's runes. In his palms was the power to blunt a sword blade, quieten cares, to understand the speech of birds, to put the sea to sleep. And all men from the high-seat to the benches gave heed to their casting.

'I behold two Kings.' Hogni Tricksleeve peered close. 'Two Kings and yet one crown. I can see a woman mourning at the lyke-wake and hear the passing-bell. The soul-bell. Tall candles burning. The end of a bloodline is nigh. Two Kings – here in this hall!' A murmur went up among the company, but Hogni, deep in a trance and having the hindsight and foresight of all eternity, wove his thin hands. 'And when one is dead – the other – the King that be yet to rule – will be loved. The love is speaking up through the runes!' Hogni stopped then on a long low cry. 'O, but there is changing that it is . . . Changing!' He put his mop-head on one side, gaping at what he saw. 'The love it has gone away . . . All is dark. Nay, twilight. And cold. And there is a wind blowing . . . And men's voices. I hear them! Those of warriors with battle shirts riven to pieces . . . Some are standing, others kneeling in the mud.' Hogni began to rock to and fro slowly then like a troll-man. 'I see the flash of massing steel. There is one who is fallen . . . O, Giver of Bracelets! – who lies, his head in another's lap. There are broken banner shafts. Black crosses upon the stars. And the men are singing and weeping and praying . . . O, I cannot shut out the sight nor the sound!' His voice rose to a shout, then he fell forward and sprawled on the rushes, not stirring. And it was Harold Godwinesson who picked up the runes and flung them onto the fire and stood whilst they burned to ashes.

Later, when the bearskins and bolsters were spread and men slumbered, Earl Leofric could see Hereward nowhere, so he climbed the winding stairs to the eaves-space and sure enough there he was.

At the sight of the Earl on the stair Hereward gave a start. 'Father?'

'Ah.' The Earl bent his head, entering that well-remembered pocket of timber and thatch. 'This used to be my cot before it was yours.' He sat down, straw and wild iris stalks clinging to his tunic. Up here was the smell of the fens. Of water and lily-pads, and fish and reeds. And that night the wind was not a tired man beneath the eaves but a roaring giant and blew a-mightily, buffeting the trunk-thick walls. Yonder the marsh was in chaos. Hereward lit a soft-rush candle and its light sprung between them.

'Where's the man Tricksleeve?'

'Hiding in the byre. He was scared you'd punish him.'

'Daft bugger. The King offered me his man-price in pure gold counted by shillings. He'd lief take him back as his sooth-sayer.' He saw the look that crossed Hereward's face. 'Don't fret. You can keep him. He's mad as the moon's-leap.'

On the bank willows were tossing wildly, cramming the horn panes, blind with rain. Leofric said then, 'The last time the runes were cast in this house was before Ashingdon. They foretold our defeat and the coming of the Danes. And my father did as Harold Godwinesson. He picked up the runes and threw them onto the fire. But they were told. It had to be.'

Suddenly then through the gale came a deep, mournful baying liken to that of a dog. They both heard it. The Earl stiffened. Hereward said, ''Tis the Hound, father. 'Tis the Shuck.'

'Aye.'

'Why does he call? Is it because of the runes? Is he angered?'

'Nay, he's not angered. He's sorrowing – sorrowing. Cannot you hear, lad?' Leofric's voice sounded different. A voice raw with the passion of youth. And looking, Hereward saw that it was not after all he but another who sat there, a stranger. And there was no wind, no rain, no sound at all.

'I'm not seeing clear,' Hereward whispered.

'Eh, dear heart! Don't ye know your own father?'

Hereward stared at him and Leofric said, 'I am the age you are now.'

Hereward beheld the dark mane of hair. The steady grey eyes giving back look for look. A sprig of lad's love was pinned to his mantle. He wore a coat of gold elf-links. And those who had told of his handsomeness had told no lie. He was close and very strong and they were breathing the same air, the fen air of the generations of their fore-elders, and forty years no longer yawned between them.

'Is it far you've come?'

'Not so very.'

'Why?'

'To see you.'

'And all the time I didn't think you believed . . .'

'In what?'

'In things beyond kenning.'

Leofric leaned forward, vital, fearless. 'Hereward! Ah, lad! D'you think I was born here without the streak in my blood? D'you think that when the green wind blows it does not draw my soul too? And you, with the wildness and the longings that once I had – that you cannot go against any more than you can hold back the mere flood nor stop the gulls from mating. Do you think I don't understand? Lad, lad, 'tis wronging me ye are. I got you from between my legs – part of me. Out there is the same sky and somewhere the same stars that used to flummox me. Your dreams were once my dreams, and the web of Wyrd governing us all. But by the casting of the runes that web's been set a-trembling this night. Do you not feel it? Its threads are our lives and we must follow them no matter what. There's no escape. Ah, maybe it is outside of Christ's teachings and has no place in Holy Writ – but this self of me is trapped in the month of October. I am from the Eve of Ashingdon. I am your yesterday and you are my tomorrow. The worlds are reeling and time turned upside down. We must wait for it to right itself. Bide awhile, my dear, there's no hurry . . .'

But it was only later that Hereward slept, to wake to a morning blown out with storm, and to an empty cot, so that all might have been but a dream, save for the sprig of lad's love, its scent still lingering fresh and green.

76

The Saint Michael-Mass Wake

With the coming of the malting-ales six months had elapsed since King Edward's visit to the Hall of Little-Bethlehem-of-the-Rushes. And it was on a day in the Holy Month at the back of the year, that Darryl swung himself over the crooked stile and said, 'Have you heard about the wrestling match in Bragi's Meadow at St Michael-Mass?'

Hereward sat on the banks of Witch-Water, now and then tossing a stone into the deeps. 'There's always a wrestling match,' he said.

'Aye, but this isn't just a scrip of coins for first prize. 'Tis a horse.' Darryl looked slantwise at Hereward. 'And no ordinary horse, neither. 'Tis the fastest horse that ever wore shoe!'

'Ah, get on with ye!'

'I tell no lie. She's a forest mare. Not much on looks but she's swift as lightning.'

'How do you know?'

'O, I had it for gospel from Hwita Clatter-Clogs.'

'I have never had a horse of my own,' Hereward mused to the browning reeds, watching the last-dance-of-summer of a great yellow butterfly, 'not that belongs to me. There are those in my father's stable for the having. But it's not the same.'

'There'll be the best men from the shires competing. No quarter given,' Darryl said. 'Are you going to enter?'

Hereward nodded. 'Aye,' he said, 'I am.' And from that moment a sudden unreasoning longing for that horse gripped him. He felt he had to have it or die in the attempt. So next day he went to Bambweare and to Aethelmaer.

At the forge in the company of the big smithy, all trouble seemed to shrink like water in a bucket. But Aethelmaer knew something to be on the boy's mind.

''Tis the wrestling match,' Hereward said bleakly. 'I learned my skill from you, Aethelmaer. You are the only one who can beat me. You've done so thrice before.'

Aethelmaer watched him and smiled his slow smile. 'What's it that means so much?' And when Hereward told him, Aethelmaer said, 'Rest easy, bor, I won't contest thee.'

So Hereward rode to Bragi's Meadow on Wynter's wagon with a heart high as a lark. Up at sunrise, they'd set forth at a shrug-trot loaded with pease-straw and apples and pears, the wicker frame of the wagon bedizened with blue luck flowers, and on reaching there before the Hour of Prime a crowd had already been gathering.

'Proper scrowge this'll be,' said Darryl.

Bragi's Meadow, with its ring of picture stones, half-swamp, half-turf, lay between Strawberry Wood and Gasp Water, and there stood in its centre the oak called the Mead Tree. So huge was it that its branches seemed to weave among the clouds and hold up the sky; dear knows how many years old it was. Said to be possessed of strange powers, it stayed green in both summer and winter, having the destinies of mortal folk written on its leaves. Beneath it the Wapentake met every fourth week and the Shire-Moot twice in a twelve-month. But that morning there was the honking of geese to be sold and goodwives with butter and hampers of hens, and mushrooms from the damp cow pastures and cherry puddings and rich country cake. Herb-women were calling:

Here's wood sorrel and marigolds!
Come, buy my nettle tops!
Here's water-cress and scurvy grass!
Come buy my sage of virtue!

And the talk was all of the horse and a dozen of the finest wrestlers from the Danelagh to the Humber had come to win her.

The mare was tethered on a patch of tumble-down grazing by the wrestling pitch. 'No beauty, is she?' said Young Leofsi.

Hereward put his head on one side. 'Doesn't matter.'

Wynter glanced from the mare to Hereward. In the green-gold light the marked side of his face was hidden. His hair spilled over his shoulders like unshuffed wheat. He was perfect as any man could be from the neck down, more so, aye, and supple. He had sparred with Wynter a week long in preparation for this, stretching his legs, loosening belly and groin and all his joints, rubbing his limbs with springwort.

'Everyone wants that nag,' said Darryl. 'I've heard that she's a

78

princess turned into horseflesh by an enchanter's spell. From a land where men have such big ears as they can sleep on one and cover themselves over with the other.'

'You're ragging us,' said Young Leofsi with a doubtful half-smile.

The mare cropped hog-weed unconcerned. She was a muddy dapple grey with a great chuckle head and a nose as big as a buck-basket and drooping hind-quarters. True, there was nothing of grace in her but Hereward saw the strength of shoulder, the thighs let down to the hocks, the flat knees and large, well-spaced hooves.

'Are you a princess?' he whispered after his kinsmen had gone to join the dancing in the bottom meadow. And the mare looked up at him with liquid eyes under a broad, sad brow, champing the herb of the field. 'Ah, lass!' Hereward felt his heart turn over for her and a lump come in his throat. 'I'll have ye, see if I don't!'

Though Hereward had no hope of getting a partner himself he would usually make his way down to the meadow and watch the men and maids dance the Kissing-Wheel and the St Mary Tydd Hop to the music of may whistles and feapers and hand-harps. But not so that day. Hereward was reluctant to leave sight of the prize as she flicked her tail at butterflies and shook her heavy mane, scattering the midges that pestered.

'Think yon dobbin will go up in a puff of smoke, eh?' said Hogni Tricksleeve, coming out of nowhere, scratching his ear and grinning.

'I'm of a mind to stay.' And thus saying, Hereward sat down under the trees and waited there until time was for the wrestling match to begin, and Hogni made his company. Cross-legged amid the long grass spangled with cuckoo-spit he played on his pipe for hours on end and the world seemed very far away, seen slanted through the Rose of Sharon and the Touch-Me-Not and the nodding foxgloves . . .

Hereward said, 'Hogni!' And he nudged him with his foot. 'Bestir yourself, man! Folk are gathering!'

Hogni scrambled up. 'Where, master?'

'About the pitch.'

'Ah, me! And there was I a-playing in the Hall of Gimli with its roof of gold and all the gods listening!'

The Wrestling Match

he reeve Eowa of Candleshoe was to judge the wrestling match and it was with a sinking heart and a muttered prayer to St Mary that he saw one of the contestants to be Hereward. But he was obliged to accept him, for any man was entitled to enter.

Mostly they wrestled in labouring shirts of unbleached wool, but Hereward stripped off to nothing but a breech-clout that all but left his buttocks bare. His skin, still richly tanned from the fen sun, was the colour of barley-wine, and his deep, hairy chest and muscle-laden shoulders, and most of all the bulge between his thighs, drew many lingering but covert glances from the women in the crowd.

'They're looking at your cock,' whispered Wynter to Hereward. 'I reckon you'd get a lover here today, bor!'

But another was sizing him up too, though for a different reason. As a rival Wluncus Moue Snake-in-the-Eye took his measure and turned blue and yellow for spite.

Young Leofsi crunched on an apple and said, 'Out for trouble, yon foul-beard friend.'

'Ah, watch out for him, lad,' said Wynter. 'He's an ugly one.'

'If he wants to fight I'm his mattler,' Hereward answered them.

The wrestling was good and hard and had the crowds watching keenly that day. Fen folk were slow to rouse ordinarily, chary of praise, saying what they thought of you in a few words or sometimes just a look and a spit over their shoulder. But not so at a wrestling match. Their hearts were behind it, solid, every one, cheering and clapping and throwing caps into the air, while the old men, some sempects very nearly, gathered like starlings on a branch, supping mead through toothless gums but with wits as sharp as frost, and after the drink-hael to the men of Edmund Ironside's blood over the water, they would be thumping the ground with their sticks and telling of the wrestlers

80

they remembered. 'Wrestled like men they did! Ah, gay days! When England was England! Ain't no more gayness now!'

Hogni Tricksleeve, meanwhile, had shinned up a wych-elm and crouched in its forked trunk had begun to sing soft, strange words, but no one paid him any heed.

By the time the bouts had been wrestled and won or lost, the competition being the stiffest seen for many years, there were but two contestants left and they were Wluncus Moue and Hereward.

The crowd was laying wagers all in Wluncus's favour for he was certain to tear Hereward limb from limb.

'Knock that young boggart all of a heap like a bull turd.'

'Ah, lay 'un out!'

'Trosh him good and proper!'

Wynter heard this and felt his heart turn cold. There had been talk of Old Skrat also and many were wearing yellow flowers as protection against Hereward's supposed witchcraft. Again he counselled Hereward to take care, but as ever Hereward heard him with only half an ear. Darryl and Young Leofsi, who had already shouted themselves hoarse, were giving their own bit of advice.

'Let him come to you, bor. Don't you seek him out.'

'Keep your elbows in and don't cross your feet.'

And up in the wych-elm Hogni Tricksleeve counted his toes and winked at Hereward, jerking his head towards the field. At first Hereward could only see that the westerly light was striking the ring of picture stones showing the hour to be betwixt Nones and Vespers. But then he saw what Hogni meant. The Mead Tree to which all others, hazel and wych-elm, dog-rose and even the holly tree – home of woodland sprites – bowed in homage, seemed to acknowledge him and smile in a kindred way, so very old and sure and wise.

They were paired equally enough and though Wluncus was somewhat taller he was running to fat with flabby buttocks and wobbly paps, whereas not an inch of spare flesh marred Hereward's body.

Soon after they were met, Wluncus got Hereward by both forearms in a grip of iron, and dropping on his hams with Hereward held fast about the thighs, Wluncus lifted him and dumped him to the ground to the shouts of the crowds. But Hereward was up in next to no time, sprung to his feet, and they were closed to a neck-and-bicep whereupon Hereward led to a head-lock, wedging his body into Wluncus's, bringing him over his hip in a wheel feat so that he fell hard with Hereward over and across him. Thus with both the baker's hands and shoulders on the turf Hereward was awarded a fall. Eowa of Candleshoe was

81

not going to let it be said he was anything but a fair man. The crowd, though, was not best pleased.

Smarting, Wluncus tried for a take-down, countered by Hereward with a cross-face and after wrestling to a stand-up Wluncus made a grab to get a wing on Hereward, who broke free. Wluncus stumbled and missed. The crowd yelled. Wluncus made a shoot-in to lay hold on Hereward and Hereward, going for a duck-under, found himself in a bear hug and tossed cross-buttock. He spun, seeing all four corners of the field at once, tripped, fell and Wluncus was athwart him, pinning him, almost laying him by the heels. Hereward blasphemed, tasting worm-sod in his mouth. An arm was doubled up, straining against the joint, near wrenching it from its socket. Then he felt Wluncus's hand thrust up between his legs and seize hold of his penis.

'Let go of my bloody cock!' Hereward gasped. But Wluncus only squeezed the harder. His mouth in Hereward's ear, he said, 'You've got a whopper, lad! I saw you sticking it up for the women to see. 'T'would be a shame to spoil it!' The agony spread through Hereward's thighs and belly. His bowels boiled. Tears of desperation streaked his face. He would not submit, not then, not ever. His spine felt as if it would break. His rib cage groaned. One of Wluncus's legs was hooked over and under Hereward's, so as best he could Hereward got one of his feet on Wluncus's thigh and with a sudden shove forced his leg back, and giving an almighty heave up from his winded belly, lamming back both his elbows, unseated the big buttocks that pinioned him, turning over onto his back and at the same time kneeing Wluncus hard in the crotch.

The baker let out a string of oaths and clutched his balls. Eowa cautioned them. The crowd grumbled. They had wagered all they had on Wluncus Moue. Why hadn't he finished off the boy ere now?

Then someone pointed to the Mead Tree. A strange half-light like that of a brewing storm was cast about it and folk swore they saw goblin faces gibber in the glow. From afar off there came a belch of thunder. 'Old Skrat!' they cried as one, and crossed themselves. Hogni Tricksleeve gave a chuckle and dropped from his perch like a squirrel.

On the pitch, Wluncus, bethinking to mock Hereward for the weaker opponent, offered him first hug and Hereward took it and got such a hold on Wluncus that the baker could not wrestle free. Hereward threw him, sending him to kiss the sod against his will, going his full length with a tremendous thud. The effort of the throw all but brought Hereward to his knees, but straightening up and turning, wiping the spit and sweat from his face, for he was all of a muckwash, he let out

82

a lungful. 'I've won! Hereward Leofricsson! Have ye no cheers for me?'

They hadn't, but they soon showed what they did have as with aught that came to hand, wormy apples and stones and cracked eggs, they began to pelt Hereward and to yell.

'Boggart! That's what he be!'

'Showing his bare arse!'

'Suffer not the cursed man!'

'Begone to your thursehole!'

A stone struck Hereward's cheek, drawing blood, a mushy apple hit him in the chest. For a moment he stood stunned, his ears full of the din that was like half a gale. Then he turned and went to the reeve's table. 'Declare me the winner!' he said to Eowa of Candleshoe. 'I claim my prize!'

Meanwhile Wluncus Moue would have come at Hereward's back had not Hogni Tricksleeve slipped in to bar his path, grinning, showing sharp teeth and brandishing a knife.

A clutch of the old men called, 'Give the lad his due! He deserves it!'

And one queer-looking fellow, tall and thin as the leaping-pole he carried and wearing a green cap with a goose feather, added his voice: 'As my name is Wulfric Raher – Wulfric the Heron of Wrokesham – I say 'twas well earned!'

But a few men had already set about tackling Hereward who lashed out with both fists. He packed a punch and no mistake! One man he knocked head over heels under the table. To another he gave a blow on the nose that had him bleeding like a pig. The old fenmen whooped and hallooed.

'Go on, give 'em a clink o' the skull!'

'Draw his snout!'

'Give 'un a ding o' the lug!'

They clapped their hands, thinking of all those who would have to be taken home on turf barrows.

But Eowa besought them, calling for order. Around the pitch there was much banging of buckets and jeering.

Sucking his raw knuckles Hereward said, 'I want the mare! I won her! She's mine!' Only to have his plea drowned by a hundred angry voices.

Eowa looked at the panting boy they called boggart and saw tears in the strange, louring eyes. He tried calm words as with a wild creature. 'We'll settle it, lad. But it would be better to let tempers cool first.' He put a hand on Hereward's shoulder.

But Hereward would not be placated.

'Nay!' he said, 'you'll give it to that other! It's always the bloody same!' The prize he had wrenched his guts for was to be snatched away. Thus with a howl of rage and despair Hereward smote Eowa and any others who would stop him, breaking free, and ran to where the mare was tethered, Hogni Tricksleeve at his heels.

Wynter came alongside in his wagon with Darryl and Young Leofsi up behind bearing a birch besom and a rake.

'Laws-a-massy-me!' said Darryl.

'Blood's up, no danger!' said Wynter.

There was no time for coaxing the mare nor using soft words. Hereward grabbed her rope bridle and hitched it to the wagon and clambered in with Darryl and Young Leofsi among the pease-straw, for Wynter had sold all his fruit. Hogni waved a gape-stick to beat off all comers, Wynter yelled at the pony to get a move on and they set off.

The crowd chased after them, some with hurdling bills and leaping-poles, but they were well on their way by then, mud clods flying, the pony's hooves going butter-and-eggs, butter-and-eggs, at a rare pace across the hay-fen, and as they gained the track to Strawberry Wood they left behind the angry faces and shouts and Bragi's Meadow dark in the eye of the gathering storm.

Mare Swallow

ereward told Lilla the chaplain about the mare and Wor-Will-Be-So made a collar of witch-bane and bitter-sweet to help keep her safe. Likewise Aethelmaer forged new shoes. By then Hereward had named her Swallow. For many days it rained and while the tracks were awash there were no visitors to Little-Bethlehem-of-the-Rushes.

But one morning Hogni Tricksleeve came running into the stable. 'He's here!'

'Who?'

'Your father's reeve.'

Hereward brushed the hay from his jerkin. Inwardly his heart forbade him. 'Where is he now?'

'In the hall speaking with your lady mother.'

A fire burned on the hearth. Thick hangings were upon the walls, woven of flax and wool in rich colours. It was only the first week in October, not yet Eldmass, but winter came early in the fenlands.

Countess Godgyfu sat upon the high-seat. She turned to see Hereward in the doorway. 'Eowa has told me,' she said, 'all of what happened.'

Hereward said to the reeve, 'If you have come for an apology then I'll oblige you. I am sorry that I struck you. It wasn't meant.'

Eowa of Candleshoe rubbed his jaw ruefully. 'I accept that, master. But it isn't for myself that I come.'

Hereward frowned. 'Then why for?'

'The folk are angry.'

'I have done them no harm. 'Twas they who sought the quarrel, not me.'

'What do they want?' said Countess Godgyfu.

'They want your son – master Hereward – to surrender up the horse. They say he took it by unfair means.'

85

'No!' said Hereward.

Countess Godgyfu bade Hereward be silent. She said to Eowa, 'And if he will not?'

'There's wild talk, ma'am.'

But Hereward could keep silent no longer. He felt his heart would burst. 'Eowa, man,' he said, 'you watched me. You saw me win. 'Twas with these very hands!' He held them out, big, square-fingered, horny-palmed.

Eowa of Candleshoe lowered his eyes. 'I know what I thought I saw. But they can throw a glamour upon the minds of men.'

Hereward whispered, 'You too?'

Eowa was reluctant to look his way again. He stared hard at the rush strewn floor and said, 'It will have to go before the Shire-Moot.'

Hereward did not answer. He swung round, balling and clenching his fists lest they fly free.

Chancing a glance at the broad, leather-clad back, Eowa said, 'I can understand your anger, master. 'Tis only natural. But consider, is it worth the trouble? It is only a drudge of a mare. Ah, I know she's credited with being ensorcelled, but I've seen better-looking nags go under the knacker's axe.'

His princess. His arrow shotten straight from Ull's bow. His heaven-crossing, river-wading, silver-hoofed one . . . 'She belongs to me!' Hereward said. 'And as God is my witness, I'll kill the first man who lays hold on her!'

When Eowa of Candleshoe had gone, Countess Godgyfu said, 'Why didn't you tell me?'

It was quiet and the sunlight turned to green through the emerald glass, and the water dripping from the thatch made a crystal echo and all was wet as with weeping, liken to when men and beasts and stones and metals did weep for Baldur. Hereward gave no answer.

'All that time you kept it a secret.'

Hereward shrugged. 'You'd not have understood.'

'Your father must be told. Hereward, O, Hereward, why did you not do as Eowa asked of you?'

Hereward looked up at her and said, 'Am I a straw man to do any's bidding?'

The Harrowing Moon

hus Earl Leofric was sent for and he rode thither from the Palace of Westminster. He had always heard grievances fairly. All troubles were brought to Leofric's hall. But then a dozen renderings of the same story had been told to him – by the Countess, by Eowa of Candleshoe and by folk who were wont to stop him on his way – before ever he drew it from Hereward.

He heard his son tell it in the twilight of the autumn evening with only the ashes of the fire between them. At first slow, tongue-tied, then gradually breaking into full honey-flood. ' "Suffer not the cursed man!" they shouted. As if I was a lump of muck. As if I had no right to be among them. A proper Molly!'

'But why do you go, lad, when you know very well they'll say unkind things?'

'There's nobbut else to do. I'd help in the fields come reaping and haymaking as you do. I'd wood-carry. Wattle-weave. But the labouring folk say that one look of me makes their blades blunt and gives 'em chalf-stones in their fingers.'

Though Hereward was coarse featured and with a jaw both too long and heavy, Leofric had seen many worse-favoured than the boy who sat before him. He felt the muscle of the shoulders that had thrown the baker and the strength of the hand that had felled the reeve. Where would his path lead? Where shone his star?

'You'll not change your mind – about giving back the horse?'

'Nay.'

'I'd let you have my own Hrimfaxi. He is of fine blood-stock. Costing many mancuses.'

In beauty far surpassing Mare Swallow. But she was his. His. Hereward shook his head.

Earl Leofric said, 'Then we'll go to hear the charges together.'

'Nay – not that!'

'But you must or else it'll go all the harder for ye.'

'It'll do thus anyway. They'll only come to stand a-gawping at me. To point at me like as if I'd got two bloody heads. For why should they listen when they have never listened before?' He brought up his eyes to his father. The lashes of them were all that was to be seen, like sickles of ripe wheat. 'But I fought by the rules, father. May the All Holy Lord strike me down dead if I lie!' Then as an afterthought: 'It wasn't my fault that the Mead Tree smiled upon me.'

'I believe you, lad.'

'Then they've not turned your heart against me?'

'You think any man could do that?'

'And to think I used to be afraid.'

Earl Leofric looked sadly at Hereward's bowed head. 'Of me?'

'Ah.'

'Was I ever rough spoken with ye? Have I ever clouted ye?'

'Nay.'

'Then why?' And when Hereward could find no answer, the Earl whispered, 'I'm glad you're not any more.'

The charge against Hereward was to be heard before the Feast of St Simon and St Jude, when all the clods in the fields were broken, harrowed by the full of the moon.

Wynter said, 'If things go bad for ye, bor, then I want to be at your side.'

They were in the orchard at Wyntering and the only sound, save the creaky wings of the wood pigeons, was the chopper bringing down the old apple boughs.

'But you have all this,' Hereward replied, 'the land. Where would be the sense in leaving such?'

When Earl Leofric rode to the Shire-Moot in Bragi's Meadow Rudgang Wolf-Cloak was at his side, though not the hus-carls. The Earl feared more trouble with the local folk. Wynter and Darryl and Young Leofsi journeyed also. They had put themselves forward as oath-helpers but had been refused. Countess Godgyfu spent the day in prayer in the chapel.

Down by the mere Hogni sat at Hereward's feet. 'Wherever you go, let me come.'

'You're not bound to me, Hogni.'

'I'd share cheese parings and scrapings of porridge pots with ye joyfully.'

'No, you must go your own way.'

'My way is thine.'

It was nearly Vespers when the Earl arrived back. He came into the hall leaving the great door open for his marshal to follow, and Hereward knew, even as he crept down the stairs from under the eaves, that everything was wrong. And as he beheld his father sitting weary and bitter among the shields, his heart smote him with pain. 'Father,' he said.

And looking up and seeing him, Earl Leofric said, 'I have failed, lad.'

'Tell me.'

Rudgang Wolf-Cloak entered then, torque and arm-rings gleaming in the dusk. 'You are outlawed. To be gone from your father's house.'

He would bear the Wolf's-Head. Any who harboured him or gave him succour would be adjudged guilty and heavily fined. None could claim vengeance for his slaying. 'Did many speak against me?'

'Aye.'

'None for me?'

'Your great-uncle Brand and Abbot Ulfketyl and a strange man in a feathered cap, claimed to be a small holder from Wrokesham. They spoke in your favour.'

The name of Wulfric the Heron struck no chord. Time would be for that later. Hereward saw a spider spin her web on the lintel. 'And none heeded them?'

Earl Leofric shook his head.

Rudgang said, 'O, my lord, if only you had let me take my hearth-troop with me! By God, there would have been another kind of judgement this day!'

The Shire-Moot had ruled that Hereward's wrongful covetousness should be punished by an exile of five years. Now in London Town there were three courts, the Folk-Moot, the Husting and the Ward-Moot, as well as King Edward's own hearing chamber at the Palace of Westminster. And it was to the King himself that the Earl was to take the case and seek his mercy.

Hereward went to Lilla's house after Compline and wept on his knee for a full hour or more until the sacring bell chimed for Nocturns.

Nothing Lilla could say or do would calm him. Lilla had been at the Shire-Moot that day when the accusations were doled out and the falsehoods mouthed by Wluncus Moue and the other mischief-mongers given credence. He had seen Earl Leofric strip gold bracelets from his arms and offer them as recompense. Heard him swear the great oath of three twelves and many hides. And Aethelmaer the blacksmith standing forth to say, 'What the lad knows is what I taught him. He

89

could beat any one of you with a hand tied behind his back. Why do you not let him alone?'

'Hereward, O, Hereward!'

Hereward got to his feet, wiping his eyes. 'Forgive me, Lilla. You must think I am daft – crying.'

'Nay, lad.' Lilla watched him, a dull ache in his heart. 'Has your father made provision?''

'He is writing a parchment to take to King Dairmaid of Baile Atha Cliath asking if he will give shelter to me.'

'When do you leave for London?'

'Tomorrow at first light.'

The Court of the Childless King

hus before the Hour of Prime the next morning with Hogni Tricksleeve slung up behind him, Hereward rode forth with his father by way of the Car Dyke and King Street and the Ermine Street – the old road of Earn's People – and thence to London Town.

When they entered the gates Hereward saw more people in one glance than he had in the whole of his life. Hogni clung on tight, his skinny arms around Hereward's waist. 'Folk must be pixilated to live here, master. Did you ever hear such a din?'

Through the winding thoroughfares – Rood Lane and Lady Lane and Bishop's-Gate-Street and St Dunstan's, home of the goldsmiths and jewel-workers – Hereward followed the earl, awed and wonder-struck by all he beheld. The open markets of Cheapside and Leadenhall and East Cheap. The inns and taverns, the smell of hot pork and chitterlings from the flesh-mongers. The tanners and besom-makers alongside shoe-smiths and bead-turners and wheel-rights. The shops of spoon-carvers and soap-makers and brand-wrights, buttock to buttock with vegetable gardens and orchards.

Earl Leofric pointed out the churches to him. St Magnus the Martyr at the foot of Fish Street Hill. St Bride's-by-the-Fleet and All-Hallows-by-the-Tower and St Clement Dane that stood between the town of London and the city of Westminster.

And coming out to the river with its teeming, barge-jammed wharfs where the foreign merchants paid their toll in cloth, pepper, vinegar and gloves, spanned by both London bridge and Tyburn bridge, lined with huts and stalls and bedecked with brightly coloured canvas, among which gaudy show were harboured tiny timbered chapels and grottoes and holy images and shrines of the saints, they drew rein to stare at the marvel of King Edward's new church of St Peter. Overshadowing the ancient church of King Sebert, that had survived

91

the Danish ravages, it stood stark and bird-haunted, flanked by the marshes of the Isle of Thorns, and to the point of sunset the Palace of Westminster reared from the morning mist, dream begirt, its towers lost amid the apple-green clouds.

Within, the main hall was already full of people. Beggars and lepers with their bells and clack-dishes, harlots and good-wives and nuns and pedlars. There was a blind girl with a crippled man. A cloth was over the girl's eyes and she was holding onto the man's ragged tunic to guide her steps. The man could not walk and was dragging himself along on small wooden trestles.

On beholding them expressions came and went on Leofric's face in the batting of an eye, and he stopped and put a handful of coins into the blind girl's bowl and his own cloak, finely woven of silk and wool, onto the crippled man's back.

In the upper storey of the palace the King had his chamber and there he was preparing for the morning's Folk-Moot when he saw his Earl of Mercia on the threshold. He turned, his mantle half undone, brooch in hand, and said, 'Why, Leofric!'

King Edward was not alone. Queen Aldwyth was with him and she wore a gold circlet over her head-rail and ear-jewels of lapis-lazuli, blue moons dangling from lobe to neck. A few members of the household, stallers and clerics both English and Norman, were in attendance. And leaning back against the sill of an open window, arms folded across his chest, was Harold Godwinesson.

Earl Leofric did not beat about the bush. He laid the case squarely before the King, and having heard him, King Edward said, 'O, Leofric, this is indeed a sad day!'

'I come to ask you, to beg you to show mercy on my son. He will not plead for himself, but I will. Do not allow them to send him away for five years. There's no right in that. No justice.'

Hereward looked at his father. He was humbling himself and it cut deep to the heart to see it.

'You do not have to beg me, Leofric. I would do everything I could to help you,' said the King. He looked to Hereward then. 'Why do the folk of your father's shire dislike you so?'

Finding his tongue, Hereward said, 'I am eye-smitten, Sire.'

''Tis superstition,' said Earl Leofric, 'nothing more. There's no harm in him.'

The Abbot of St Riquier, a monastery under the King's patronage, suggested Hereward should serve the Church.

Whereupon Queen Aldwyth said, 'What? Would you trap a wild

thing in a cage? He is old enough to be wed. He would soon make you a grandsire, Leofric.'

'Women shy from me, ma'am,' Hereward said, dazzled by her.

Queen Aldwyth contemplated the size of his shoulders. 'I find that hard to believe.' And she whispered in the King's ear then.

King Edward said, 'Aldwyth's taken a fancy to your lad. If he'll admit his wrong-doings she would have him for her staller.'

Aldwyth smiled and her mouth was like the juice of strawberries. 'Be my dish-thane or bower-thane. Make your choice, Hereward Leofricsson.'

'But I did no wrong,' Hereward blurted out.

'So sure of himself. He delights me, my lord!'

Harold Godwinesson moved forward then. For all he was so big it was easy to forget he was there, watching and listening and biding his time. A jerkin of lambskin fitted close across his shoulders. Twin bracelets of gold set with lumps of raw amber gripped his mighty forearms.

''Tis no bootless crime,' he said slowly, 'if crime it was at all.'

King Edward looked up to see him. 'What do you suggest, Harold?'

Harold bowed his head beneath the low beams. There was already sweat in the armpits of his shirt and hay on his trousers, bespeaking of stables and labouring and muck. His voice was like a summer full of Julys. 'Well, Sire,' he said, 'it is in your power to bring the sentence to two years without overruling the Shire-Moot, and the petitioner still having the right of appeal. I'll sign as witness. Would you accept that, Leofric? Two years passes quickly, and in the meantime you can be working for his return.'

Queen Aldwyth looked from Harold to the King. Harold was the power, the strength, the force. She twisted an ear-jewel, humming softly, disappointed at losing the chance of seducing Hereward. But Harold's suggestion was met gladly.

'Then let it be done,' said King Edward.

'I shall ever be beholden to ye, Harold Godwinesson.' Earl Leofric faced him squarely.

Harold shook his head. 'Ah, no,' he said softly. 'Not that, not from you, Leofric.'

The Lane of Goblin Feet

ogni Tricksleeve burst out crying when he knew and wept all the way back back to Little-Bethlehem-of-the-Rushes.

Countess Godgyfu, her mass book set aside, said, 'How many days grace have you?'

And Hereward answered, 'Seven.'

He had already taken his leave of Aethelmaer the blacksmith at Bambweare and of Wor-Will-Be-So who had sung a journey-charm for him and given him a toad-bone which he wore then round his neck, tangling with the red spinel prayer beads.

He stood in his mother's bower by candlelight, her maids having been only too ready to leave when he entered.

'I scare them,' he said, touching the bed coverings of thrown silk and otter pelts, 'yet they watch me from the window, times, when I'm swimming, eager to see a naked man.' He brought an earth-sweet smell with him and hair bristled at the open neck of his shirt.

'You will not go a-Viking, will you, Hereward? Become a berserker – a sea-rover – and shame your father?'

'I'd not thought of it.'

'He is heart-broken at the losing of you.'

'Are you?'

'His sorrows are mine.'

Hereward said, 'I'm not fit to tie his thongs.'

'Then you'll promise?'

'Maybe I don't belong to him nor to you. Maybe he grieves for no reason. For a changeling.' Hereward shrugged. 'No matter. But I promise.'

Godgyfu gave a shuddering sigh and rose and went to her tow-chest. Opening it she brought out tunics and shirts and belts of gold links and jewelled buckle-loops. 'You will need these,' she said. And Hereward looked at them, then at her. 'That's how the poor folk must see

94

you at the gate. Dealing them out clothes and bread. Only 'tis home-spun and not fine velvets.'

'You have money?'

'Father has given me some.'

Countess Godgyfu opened a smaller chest and the inside of it glowed with the reflection of gems. 'Take of these what you will.'

'They'll be of no use to me.'

Silver bracelets. A brooch of garnets and gold. Beads of amber, amethyst and coloured glass. Gold necklaces.

Countess Godgyfu cluttered Hereward's pockets. 'Will you refuse my parting gifts?'

The chapel bell was sounding for Matins and Lauds as with sword Brain-Biter on his thigh and his saddle-bags stuffed with provisions and a gipsire of bow-strings and arrow-heads and the rich bounty of Countess Godgyfu, Hereward made ready to leave.

Earl Leofric was dry-eyed as he bade him farewell in the hall yard. He gave him a pledge-ring of ravens rampant and held him hard and close. 'I'll have ye back before the leaves turn again.'

Then would be the ploughing, the reaping, the mowing. The feasts for the making of hay-ricks and the corn-ricks. The gathering of the wood. The hus-carls, led by Rudgang Wolf-Cloak, had harped their lament in the hall over ale cups. And each morning small bunches of flowers had been found on the stairs. Gift of the elves.

Wynter and Darryl and Young Leofsi followed behind Mare Swallow to the priest's house where Lilla waited. His tithe of glebe-land had flourished all the year, full of vegetables and herbs and fruit, sown with madder, linseed and woad. Now it was brown and dripping and forlorn. And that was the picture Hereward was to carry in his heart.

'God go with you and keep you,' Lilla said, taking Hereward's hands in his own across the wicket gate. He had shriven him that morning after Nocturns. As a priest there was no more he could do.

Hogni Tricksleeve was there, scrawny and bright-eyed. 'Give us a leg up, master!' he said.

Whereupon Hereward leaned over and hauled him up by the seat of his breeches.

Then he said to Wynter, 'Ah, do not weep, man, or you'll start me blubbing too!'

And so after they had exchanged prayers and blessings, Hereward left his kinsmen and rode down through the fen fields, and thence to the paths he knew so well – the lane of goblin feet. And Hogni began to play on his pipe, strange, wild, music. And away out, the birds, winter-stayers, rose up in their hundreds from the mere.

The Ears of Corn

n the beginning of the year after Hereward was outlawed, as with the liriconfancy to the meadows, so came Hwita Clatter-Clogs the minstrel to Little-Bethlehem-of-the-Rushes.

Strange it seemed to Hwita without the boy hanging about in the doorway or watching from behind one of the god-pillars. But he unslung his harp and told of the news he'd brought. That of the death of Earl Siward Digre of Northumbria.

'What death did he die?' asked Rudgang Wolf-Cloak.

Hwita answered, 'It would have been a cow's-death, had not he bidden his hearth-troop stand him up on his feet and harness him for war.'

And so the north was left open and in time was disputed between Aelfgar and Tostig Godwinesson. But it was Tostig the favoured one who was King Edward's choice. 'As though the sun shone out of his arse!' And so saying, Aelfgar had stormed out of the counsels and gone to wreak his vengeance on the English–Welsh border, with the help of Gruffyd ap Llewellyn, who had ousted Gruffyd ap Rhydderch to become Prince of both Gwynedd and Deheubarth, and to whom Aelfgar had given his daughter, then a five-years child, in marriage. They had put to flight the local fyrd under the command of Raoul the Timid, Earl of Hereford and a royal kinsman, laying waste with fire and sword.

Tightening the pegs of his harp, Hwita Clatter-Clogs did not think much to Aelfgar. Not then nor in the months following when he'd come back to Westminster seeking forgiveness yet again. Couldn't tell the truth if his life depended on it. Just give you a greasy, buttery tale. And he wasn't worth the pleading that Earl Leofric had done for his sake. Now there was a man. 'Took his sins upon him, he did.'

'And?' said Countess Godgyfu.

'He got him his pardon and East Anglia. "I would do it for no one

96

but you, Leofric." Those were the King's very words. And all the time with his hands on the cross at his breast and big tears in his eyes.'

'But what of Earl Harold? They are his lands. Surely, he is wrath?'

'Wrath, lady? Him?' Hwita tucked the harp under his chin, feeling the wood-soul move. 'Nay. Temper like honey. Gave them up without so much as an argument.'

And that was what had so grieved Tostig Godwinesson when he heard of it. He'd said, 'Christ, man, are you daft? What do you expect to gain from it?'

And Harold calmly answered, 'I do not know.'

The puzzle was that you could never be sure with Harold the Deep-Minded just what his true motive was or might turn out to be. At first glance he looked to be easily won. The appeaser. The peace-maker. The ruthful. But Tostig knew well that he could be stubborn, aye, even without mercy, when it suited his purpose.

As luck would have it, Hwita Clatter-Clogs had his harp strung to fine voice when he played at Aelfgar's heir-ship ale, held amid the blazing fires in the Hall of Blickling, among the north folk of his earldom of East Anglia.

It was middle-winter with snow upon the ground. Hwita had happened on the feast as he happened on most things; the chance of food, shelter, a bed for the night, in return for his songs.

And though it lacked the King, the company at the festal board had been great. Earls and thanes and churchmen, and after Harold Godwinesson had tossed him a gold ring, the pickings were rich.

Tostig, so as not to be outdone by Harold, had likewise given gold to the minstrel, but all the while he had the raging mind and aching heart of an unhappy man. That night he'd watched good fortune rain upon Aelfgar Leofricsson. And to have to drink the heir-ship ale in his praises had well nigh choked him.

And thus it was he sat pondering on his empty cup – gold the thickness of a goose-egg – when Eahlswith, the young daughter of Aelfgar, who had been larking with her brothers Eadwine and Morkere, tripped and went tumbling headforth.

Harold happened to be nearest. 'Are ye hurt, lass?' he said, and bent to pick her up. The child's cheek was warm-shaded as an autumn nut. Ears and neck and wrists gaudy with Welsh gold. 'You must be more careful, pet.' The floor rushes had softened her fall. Harold brushed the husks of dried flowers from her smock. Kindness was in his huge hands.

97

Looking on, Aelfgar said, 'And what do you say to Earl Harold?'

Whereat the little maid only hung her head so that her tresses hid her and was tongue-tied.

Countess Godgyfu made light of it by a whispered, 'O, ware lest she fall in love with you, my lord!'

Harold smiled and shrugged. 'Why, she's nothing but a babe.'

Though in truth the child's rapt gaze was often to be seen on Harold during the next two days and it afforded the company amusement that she blushed for him.

When Harold rode back to Westminster with Tostig, the church-men travelled in the same train as the hus-carls. Aelfgar came to see them off. His words were mostly for Harold, smooth-tongued as if he'd got melted butter in his mouth.

'I'll teach my lads to be friends with you, Harold,' he said. 'The sword shall rest in the scabbard.'

'So be it,' Harold replied.

Even beneath the shelter of the low-hanging eaves gusts of snow blew sharply between the two, eyeball-stinging, cheek-lashing. Astride his horse and cloaked and hooded in the skins of grey wolf, Harold took up the reins in a leather-clad fist.

Aelfgar said, 'Eahlswith weeps to see you leave. Poor lass. Did you find her comely, Harold?'

'A fair maid,' got Aelfgar in answer.

Aelfgar lifted his head, heedless of the snow, to meet Harold look for look. 'You could have her if you wanted, when she is ready for bedding.'

Harold's reply was equable enough. 'You must have lost your wits in the mead-cup, man,' he said.

'Nay, 'twould join our two houses. Her marriage to Gruffyd was of no consequence. He was but a foster-father to her.'

'I have my wife.'

'Only in common law,' Aelfgar said, gripping the horse-harness. 'You are but hand-fasted to the lady of the Swan-Neck. Nothing holds you.'

'You do not know me.' Harold's voice was suddenly hard beneath the gentle southern brogue.

'But you have done something for me. I would like to repay you.'

'I want no payment.'

Aelfgar loosed hold of the bridle-rings. He stood back so that Harold could pass. 'Very well, have it as you will,' he said.

Tostig strove to keep at his brother's side. The hus-carls bringing up the rear chaffed each other and swore much. Bold men in battle, they were, but they went in fear then as they passed through the Forest of the Souls of Dead Children.

'Living here must do something to a man,' said Tostig.

'I lived here a time. I liked it,' answered Harold.

'You did?'

'Aye.'

'I'll be glad to be quit of it! Three days was enough for me!'

'Ah, but was it not you that upbraided me with that tongue of yours the night long for giving these lands over to Aelfgar Leofricsson?'

'That was different!'

'How?'

'Because through it you have lost face, aye, and power!'

'You take it too hard.'

Tostig stared sullenly ahead, eyes narrowed against the snow. 'It wasn't even as if you were obliged to stay here. You had the court – Nazeing. These estates can take care of themselves. You have but to collect the dues.' And they were rich; for many was the time Tostig had seen the bringing in of the first fruits of the grain at Martin-Mass.

Harold said, 'Wringing wealth from the land isn't everything. You must be prepared to give also. Maybe if you tried staying a while among the folk of your own earldom you'd understand my meaning.'

'In Northumbria? They hate my guts!'

'You have to make an effort, lad. None of it is easy.'

'I'll suck up to no man!'

Harold shrugged.

At length Tostig was the one to speak, in gentler tones this time. 'I can never anger you, can I, Harold? Even when we were lads together and me such a cross-patch – you'd never strike me. Always so calm. So full of patience. You know, you made a good impression on the Mercian men. They like you. But tell me, brother, what was it that Aelfgar Leofricsson was speaking to you of before we left?'

Harold did not turn to look at Tostig, but he could feel his eyes hard and paler blue than his own, searching. 'He wanted to repay me.'

'Did he, then? And what did you say?'

'I told him I wanted nothing.'

And Hwita Clatter-Clogs had got himself a ride on the back of a wagon, his harp well hidden beneath a pile of pease-straw sacks.

99

The Wolf's Head

ereward bided at the great yew-tree-timbered hall in Baile Atha Cliath belonging of King Dairmaid Mac Mael na mbo for the space of two harvests. Rich in cows and men, King Dairmaid was one of seven Kings who ruled many under-Kings, each disputing the title of High King of Erin.

In the early days Hereward had thought of little else but going home. When it was the Mead-Month his heart had yearned for the honey-gathering at Wyntering. 'Don't you want to go home?' he'd said to Hogni Tricksleeve.

Hogni had got himself a corner of the hall as his own, ousting the two sprites who already lived there, and seemed happy enough. 'Home? Home is where you are, master.'

Thus as time passed, Hereward made friends, the closest among them being Padraig O'Connor, a boy about his own age and a foster-lean of King Dairmaid. They were always together. They rode and wrestled and fished, and played fidchell by the hearth of nights. And so it was that Hereward learned of the Gaelic ways and language. So quickly did he pick up the tongue, that laughing, King Dairmaid had said, 'We'll make of you one of the Fian yet!' And Hereward, knowing the Fian to be the highest rank of Irish Warrior – from the tales of Fian-lore told to him by Padraig – answered, 'I'd lief that was so.'

Being a Wolf's-Head was no bar to Hereward submitting himself for the ordeals of the Feinnidh, a wondrous belt of animal heads and bird-masks of gold to be his if he succeeded, empowered with magic and worn only by the followers of Fionn Mac Cumhaill.

''Tis a terrible hard thing,' said Padraig. 'You can count on the fingers of one hand the number of men who survive it.'

'Did you try?' said Hereward.

'Aye.' Padraig shook his red head ruefully. 'And failed.'

But Hereward was not to be put off. He came through the first trial of having nine warriors cast their spears at him whilst he defended himself with shield and hazel rod. And Padraig, braiding Hereward's hair for the next, said, 'What if you're killed? By the Oak of Mughna! What are we to tell your father?'

'By the sun, moon, stars and wind, you'll tell him nothing!' Hereward replied.

Stripped, but having both spear and knife, Hereward had to run through the woods of the province, with all the finest warriors of Leinster in full chase at his heels. If overtaken or wounded, he would not be accepted. Nine days and nights did this last and Padraig O'Connor gave a great sigh of relief and a glory be, to see Hereward return, having outrun and outwitted his pursuers.

He walked, limping a might, into Dairmaid's hall, naked, heedless of the company. And when it became known that in all that time his weapons had not quivered in his hand and that no dead branch had cracked under his foot, that he had leaped over a bough as high as his head and passed beneath one as low as his knee, those gathered in the hall called for the belt of Fionn to be girded upon Hereward that very hour.

Thus, his prize got, as with Mare Swallow, so likewise the belt joined sword Brain-Biter as his most treasured possession.

Hogni Tricksleeve grinned up at Hereward. 'The way those maids looked at you! Gobbled you up with their eyes, they did!'

And King Dairmaid was to echo Hogni's words in the hall not so long after. 'You're famed, lad! Known by the men of Ulster and Connacht! The only Sasanaigh to be one of the Fian!'

Hereward fingered the belt. ''Tis proud I am to wear it.'

Whereupon King Dairmaid leaned closer, gold brooches aflame, filling Hereward's cup, and said, 'And we've many a fair heifer eager for a young bull like yourself!'

Hereward's heart beat quick and hard at that. 'I'm shotten,' he said. 'I'm no woman's man.'

King Dairmaid looked anew at the strange scar half-hidden then by the growth of beard. 'As though that mattered!'

Hereward's hand went up to his face and he ducked his head in the old closed-in-unto-himself way. 'I don't need anyone,' he said. 'I can get along by myself. It doesn't bother me.'

Hogni Tricksleeve chuckled into his bowl on hearing this, for almost every night Hereward soaked himself in his dreams, creeping out in the dawn to wash the seed from him in the waters of the Lough of Enchanted Birds. Maybe sweet talk was beyond him. Plamais they

101

called it. But curled up out of sight under a fairy bush, Hogni had seen Hereward lying on the bank, looking down at his reflection, then smashing it with the flat of his hand. And heard him utter the words he'd likely always wanted to say, 'O, woman! Will you have my baby? And live with me till I'm an old, old man. Till I die . . . '

But Hogni's chuckles soon stopped when Hereward began to talk of leaving. 'What for?'

'Just to go.'

'But, master –'

'You don't have to come. You can stay here.'

This threw Hogni into a right panic. 'You know I cannot! My life is yours!'

'O, shut up about that!'

'Master – folks are kind here. We mayn't find no kindness anywhere else.'

Hereward had been polishing sword Brain-Biter and he lammed it down hard in the straw. 'Stay then! It's nowt to me! I don't own you! And I don't want you following me! So sod off!'

A King Shall Win a Queen with Goblets and Gold

T he Church of the Nuns at Wilton was founded by Queen Aldwyth during the first year of her marriage. Her dowry from the King had consisted of the city of Winchester, all of Martinsley Wapentake as well as the sokes of Leominster, Leighton-Buzzard and Houghton Regis and the blessed Old Sarum, making her the wealthiest and most powerful woman in England.

'You will do us proud, lass!' Earl Godwine had said upon her wedding eve. 'Yea, you truly are the rose of my thorn.' He'd his hand beneath her chin, big and well-ringed, chiefest among them the Seal of the White Horse of the Leets of Kent. It was no easy task in those days to build up a landed inheritance. But Godwine's father had throve from villager to his thane-right and Godwine himself from thane-right to earl.

'I cannot love him, father.'

The King's nuptial gift had been a necklace of agates, each stone the size of a mistle-thrush egg and the colour of pigeon's blood.

'He is kindly. Mayhap you'll grow to be fond of him.'

And thus King Edward had become like a second father to her. Members of the clergy had praised this, for Aldwyth, under the King's guidance, had been brought further into the service of God. But watching, the men at court were wont to remark over their mead cups that no woman ever turned to religion if she had a good man in her bed.

With the foundations laid and the masons and wattle-weavers begun work, King Edward would often accompany his bride to Wilton, riding thither with his retinue, gold and scarlet thuuf borne aloft before him, to see the building in progress. He indulged Aldwyth's every whim in those days, taking a celibate pleasure in her youth and beauty. He could give her love, deep affection and above all, faithfulness. There were even times when he felt the need for her. The need that shamed

103

him. The act he could never perform. He was a man – equipped to mate as well as any, to hunt and ride and hold his liquor – and yet he could no more copulate than the carved stone angels. Marbled, sightless, genderless. Physical contact, the feel of living flesh all but repulsed him. His mother had known. The Norman Queen Emma-Aelfgyfu, widow of Ethelred Evil-Counsel, Edward's own father, and afterward Consort of Knut the Wolf-Feeder and by him the mother of Harthacnut. For years Edward had suffered her mockery and bullying and been forced to drink mint water to make him lusty.

The measure of a man to the Saxon way of thinking was plain enough. Strong of arm, true of heart and tireless with a woman. Thus it had not been long before Aldwyth was given her own bedchamber and bower, and if she waited his coming in unto her then she waited in vain. She never spoke of it nor did he. He kissed her cheek and cluttered her fingers with many rings. He sat her beside him in the hall and saw her draw the eyes of those husky, brawny, fecund shiremen with their bulging muscles, great stiff cocks and shaggy gold manes. They envied him and it pleasured him that it should be so, and for those first few years he cosseted and coddled her. His child. His pure vessel. His chaste Susannah. She whose price was above rubies. She did not reproach him, demand from him. For why should she when she had no knowing what it was she lacked?

One day, chiding Aldwyth for walking in the woods barefoot, he'd said, 'Child! Child! At least put on your slippers. What if you should be bitten by a snake or stung with nettles?'

Braiding up her hair, Aldwyth had answered, 'I shall be well, Sire. O, do not fret!'

The grass had been lush and warm during that time, it being the Dry Month, scented with meadowsweet and dodder-of-thyme, the tiny buds like elves' thumbs. And among it had come Aldwyth's belated sexual awakening. One of the hus-carls, a Dane and of the King's own troop, had waylaid his royal mistress in a lonely spot dense with blackthorn blossom, and putting his big arms around her he had overpowered her very gently and lain with her. Her skirts he removed carefully, hardly creasing the flox-silk. His trousers he tore open and for the first time Aldwyth felt what lay between a grown man's legs, before he entered her. His mouth had silenced her first cry of pain, for she was virgin still as was rumoured. But after a few moments when it became clear that she would not scream nor try to fight him, the young hus-carl had cradled her tenderly as any babe, whispering in his Danish tongue, working his cock in even deeper, thrusting fierce, unrelenting.

When he'd finished, Aldwyth opened her eyes and murmured, 'You have raped me!'

Freeing himself from her body, breathing hard, the hus-carl said, 'O, my lady! I ask no pardon. I had to do it!'

'Why?'

He was handsome, his hair the colour of water-lily hearts. ''Twas seeing you thus – like a peach for the plucking – and the knowing that I'd be the first man into your soft, sweet cunt . . .'

Joy coursed through Aldwyth's veins. She whispered, 'I could have you castrated for this. What if I should tell the King?'

To which the hus-carl shrugged and gave answer, 'I cannot stop you, my lady. But it won't be just me. Many other men are going to hunger after you and want you. You were made for love. Not to be hidden in a cloister.'

Years after she had heard that the hus-carl had been killed fighting in the campaigns against the Viking-Irish and Gruffyd ap Rhydderch. And when Earl Godwine had asked her why she sorrowed, she had told him, 'He once made love to me, father, on the earth at Wilton.'

The Earl had looked at her with knowing blue eyes. 'That stroppy young bugger! Right under the King's nose! And ye enjoyed it?' He smiled, then said thoughtfully, ''Tis a pity Edward cannot do the same.'

Queen Aldwyth's fortunes were mostly decided by the King's relations with her family. If good he was doting and considerate towards her. If, however, he'd been at logger-heads with Earl Godwine, as often happened, especially in the later years, King Edward could be spiteful and petty as any woman. One minute he would be liberal with jewels and gifts (Aldwyth then possessed all the jewels once belonging to Queen Emma-Aelfgyfu). The next he would be in a passion, threatening to take away all that he had given.

But in the winter of the year when Aelfgar Leofricsson drank his heir-ship ale at Blickling, Queen Aldwyth's position was assured. She could do no wrong. Thus she bethought herself of journeying to Wilton to see the progress of her abbey-church. It was sudden, that desire to be gone; to be quit of the summons of the chapel bell and the kneeling mat. King Edward, residing at the Wardrobe Palace, showed little interest in what she did and seldom questioned her. The novelty of having her to wife had long since ceased to be. Aldwyth reflected on it without regrets as she came by way of the Painted Hall aglow with Advent candles hanging in their evergreen wreaths and into the icon-studded chamber.

'I shall be gone for a few days, my lord.'

The King looked up. He was sipping malvoisie, warming his buttocks before the fire. On every finger he wore a ring.

'Where is it you go, my dear?'

'To Wilton, my lord.'

'Ah, yes!'

Even the religious devotion they had shared (or at least, she had pretended to share) when she was a young girl and he two and twenty years her elder, had resulted in a barren rivalry. For he already had his abbey-church, his minster foundation, that of St Peter upon Thorney Isle. Based on the style of Jumieges, its stone that of Reigate and Caen, it was the greatest church built entirely without timber yet to be seen in England.

The King sipped and said, 'The weather is so bad, alder-liefest. Would it not be wiser if you stayed here until it cleared?'

Aldwyth looked away to the window where the snow crowded the panes of red glass. 'I shall manage, my lord,' she replied.

'Your brothers Harold and Tostig are due back any day now, big with news from Mercia.'

'Aye, I know.'

'You do not wish to wait them?'

'They will deal well enough without me,' she answered.

Upon taking her leave of the King she called Njal Uggarsson, one of the royal stallers, to her. 'I want to be gone from here by tomorrow.'

He was an Icelander and young to have a valued position in the household. But with the candour of his breed he said, 'You will find nothing to your advantage there, ma'am. The snow lies two foot deep. Unless of course 'tis soaked to the skin you wish to be.'

'Do not counsel me, Njal! Just do as I tell you!'

He bowed and left her. But his counsel was proved right. The site of the Church of the Nuns was deserted, with hollow walls and gaping pits dug for the hung-floor, the local men having abandoned work for the winter. Queen Aldwyth's household, with baggage-wain and sumpter-mules, was aggrieved at leaving London Town and stood about in huddles of two and three. Before dark the tents would have to be pitched and fires lit.

'How they must curse me!' Aldwyth said.

106

'No doubt, ma'am,' Njal the staller answered her.

'Do you?'

'I am your loaf-eater, ma'am.'

'It is the devil's weather!'

'Aye, 'tis said it will be as the mighty Fimbul-Winter of the old legends.'

Lapped in a cloak of heavy wool, the hood of which was sewn with tiny glass beads, Queen Aldwyth shivered. Njal said, 'You'll catch your death of cold, ma'am.'

And the Queen smiled. 'Better that than to suffocate at Westminster.'

'Is that how it is for you, ma'am?'

She looked up at him. Her hazel-gold eyes were like those of a cat, the lashes snow-spangled. Indeed, her adversaries, though few, were wont to call her Puss Velvet-Paw. He judged her age to be about three and thirty.

'I am as the King's daughter and I sit upon the stool at his feet.'

'The King is a lucky man.'

Aldwyth laughed softly in her throat, wondering if Njal Uggarsson's chest was smooth or hairy and how big and red his cock was. She said, 'You speak your mind.'

'In my country all peasants would be princes.'

'How long have you been a staller?'

'Since a year last Barnabas-tide, my lady.'

'You please me.'

'Ma'am.' Njal doffed his fur cap.

'I wish you to attend me at supper.'

The queen was closeted in the royal tent for her supper of partridge pie and mulled ale. Afterward Njal cleared the platter and began to prepare a bed for his mistress; a bolster of duck feathers and ample bearskins. Aldwyth watched him. Deep scars showed above his leather wrist-bands. She knew he had seen hard fighting, that along with Tostig he had joined the army of Earl Siward Digre to bring Macbeth to battle by the Tay.

'Njal.' The Icelander stood up straight. She noticed that the blue iris of his eye was rimmed in black. 'How many years have you?'

'Four and twenty, ma'am.'

Battened against the night the tent shuddered. The wind was as the howl of wolves. Slowly then Aldwyth undressed, letting her garments drop from her. 'Could you desire me, Njal?'

And his answer was all that Aldwyth had hoped for and much more. Thus for his prowess Njal Uggarsson became the Queen's bower-thane henceforth.

The Lay of the Magic Blasts

ith his belt of the Fian, Hereward had once thought of going in search of Aelfgar. 'Will ye both be as the breaking of your father's heart like a nut in his breast?' King Dairmaid had said.

Then news had come that Aelfgar was in England again. 'There's no reason for you to go, cara,' said Padraig. 'Bide with us.'

But Hereward had the wanderlust strong upon him. All the places he'd heard tales of beckoned. Gothland. The Meadows of Boulom and Skania. The Amber Isle of Abalus and the Blue Mountain. His lack of woman would go unnoticed there.

When King Dairmaid knew of his plan, he said, *'Cad fath?'* What for?' It was a rainy day somewhere between the Feasts of La Samhain and La Beal-taine. The plaid-clad old warrior sat upon his hearth-seat. Peat burned, mended with fir cones. Bearskins and heavy wool hangings woven of the great wonders of the two battles of Magh Tuiredh shut out the clay-daubed walls. Bidden to come forward, Hereward obeyed, kneeling on the floor at the King's feet.

'Has aught happened to make you feel this way?' Hereward shook his head. 'I've grown fond of ye, cara. We all have here at Baile Atha Cliath. We'll all miss you.'

Hereward split straws. 'You have a busy court. Men come and go.'

'That is true,' King Dairmaid replied. 'I have been wedded to my kingdom a long while and was chosen by the bull-sleep. I have seen many pass. Some good. Some bad. I took in Harold, Godwine's son, and those two brothers of his. They were not much older than you then – at least Gyrth and Leofwine were not. Harold was like a man twice his years.' Dairmaid smiled sadly then. His coarsely veined hand was no longer steady, a far cry from the day when it had clamped iron side by side with Brian Boru. 'So your mind is made up?'

'Aye.'

The King's watery blue eyes were suddenly sharp. Skene-dhu bright. 'You are not by any chance thinking of going to O'Dea of Slievardagh or MacCarthy of Cashel?' Hereward shook his head. 'Nor O'Sullivan of Knockraffin?'

'Nay.'

'Ah! Then that's not so bad. For they're rogues, every one!' King Dairmaid gazed long on Hereward then. Thinking of when he had walked sky-clad into the hall to claim his feinnidh. Usha! What a sight the lad would have made going into battle like the warriors of olden times, naked but for his weapons and a neck-ring of fine gold. 'Well, so be it. I'd not be the one to keep ye. There is a ship leaves for the northern lands two morning tides from now.'

Getting up, Hereward said, 'I pay my own passage.'

King Dairmaid's burly shoulders sagged. '*A mhic!* My boy!' he said, and smote his hands together. 'You know you can come back whenever you want.'

Hereward said, 'I will remember that.'

It was a Danish cargo ship, a knorr, the maid-of-all-work of the northern seas. Shorter and bulkier than a warship, with a sail and a few oar-holes, it was built mainly of pine with a half-deck fore and an open hold amidships for provisions.

And it was with a sinking heart that Padraig O'Connor stood on the quayside to see it off. The night before, in the witch-hour and uttering a witch-prayer, he and Hereward had cut their wrists and mingled blood. 'May it not be long before we see you again!' he called through the screaming of the gulls. '*Go mbeanni Dia dhuit!* May God bless you!'

Hogni Tricksleeve had come aboard stuffed in one of Mare Swallow's saddle-bags. Upon unpacking and beholding him, Hereward said, 'What do you want?'

'Crusts off your platter.'

'Ah, you're crazy. I've got a good mind to chuck ye over the side!'

Whereat Hogni snickered and found himself a cupboard no bigger than a hen-coop, in which to squat out of Hereward's reach.

But it happened that after a day's journey, the ship could no longer keep to its course. A strong tide had it, carrying it into strange waters. The bearing devices were awry and men wondered that it should be so. There was talk of sighting the White Serpent and trolls riding the mast. And by the twilight of the second day all aboard were ghost-pressed.

Picking his nose in his cupboard, Hogni Tricksleeve began to have second thoughts on the venture.

''Tis too late now,' said Hereward. And he felt the great weight of the night bear down on his shoulders.

'What're we to do?' said Hogni.

'How the hell do I know?'

'There's hundreds of rats and mice in the hold – only they're not rats and mice, but elf-folk in travelling clothes!'

Soon after a weather-bag was shaken and a fierce storm wind was loosed. Rain the colour of fire lashed down, dancing on the water and quenching the moon and stars. Hereward was up on deck trying to calm the restless Mare Swallow when Hogni appeared at his elbow, clinging to him. 'I can hear the singing of women. They'll be out for souls. Lordy me! I cannot swim, master!'

Ahead then loomed a mass of howling green rocks and the ship was flung against them. The timbers groaned and split wide. Men were swept into the raging sea, their screams blotted out by the wind.

Hereward knew Hogni would be a lead weight. He could not support the both of them. He grabbed a length of rope and yelled, 'I'm going to tie you to Swallow!' Whereupon Hereward slung him across the mare's back, along with his saddle-bags and sword Brain-Biter, and began to strap him tight. Hogni struggled, terror-stricken, and Hereward hit him on the jaw, knocking him out.

Within minutes they were in the sea and the waves were smashing over them. Hereward clung onto Mare Swallow's reins as long as he could, keeping Hogni's head above water. The ship had vanished by then. He could see the rocks above the spewing surf. Wood and rigging were hurled to heaven as the waves covered the hag-ridden sky. Hereward tried to strike out but it was impossible and even his strength was soon exhausted. His body was numb with cold. The black depths gaped beneath him. He lost his grip on Mare Swallow's reins. The waves tore him from her. Wildly he fought to reach her. He screamed, 'Mare Swallow! Mare Swallow!'

Freezing water filled his mouth and ears. He went under, then surfaced again. He felt weak suddenly and very tired. He lifted his voice in a last vain shout: 'Mare Swallow!' One of the lumps of driftwood struck him on the head then and he was nothing any more.

The Hall Among Thorns

A t the Palace of Westminster the thanes began to gather for the Christmas festival. Earl Leofric came with his hearth-troop and thither too Aelfgar, and it was not long before he was winning men over. Even the King grudgingly acknowledged his presence amongst them and his charm was as heady wine.

Tostig was proof against it, though. 'Strutting like a peacock! Who the bloody hell does he think he is?'

And Harold, appealed to, would shrug, letting it pass. His mind was on other things then, for he had lately received word that Eadgyth of the Swan-Neck was nearing the time of her confinement. So preoccupied was he that even when the King spoke to him he made no answer.

'What ails you, Harold?' the King would say. And dragging his eyes from the window, Harold would reply, 'I am sorry, Sire.' Then he would be attentive and hearken to his royal master's talk so that Edward would be placated and cease to watch him closely, and so leave him free once more to think of Eadgyth. He remembered well the night he had gotten her with child. That of the Ploughing Ale. So seldom was he to have her that each time of lovemaking was a clear image in his mind. He remembered the moonlight on her face, tracing the long, pure line of her swan's throat, uplifted, all open to him, and the natural easy way it had happened between them, with the soft shedding of tears afterwards.

Standing in the low-roofed chamber of Westminster Palace while the winter-light darkened, the world of Nazeing seemed to Harold then to be very far away. That world of corn-bells and ripening fruit; of furrow-chucks and drowsy scented lilac and shiny rose-hips in the Weed Month. Of Eadgyth slumbering in his arms, the smell of her like milk wine.

112

But the King was speaking, his voice sulky and vexed: 'O, how many more of these must I sign?'

And in answer Harold laid a parchment on the table before him. 'This is the last, Sire.'

Nearly all afternoon he had been with the King while he signed manifold documents – a task he hated and usually left to Harold. With the Great Seal stamped, King Edward leaned back in his chair and yawned. He watched Harold move. Neither lumbersome nor quick footed, he had a certain grace rare in such a big man. In his veins ran the blood of swineherds and Knut the Great, of cottars and of Edmund the Martyr, King of the East Saxons.

'Harold.'

'Yes, Sire?'

'What arrangements have you made for the Christmastide?' And when Harold told him, the King said, 'I suppose Aelfgar Leofricsson will be at the festal board?' He spoke testily. He still had no good opinion of the new Earl of East Anglia.

'Doubtless, Sire,' said Harold.

'I do not like him. I cannot forget and forgive what he has done.'

'Nay, Sire.'

'Yet you gave up your earldom for him!'

''Twas his to begin with.'

'You favour friendship between the houses, do you not? Yours and Leofric's and the scions of the North?'

'I am not willing for any to be my enemy.'

Aye, that was true. Harold had not even been in favour of the bid to overthrow Macbeth's power in Scotland three years previously. He had counselled against it. Stroking the vair pelts that hemmed the sleeves and edges of his mantle-cum-coat, King Edward said, 'Do you covet for yourself the role of Land-Father?' This was the name the folk of England had bestowed upon Earl Godwine and King Edward had ever grudged the love borne him.

Harold stopped in the doorway, his head bowed beneath the lintel. He said quietly, 'I covet nothing, Sire.'

The King looked at his Earl of Wessex, massive in the gathering dusk. 'You are determined upon peace, are you not?'

'I believe in peace, Sire.'

'At the expense of all else?'

'It depends.'

'Do you intend more wooing?'

'I know not your meaning, Sire.'

'Of the men north of the Humber.'

'The North is Tostig's concern, Sire, not mine. He has his own peck of troubles.'

Harold met Archbishop Stigand of the Mother Church of Canterbury on the stairs. His right to hold the office had long been disputed since it had been confiscated from Robert Champart of Jumieges, the former Norman Archbishop and confidant of King Edward. Stigand's pallium had not yet been granted by Rome, and he lived in hopes and by his wits. He was a small, mild man, more given to gossip than to quarrels. Unlike many of the English clergy who wore their hair long and had both beards and moustaches, Stigand's sparse grey locks were shorn to the crown. He had come to discuss the Christmas alms-giving with the King.

'What mood is his Majesty in?' he said to Harold.

'Bloody-minded, if you'll pardon me, Father,' Harold answered him. The Archbishop clicked his tongue and burying his chin deeper into his collar, he passed on.

It was Christmas Eve when a message came from Nazeing to say that Eadgyth had been safely delivered of the babe. Harold's three younger sisters and his foster-sister, Ragnhild and Freawaru and Gondul and Menglad – his little maids as he was wont to call them, each having a chunk of his heart with which to hold him ransom – were with Countess Gytha in her bower, and Aelhhunn the mass-priest in attendance.

As one they ran to Harold and he was drawn awkwardly, stooping beneath the rafters, to the hearthside. The difference between his age and theirs was much. Ragnhild of the golden hair whom Aelhhunn devoted his time to tutoring had fourteen years, while Freawaru and Gondul at six and five were the children of the Countess's life-change, with scarcely a summer separating them. Menglad the foster-lean, the orphaned granddaughter of Earl Godwine's brother by his marriage to a kinswoman of King Ethelred, was just thirteen. They were all speaking together, anxious to give their gift for the new baby. From the quiet, religious-minded Ragnhild a tiny crucifix. From Menglad a string of eye-beads. Freawaru and Gondul both gave lucky charms of coral. Harold turned to see his mother then and beheld her as a seeress by the hearth. At her feet had wonders been learned. Her head-wrap was daffodil yellow silk woven with gold threads and encircled by a crown showing her descent from the ancient Nordic blood-royal. She delighted in necklaces of big lumps of amber and rock-crystal and amethyst.

114

'You will give my excuses to the King?'

'Hurry now! These walls will support themselves a while without you!' The Countess smiled to see Harold flush at her gentle mockery.

'Do I take your blessing, mother?'

'You ask that of me?' Whereupon Gytha gave him a silver spoon set with garnets. 'Make sure Eadgyth has to eat of plenty of caudle.'

In answer Harold bent and kissed her hands and then was gone.

Aldwyth, upon her return from Wilton, had also heard of the birth of Harold's child, and as she sat reading to the King as he dozed on his day-bed, her heart was a leaden thing within her breast. Once she faltered and King Edward opened his eyes. 'Are you tired, my dear?'

'Nay, my lord.'

'I thought perhaps we would hear midnight mass together.'

'As you wish, my lord.'

'We have not done so for many years, child. Not since we were first married, do you remember?'

'Aye, my lord,' Queen Aldwyth said. 'I remember.' But all she could think of was Harold's frilla. His swan-necked mistress or so-called wife. Daughter of the holt-reeve of Swaffham, she had held some land of her own and Harold had since given her more, including the manor of Harkstead. She was said to be beautiful, though Aldwyth had never seen her. Harold kept her at Nazeing with a houseful of servants and her foster-aunt Hag Annis the Wise Woman, no more than a rich man's whore.

Yet rather that than to be a Queen anointed, crowned and alone.

Meanwhile Harold had given orders for a horse to be saddled and it was as he crossed the hall yard to the stables that Modred the marshal of his own hearth-troop came upon him. The bells had begun ringing for Vespers in St Stephen's chapel.

'Will you go by yourself, man?' Modred said. 'The beggars are all in the roads to the town and without, come for the King's alms-giving. Better that I ride with you.'

Harold swung himself into the saddle. He chaffed his marshal for a watch-dog but care seemed lifted and he was smiling. 'So you shall, Modred,' he answered, 'and if the babe be a boy then he will be your name-sake!'

It was dark when they reached Nazeing, coming upon the house, tall and gabled of timber clamped with iron, by the chestnut copse. Harold's wood and the surrounding forest and fields lay silent beneath

115

a sky of frozen stars. At the sound of hooves clattering into the yard a stable boy hurried forth with a lanthorn, wolf-hounds at his heels, and the shutters of the bower tucked up beneath the eaves were unlatched and a maid-servant's railed head peered over the snowy sill.

'A greeting, Lintrude!' said Harold to that damsel.

And she opened the shutter wide. 'Earl Harold!'

'The lady Eadgyth – how fares she?'

'Well, my lord.'

'And the babe?'

'It is a boy.'

Kneeling by Eadgyth Harold watched his son feeding at her milk-heavy breast. The bed was hung with curtains dyed of ling and gall apples. Hag Annis sat nearby making titsy-totsy balls to hang over the crib.

'He's already taken honey from the tip of a sword,' she said to Harold. 'Born upon the stroke of twelve. A chime child!'

Eadgyth met Harold's eyes and whispered, 'I did not think you'd come.'

'Nothing could keep me away, dear heart!'

'How long can you stay?'

'As long as you want me.' Harold kissed her then and she clung to him, gripping his snow damp cloak.

Presently he went to the head of the stairs and called down to where Modred the marshal waited by the blazing hearth-side. 'Come you up, man! Come and see Modred Haroldsson!'

Stranger of the Fairy Shore

he was looking down at him. Her hair was long and black and her face was thin in the midst of it. And her eyes were dark too, with the big hollows of her cheekbones beneath them.

Hereward lay on his back, one arm across his face. The shingle of the beach dug in hard. He tried to move but his head pained him so he stayed still. His eyes focused on the low heavy sky. He saw birds circle above. He heard the sea. The relentless pounding of the waves on the shore. And it all came back. All that had happened.

The woman spoke then: '*Cad is ainm duit?* What is your name?'

Hereward gave a slight shake of his head, his understanding dulled. '*Sasanaigh?*'

Hereward nodded. She pointed down the beach. Hereward shifted, heaving himself up on one elbow. There a few yards away stood Mare Swallow cropping dune grass and Hogni Tricksleeve lying close by. Hereward could have sobbed with relief. The woman touched his hand. His right hand. Because it was bleeding and because he wore the pledge-ring. She said very softly, '*A chréatuir bhoicht!* Poor creature!'

Hereward started to get up and the woman helped him. Her shoulder was frail as a thistle under the plaid she had wrapped about herself, so he tried not to lean too heavily upon her.

Getting Hogni to his feet was a different matter. He was still muttering his prayers and crossing himself. Sorting out his seemingly boneless limbs Hereward shook him so hard that his head all but snapped off his neck. 'Are ye hurt?'

'No, master.' Hogni looked at him, glazed and stupid. 'I don't think so.'

Cursing him for a bloody shanny, Hereward slung him cross-back like a shot deer. The woman gestured for them to follow her and Hereward did so, trudging slowly with his burden.

A mud hut, a little, hidden, lowly hut, covered with the wings of many coloured birds with a yew tree beside it, and a holy well with rags and flowers and gew-gaws tied to it was what he saw in a silvery land rained upon by dragon stones and crystals.

He crawled beneath the hide flap, letting Hogni drop to the beaten, leaf-strewn floor, and the only glimmer was the red mouth of a peat fire. Bone-chilled, holding out his hands to the poor warmth, with Hogni snivelling at his side, Hereward grew used to the half-dark. He saw a cauldron and a flesh-fork, a loom hung with clay weights, and all about the rest of the small space was full of bunches and bunches of drying herbs and flowers, scores of them, so sweet and thick as to clog the brain. And two cats peered out at him with eyes like gobbets of amber.

The flap opened and the woman came in. With more gestures she made it plain that Hereward should take off his wet clothes to be dried over the fire. Hogni wouldn't. Not even threats would make him remove a stitch. Hereward turned his back and stripped naked and wrapped himself in the skin she gave him. She could stand upright but he had to bend his head and hunch his shoulders lest he knock into the walls. As she hung out his clothes he saw her finger the fine linen of his shirt, the yellow combed wool of his tunic, and gaze long upon the belt of the Fian. But she said no word. She just gave them black bread and milk and let them rest up all that day.

Lying by the fire Hereward slept fitfully. Times he would wake with a jolt as though he could still feel the water flooding over him, down into his lungs. Then he must have dozed again for the next thing he knew was that opening his eyes he saw the woman kneeling close by him mending the fire with lumps of peat. She turned her head then and smiled down at him. How could he ever have thought her eyes were dark? They were hazel and grey with green in them too, and having the look of hyacinths.

'You're kind,' he said awkwardly. 'I'm grateful, truly . . .'

The woman frowned. Hereward sat up, the skin, a cobble of rabbit pelts, fallen away from him, leaving him bare to the waist. Her eyes took him in, every inch of him. '*Gruagach*,' she said. Hairy One. For his chest and arms. She didn't seem to be put off by his face or the mark. '*Ní mór liom duit é!* I do not grudge it to you!'

Hereward rose naked whilst Hogni snored and putting on his dried clothes crept to where the woman sat cross-legged the other side of the fire. An old carved bronze pin held the plaid at her breast, plaid of rich red and blue and yellow, brighter than the hue of any flower.

118

Strands of beads of polished nuts hung about her neck and wrists, and coloured sea-shells dropped from her ears. He glimpsed feet without shoes beneath her coarse smock, the fringe of which was sewn with tiny bells. And when she spoke to him it was with a tongue he knew well but the lilt and the way of the words was strange, and so at first it was with some difficulty that he made himself understood and had the understanding of her.

'What do you call this place?'

'*Emhain Abhlach.*'

'Where does it lie?'

'Three times fifty distant islands to the west.'

'Do other folk live here?'

She frowned, then smiled. '*Mé féin.*'

'You must crave a mortal voice.'

But she only shrugged and said that she had all the music she wanted from the trees. Then she called softly, 'Morrighan! Badbh!' And the two cats, answering, came fussing round. Hereward put out his hand to them, bending to stroke them. The woman gazed at his bowed head, the hair of it golden fair like a field of wheat. Then she touched the big main muscle of his upper arm where it bulged like a warm yellow apple.

'*Tá sé mór láidir!* He is big and strong!' she whispered. And her eyes sought his hand, looking for the pledge ring. He let her see it and told her what it meant and the name by which he was called. She took his name on her lips, saying it softly, slowly.

'A great chieftain's son! And a feinnidh! What of him yonder – is he your man?'

'Aye.'

'And that horse. She has a bridle with rings of gold. An Aughisky?'

'Nay, she's no water-horse. A forest mare.'

'Come far? A long way from home?'

'I am a Wolf's-Head.' And he told her how such a man as he could be slain and his worth paid to his slayer.

'*Na raibh se mar sin!* May it not be so! *Nar lige Dia san!* God forbid!' Then she looked into his eyes. 'There is no bad in your heart.'

'You talk like a wise woman.'

'I have the Sight. Tell me, cara, have you a wife or a lover that waits you?'

'Nay.' And he poured out the rest of his story to her. Of his life and his home. Of Mare Swallow. Of all that had befallen him, big hands making word-pictures in the air. He confided in this woman he had known only a few hours more than he had ever confided in a human being before. Looking up from the earth floor, he whispered, 'Now you know. Everything about me. Won't you tell me what is your name?'

Liquid-lipped, her voice like many leaves was murmurous as she said, 'Muirgheal.'

Hereward went out next morning to see Mare Swallow where she had been put in the byre and to get his saddle-bags and sword Brain-Biter.

Hogni Tricksleeve tagged behind. 'I wonder how old she is?'

'Who?'

'Her. The wood-woman.'

'Not all that old.'

'Had thirty years, I'll wager.'

'So?'

Hogni tapped his nose and grinned. 'Not as thin as you'd think, neither!'

Hereward said suddenly, 'You mind what you say to her! I don't want any of your bloody cheek.'

'Who? Me, master?'

'Aye, you!'

Hogni's sharp eyes narrowed. 'Why, master, you are red as lally-low and ashy pale all in a minute. What ails ye?'

'Nothing.' Hereward chucked the saddle-bags over his shoulder. 'But if I ever hear you use a wrong word to her, I'll brain you, see?'

Hogni watched him go and smiled to himself. Then he trotted after.

For a couple of days wreckage was washed up on the shore. The morning tide left it strewn on the shingle. Pieces of rigging, lumps of wood. Grotesque, sad offerings. An axe shaft, a bit of sail. A broken oar. A shield . . .

Hereward split the drift timber for burning, the other he left for the sea to claim, all save the shield. There was not a mark on it. It was solid linden wood, embossed and gilded in the true Danish style. He took it and put it near the fire to dry out. Its brilliant colours had withstood the rocks and water. Not a chip of dye paint was missing.

'Cad fath?' said Muirgheal.

'What for?' Hereward shrugged. 'I don't know. But 'twould be a shame to leave it.'

120

When all the Trees were Green

With the passing of Christmas and the wassailing of the Orchard Robin, men began to return to their lands and Earl Leofric was among them. He took his leave of the King one bright morning before Passion-Tide. Tarrying then in the cobbled yard by the gate, his grey head bare under the April sun, the Earl spoke his heart to Harold Godwinesson. 'I would Aelfgar keeps faith. He is gone to Blickling again – full of promises. But I fear, times, 'tis only a game with him – like life!' Earl Leofric sighed, contemplating the Ring of Oaths on his forefinger. 'Ah, but then I can do no more!'

'He is your heir, Leofric. He stands to inherit Mercia.'

'I know. That is why I wanted him back.' The news that Hereward was drowned had reached Little-Bethlehem-of-the-Rushes the year before and Earl Leofric had mourned his loss greatly. Otherwise, few things had changed, save that Wynter was married with a baby son and Young Leofsi had taken the robe of black burel to become mass-priest to the household. And Darryl – he would have already forsaken the ploughing on such a day as this to go to the fair, gaming and wenching, just like his father.

Earl Leofric said, 'For good or bad Aelfgar is all that I have left now.' A stable-keeper came forth with the Earl's horse, Hrimfaxi. His hearth-troop was already mounted, breast-plates gleaming, awaiting their lord. Rudgang Wolf-Cloak in command.

'The King will miss you this festival,' said Harold.

Up in the saddle Leofric smiled and shook his head. 'Nay, lad. The King will have forgotten me ere the night comes and I shall think no more upon Westminster!'

*　　*　　*

121

Tying rags to the well in appeasement of the fairies, Muirgheal greeted him, '*Dias Muire dhuit!* God and Mary to you! You'll be wanting to be on your way in another day or so.'

'I am in no hurry,' Hereward replied.

'I thought you were bound for other lands.'

'I was.'

'Not any more?'

'Nay.'

'Where then? Back to Baile Atha Cliath?'

'I'd as lief stay here.'

'There is nothing for you here, cara!'

Hereward wanted to say, There is you. But his tongue cleft to the roof of his mouth. 'I will be no trouble,' he whispered. She seemed reluctant, somehow. 'Is it because I am not a man of Erin?'

'*Erineach?* O, no!'

'I'll work. You'll find few as strong.' He offered up his big horny fists. 'That is if you do not mind.'

Muirgheal looked away, muffling her chin in her shawl. '*Ni miste liom.* I do not mind,' she said.

That night Hereward dropped something into Muirgheal's lap. 'For you.'

She picked it up and looked at it in the sheep-grease light. It was a brooch. The garnets were blood-drops. 'Cara!' she breathed. '*Go raibh maith agat.* Thank you. But I cannot take such a thing!'

Hereward closed her hand over it, feeling the fragile bones. 'Do not think I am pushing in. I don't mean it that way.' His gaze met hers. 'I just want to bide alongside you.'

When Queen Aldwyth combed wool – dyed of bird-cherry and St John's-wort and sloe – she had at her velvet-shod feet a boy red-haired as herself to labour over his wax tablet, muddling his scriptures. He was Haakon, the base-born son of Earl Sweyn and Abbess Eadgifu of Leominster, for whose foster-lean Aldwyth had made herself responsible.

Soon they would be moving court to Oxford and there the King would wear the crown and cause the Paschal candle to be lit. As usual Harold had made the arrangements. But that year he had plans of his own to go before the Easter-Moot for the building of a new fleet of ships. Long ships of oak and pine supple enough to ride the heaviest seas, with carved masts and weather-vanes and hung with bright shields. The ship-geld of a silver shilling a hide would pay for them and the King would agree, that much was certain. He always did with Harold. Ah, an iron will lay behind those calm, seemingly guileless blue eyes.

So thought Tostig, travelling with the baggage-wain. 'Another notch on your belt, brother!' he'd said. And though he smiled, his lips were crooked and sly and malice was in his speech.

The hunting was good, the forest teeming with game, and it was after a strenuous day among his hounds that the King, in the midst of devouring a platter of oysters at the table, was seen to turn purple in the face and collapse. Azur his stag-huntsman carried him to his chamber and there Fitz-Baldwin, the French bishop of Bury St Edmund's and his own physician, duly purged him, ordering rose cordial to wash the mulligrubs out of a moody brain, but was loath to bleed him as it was only the fourth day of the moon.

Though recovered and prescribed goat's milk and fasting, King Edward began to speak openly for the first time about the succession. And while still at Oxford he summoned Harold to him and told him of his decision to appoint an heir. It was to be the King's nephew and name-sake, Edward the Aetheling, the only survivor of the twin sons of Edmund Ironside, smuggled from England after the loss of Ashingdon and brought up at the court of King Stephen and Queen Ghislaine in Hungary. The men of the Witenagemot, though, viewed the choice with mixed feelings. And Dagobert, the marshal of the men of London, made his voice loudly known in the company thus: 'For God's sake why does the Ethelredsson send to Hungary when the man to be King is here under his nose?'

Harold rode to Nazeing before Warning Eve and there seeking Eadgyth in her bower he knelt at her feet and let rail against the world. 'After I have worked myself to death doing his duties! Kicking the stones out of his path! Making life easy for him! Doing all for him! Now he passes me over for some foreigner! Where the hell does he think he would be without me? I run this bloody country for him!'

Eadgyth put her two hands over Harold's. 'But you do not do it just for that – just for power. You do love the country.'

Harold looked up at her. 'It is the same thing.'

'Nay, it is not.'

'I want what is best for England. I served my apprenticeship under a good master. A wise master. My father trained me for this,

123

Eadgyth. He knew all the snares. The weak spots. He taught me to grab life with both fists and to win!'

'And there is bitterness in your heart because you feel you are losing.'

'I have a right to be bitter. The Aetheling will just take over what I've done. It will be easy for him. Never mind the struggle, the hard sweat I have put into it over the years.'

'Perhaps the Witenagemot will not elect him.'

'They will – in the end. They fear the absence of an heir. The Aetheling will be their safeguard against any claims of the Norman Bastard and the lust of the Viking Haardrada.'

'But what makes the King so sure he'll come? He might not be keen to venture.'

'Edward has the belief that his days are numbered, though Fitz-Baldwin says he's hale enough. The Aetheling will be expecting an empty throne.'

'But what of you?'

Harold shrugged his huge shoulders. 'The faithful subject once more.'

'You are as the King. The men follow you. Their loyalty is to you, not Edward.'

'But the crown, Eadgyth. The crown. That is not mine!'

'Not yet.'

'Not ever – now. The Aetheling has children. One of them is a boy.'

'But they can only be of tender years.'

'Their stock is royal.'

'So is yours. Your mother is a princess. Your grandfathers were kings.'

'The Aetheling was spawned by the Ironside.'

Two days later Harold went back to Westminster only to find that bishop Ealdred of Worcester had already been sent to the court of Emperor Henry the Black of Germany, bearing royal gifts, in the search for the Aetheling.

The good bishop stayed for a year, at the end of which he was obliged to return empty-handed. King Edward was disappointed and took counsel of Harold. 'What would you do in my place?'

And with an effort Harold swallowed and replied, 'I don't know, Sire.'

The King grunted and chewed on his thumbnail. 'I suppose you think me hasty, sending for a man to be my heir whom I have never

124

even seen. But I feel it is my duty to provide, as God in his wisdom has not seen fit to bless me with children.' He sighed. 'The end of the line of Cerdic! I cannot tell you how it burdens my heart.' And even as King Edward spoke, his eyes suddenly clouded with memory. That of a rush-lit cavern where a flibbertigibbet had practised his goblinry. Yea; it had been in Leofric's house that the runes had been cast . . .

Harold remembered it too. Two kings, so had said the prophesy, both in the same hall. What a fool he'd been to believe in such old magic! The King was good for another ten years – perhaps more – no matter what he said. Any who saw him relishing karum pie and his favourite borage wine could be in little doubt of it. And the Aetheling, exile and stranger though he was, would by that time have gained acceptance.

But the final irony was yet to be when news came of the death of the Emperor of Germany and Harold journeyed thither to attend the funeral at Spierers. Before he left King Edward summoned him and gave him the fabulous sapphire ring of the Pilgrim, that which men called the Midnight Star. 'I want you to send this as a pledge of heir-ship to my kinsman in Hungary. I want you to bring back his answer. You will do this for me, will you not, Harold?'

Three months later and returned to England, Harold reported to the King at the Wardrobe Palace. The Aetheling would come.

'You are sure? You say the Mass of St James?' King Edward clapped his hands. 'O, Harold! It is well! And you – you will be of great worth to him as you have been to me!'

No more than a hyre-man, ever at his beck and call. Harold said, 'I suppose you know that he speaks no word of English, Sire.'

The King filled a goblet brimful of sweet malvoisie and smiled benignly up at his Earl of Wessex. 'Nor could I when first I came. My kinsman shall study your Saxon tongue, Harold.'

125

The Months of Meadow and Weed and Rye

he place of Prior Wulfstan whence Harold had accompanied Bishop Ealdred that day was a lowly one. And it was there on Botolph's Wharf, among croziers of walrus ivory and rich vestments, that Harold saw him. He had known and loved the Prior since his youth; Wulfstan had begun as house-father to Earl Godwine's family. Thus shouldering his way through the press – for already many score were gathered, it being the Hour of Tierce upon the Mass of St James and London Town astir before cock-crow in readiness to welcome home the son of Edmund Ironside – Harold greeted Wulfstan, stooping to kiss the crucifix at his belt, noting that as always he wore the cow-bell and sprig of basil, herb of poverty, and carried the staff, a knotty wand of limewood.

Prior Wulfstan, though gladdened to see Harold wore his crucifix beneath his warrior's trappings, was not fooled by his apparent subjection of himself. It was a day for which he must anguish keenly, cut to the heart, especially as King Edward, awaiting his long-lost kinsman in his house by Cow Cross, had bestowed on Harold, whether by magnanimity or mischief-making, the honour of escorting the Aetheling through the streets of London.

And so it was that the barge which had set sail from Flanders the previous night hoved into the Thames, oars cleaving, to the blaring of lurs and the roll of drums and clatter of cymbals. Along the miles of river bank, from stall and workshop, mill and field, the people of town and village crowded to watch its progress through winding, weed-clogged reaches, out into the broad, flowing stream. Past the cottage gardens fragrant with lavender in flower and sweet-briar, the thousand orchards of cherry trees and lime-blossom and early pears and apples.

Harold heard the cacophony of sound that sent the birds scattering from the marshes. Felt the gut-churning sudden fever of excitement

126

that gripped the throng from Garlickhithe to Dow-Gate, and with men of his own hearth-troop, mail coats a-glitter, cheek-guards flashing, did he walk slowly down the steps to board the royal barge. '. . . And?' said King Edward.

'Holy Mary Mother of God! He's sick!' Modred the marshal came in unto the King bearing his tidings, having ridden thither with all haste. He could still smell the noisome cabin below deck where the Aetheling had lain and see the dark, strange, frightened faces of the Magyar followers uplifted in the gloom.

'Is it the quartan ague?' the King demanded, and Modred shook his head. 'Nay.'

'Summer-sickness?'

''Tis the lung-rot. He's coughing blood.'

And so from the barge Edward the Aetheling was borne to the garret chamber where a couch was made ready and peach-wort strewn. Men came and went. King Edward, stunned, saw them in a daze, until one, more massive than the others, remained solitary between window and door and he recognised it to be Harold Godwinesson. 'How came he to be thus, Harold?'

Harold's deep voice answered slowly, 'He has been ill a long time, Sire. The rot has got a hold on him.'

'And yet he journeyed here?'

'You wanted him, Sire,' said Harold.

Queen Aldwyth came then with the Aetheling's wife Princess Agatha and two daughters Margaret and Christina. Gyrth followed carrying the boy Edgar, a four-years child, already half asleep on his shoulder. They knelt before the King, who bade them rise, calling them his kinswomen and the slumbering boy his foster-son.

Fitz-Baldwin strove to revive the Aetheling, surrounding the couch with pans burning purifying herbs. He had lung-salves; hyssop and honey, elf-wort and saffron. But when all remedies had been given and the old, strong cough still racked the chamber and rotten phlegm and blood was still being cast, nothing but prayer was left to them.

Thus Edward, son of Edmund Ironside, died that same day before the Hour of Vespers. And the bells began to toll in the churches of London Town and the nearby villages. That night the Aetheling was lain on a bier decked with rosemary in the small candle-lit hall of the house by Cow Cross and the doors stood open for all those who wished to come.

Who could sing his praises in the time honoured way? Or bewail the loss of his virtuous life? No one. He had spoken not one word nor been known to any. Only in the far off Kingdom of the Magyars had he walked, laughed, loved and fathered children. His memory was theirs. The monks from the Abbey of St Mary Overy chanted their monotonous dirge. Incense from a dozen holders creaking on thin brass chains made a sweet fog through which the candle flames glowed as stars.

'They take him to Westminster tomorrow.' Harold turned to see Leofric. He had a simple wool cloak over his shoulders. 'The King plans a royal funeral.'

'Where?'

'In St Paul's Minster.'

'Nothing could have saved him,' Harold said. 'He was too far gone.'

Earl Leofric lifted his eyes from the bier to Harold's face. ''Tis no one's blame.'

They spoke in low voices. The monks were singing the lyke-wake carol. The third watch of the night was not yet past. Harold said, 'Leofric, I begrudged him.' Leofric was a long time considering. Harold wondered where his words fell. He said, 'I'd hate of him, though I did not even know him. And now he's dead.'

'It was meant to be.'

'But I wanted it.'

'Talking like that gets you nowhere.'

'I've got to tell it to someone.'

'So you've told me. Is your heart eased?'

And when Harold took his place at the bier they were to comment upon his still bearing and show of reverence. He held his rosary in one hand and as his fingers moved among the decades of aves, the glorias and paternosters, a slow exultation rose unbidden inside of him. Swallowing it down he tried to pray, and he could have made no better impression on the watchers than as the granite-hewn warrior kneeling, his sword ungirt by his side.

'. . . So now the way is open,' said Tostig. He rode with the great company behind the solemn mourning rade that wound under the thatched eaves of the houses. Pressed about with the crowds in Candle-Wright street there was scarce room for the wheels to roll and the wain bearing the coffin clad of purple was halted at every church. To the King's hall at Kennington had already been taken the treasures of the royal barge. Casks of precious stones and narwhal ivory and an age-bitten black rood.

'Aye, but who for?' Aelfgar Leofricsson was quick to ask.

128

Whereupon Gyrth said quietly, 'The Witenagemot will choose if need be.'

'When half of them are Godwinesson men?' Aelfgar said. Giving all men his larkspur blue eyes, Tostig said, 'Do you propose yourself, then, as England's next heir?' His voice was soft, belying, dangerous. 'A Wolf's-Head?'

'Better that than a tyrant!'

Archbishop Stigand murmured, 'My sons, this is no place to argue.'

Harold rode in front, neither turning his head nor speaking. Flowers were thrown from windows above and wreaths of apple blossom borne in profusion. Brushing petals from his hair Tostig kept at Harold's flank, making play with the elaborate ornament of his horse-brass until Aelfgar felt he could have throttled him with it.

'Ah, you men north of the Thames think you are a law unto yourselves. You baulk at discipline. At least I've brought the mulct and infangenetheof to my earldom!'

'And men afraid to spit!' said Tostig.

'You had no care for such as they when you put Hereford town to the sword!' Earl Leofric was powerless to stop Aelfgar from rising to Tostig's bait. Aelfgar lunged across, grabbing Tostig by his cloak. He was hot tempered as ever. He would never keep his counsel. Never learn . . .

'Aelfgar, lad!' the Earl besought him in earnest, wrenching gloved hand from cloak front. 'Hold your jaw! O'er God forebode! Have ye no respect? Be still!'

'And be talked down to by him?' Aelfgar's blood was up, his nostrils pinched and white. 'I know you think I am not responsible,' he said, 'that is why you've got your men on my estates. So they can spy on me! Trying to govern my life!'

'They are there to help ye.'

'God damn your help!' And Aelfgar pulled out from the rade, steering his horse free, and rode back the way they had come. Turning in his saddle, Leofric watched him go.

Archbishop Stigand crossed himself. 'Angry words at such a time!'

And secretly Tostig smiled, seeing the devices on the horse-brass writhe and squirm, cunningly carved lind-worms, mouths stopped with beryls.

Dagobert the marshal offered to take the tidings to Nazeing. Harold's sister Ragnhild was staying with Eadgyth and it was a rare chance for

Dagobert to feast his eyes on the maid. She bloomed in secret, that one, and his bowels yearned for her.

Eadgyth made Dagobert welcome at the house, its mellowed walls overgrown with traveller's joy, and heard the great news he had to tell.

'The Aetheling dead?'

'And buried in a stone tomb alongside his grandfather,' said Dagobert, thinking back upon the packed Minster of St Paul's, echoing to the Mass and reeking of incense, rags and riches seeming all to be one in the gemmiferous light.

Eadgyth said, 'What does this mean now?'

Dagobert looked at her, at the famed white swan's neck spun about by buttery tresses and gauzy head-veils, seeing the gymmal-ring, amongst many others on her fingers, twin to Harold's, signifying heart and soul, life and death, and he knew that she understood only too well. 'That there is no one but Harold,' he said.

It was then that Ragnhild spoke. 'But has not the Aetheling a son?'

She wore no jewels, not even a girdle-hanger or purse, and her hair was bound in ropes to her knees. Near her sat the mass-priest Aelhhunn, the black burel robe fitting across shoulders more worthy of a war-coat than a monk's habit. He was always with her, nagged the jealous sprite in Dagobert's ear. He looked at Ragnhild and said, 'A babe. Smaller than those two.' And he pointed to Godwine and Edmund, Harold's eldest sons – then nine and six – who had come in from playing to stand behind their mother's chair, armed with blunt-edged, wooden swords and tin shields. 'And the men are not keen.'

'Has King Edward made the boy his heir?'

'He has. But 'tis a mere formality. Only the Witenagemot can decide what's to be.'

'What support can Harold expect?' said Eadgyth.

'He has Wessex. There's not a man there who would not but follow him to the earth's end.'

'And Mercia? The great Leofric?'

'He's a reasoning man and nobody's fool. He wants only what is good for England.'

Eadgyth knew of Dagobert's love for Harold – they had known each other since boyhood. The same as Modred. She knew the fierceness of their pride, their protectiveness, their loyalty. Dagobert's comely face was flushed with it, his eyes, times, tear-bright. She said, 'What of Tostig and Aelfgar Leofricsson?'

He answered her in uncommon wrath: 'Those two bleeders! Excuse me, ma'am, but they raise my bile. They'd cheerfully ruin this country if they thought they'd get so much as a gold bangle for it.'

Muirgheal of the White Hands

ereward took over the jobs that Muirgheal had always done, save those in her herb garden. His lot was to fetch water from the holy well and cut peat and logs, but only from the east side of the wood for the west was sacred and inhabited by the Folk of the Sidhe. He caught the fish and mucked out the beast housen and tended the few animals she kept, one of which was a magical red-eared cow. The thoughts of his home, the people he had once known, his father – even his voices – they began to fade. He was content to live near Muirgheal, to watch her and worship her, holding out his hands for whatever crumbs might fall.

Folk came for healing – for Muirgheal had that gift also – from the villages beyond the hills of Draoiachta. They ventured thither in dread. Yet her hands held only goodness. Her hands, her beautiful, thin white hands, one of them having the special power with its long leech finger . . .

Once, Hereward had lain them on the marked side of his face. 'Ah! if you could but rid me of it!' He had then grown used to her speech and she to his.

'*Slán mo chomhartha!* God bless the mark! You have a nice face, cara!'

'Now you're joking me.'

''Tisn't joking you I am at all.'

Hereward thought of what she'd said while he worked. It wasn't so bad during the day. He'd got something to take his mind off her. It was the evening times that were the worst when there was nothing to do save to sit with her – for Hogni had betook himself off to the turf shed where he liked to play his pipe and have as audience the night stars that peeped through the slats. And after a while Hereward wasn't satisfied with sitting any more. He wanted to put his arms around her and hold her to him and smell the scent of her that was like wild comel in the rain. But he slept by the fire and Muirgheal on the straw behind the plait of rushes. He envied that oat chaff pillow where she laid her head. The cloth she dried herself on. In the silence he'd hear her move. He knew the poetry of her form – for though she was wand-slender, her breasts were full. He imagined her taking off her smock, pulling it over her head, and as she lifted her arms her breasts would lift too . . . Hereward turned over onto his stomach and buried his face in his hands, his penis thickening and stirring with the want of her.

Living so close by each other there was an everyday intimacy. After work Hereward's shirt smelled of sweat. His arms were bare, veined and hard. Dirt caked a scratch on his cheek. He'd say, 'Shall I fetch some more peat in? And water?' And Muirgheal would give him the bucket and as he took it his hand would touch hers.

One morning Muirgheal had gone out early to gather flowers, and it was returning with her trug that she came upon Hereward washing by the well. He was stripped naked and he turned to face her, all without shame, making no attempt to cover himself.

He'd watched her go, barefoot, walking up on her toes with the grace of a sunbeam, the little bells tinkling on the hem of her smock. He knew she would be back before sunrise, coming by that same lost, thin path, and her trug spilling over with flaxweed and marsh-mallow, mugwort and horehound, blue-flag sprent with dew.

'*Dias Muire dhuit!*' she said. She had to pass him to get to the hut and as she did so he reached out for her, putting his arms round her. She felt his breath on the back of her neck and the great power of him.

'Ah, Muirgheal!' he said.

'Hereward – *cad tá vait?*'

'You,' he answered simply.

'No, cara!'

He turned her against him. Water clung to the hair on his chest. He smelt raw and good and she guessed he would taste that way too. 'Why not?'

'Let me go.'

'Don't you like me?'

'Aye, of course!'

'Then what's your hurry?'

'I've things to do. The cow to milk.'

'I've milked her,' Hereward said.

'There's my plants . . .'

'Can they not wait?' And he gathered her into his arms as she'd gathered the flowers and kissed her. It wasn't much of a kiss but it was the first and in that moment she didn't resist him. So he kissed her again, deeper, until her mouth opened under his.

But then she began to push with her hands against him and cried out, 'Loose me, Hereward!'

'I can't!'

'You can very well!'

'What's wrong? Is it my looks? We could go in the woods. 'Tis dark there. You'd not see me . . .'

'You're young. Too young!'

'I've been eighteen years a-growing,' Hereward said, and taking both her hands he put them up between his legs, holding them there until Muirgheal groaned aloud. 'Am I not man enough for ye?'

'You are hurting! Let me go, Hereward! O, you're so big – all over me! You're hurting!' And she broke free of him, backing away.

Hereward stood staring down at his empty, shaking hands. Then he said, 'I'm all buggered up over you. I love you, Muirgheal.'

Muirgheal had picked up her trug of flowers. Many of the blooms were spilled and broken, their healing-magic gone. 'Love me?' she said, and looked at him as though he'd struck her. 'No, it cannot be, Hereward! Not that. O, your mouth is sweet. You'd stop a woman's heart. But you couldn't ever love me – because you don't know me. You think you do – but you know nothing at all. *Go mbeannai Dia dhuit!*'

Sharpening a stick, Hogni said, 'Any luck?'

Hereward shook his head. 'It's as if she's always waiting for something that isn't me.'

'Then don't let's stay, master. 'Tis plain she doesn't want you to.'

'But why?'

Hogni spat on his knife. 'She has her reasons, I suppose.'

The Months of Wine and Blood and Cakes

ꝏ aving put tinder to dry faggots, coaxing a cheerful flame, Ywar the Churchwarden, one ear full of the tolling bell, listened with the other to his master Abbot Brand of Peterborough and Ulfketyl the Good of Croyland. Like two sagacious plovers they warmed their shanks and creaky joints by the fire. They wore eel skins beneath their robes to ward off the agues and black fevers of the early fenland winter. 'Bring mead, Ywar!' said Abbot Brand. Only in the bitterest weather did the fathers call for strong drink. And as they sipped they spoke of Earl Leofric buried that day in Croyland Minster with nought but his ash-spear. Ah, me! thought Ywar. At the boon-work a few months before had the Earl looked fit as ever, nut-brown from labouring in the fields. Though folk said as how his heart had never truly healed. That he'd been unlucky with his sons. And suddenly his health had failed him and by the first week in Advent he was dead.

'And now Aelfgar will inherit,' said Ulfketyl.

'Mayhap he'll prove himself worthy.'

'Mayhap,' Brand agreed with reserve, 'but whatever, he cannot hold a candle to his father.'

'The Countess will keep the Hall at Little-Bethlehem-of-the-Rushes. It was Leofric's wish.'

She would continue to preside over the Moots and Wapentakes as she had always done in Leofric's absence. And hers was the right as with all land-owning women to take her place at the Witenagemot. Nodding, stretching his toes closer to the fire, Brand said, 'I remember when Leofric first brought her home as his bride. Just a slip of a lass up on his saddle-bow.' Lammas. Birds guzzling red-currants. Dog-rose time. Lanes ablaze with crimson shoe. The weather of crab-apples and quince and fairy-shot . . .

*   *   *

135

Wynter told the bees of Earl Leofric's death and asked them kindly to stay. It was a cold twilight and Darryl and Young Leofsi were with him.

'D'you think they heard?' said Darryl.

Wynter shrugged. 'Can't be sure. Have to wait for them to make up their minds.'

Holding a hedge-taper, Young Leofsi said, 'I'd lief they don't go. Funny things, bees. Each one a soul.'

Rudgang Wolf-Cloak sat by the hearth polishing Leofric's armour. Hand-linked, it was, and hammered, unworn since the battle of Ashingdon. For days and nights Countess Godgyfu had wept and would take comfort from no one, not even from Lilla the chaplain, her foster-son.

Mercia was Aelfgar's then. He possessed the Chain of the Folk-Founder and the Ring of Oaths. 'But dear as he is he shall not have thee!' whispered Rudgang to that war-coat of fairy-gold. And by night many were the bunches of flowers left on the stairs.

And before the year closed news of a third death smote King Edward. That of his nephew Earl Raoul the Timid, stricken of a putrid fever. 'First the Aetheling – then Leofric – now this. O, what a twelve-month of woe!'

Earl Raoul left an English widow and a son, a babe in arms, and his lands were granted to Harold. But only for safe-keeping. Harold, who was the babe's god-father and the boy named after him, would hold them in trust until he was of an age to inherit. Also an earldom made up of the seven lathes of Kent went to Leofwine. The earldom of East Anglia had already gone to Gyrth. Aelfgar as Earl of Mercia ruled from Chester. And thus St Clement's-tide passed and the wind brought the first heavy snows of winter.

Tostig's thoughts had been upon Mercia. In the change of earldoms he had gained nothing. Unsatisfied with his own lot he sought someone to tell his grievances to. He found a willing listener in his sister the Queen.

'Aelfgar Leofricsson gets Mercia to himself just as easy as that!' And he snapped his fingers.

'He was chosen.'

'Aye, but he doesn't deserve it. God damn it! A plague on the sod, he's worthless!'

Tostig only blasphemed when the King was out of earshot. He sat with Aldwyth in her bower sweetly fragrant with burning apple wood and aglow with tapestry hangings. It was Christmas Eve and the bells of London Town were ringing across the frozen river.

'You would have governed it better?' Aldwyth looked up at her brother. Strings of crystal beads and amber were slung across her bosom betwixt twin gold brooches. 'Dear Tostig!'

'You know me, my honey.'

'I ought to!' Of all her brothers Tostig was the best beloved. He was certainly the handsomest. Big without being muscle-bound, healthy-skinned without being weather-beaten. She was fond of Gyrth and Leofwine – and Harold. But she had a secret language of eyes with Tostig. She could interpret his mood in a glance. Often they had no need of words, though sometimes she wondered if he felt for her as she did for him.

Tostig was saying, 'Mercia is the next richest shire to Wessex. Why should it be given to a Wolf's-Head?'

Aldwyth herself had been at the Witenagemot but had held her tongue. 'Aelfgar was inlawed by the King's grace.'

'No good will come of it. Aelfgar Leofricsson is a treacherous bastard!'

'Perhaps. But he is Earl.'

Tostig thought of his own lands north of the Humber where he should have been travelling to spend the Christmas-tide. Those wild hidages in whose thorny heart the Word of God had first taken root, causing them in a brief blaze of glory to become the foremost kingdom of England. Since then Mercia and Wessex had risen, and Northumbria had dwelt alone with itself, dreaming its old dream. In the governing of it Tostig had brought a semblance of order and introduced new laws, trying to stamp out the feuding of the families, with sons and brothers slaying one another in revenge for the death of a kinsman. He had done right by them, he felt; hard, aye, but fair. And what had been his rewards? Nothing but sullen disobedience, the ever-smouldering embers of hate fanned by the hostile northern thanery, in particular Gamel the son of Orm, and Ulf, son of Dolfin, and the sprawling broods that would rise to challenge him – among them the many sons of Uchtraed, thane of Durham.

'Why, even Gyrth, who has never yet raised sword against any man and shies the hunting field, aye, and Leofwine, that wench-chasing good-for-nothing, have better earldoms than mine, and I am older than the both of them. There's no right in it.' His blue eyes clouded. 'No justice! No forgiving!'

137

And even when he was home at his house on London bridge with his wife Countess Judith and his two sons Skyle and Ketil, Tostig could not rid his heart of resentment. He dwelt much on the wrongs fancied done to him, answering Judith's soft 'What troubles you?' with a terse 'Why should aught trouble me?' And of nights he'd lie still, his head between her breasts as though elf-shot.

Midsummer to Midwinter

Before the Mass of St John news was brought to Westminster which pleased the King. It was of the defeat of Macbeth's forces at the battle of Lumphanan and his death at the hands of Mael-Coluimb, Prince of Lothian and Cumbria.

Meanwhile Queen Aldwyth had taken it upon herself to see to the welfare of Edward the Atheling's family and retainers. They were treated always with great honour. Princess Agatha would have difficulty learning English but Aldwyth turned her attention to the children and spent hours with them as she was wont to do with Haakon, loving him sorely for his likeness to Sweyn. But of late there had been grief in that love, gnawing at her heart as a worm at an apple. Haakon, her very own foster-lean, who though fed at his mother's breast had been hers for all of his twelve years, had begun to look outside the tranquil walls of her bower to the sweaty, muscular world of the beer-drinking hearth-troops. Every other word on his lips was Harold. Blooding him, setting a falcon on his wrist, crimson-jessed, talons flashing. Lengthening his stirrups, encouraging him to piss boldly and think deep thoughts whilst watching his spit float on water.

'They are well endowed, your Saxon men,' Mahault, the Queen's Caen-born mistress-of-the-robes would say. She was married to the wealthy Aelfweard, one of Harold's thanes. 'Ah! The English dames – do they know how lucky they are, I wonder?'

After supper when the fires sank and the harp was passed from hand to hand in the hall, Aldwyth would retire to her bower and call to her not her maids nor Mahault with her quick brown fingers and starling's chatter, but Heardwin the cup-thane, son of Eadnoth the staller. He was present when she bathed, filling the tub with water of roses and lavender, bringing her drying-sheets. Then, banking the fire with pine logs, he would say, 'You wish me to leave ye now, ma'am?'

'Nay, Heardwin, stay . . .'

In bed that night the Queen was starved and Heardwin satisfied her well. He was not the half-tamed Viking like Njal Uggarsson, and even in that moment of man's supreme mastery over woman, he was tender and worshipping. As she lay feeling his sperm run between her legs, Aldwyth whispered, 'If I were to bear a child it would be England's heir.'

Heardwin propped himself up on one elbow, gazing down into her face. 'My lady,' he panted, 'you're not . . .?'

'Nay,' Aldwyth spoke wistfully. 'I am not with child – yet.'

'I'd like to give you a baby,' replied the young cup-thane. 'We have fucked enough to make one, that's for sure. But what of the King?'

'The King would have to acknowledge it as his.' Or stand humiliated as an unman and a cuckold . . .

'D'you think so?'

'How could he do otherwise?'

As usual there was a great gathering in London for the St Clement's-tide sheep fair and the Christmas festival was kept at the Wardrobe Palace. Churchmen in abundance were petitioning the King for bishoprics and land.

'More of the psalm-singers than you could stick a pin betwixt,' was the way the forthright Wendelwulf, marshal of the men of Kent, saw things.

Harold glanced up. The reading and signing of documents would fill his days from Tierce to Compline. 'The King always rewards them.'

'And some holding office in plurality. Isn't that a sin?'

'Carnal lust is the only sin the King knows,' said Harold.

'Ah, yes. Chastity and celibacy. Do you believe he is a saint?'

'No,' said Harold. 'I don't.'

Haakon, who had been sitting by the fire, got up to fetch some wood. 'Abbot Gervain says that the King lives like an angel in the squalor of the world and he should receive beatification.'

Wendelwulf said, 'Well, as to the yeas and nays of that . . .' and he shrugged. 'But what I do know is that some of his servants are profiting mightily by selling his bath water to the blind and the sick.'

Prior Wulfstan had journeyed to London and before returning to Worcester whence he had come, he said to Harold, 'Visit me when you can.' Wulfstan was not an overly tall man but he gave the feeling of height. His back was straight as a measuring rod, and with his head

140

upheld there was no escaping his eyes, heavy-lidded, weak-sighted, kindly. It was known that he wearied himself by watching through the nights in prayer. That he worked with his hands making braiding nets to keep awake. That he wore plain clothing without colour and seldom changed his boots. They called him Pastor of Souls.

Harold gleaned peace from his look. 'I shall, father.'

'It has been long since we spoke at ease together.' Wulfstan put out his hand and Harold took it, then bent to kiss the crucifix at his belt. 'God bless you and keep you, my son.'

And Harold stood on the steps and watched the Prior and his small band of monks ride away.

One night, Hereward said to Muirgheal, 'You never wear that brooch I gave you.'

'What if I lose it?'

'You can have another. Anything. I mean it. They're in my saddle-bags. Lots of things.' Maybe she did not believe him. He would show her. She could have everything he owned. Emptying his saddle-bags onto the floor, brooches and bracelets showered gold. An amethyst pendant gleamed. Beads of red glass.

'They are yours.'

'You have no need – giving me such.' Her face showed no pleasure. Her voice was soft and sad. He put a string of beads round her waist, hanging another about her neck. He was kneeling close by her. Rainbows came to him through her hair.

Muirgheal said, 'You have never had it before, have you?' Her breath was the breath of cowslips. Hereward shook his head.

'And you want it with me?'

'Don't you? O, Muirgheal, I'd give my soul to have you but once!' Muirgheal shut her eyes. 'Is it because you think I'd be clumsy? That I'd hurt you?' Hereward dropped his head in her lap. 'I'd be as good as any. You've seen what I've got. I could warm you. Make you happy.'

'Ni mar a siltear a bitear!' she whispered, and began to take the beads from round her neck.

He looked up at her, powerless then, his senses somehow deadened. 'You treat me like a child!'

'You are a child – sometimes. You are so innocent!'

'I wasn't trying to buy it!' He got to his feet. A mist like blood came into his eyes, blinding him. He went from the hut. Rain was gusty from a black sky. He blundered through it, cursing, until at last

141

he found a refuge of sorts by the byre. And there he crouched to open his trousers and bring out his cock. It was greatly swollen then, bruised and aching. 'Muirgheal,' he gasped, 'O, Muirgheal . . .' He shut his eyes and put his head between his knees. The rain beat on his bare neck. He jammed his fist in his mouth and sobbed.

Muirgheal would have liked to have sobbed also but the tears would not fall. Since before the age of ten, before her mother, a Seeress, from whom she had inherited the skill in hidden knowledge and enchantments, had died, men had sought her body for their own needs. They called her a cailleach. A Hag. A Witch-Woman. Her bronze pin was in truth a *bar an suan* – a slumber-pin. She could speak with the spirits. She could read hands. She could bless and banish and bid as well as heal. From her was got purification, the riddance of shooting-wens, venom-blisters, scabs and blotches. She brought good fortune, keen eyesight, and provoked the running of the seed, and in most just satisfied plain lust. At the times of La Bealtaine and La Samhain and La Lughnasa, they would come to lie with her on her heap of straw, a dozen men, maybe more, in turn. For when she had taken all being within herself and was one with the Fairy Queens Aoibheall and Aine and Cliodna, coition ensured protection against the Evil-Eye and the woe-working of the Foimhoire . . .

But now there was Hereward. Hereward. Yerrah! How could she explain it to him? Her purpose and reason for being? He'd never understand. She guessed that man of his already knew. His ferret eyes missed nothing and he made her feel uncomfortable . . . But the Earl's son! She could have had him almost from the first night for her love-man, and she no longer the apple left on the tree, but supple in the cradle of his hairy arms and sweet to his kiss . . . But when he discovered her true self – what then? O, she wanted him, yet she didn't. She yearned to bind him yet also to see him go . . . 'You'll be lonely without him,' she whispered to herself, 'but you've been lonely before . . .' And so she gathered her salve plants in a bowl, elf-leaf and moon-wort and sage and Virgin Mary's Milk-Drops and began to crush them and to bless them and to sing, and as she sang, to weep came easy.

142

The Months of Earth and Milk

 t had been after the Welsh wars that Harold had founded his own church – the abbey of Waltham, by the water meadows of the Lea – to house a relic of the True Cross. And when Countess Gytha knew he was to journey there in the spring of the year, she said, 'You'll go to Nazeing?'

'Aye,' Harold answered.

So she brought from her tow-chest a shawl woven of an ancient Danish pattern, nut-gall and lichen-dyed. 'A tooth-gift for the babe.'

Menglad pleaded to come. At sixteen, with her crop-yolk yellow hair, she drew the eyes of many men, not least of them Wendelwulf the Marshal.

'And why not have Ragnhild to go with you also?' said the Countess to Harold. 'Maybe she will take a fancy to one of your handsome hus-carls. It is high time she was betrothed.'

At Nazeing, in Eadgyth's bower, Ragnhild said forlornly, 'And mother would see me married to some great bear. One of Harold's men.'

'You could do worse.'

'I seek no bed-mate.'

Eadgyth was doing sprang-work. She glanced up from her wooden needles. 'But Dagobert the Marshal seeks you. He watches you constantly. You must know it.'

Ragnhild did. 'I give him no cause,' she said.

Menglad said, 'He is good looking. I'd lief find him beneath the kissing-bough!'

Wendelwulf had ridden thither with Harold and he sat in the bower rocking the cradle in which Modred slept, covered then with the Countess's shawl-gift. 'Ah!' he said, 'and I'd hoped you'd care for me!'

Menglad flushed, aware and not for the first time of the heftily handsome Wendelwulf.

Eadgyth chaffed her, 'You have a sweetheart there!'

And Wendelwulf said, 'Yon maid has always had my heart, ma'am. But I'm a plain man and know not how to tell her.'

Whereupon Menglad said boldly, 'If you had me to wife, what would my morning-gift be?'

Though no match for her quick tongue, Wendelwulf answered, 'Ask me that when thy wakes in my arms, lass!'

Ragnhild got up and went to the window. From without came the scent of hedge-rose and plum blossom. 'Is that all there is to life?' she said. 'There must be something else!'

'What more?' said Wendelwulf. ''Tis life. Natural.'

'Then that's why I crave the cloister. To serve the Holy Mother Church. Aelhhunn is preparing me for it.'

'I'll wager he's not blind to your golden hair, either!'

'Aelhhunn is a priest.'

Wendelwulf shrugged and said, 'He's a man.'

Though Aelfgar was Earl of Mercia he stayed in the north of his hidages, having all the Danelagh and never setting foot inside Coventry Minster or Croyland where Countess Godgyfu still heaped silver on the twelve altars and gave many mancuses of gold for masses to be said and psalms sung for the soul of Leofric, his father.

Times, he grew restless for the summer-leding season, wishing he had joined the army of Mael-Coluimb in Scotland that had lately brought Lulach, son of Macbeth and Gruoch, to battle, defeating him with great slaughter, and thus seizing the kingdom. And looking round at his treasures he'd see Eahlswith, his ewe-lamb, the most precious jewel of all.

'You'll mate with a thane, my yeanling. Nay, an earl. What do you say to that?'

And Eahlswith, wheedling honey-plums to suck and glass beads for her hair, had smiled a woman's smile. 'I'd rather mate with a King!' she said.

The Priory at Worcester was in an upheaval for Bishop Ealdred was enlarging and rearranging his ancient house. Away from the tangle of rope and dust and men humping wood and stone, Harold sought Prior Wulfstan where he tended the vegetable garden. The beans were sown, and cabbages and onions and peas. The vineyards set, the thorn hedges made good.

'Father!'

Wulfstan straightened up, pushing an old broken-brimmed straw hat from his face. 'Harold, my son!'

'You said to come.'

'Aye, of course!' Wulfstan took Harold's hands in his own, warm and earth grimed. 'Be welcome!' He asked after Eadgyth, the children. Did the new babe thrive? Was he baptised? Harold gave answers that pleased Wulfstan greatly.

Ealdfrith, a lame monk, worked with the Prior. He leaned on his hoe. He had a long-jawed, raw-boned face that had seen rather more than two score summers. His hair was a mop of grey-blond, shorn and tousled, as in true humility no comb nor looking-glass was ever used. 'You find us mucky at our labours, Earl Harold,' he said. There was a bed of dung, newly mulched, a-buzz with flies.

'For cucumbers,' said Wulfstan.

Ealdfrith sighed. 'We grow them but the yield is scant. The seed should be sown by a naked man in his prime before midnight on May Day Eve. The bigger the man between the legs the bigger the cucumber. 'Tis earth magic!'

Wulfstan shook his head at his mass-thane's tattle of superstition and turned his attention to the herb garden. Then there was heard a sound familiar to all at the Priory, that of shuffling, dragging, hopping footsteps, as along the path came hobbling Cwichelm Crookback, Child Master of the novices. His arms were full of Easter flowers — yellow boots and April's darling and fairy cups – for the chapel.

He greeted Harold and Ealdfrith said, 'I was just telling him about our cucumbers.'

For all that his monstrously humped spine threw his whole body awry and he was often in pain, Cwichelm's smile was wide and warm. 'Ah, yes!' And he nodded. 'We are in a sorry case for virility here.' Then he looked up at Harold. 'Unless, of course, you would sow them for us? I'll wager our crop would be the best seen!' Harold laughed and said, 'I'd be glad to.' Then he told of the building at Waltham.

'It will be a worthy shrine,' said Wulfstan.

''Tis only small,' Harold said.

'Cubit span matters not in the eyes of God.' Wulfstan sat back on his heels. 'My lord Bishop seeks to outdo Archbishop Stigand and Bishops Aethelwine of Durham and William of London. Reorganising their cathedral chapters, adorning and enriching.'

'Is that not good?'

'Not at the expense of the soul.'

Harold turned to look at the buildings of the Priory through the misty trees, low and rambling and at harmony with itself. Where no hawk flew and no hound sought its quarry. Hart and fox, stag and hare all found sanctuary within those blackthorn and raspberry hedges.

Wulfstan said quietly, 'Rather than rood-screens and fine altar-cloths, the apothecary needs re-thatching. New straw mattresses for the novices. Tools for the workshop.'

When Cynesige of York died – which could not be long, he being old and full of years – Ealdred was next in line to become Archbishop and Wulfstan would succeed him to the Bishopric of Worcester. We both await the death of a man, thought Harold, to enable us to work our will.

And the chapel bell rang for Sext then, a crystal chime in the quiet.

La-Mas-Abhal

I n the Month of the Fruit Spirit Hereward had begun to patch and mend. He fixed the leaking buckets and the broken fence and the hole in the roof. He chopped wood to make a sheep-pen and as he swung the axe, it barked in the dismal hanging of the autumn air. All the one day it went on and into the next, and Muirgheal did not give much thought to it when suddenly it stopped.

Then she looked up to see Hereward bending beneath the flap. He said, 'There was two men asking for you.'

'*Cath ain?*'

'Just now. They weren't so keen when they saw me.'

'Have they gone?'

'Aye.'

Muirgheal turned, trembling, stooping to the peat fire.

Hereward came in up close behind her, hunching his shoulders. 'Is something the matter?'

Muirgheal bit at her white knuckles. 'Hereward! Ah, *cara!*' Hereward had not seen her this way before. Tenderly as he could he laid a hand on her hair. 'What is it, love?' he said. At his touch she gave a soft moan. 'Muirgheal . . .'

Then she turned round on him suddenly. 'You have no right to question me!'

Hereward drew back, puzzled. Then he wiped his nose and said, 'Now ye're mad at me.'

Muirgheal wanted to injure him then. To see the hurt in his face. That he should stumble into her world and turn it upside down . . . '*Gommagh!*' she said. 'You'd not go, would you? You'd not leave well alone. I warned you!' She gave a bitter little laugh and a shrug. 'But you might as well know. Men do come.'

'To you?'

147

She nodded.

'What for?'

'I lie with them.'

Hereward stared at her, uncomprehending. 'But why?'

'It is my craft. It is of making holy. I harm no one.'

'Sod that! One of them had got no teeth and the other was all scabby!'

Muirgheal drew a shuddering sigh. Hereward said slowly, 'So that is why you didn't want me. I have money. You would not have to do anything for it.'

'I don't want money from you!'

'But you'd take it from those swine! I thought you were a healing woman. An angel. I kissed the ground you walked on. But you're naught but a bloody whore!'

Muirgheal gazed at him with huge tears in her eyes. 'I knew you'd not understand.'

'D'you have 'em in here?' And Hereward took in the walls. The heap of straw he'd longed to share with her. Other men had lain on it, wormy, pawing, groping. They had mounted Muirgheal. Rutted on her. And she naked beneath them, doing nothing to hinder them while they had of her the one thing he craved . . . He ripped down the plait of rushes and tossed the straw onto the fire, scattering it, burning it. Then he snatched down all the herbs and flowers she had set to dry, collected so carefully, tied so lovingly, trampling them, grinding them to dust under his heel. Then he swung round on Muirgheal where she crouched in the corner behind the loom. 'There! You'll have to do your fucking elsewheres!'

'*Go maithe Dia dhuit e!* May God forgive you!'

'I'd like to kill every one of those bastards who ever touched you! You are mine! You belong to me!'

'I belong to no one!'

'You abase yourself with them! Let them use your body! Sell your cunt! That is belonging. Why cannot you do it with me?'

'It isn't what you think . . .'

'You'd rather let some stinking, warty bugger . . .'

'*Greadadh tri lár do scart!* May the midst of your entrails be tortured!' she yelled at him. 'Could you do it any different?'

'Try me!' And so saying, Hereward grabbed her thin wrists, both in one hand, and dragged her out of the hut and down into the fastness of the wood. The sacred wood of ash and oak and yew. It was raining then, spattering among the leaves, making a fragrant wet bower. She fought him, striking at his chest and shoulders. He was strong as the boar of the mountains, and she knew that she could scream until her lungs burst and no one would hear her, save perhaps that man of his and he wouldn't care.

Then turning her suddenly, savagely against him, Hereward said, 'Did you enjoy it with those others? Did you like them mauling you? Tell me, Muirgheal, did you?'

'Why should I answer you anything? You said you loved me, but you don't – not now! Because you're so stupid and so blind!'

But the time for reasoning was past. Hereward took her down into the bracken, landing hard on top of her. Crushed beneath his rib-cracking weight, Muirgheal had no chance against him. He tore her smock with one hand, baring her white belly and fragile, silken-haired cunt, while he ripped open his trousers with the other. He was straddling her, panting for possession, ramming his knees between her legs, forcing them far apart, and she felt his cock – Usha! the size of it! – start to push against her, trying for her opening. The power of him lapped about her, his muscle-heavy thighs bearing down on her and it was like drowning. The impulse to cling to him, to drag his head to her breasts was great, but while surrender to Hereward's brute strength would have its sweetness, she didn't want it with him like this – not in a miserable rape. Thus with all the fight she could muster, Muirgheal hit up into his face with her clenched fists again and again, clawing at his arms with sharp nails, tearing his shirt. Caught unawares, Hereward lost his grip on her and in those moments Muirgheal struggled desperately to escape, but he was quick to seize her again, to pin down her flailing arms, and in so doing, one of her hands – the leech hand – was scored cruelly on a thicket of thorns. Muirgheal cried out loud in pain and anguish, blood running between her fingers.

Unable to hold back any longer, Hereward climaxed and the sperm shot out of his pumping cock every which way. He was slumped half across her. Raindrops soaked his shirt. She was breathing. He felt her but he was nothing. He wasn't alive or dead. Just empty. The clamouring in his balls had gone. He smelt the rotten-sweetness of his sperm. He'd spattered it all over. Filthy sod, him. Mary, Mother of Christ! He took her hand, pulling a thorn out of her leech finger with his teeth, sucking the blood, cleansing the deep scratches with his spit as if he were doing it for his own body.

'I'm sorry . . . sorry . . .' She did not stir but she was weeping, he knew. 'Muirgheal, O, Muirgheal. I'm dirt. I'm not fit any more. I'm dirt . . .'

149

'Get off from me,' she said.

He shifted and she groaned. He'd snapped her beads and her smock gaped from neck to hem. Many of the little bells were missing and she grieved for their loss.

'I didn't mean it, lass, honest. I don't know what came over me.' Hereward wiped himself off with handfuls of grass. 'Forgive me.'

Muirgheal drew her plaid about her. The rain, heavy then, plashed through the trees, the branches showering, washing down her cheeks with the tears. 'For being a man?' she said.

Hereward could not weep. He had gone beyond tears. 'But I do love you. I do . . .'

Her eyes were all colours of the rain and leaves, the lashes like black webs spun with drops. She shook down her sopping hair. 'And I am supposed to be grateful – to forget what happened. Just because you say that. To talk of love as if it makes everything all right . . .'

'Would you not have liked me fucking you?'

'Ca bhfios dom? How do I know?'

'Do you hate me?'

'No.'

Hereward kneaded the earth with his fists. 'I hate myself. O, Muirgheal, I'm so ashamed . . .'

And so he cleared the hut and brought fresh straw. And when he'd gathered and plaited a swath of rushes, he laid it at Muirgheal's feet. Like a love-gift.

'Things won't ever be the same, will they?'

'Conas?'

'You and me.'

'They cannot.'

'I have spoiled it.' He squatted down, the curtain of rushes between them.

'Mind Morrighan and Badbh.' The cats hid behind her skirts. Hereward felt them to be vaguely hostile then when before they had been friendly.

Without lifting her eyes, Muirgheal said, 'You'll go then?'

'Where?'

'Leaving me.'

'You want it so?'

'Fágaim fút féin é.'

'I wish I could die for you.'

'Nár lige Dia san! I'd still be the same.' And she looked at him then

150

and he felt a flight of birds pass over his face. 'You are so innocent!'

'Don't keep saying such!'

'But you are. It is true. O, you have got big broad shoulders and the strongest arms. *Fearuil!* But you are pure as the rain that is yet to fall!'

'O, Muirgheal, let me stay by you. Let me look after you, protect you. I won't ever touch you nor bother you again – unless you ever had need of me.'

'Without sin? Without lust?' Muirgheal shook her head. Tears trickled down her hollowed cheeks.

Hereward took her hand, the injured one, kissing it tenderly. 'I love ye.'

'What understanding do you have?'

'All. There's no secrets between us.'

Muirgheal felt despair at his dumb acceptance of her. 'You are the son of an Earl. You could not go back to your home with me.'

'I am never going back. This is my home. Where I belong.'

151

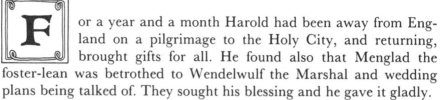

The Feast of All Souls

For a year and a month Harold had been away from England on a pilgrimage to the Holy City, and returning, brought gifts for all. He found also that Menglad the foster-lean was betrothed to Wendelwulf the Marshal and wedding plans being talked of. They sought his blessing and he gave it gladly.

At Nazeing Eadgyth clung to him, whispering, 'You are the only gift I want,' unfastening his heavily-ornamented belt, the straps of his jerkin . . .

He had remembered everyone, and Margaret, Edward the Aetheling's eldest daughter, sat gazing on the strange and lovely gift that Harold had given her. From the Campus Martius in Rome, it was a set-piece of a golden king and queen and courtiers all lit by a single carbuncle and guarded by a golden boy with a bent bow. At first she would rather have had what was Christina's – a many stranded prayer-rope of jewelled icons – but looking at her own gift again she thought that she would not have exchanged it for the whole world.

And what was it that the Earl had said to her? Stooping, with his immense shoulders and his gentle blue eyes: 'It is important that you just never take anything from it nor disturb it. Not even one of the tiny arrows from its quiver.'

She blushed when she remembered how shy she had been with him, clutching her gift, overwhelmed by the size and the raw male smell of him. What must he have thought of her? Did he ever think of her? He must have done, and kindly, to have chosen such.

'Seen the lass look at him?' Modred said. ''Tis a shame. For I hear the King is trying to match her with that young cub of the Scots.'

And thus it was that the novice monk Cumbra came to Archbishop Stigand's house with an armful of parchments and a tale.

152

'Mael-Coluimb?' said Stigand. The Scottish King had spent the Blood Month at Westminster.

'And she has no liking for him,' said Cumbra, bending to put an apple log on the fire. 'Her eyes are for Earl Harold.' The Archbishop chuckled and shook his head. Cumbra, grown bold, whispered, 'In the hall a few nights ago 'twas said that there's not a woman at the court who wouldn't go to bed with the Earl given the chance.'

'So you eavesdrop on the mead-benches?'

Cumbra flushed. He was but a lad feeling his manhood struggle against the vows of abstinence. Smiling, Stigand began to sort among the parchments. 'It is his brawn, my prattle-tongue. It's a sure attraction for the women.'

Looking up through the smoky rush-light, Cumbra said, 'Why do God's thanes have to be chaste, my lord?'

The Archbishop replied, 'Because it gives the Devil a pin-and-web in his eye!'

King Edward was not best pleased to have his plans thwarted. Was Mael-Coluimb not a handsome enough lad to please any maid? Yet Margaret would have none of him.

'I cannot understand it,' said the King to Harold.

And Harold answered, 'She's but a little lass. Not half grown.'

'She eats my bread.'

'There's no forcing her.' Edward watched his Earl of Wessex. Harold had always kept clear of affairs outside England. Yea, he had been downright disobedient, shirking the task of marching against Macbeth. ''Tis no business of mine,' he'd said. 'I've no quarrel with the man . . .' Leaning back in his chair, nibbling a be-ringed forefinger, the King said, 'He'll marry Ingiborg, heiress of the Orkneys and Caithness.'

'Then let him.' Harold was equable.

'I wanted him brought under the southern influence, or else he'll begin to side with the Haardrada and those Norse chiefs.'

Harold shrugged and said, 'I don't think it would matter who his wife was, he'd give his allegiance where the pickings were best.'

Edward's jaw dropped. 'My foster-lean?' And struck by this new thought the King was seen to be in a silent mood the rest of the day.

Relieved that Mael-Coluimb was returning to his own court without any more attempts at wooing, Margaret brought out her golden treasure to gaze on.

153

'That you don't travel at the Scotsman's side is due to Earl Harold,' said Christina.

'How so?' Margaret said, her cheek grown the hue of the foxglove.

Christina was also gazing at the treasure. 'He counselled the King against it.' With the lustre of gold in her eyes, she said without turning, 'You like him very much, do you not, Greta?'

'I suppose so.'

'They call him charmer of women. Yet he has no looks.'

'He is kind.'

'He also has a hand-fast wife.'

And before Michael-Mass news was that Eadgyth was with child again. At Westminster men said, 'It must be his fourth. Would that he could teach the King how to do it!'

Thus with the boon-work and the malting-ales over for the year, it was November once more, the Month of Souls, and men came in from the outlying hidages to seek bracelets of their lord. And it was at the lodge of Savernake or Sweet-Fern Oak that they gathered, a favourite hunting forest of the King. And there also that Tostig, with a laugh better, sweeter than any hawk-bells, took pleasure in nightly goading Aelfgar Leofricsson into such a rage that in the end he upped and struck him, giving that mocking, handsome face such a clout that the blood gushed.

That his peace should be broken threw King Edward into a black temper. He sought to punish Aelfgar, calling for him to be brought thither, only to be told by Harold, 'He's gone, Sire.'

'Gone? Gone where?'

'He rode with his hearth-troop.'

'And you let him?'

'I had no orders to stop him.'

'Orders!' the King flared out. 'When have you ever needed orders?'

Harold shrugged. 'There is Tostig.'

'The blame was not his.'

'Then you had best tell that to the Mercian men, Sire. They outnumber us at this feast. Feelings are running high and he's not making matters easy on himself.'

'Tostig has never done a base thing!'

Harold said, 'He is a quarrelsome sod.'

'Your own brother!'

154

'Aye, and as he is my brother you'd better put him in your own chamber under lock and key for his own safety . . .'

'I don't know what the bloody hell they'd do without Harold to wet-nurse them!' said Dagobert to Wendelwulf.

'Find some other soft bugger?'

Dagobert sighed and shook his head. 'D'you think anyone else would ever be that daft?'

The Honey-Thief

O ne dark morning of rain and wind at the Vigil of La Samhain when the spirits of the dead walked, Hereward went to feed the animals and to fetch water and chop kindling. And it was when he'd stacked a pile that he looked up to see Muirgheal. She was wearing a plaid dyed of woad and all sad colours both as shawl and cloak, clasped by the old bronze slumber-pin. They had spoken little during the past days.

'How long have you been there?' said Hereward, straightening up. She wore no bells on the hem of her smock and Hereward had not heard her come.

'Not very long.' She glanced at the wood. 'You have been gathering.'

Hereward kicked at a piece of kindling with his foot. 'Aye.'

'And to think – I used to do all that before you came – and all the while wanting to be white-souled and fair as St Brighid and to hang my wet cloak on the rays of the sun!'

Hereward looked down at her skin, crystal-clear in the rain. Like lilies. 'You need never do such again. I'll fetch and carry. Do your bidding.'

Muirgheal said, 'An Earl's son – my servant.'

'Aye, and more.'

She bowed her head. '*An mor* – what more?'

'To be your lover.'

'Hereward! *A mhic*!'

'Why did you come?'

'Because I knew you would be here.'

'Have you changed your mind?'

'About what?'

'About having it with me.'

'That is all you want. My body.' She appeared resigned. Hereward longed to see her eyes as she lay beneath him, looking up into his, full of joy and desire.

'Aye, I want your body. Do you not want mine?'

'Where? Here in the mud? For that's what it is. Rain and mud and grass. *Ana-salach!* So dirty!'

''Tisn't dirty. You like me. You've said so. I'm not asking you to feel a great love. I'll not cry for the moon. But just let me warm ye. Come into the shed, lass, just for a little while . . .'

Hereward's voice was so calm, so gentle, that her legs went weak. That he should have this effect on her. To have her bowels move towards him. Just a boy . . . He pushed the door open for her and she went in, passing beneath his arm and he followed behind her. It was dry and deep-scented in there, heaped with hay and laden with grain-mote, and the calyx of springs past breathed of a floral rain. There was barely enough room to turn round.

Hereward put the bar across the door and thus they faced each other for what seemed an age until Hereward started to unfasten his wet jerkin, then he took off his shirt. Unbuckling his belt, he shrugged down his trousers, and naked in the rainy gloom, a few paces the distance between them, Hereward was conscious of himself, head bent under the low roof: of his calloused hands and chipped nails, his thick wrists and shoulder muscles, and his cock hanging heavy from amidst the bush of dark gold hair, stirring and reddening then as the blood pulsed into it. And his balls began to sing.

Muirgheal offered no resistance as he reached out for her and drew her to him. He would have gone down on his knees to beg – anything to get her to come into his arms with no struggling, no crying. But there – she let him take the old bronze pin from her plaid and strip the smock from her.

'Muirgheal!' he whispered. 'Ah, Muirgheal!' His voice was plaintive and choked. 'You're so lovely! O, lass, lass!'

She dazzled his eyes. He'd never seen a woman's breasts before. They were not round, but drooped, large on her thin body, flower-white gourds without blemish. With big, coarse, trembling hands he lifted them, fondling them, and bent to suck on her silky-brown nipples. Muirgheal sighed, her head lolling back, feeling her nipples quiver and grow to the size of small plums in the warm wetness of his mouth, and for long moments she could utter no word, so great was the pleasure. And he hadn't half begun. Crudely masculine, he was trying to be gentle, kissing her neck and throat with deep, devouring kisses. She did not gainsay him her mouth. He covered it right over with his own,

157

shoving his tongue between her lips, forcing apart her teeth, seeking her tongue in mute hunger, as if to find honey there. They mingled spit, tasting each other, and Hereward's tongue crammed the whole of her mouth. He was sinking down onto his knees and taking her with him, and Muirgheal was panting then with being held so tight against the bruising bulk of his penis. She cupped his balls and they filled her hands, lumpy and teeming and tender.

'My cock!' he muttered through clenched teeth. 'It'll burst!' He was almost in tears. He'd already risen so high, hugely engorged with excitement, that his penis, straining from its foreskin, was flat up on his belly, and the veins stood out like knots, purplish-blue and throbbing on its rigid length.

'*Is mithid dhuit!* It's time for you! *Na biodh eagla ort!* Don't be afraid!' whispered Muirgheal, beholding him, and brought her legs up over his thighs, almost squatting on the swollen head of the cock, baring herself, opening her cunt wide for him, aching-wet, pushing herself onto him, and then suddenly he was there, entering, shoving all the way up inside her, deep into her womb, and strangled by the joy of it, Hereward let out a great, howling groan.

Second by second the cock was growing even bigger and hotter and harder, filling her, and it began to jerk and thrash.

'Hereward!'

'I'm fucking ye!'

'Sure ye are!'

'It's bloody wonderful!'

'You're doing fine, cara!' Muirgheal gasped, dazed, half-collapsing on his neck from the size and pressure of him within her. '*Acushla! Acushla!* O pulse of my heart!'

Then he bore down on top of her, flattening her beneath him in the hay, and she clung to him, gnawing at his shoulders, seeing the pain and bewilderment and lust on his face.

Musha! How fiercely he beat! How hard he thrust! How young he was! The rhythmic thud of her buttocks was muted in the piles of dried grasses and dusty barley. She pressed the heels and soles of her feet against the calves of his hairy legs. She smelt the clove-gillies and matted pinks and little wind-roses – flowers of paradise – that wove her pillow. But soon they were overpowered by the smell of Hereward's sweat. It fell on her like his spittle as grunting and heaving, he strove to hold back his sperm, but couldn't, and he yelled out as he lost it, and Muirgheal, all yielded up then, her soul washed transparent, felt the warm, oozy stickiness trickle between her legs. Still half-hard within

158

her Hereward's cock continued to move, pulsing very softly, but he'd sagged on her, crushing her with the whole of his weight.

And so he was a man.

After a time, he whispered humbly, 'Shall I get out of you?'

'Not if you don't want to.'

'Did you like it, maybe?'

'Ah, jewel, was it not a fine thing?'

'It'll be better – next time.'

Muirgheal reached up to stroke the sodden mass of his hair. 'When'll that be?'

'Whenever you want.'

The rain was still falling yonder and the old wood of the shed creaked. Muirgheal tasted his salt-sweat on her lips. Her hair was damp and tangled and her flesh seemed gummed to his.

Hereward said, 'That's my stink on you. I've made you mucky. I'm sorry.'

'*Is mó duine ná féadfadh é a dhéananmh!* Many a man could not do it!' Muirgheal answered him.

'D'you mean it?'

'I'd not lie to you, *cara*.'

'Ah, Muirgheal! *Mo bhean!* Would you mind if a baby came of it?'

'I do not think I can conceive.'

'All women must.'

'Not if they're barren.'

'You'll bear.'

'So sure of yourself, are you not?' Muirgheal chided gently.

'My seed is ripe.'

'And you'd give all that to an old *cailleach* such as I?'

'You're not old. You're beautiful. With those white tits of yours and that darlin' arse – it sticks out right proud!' Tears were trickling down his face. He sniffed, wiping his nose on the back of his hand. 'I love ye fit to die, I do!'

And thus with the days being so cold and forlorn, Muirgheal spent most of them in the shed with Hereward, craving his arms and his strength. Better than sitting alone, lying with him afforded warmth and solace, and besides she was weak for his maleness. He used his white bearskin cloak for their cover and she would be forgetting the wind and rain when his body came into hers . . .

In the hay, damp and bruised with the boy's passion, weary with her own, she opened her legs to give him entry. Putting her mouth to

159

the apple of his throat she could see the dark winter-light through the gaps in the wattle, the bleak, comfortless world beyond the refuge of his great, hefty shoulders.

'I do try,' he said, 'to keep away from you. Not to bother you. I think to myself – you randy bugger, that's all that's ever on your mind. But I can't help it. Fucking you is so good!' And then, looking down into her eyes, 'You do feel the same, don't you? You're not just letting me have it, despising me? You've a bit of love for me, have you not?'

He always asked this of her, forever seeking reassurance; he was childlike in so many ways, yet in others so much a man. The child part of him with its mixture of innocence and sensitivity appealed to her heart, awakening compassion – but the man! He brought response in belly and breasts and womb, and all that she had went out to him. He offered a sexual fulfilment she had never known before. And though so many had entered her body, none had ever blundered on that inner peace, that secret part of her. Claimed her soul.

From the Feast of Fools to the Winter Solstice

I t was just past the Hour of Prime and the morning light made a path across the shallows of the Lea to where the newly-finished Abbey of Waltham seemed to float all of a dream among the fairy bells and stiff green rushes.

''Tis a sight to behold,' said Modred, looking at it on that April day. 'It does ye credit, Harold.'

And sitting his saddle easily next to the marshal of the hearth-troop, Harold said, 'It has taken ten years.'

'When is the hallowing?'

'The third day of May.' The day of the Invention of the Rood . . . And the sunlight brought out the colours of stone and the honeyed shades of the wood, and the dew clung to the split oak roof shingles, dripping slow as Freyja's tears.

'You will go, my lord, to see this hallowing?' said Aldwyth.

The King looked at his Queen. 'Yes,' he answered her, 'for I've heard that the Minster is to be filled with all manner of wondrous things.'

Njal the Icelander said, 'Do you wish a litter, ma'am?'

'A litter?'

'To journey to Waltham.'

Aldwyth sulked and shrugged. Bloodstones hung from her ears. 'What of my Wilton? It should have been hallowed first.'

Njal considered his royal mistress, then said, 'Do you think God cares?'

Aelfgar Leofricsson had retreated into his Danelagh and held court at Chester like a chieftain of old, putting a scrim curtain betwixt himself and the world. 'A Godwinesson world!' he'd say bitterly to his two

161

sons Eadwine and Morkere, and they listened at his knee and marked him well.

Tostig went to the hallowing performed by the aged Cynesige of York on a day of sunshine and early butterflies. And the company of thanes led by the King and the clergy with Archbishop Stigand at their head, prepared as they were for the treasures with which Waltham had been endowed, could not but gasp and marvel at the sight that met their eyes.

Vessels of gold and silver. A rood of gold and a crucifix carved of the black wood of the True Cross on which hung the figure of the suffering Christ chipped in black flint. The thick walls hung with tapestries of matchless design and worked by English needles. The altar cloths and dossals of lace; the rood screen ablaze with emeralds. The Eucharist was celebrated. Tostig knelt and crossed himself, dumb in that House of God, whose very timbers seemed to flash fire. Sodden, drenched in beauty, his brain ached trying to measure and weigh in mancuses and sestiers.

'It is like Fafnir's hoard!' he whispered. 'Will he lock and bar the doors?'

Archbishop Cynesige laid crosses of aspen wood before the altar, calling upon the blessings of the saints. 'Crux Mattheus, Crux Marcus, Crux Lucas, Crux Sanctus Joahannes, Sanctus, Sanctus, Sanctus . . .'

Leaning back against the wall, arms folded, Leofwine said, 'The doors will never be closed. The village folk will come here for Mass.'

Tostig stared at his younger brother. 'You mean they'll tramp among all this with cow dung on their boots?'

Leofwine smiled. His usual high spirits were sobered, tawny hair kept in check by a rich-woven band. 'Christ was born in a stable,' he said.

'Was he there?' said Eadgyth.

'Tostig – aye.'

'Did you speak together?'

'Nay, he was waiting on the King.'

Eadgyth was seven months gone with child. She seemed anxious, picking up her stitching, then putting it aside. 'O, Harold, if only you were friends with each other!'

'I have never been aught else.' Harold, usually slow, often mum, was the more so that night in her bower after the strain of the great day.

162

'I know,' whispered Eadgyth. 'I know.'

Then Harold knelt down at her feet, the might of him seeming to fall and tumble about her. 'Do not let us talk of him – God knows, I'd cut off my right arm for him, but he vexes me sore. Let us talk of the baby.' And he put his hands on her stomach, bending to listen. 'Does it kick?'

'Aye.'

'D'you think it's a lad?'

'My belly is sunk low – with the boys it was high up. Hag Annis says it will be a girl.'

'A girl! Ah, but I hope she doesn't look like me!'

'The Swan-Neck must be near her time,' Queen Aldwyth said, dismissing her chaplains and turning to the King.

And Edward nodded, but his thoughts were elsewhere on that spring day. News had lately come from Normandy, where for many years he had followed the fortunes of his distaff kinsman Duke William. After constantly warring against his neighbours – France and Anjou and Maine and Brittany – it seemed that all was now quiet. But for how long? William was by nature both greedy and cruel and men feared him. And he still held Wulfnoth Godwinesson hostage, for whose freedom Countess Gytha petitioned each Jesus Day.

Remembering William's visit to his court in that snowy winter long ago, the King smiled to himself. How covetous those black eyes upon tapestry and plate! How well, he, Edward, had played upon his kinsman's greatest weakness.

'What would you do if this kingdom were yours?' he'd asked of William, whilst pouring malvoisie by candlelight.

'Mine?' had come the reply on sharply-drawn breath.

'Who knows what the future may hold?'

And William, non-plussed, but shrewd, had said, 'Eh, kinsman, you jest with me?'

King Edward had given neither a yea nor a nay. He let William think what he would. Let him boast ever after to friend and foe alike of the promise of his English inheritance.

Ah, the ravening for that crown! Edward enjoyed the feeling of power it gave him. Power over men he could not better by physical strength. Power over a man like Harold Godwinesson who could make him feel palsied and useless just by standing in the same room.

Aldwyth left her lord to his wool-gathering and said no more.

The Feast of St John the Baptist passed and the mowing and scything ales. Then she heard that Eadgyth had given birth to a daughter. Gytha, she was to be called, and the Countess herself travelled to see her first grand-daughter and namesake.

Njal Uggarsson the bower-thane told his mistress as he lay abed with her.

Aldwyth said, 'To Nazeing? My mother?'

'Aye,' Njal replied. 'The Countess left before Vespers with the lady Menglad.'

Menglad the foster-lean, given last Candle-Mass in marriage to Wendelwulf the Marshal and already with child. And did not tell me, thought Aldwyth. Did not ask whether I would accompany them or nay . . .

But what would have been the point? Countess Gytha had self-counselled. She would only be met with refusal. Often she wondered what Aldwyth wanted from life. What made her star so angry and lost. She had brought her grand-daughter a bracelet of amethysts and a glass drinking cup. Menglad gave a bearing-cloth she'd worked with her own hands.

Charms and tooth-gifts gilded the cradle wherein the babe slept, watched over by Hag Annis, whilst Eadgyth stitched and Lintrude the bower-maid wound yarn. And seated among them the Countess said softly, 'Womb-want!' As if she had answered her own question.

Towards the end of the year, betwixt the Mass of St Luke and the Mass of St Stephen, Archbishop Cynesige died and Ealdred succeeded to York. Worcester thence fell to Wulfstan.

'Where are your Bishop's vestments, Father?' Harold said as he beheld Wulfstan in his coarse wool robe.

Wulfstan smiled. 'Did you expect to see me in finery, my son?' The new Bishop had just heard Nones on a bleak December afternoon in the chapel at Worcester, and risen from his prayer-mat. Harold had Gyrth with him. Wulfstan held out his hands, strong, the nails broken with work, and they clasped one each.

'I thought perhaps you'd wear a chasuble or a gold crucifix . . .'

'We worship God with our hearts, not our outward seeming.'

Rebuked, Harold gazed at the simplicity of the dark carved wood, scrubbed stone and plain crystal-glazed windows. There were tapestries, it was true, wondrous-wrought, and shining lamps and a chalice that lacked not gold, yet withal humility shone in that place, the absence of pride. And he thought of the glory of his Minster at Waltham.

As if reading his thoughts, Wulfstan said, 'But then nor is the Lord blind to beauty lain before his altar nor the sight of the good Archbishop of Canterbury at a loss for words!' There was a twinkle in his eye as he spoke and Harold laughed.

Over mead in Wulfstan's tiny room beneath the thatched eaves they talked of old times and people known to them. The news of Harold's growing family was of great interest to the Bishop.

'And what of you?' he said to Gyrth. 'When shall we drink at your wedding-feast?'

Gyrth said, 'Women don't bother over much with me.'

Harold downed his mead, wiping his hand across his mouth. 'Ah, he is better-looking than any of us!'

It was true; neither too lissom nor too muscular, and eyes the colour of drowned violets, Gyrth was enough to make any woman's mouth water.

'And Tostig? Where is he?'

'In the north, Father,' said Harold.

Wulfstan put his hands palm-down on his knees. 'Do you consider him diligent in the welfare of his folk?'

Harold answered quietly, 'He holds sak and soke. Takes toll and market dues.'

And all those snow-bound miles away in York city, that was the burden of a moot of local thanes held unbeknown to Tostig as he sat in his hall liken to that one with many doors, its rafters like spear-shafts, filled with mail-coats and haunted by the wolf and the eagle.

'Our taxes! That is all he cares for,' said Waltheof, son of Siward Digre.

'We cannot even get close enough to the southern bastard to slit his throat!' This from the Gospatrics, Snow and Gulla.

'He never stirs an inch without his hearth-troop.' Ulf, son of Dolfin, spat on his thumb and stroked his axe blade. 'Would that I could meet him alone on the fell!'

But Tostig had Copsi, his deputy and shadow-dancer, known and hated throughout the Thrithings. And Amund and Raevenswart and Frodi and Thorbrand and Eilifr the Long-Tooth . . .

'Perhaps he is over zealous,' said Bishop Wulfstan.

The rents were paid in renders of malt, grain and rye. In un-coined silver, gold shillings and the church-scot, and not forgetting the half-pennorth of wax from each hide at Passion-Tide.

Harold said, 'There's never been a man yet that could tell Tostig he was wrong. There's times when he's so sure of himself he makes me afraid.'

From the Bells of Candle-Mass to the Paschal Moon

n a day in the spring when violets peeped from under the bracken and wood moss, Muirgheal came and knelt where Hereward worked, clod-turning in the herb garden, planting afresh.

'I have not bled this month,' she said.

Hereward stopped, his hands earth-mucky. 'How much overdue?'

'Twenty days.'

His heart missed a beat. 'Do you think . . . ?'

'Maybe.'

'When will you be sure?'

'A few weeks.'

And with the passing of those weeks Muirgheal knew for certain that she was pregnant. And she both loved and hated Hereward for what he'd done. At her age to be gotten with child by a boy . . .

When Bishop Ealdred journeyed to Rome to seek his pallium in order that he might return sanctified Archbishop and bearing the blessings of the Holy Father, Tostig decided to accompany him. As was his way the issue was settled in minutes. Judith would come.

'You always wanted to visit the Holy City.'

Judith looked up at him. She said, 'What of our sons? Ketil will fret.'

'They can go to Winchester. Mother is always eager to have them. I'll give them a falcon apiece. Leofwine will teach them how to fly it.'

Tostig noticed the gold cross set with peridots at Judith's throat. A gift from Rome of Harold's bringing. He frowned, touching the chain, gossamer-fine. 'I will bring you a better one than that – set with emeralds. Fit for a princess!'

'Hah! You grow boastful!'

167

'What of a crown for a Queen?' Judith watched his eyes roam and challenge the night. Then he smiled. 'Well?'

'You talk as one beguiled.'

'Have you ever thought of when Edward dies – who will follow?'

'He has named Edgar the Aetheling as his heir.'

'At nine years old? A lamb among the wolves.'

Judith said, 'There is Harold.'

Tostig thumped his fist into his palm. 'Harold!' There was a sudden, hard, cold anger in his voice. 'You may as well say there is your brother-in-law William of Falaise. There is Harald Sigurdsson. What of Svein Estrithsson, my kinsman? He is King in Denmark now. What of me? Am I not battle-worthy? Trustworthy? Power-worthy?' Judith nodded, held by his beautiful, dark-lashed eyes. Tostig whispered, 'Does the King not love me? Have I not been as a son to him? Why should it not be me?'

When Muirgheal's pains started in the winter of the year – the time of La Samhain once more – she betook herself to a cleft among the rocks by the shore and there scraped a hole in the dried leaves wherein the babe could be dropped when she was delivered.

Hereward woke to find her gone and ran to the woods in search of her, calling her name, even trespassing on the ground sacred to the Sidhe. A solitary May tree grew there. Centuries-hunched, fairy-hallowed. 'She's having my baby!' he panted to the web of rattling, dry branches.

Baby . . . baby . . . they echoed. Not mocking, just mournful. And with cheeks lashed by sudden rain and bramble-stung, Hereward stumbled from that brooding, enchanted place.

It was not until much later that he came upon Muirgheal crouched in the tiny hollow overhung with trees, whimpering, her black hair tangled about her face. She would have bitten him, would have scratched him, she pleaded for him to leave her. But he caught her up easily in his arms and carried her back to the hut, and there, with the hide flap down, shutting out both wind and rain, he laid her on the bed of straw. He rubbed her hands and feet, trying to warm them. She looked waxen and pallid as a snapped stalk.

'What a fright you gave me!' he whispered, and pulled up her smock, baring her swollen belly. 'Don't ye know you are dearer to me than my own life?'

Muirgheal heard him in a daze of pain. Spasms wrung her body. Weakly she besought him to set charms about the hut and to write charms on scraps of paper and hang them round her neck. To bring the ache-no-more, blue flower of childbirth. Hereward did as she bade him, and lastly laid her not upon the straw but on the bare ground so that she might draw strength from the earth.

Once when Hogni Tricksleeve appeared at the flap, Hereward threw a pot at him. 'Get out, you silly bugger!' he yelled. And his heart was in his throat for fear she'd die. Tossing, moaning, heels and toes dug into the mud floor, hands clenched, Muirgheal cried out in travail.

Hogni was at the flap again, eye to the crack. 'Do not forget the afterbirth!' he was saying.

Hereward looked out to see him perched on a stump in the shelter of the trees. He'd found himself a length of witch-wicken – break a piece and power is in your hand for a thousand purposes – and was making a wishing-wand for his own use. He grinned. 'Babe'll come by itself! You must bring out the afterbirth!'

With that Hereward went back to Muirgheal, to squat and watch and wait. 'I'd like to kick him up the bum!' he said, for the relief of hearing his own voice. 'Talking daft! I'll wager he knows no more'n me!'

But after Muirgheal's water broke, the child was soon born, sliding out from between her legs, bloody and dripping in the caul. Hereward cut the birth-cord and tied it to the scrap of a puckered navel and saw the babe to be female. She was perfect. Without blemish. He crossed himself hurriedly in thankfulness. The first cry was as magic. Lardy and wriggling-red, he let her bawl and thresh in the straw, while following Hogni's advice he pressed with both hands on Muirgheal's belly to rid her of the afterbirth. Then he washed her limbs and fetched clean straw for her bed, mended with fern and elf-grass, heaping it softly beneath her head, covering her with his bearskin cloak. He breathed life into the fire of crumbly peat, coaxing the red heart of it with a stick, whereupon Muirgheal opened up her eyes and whispered, 'The baby!'

''Tis all right, *mo bhean!*'

'Hereward!'

''Tis a girl! A little lass!'

'O, let me have her!' Muirgheal said, struggling to sit up. '*Tabhair dham!*'

Kneeling by her, Hereward put the babe into her arms. Muirgheal smiled softly, tearfully, and Hereward, dying inside of his heart for those tears, whispered, 'You need rest, love!'

'And she needs milk.'

'Will you be able?'

'I must!' And so saying Muirgheal squeezed her long brown nipples between finger and thumb. 'O, rub me, cara!' she begged. And Hereward did, pressing on her breasts gently, until in wonderment he saw the first drops of milk spurt from both nipples. 'Wisha, then!' Muirgheal gasped, smiling and brushing the hair from out of her wet eyes. 'Wisha then, mavoureen!' And thus, cradling the tiny head in her hand, she began to suckle their daughter.

She was called Blathnad. Little Flower.

In order to have treasures to surpass those brought by Harold, Tostig spent much gold in the Holy City. And it was the task of his hearth-troop, armed to the teeth, to guard them on the perilous journey back to England.

And so, when Tostig came into King Edward with altar-cloths and precious vessels – gifts for his church – it was the time of the Paschal moon. Archbishop Ealdred had brought back little that was of worth, save the oil of his consecration. But it was Judith who was on Tostig's mind. Even as he bowed to the King and prepared for his endless prattle, he puzzled over her, at a loss to understand why whilst riding up in the saddle before him, she had been so unwilling to bear the translucent weight of the costly topazes he had sought to hang in her ears.

From the Twelfth Night Fires to Eldmass

At the end of harvest time Gruffyd ap Llewellyn had begun raiding once more across the Severn, and Aelfgar Leofricsson, instead of rallying his shire-fyrd to beat off the marauders, had gone to join them, and together with the Welsh King and his forces and a rabble band of mercenaries, they put the border lands to fire and sword.

'Will he bedevil me all my days?' cried King Edward. It was Christmas then and the court held at Gloucester. And from his high-seat he bade Harold Godwinesson to raise an army and put an end to the Welsh threat.

'But this weather will bugger it up, Sire,' Harold answered slowly.

Without it was bitterly cold and snowing, and beyond the hand-breadth windows a strange, pale winter-light glowered.

King Edward fixed Harold with a look and said, 'Do you advise that I sit here whilst they burn my Kingdom down about my ears?'

The bite in his voice was not lost on Harold. But he squared his shoulders and reasoned, 'Gruffyd has pulled back into Rhuddlan. The danger is still there, I grant ye, but if we could just tarry till the thaw . . .'

Tostig was among the company. 'He wants to wait until the daisies bloom!' he said, narrowing his eyes and smiling.

'Tarry? Are you mazed?' King Edward burst out angrily. 'Tarry until Gruffyd ap Llewellyn is lord of the Gyrwe? Until he has Mercia in thrall? What next? London? Your beloved Wessex?'

So Harold raised an army and with great difficulty Rhuddlan was gained. But Harold found that Gruffyd ap Llewellyn had made off into the Clwydian mountains to the southeast.

The English army surprised and burned some ships in the nearby haven and destroyed Gruffyd's hall, but for the rest of the campaign, bogged down in ice and snow, they caught not so much as a glimpse

171

of the Welsh King nor the Loki-guised Aelfgar Leofricsson. At a snail's pace they straggled along the northern coast, then turned southward into the valleys. When the gales were at their most fierce in February, Harold called off the campaign and headed back for home.

Colossal in his bearskin cloak, his boar-crested, dragon-rampant helmet glittering with snow, he faced King Edward at Westminster. 'I will lead your campaign for ye, Sire. But I will go again in the spring and not before.'

Tostig waylaid Harold in the passage. Harold was warming his hands over a smoking brazier of burning damson wood and rubbing together his great leathery palms. 'Your reputation has grown a-pace yet again,' Tostig said.

'I don't see how,' Harold answered. Usually he was easy-going as the butt of Tostig's tongue. Others, he'd catch him on the raw. ''Twas all buggered up, like I said it would be.'

Tostig leaned close. 'There'll be no respite until the King gets that Welshman's head!'

'He'll get it,' said Harold, 'and his gut and liver if he wants it!'

Tostig grinned. 'Split the command between us and we'll show the Cymry who is master!'

'Eadgyth is so full of worry for Harold,' said Ragnhild to Countess Judith where they sat late in the Countess's bower.

Judith said, 'So would I be were he mine.'

'Do you fear for Tostig?'

'Of course!'

'And love him?'

'Yea, I love him.' Judith's head-wrap was held by twin ouches of gold and blood-red jade, pinned over her heart. Part of her morning-gift, they bespoke of Tostig's taste, rich and bold and bright. 'Though he really understands so little of women,' Judith said. 'Whereas Harold . . .' She fingered the jade stones thoughtfully. 'Harold is a woman's man . . .' Then she shrugged. 'But I suppose I was luckier than Matilda. Claimed by that tanner's grandson with the wrath of the Pope on both of their heads!' Judith and Matilda were daughters of Count Baldwin of Flanders and Adela of France, and Judith had always thought such a coupling with barbarous Normandy beneath her sister. Matilda had already been married and divorced from her first husband and had a daughter, Gundrada. Duke William of Normandy had his lemans and two bastards at the last count – William and Adeliza.

172

'Though to do him credit he does not flaunt them in Mald's face too much.' Judith sighed. 'Ah, but then Mald was no virgin and none could call it a love-match!'

'Yours was,' said Ragnhild.

Judith gazed down at her hands, at her troth-ring. 'Yes,' she said softly, 'my choice was best at the time. But . . .'

'But what?'

'Tostig. His moods. His rages. Always wanting what belongs to another. Like a magpie. A gem-thief!'

'He is all in the world to the King,' said Ragnhild.

Judith nodded. 'But it is not good. Men glare at his back. Make ugly sounds. Especially in the north. O, where is the warp in him? Why cannot he make himself agreeable?'

When Harold brought Aelfgar's war-hoard back to Little-Bethlehem-of-the-Rushes it was October and the Month of Wine.

And it was with a leaden heart that Rudgang Wolf-Cloak watched him walk into the hall and lay it at Countess Godgyfu's feet.

'Then he's dead for sure,' whispered one hus-carl to another.

Lilla the chaplain crossed himself on hearing this and went to light candles in the chapel.

There had been so many rumours, Hwita Clatter-Clogs the minstrel carrying most of them, his tongue only too willing to be loosed for a bed and a mug and a pudding-pie.

And as Countess Godgyfu raised her eyes from the glitter of mail and shield and sword, she had no need to ask, and the compassion in Harold's steady gaze as it met hers made it all the harder to bear.

'What now, my lord?' she said softly, wearily.

'Your eldest grandson is to be Mercia's new earl, ma'am.'

'In spite of his father's wrong-doings? The paying of the mulct?'

'The Witenagemot are agreed on it.'

Godgyfu had her three grandchildren with her, sitting on the steps of the high-seat betwixt the pillars. Eadwine shot up so tall, almost a man, with Aelfgar's cloudy, sly charm. Morkere, smaller and thick-set, was fair-skinned and comely. And Eahlswith, sobbing to lose her father, she being his favourite and much spoilt by him, whilst forgetful of King Gruffyd ap Llewellyn, slain then by the men once loyal to him, but who had also shown her kindness as to his own child.

She had begun to cover her hair like a woman grown, with a rail and brooches. Harold noticed her body was blossoming; rounding breasts, a curve to her hips, the swell of full buttocks . . .

Countess Godgyfu saw his eyes rest that moment on her grand-daughter, but then she guessed he would have looked at any female that way, having been nearly a year at the Welsh wars and without a woman. He would think of her no more when he held the Swan-Neck in his arms.

With the bed curtains drawn back and the light of the moon filling the bower, Eadgyth could see Harold clearly above her, his vast shoulders hunched, cave-like, shutting her in.

Her nipples were ruby-red and wet where he had sucked on them for the past quarter hour. Her breasts – two doves, he'd called them – pushed at his face, begging his mouth. 'Thy cunt's a lily!' he'd breathed as he'd taken her slowly, inch by inch, easing the whole length of his penis upward into her, and Eadgyth had arched her back and opened her legs as wide as she could to receive him.

And then as his cock pounded with blood, growing hot and mon-strously swollen, she heard him moan, 'O, God, I'm like a churn-staff!'

Eadgyth loved him best when he was like this, confused, afraid of losing control, of his own hunger.

'Do it,' she sobbed, 'O, Harold, do it now!'

And Harold felt his cock start to leap and thresh whether he would or nay, and Eadgyth hung on his neck, crooking her legs up either side of his straddling hairy thighs, almost to his waist, heels digging into his buttocks.

His motion, slow at first, grew stronger, harder, deeper, the thrust-ing unrestrained. Her womb yielded to, and enfolded its huge scarlet intruder. 'My darling! Oh, my heart!' Eadgyth cried out aloud, exulting that his control had at last weakened and ceased to be. He was grunting and groaning then as he laboured on her, powerful knees spread, taking the whole of his massive weight on both forearms, rocking the bed, bringing down the stars. And when at last he sprang his sperm, he felt the last drop go out of him, leaving him tearful and shaking like a boy.

'Eadgyth!' he panted, 'Eadgyth!' and he dropped his head on the pillow above her. He was all without shame in the dark, his soul laid bare.

As if in answer, Eadgyth turned against him, her mouth open at his throat. 'Harold!' she whispered, 'O, Harold, I love you so!'

'Do you?' His voice was smothered, husky. 'And me such a slum-mocking great clumsy bugger!'

'You're gentle.'

174

'My heart's thy bond-serf, lass!' And he hugged her, all but squashing the breath from her in his arms.

'Ye'd pleasure?'

'Would I lie with you otherwise?' Eadgyth bit his ear gently. 'You must know how well you do it, Harold Godwinesson!'

To which Harold answered, 'Only a woman can tell that of a man.' And rubbing his bearded cheek against hers, ''Twas never just fucking, lass. Not just for the sake of it. Not even from the first time. 'Twas always meant.'

'Harold . . .'

'Aye?' He stirred against her. 'What, love?'

'You and Tostig. Did you fare well together?'

'Ah, just like in the old days.' Eadgyth knew that in time she would learn of the happenings of the past twelve months from Harold. But it would be slow, for to him words did not come easy. 'And the new earl – the young Eadwine – he has a sister, has he not?'

'Aye,' Harold answered. 'Her name's Eahlswith.'

'How many years has she?'

'Thirteen or so.'

'Is she sightly?'

'Aye, and knows it well, I reckon!'

Chance-time, looking at Eahlswith, Countess Godgyfu would see something of herself in the child, as she was when first betrothed to Leofric long years ago. So she spun to dull her sorrow through the Ember Days, and wove wool, combing the shaggy fleece upon the Feast of St Aethelthryth.

And it was to her there at Little-Bethlehem-of-the-Rushes that Eadwine, down from his father's house in Chester, came at the time of Eldmass. He was a fledgling no more, but bearded and having many bracelets. Surrounded always by men twice his age, he repeated the gossip of the mead-benches: 'I have heard that Radnor on the Marches and all the lands betwixt the rivers Usk and Wye have been merged with England – and most of it has become part of Harold Godwinesson's earldom.'

'I liked him,' said Morkere from where he sat by the hearth. 'He did not have to return father's war-gear. I wonder how many times his nose has been broken? It's battered as a leather bucket.'

'And what wads of muscle he has on his arms!' Eahlswith whispered. 'And his eyes – did any notice? They're cornflower blue!'

175

Eadwine looked down at the bracelets on his wrists, the jewel-work scumbled in the rush-candle glow, then said, 'Ah! but these are nothing to what Harold will give soon! They speak of him thus already!'

Rudgang Wolf-Cloak kicked at a smouldering log with his foot, sending sparks flying. 'You sound as if you're fallen under a spell!'

When in London Eadwine had seen Harold nearly every day, in the moot-chamber and the hall and the streets, and often shared a platter with him at the table. 'You know what's being said? 'Tis common knowledge that he will be King.'

Countess Godgyfu stilled her shuttles and seemed to dream to the fire, though in truth she thought clearly and calculated boldly. Eahlswith. She had already begun to bleed and cast shy, meaningful glances at the young hus-carls. She would soon be ripe for a man. But not just any man. A man among men.

She was a sweet white rose scarce out of bud. A perfect sacrifice to Harold Godwinesson's virility . . .

At a feast in the Wardrobe Palace, King Edward said, 'Name your reward, Harold, for ridding me of Gruffyd ap Llewellyn.'

'Tostig did as much as I.'

'Tostig already has his reward. A war horse and saddle with gold stirrups.'

Tostig winked at Harold from behind his mead-horn, his face flushed with triumph.

How should he answer? For what should he ask? He wanted for nothing . . . Then came the image of his mother weeping at the close of each Jesus Day. He said quietly, 'With your leave, Sire, I want to bargain for the release of the hostages.'

The King looked up from under pale lashes, a cup held half-way to his lips. Reaction among the men in the hall had been swift. A gust of approval liken to a roar. The request was made. King Edward could do nothing but bow assent.

Turning from the fire, Countess Gytha said, 'O, Harold! You are to go?'

'Aye, mother.'

'After all these years!'

And their thoughts twinned unspoken to the bleak November day when Wulfnoth had been sent from them. To the rain-swept deck of a ship and a small boy sheltering beneath the cloak of a young altar-thane,

176

Ecgwynn of Winchester, who had offered himself as a hostage so that he might care for the lad.

Upon hearing the tidings many was the man who volunteered to go with Harold to Normandy. But Harold would do it his way, and without the company of kinsmen. Silencing Haakon's pleas with, 'We want no more Godwinessons in Normandy than we can help!' he chose Modred the Marshal and a half-score of his own hus-carls and a stout ship for them to crew.

Preparations went ahead. Messages were sent and received, the last being from the castle at Rouen, from Duke William himself. 'He is looking forward to your coming,' said King Edward, reading from the parchment, 'and has made all provision.' He looked up at Harold. 'You had better take some gifts from me. He will expect them.' And thus saying, he beckoned his staller Ralf the Norman and bade him to secure a chest, and that chest to be filled with the finest examples of English work. Jewelry, drinking horns, glass.

Thus King Edward poured himself a cup of wine and said, 'I suppose you think you have been clever.' He was alone with Harold then, and Harold stood with his back to the shuttered window, enormous, immovable. He said no word. 'But you will find much treachery in Normandy. Many traps for a stranger.'

'I can look after myself,' Harold answered his lord slowly.

Edward mused, 'You believe so? Just because you can knock the life out of a man with one of those hands? There are more subtle wiles!'

Ragnhild said, 'Do you not rejoice for what Harold is doing?'

Aldwyth hung rings of gold through her ears. 'Doubtless he has his reasons,' she said.

Ragnhild looked at her sister. 'You are an unnatural kinswoman.'

Aldwyth turned her head and glanced slantwise. 'Because I am not in thrall to his maleness? Nor worship those hulking shoulders?'

'You do not seem to mind hulking shoulders on your bower-thane and cup-bearer!' Ragnhild said with a sharpness of tongue. 'Indeed, I doubt that you chose Heardwin, son of Eadnoth, or Njal Uggarsson the Icelander for their brains!'

Aldwyth smiled slowly. 'My little wasp!'

And afterward when Tostig came to her bower and flung himself on the rushes at her feet, Aldwyth whispered, 'The court is Harold's this night!'

177

'God damn and blast him!' Tostig smote his clenched fists.

Aldwyth ran her fingers through his dark wiry mane. 'I thought you'd grown close, you two, on the Marches . . .'

Next to the seat of power once again, the reliance upon each other, the sense of brotherhood had begun to fade for Tostig, become a thing of the past like the blaze of the yellow Welsh poppies.

'He irks me!'

'Ah, Tostig!' Why did she love him so? There was no accounting. He came to her with his wants, his woes, his hatreds and suspicions. His arms were hard and smooth, the colour of chestnuts after long months in the sun.

Tostig was saying, 'In Wessex they've begun to call him Land-Father.'

'That was our father's title!'

'He's waxing strong, Aldwyth, is Harold . . . And it should have been me!' Tostig's jaw was mutinous; his eyes robbed of the gleam that made them sapphires were hard blue stones. 'All I have is that accursed, barren wilderness!' And he continued to berate and fling scorn on the thanes of the north.

Aldwyth stroked his cheek and whispered, 'Could you not rid yourself of these troublemakers?'

'How?'

'Do you not have men of your own – men you can trust? Who will obey you without question?'

'Aye.' Tostig looked up into her face. 'You mean kill them?'

'Why not? If they threaten you – plot treason.'

'But I'd have the fury of Northumbria on my head!'

'Your reeves could handle the deed in York.' She brushed the hair from his forehead. 'And there is Westminster.'

'Harold has Westminster. He has the whole bloody country!'

'But Harold won't be here . . .'

The Cot of Rushes

hen Hogni Tricksleeve cast the runes for Blathnad he saw the Norns by the Well of Urd, faces hidden by cloudy grey shawls, as they spun the web of life. Then he looked up at Hereward and said, 'Babe was born on the first day of the moon. A lucky day!'

Also Hogni had woven a cot of rushes and lined it with moss and stuck it all over with angel-flowers. Within it the baby slept sound. 'She favours you, master,' Hogni said, and winked.

Her features were Muirgheal's but her colouring was Hereward's. She absorbed him heart and mind and muscle and he was loath to leave her, to cut peat or fetch water, coming back at the least opportunity, to watch her feed at Muirgheal's breast, the tiny fists like cherry buds seizing the nipple of the milk-heavy tit in a world-old grasp.

Hereward tied wild garlic and primroses and golden fern to the holy well to ask the blessings of the fairies for his daughter. Her chrism-cloth was the fleece of a sheep he'd shorn for her. And coming back from fishing, knife in belt, he'd hear Muirgheal's voice crooning softly:

> *Séothó, a thoill, ná goil go fóill,*
> *Séothó, a linbh, a chumainn's a stór*
> *Séothó, a chaillin bhig . . .*
> Hush, darling, don't cry just yet.
> Hush, baby, my love and my treasure.
> Hush, my little girl . . .

And that smoky-dark hut, sung about with spells and drugged with the sweetness of herbs, was the most desired place on earth for him then.

Muirgheal's feelings for Hereward caused her to search her heart. Ever since the birth of Blathnad he had made no move towards her, but instead had begun to clear a patch of ground near the sacred woods so that it could be put to the plough. And she knew that it was lust for her body that he worked off on those stones and brambles. He laid on the straw with her at night, tired from his labours, but never once did he try to take her in his arms.

One day when he came into the hut for food, Muirgheal said, 'Cara!'

And Hereward turned. He wore only a labouring shirt of coarse wool she had woven for him, patched dark then with sweat. Over his shoulder he carried his wood-cutting axe.

'Is it that you have no more love for me?' And even as she spoke he had started trembling.

'I thought you had no more love for me,' he answered. 'That you'd not want to be gotten with another child. Anyhow, what of your milk?'

'You'd not harm it.'

But he looked at the axe blade and said, ''Tis blunt. I must sharpen it.' And he went out.

Later, in the wane of the sun, Muirgheal went to where he worked, and slipping off her smock, walked naked towards him through the leaves. The air was full of midges and set singing between them. At the sight of her Hereward's heart beat so loud that he could scarce breathe. He straightened up.

'O, Muirgheal!' he said.

Her breasts were white and lush as was all the rest of her save for the cluster of dark hair on her cunt. He laid aside the axe and she came into his arms. He needed no rousing, no bringing on, under his shirt his cock was already risen, and as he bared himself Muirgheal saw the head of it to be fiery red and double its size.

'Here!' she whispered. 'Quickly!' And he lifted her as he'd have lifted an armful of sweet grass, so that her legs were either side of his thighs and brought her down onto his cock. She was wet and he went in easy. Shudders of joy passed through both of them and Muirgheal folded her arms tightly round his neck, panting softly, and soon Hereward was thrusting and plunging up inside her and within moments he'd sprung his sperm.

'O, Muirgheal!' he groaned, '*mo bhean!*' and buried his face in her hair.

Hereward did not question her change of feelings towards him. He was just grateful that she wanted him. And Muirgheal knew that at his age, being on the very cusp of manhood, he could take her anywhere,

180

and up against the wall of the hut became a favourite love-spot for them.

But if Muirgheal had thought to conceive by Hereward again, it was not to be. Even her spells it seemed were thwarted, and the months passed and there was nothing.

The Lay of the Killing Candles

In the timbered hall of York, Tostig's two reeves, Amund and Reavenswart, washed the blood-stains from the floor and strewed fresh rushes with their own hands. Their swords, wrenched from the bodies of Gamel Ormsson and Ulf Dolfinsson, had been scrubbed clean with snow from the garth. They could trust no man with the knowledge of what they had done that night. The corpses of the murdered thanes they took to the fells and left them for wolf-meal, rich cloaks, gold bracelets and all.

Gospatric Gulla's end was only a little sweeter as Queen Aldwyth welcomed him into her bower and her bed. It had not been difficult to encourage and entice him.

'My lady!' he said, as the Queen folded her arms behind his neck.

'I hunger for you!' Aldwyth whispered. And quickly she helped him to strip off his tunic and trousers, sadly delighting in his hard, well-muscled body, keeping his back open to the tapestry-hung walls, so that when the seax struck him it was between the shoulder blades. Then a sword drove through his bowels. His life blood gushed from his mouth and he fell forward onto her. Aldwyth stifled a scream and sought to escape from his death-embrace. He was so heavy, so limp, so warm . . . and he slumped to the floor, face upward, eyes glassing. And wrapping herself in the velvet bed-curtains, Aldwyth watched as three men of Tostig's hearth-troop, led by his deputy Copsi, sheathed their weapons and dragged Gospatric's body out.

'He tried to rape me,' Aldwyth said.

Njal the Icelander gazed about the chamber. 'How came he to be here?'

'I let him in all unwitting.'

'Will you tell the King?'

'Nay, let it be known he was killed in one of their northern feuds

182

or a drunken brawl.' Aldwyth was quite composed by then, if trembling, a gold circlet on her head. A rail held by twin brooches of rose-quartz covered the breasts that had so bewitched the young Gospatric.

When Tostig came in Njal withdrew, his heart grim with misgivings, his jaw set.

'It was all for you!' Aldwyth cried as she and Tostig fell upon each other, clinging together.

'They won't know,' Tostig said. 'They won't suspect . . .'

'What of York?'

'It's done.'

The bells had begun to ring then. Aldwyth looked up into her brother's face. 'The Hour of Matins.'

Tostig said, 'I must go to the King.'

'Not now.'

'I have to. I am his wardrobe-thane.'

And even when Harold's return from Normandy in the February overshadowed all else at Westminster, in York city the loss of three of their leading thanes tore open a wound that festered into a foul-running sore.

The Lay of the Gongeweafre

'd have rather taken my chance in a snake-pit,' said Modred the Marshal to Aelhhunn where they sat by the hearth at Nazeing. 'It was a bloody cock-up from start to finish, if you ask me! Foreboded!'

And Aelhhunn listened and thought of how the tower of Bosham church had collapsed the night Harold had sailed for Normandy. And how the wise woman Hag Annis had cast a nativity and been reluctant to tell of it.

'Blood, spittle, piss – the soul powers of the man!' Hag Annis had said. 'Eadgyth, my hen, get whichever you can!'

And to please Eadgyth Harold had pissed into a bucket and from it she had filled a thumb-bottle. And his man's water had stayed clear throughout the long months he'd been in Normandy, and so Eadgyth had known him to be safe.

'I never let him out of my sight,' said Modred. 'Ah, he chaffed me for ever being up his arse – but I'd good reason. His back was a big and easy target, and he never gave a thought as to what they might be putting in his cup. Whispers, knives and itchy fingers. I tell ye, after four months I'd had a bellyful!'

'And Wulfnoth?'

Modred shrugged, his worn, scarred face dark in the fire glow. 'Hair shorn in the Norman way, dressed like them too. Open-hearted enough, I suppose, and speaks a sort of English still, and thanks be for that to the priest Ecgwynn. Ah, but he's a stranger . . .'

'I'd never have known him,' Harold said to Eadgyth.

Her bower was candle-lit, the floor bestrewn with woodruff and sweet fennel. Harold had ridden straight away to Nazeing with his troop, and his disappointment was both deep and bitter, and he showed it plain, which for him was rare.

'And you thought to bring Wulfnoth home,' said Eadgyth.

'Bloody right, I did!'

'What more does the Norman Duke want?'

And Harold, the weeks of haggling still fresh in his mind, said with more weariness than anger, 'More money, more gold, more oaths. More bloody everything! I'll have to ransom Wessex!'

'And if that's not enough?'

''Tis all I have.'

Eadgyth laid a hand upon his arm. The muscles were bunched and tight. Harold looked at her. She said, 'But are you so sure that Wulfnoth wants to come?'

'Wessex!' said Countess Gytha when she knew. Her eyes shone with tears. 'Harold, you cannot mean to.'

'How else?'

Queen Aldwyth had been at her mother's house that night, and as Harold turned to go, she followed him to the door. He was fastening his cloak, made of cloth so shaggy it looked like fleece. Aldwyth said, 'So you did not get everything your own way. The Bastard drives a hard bargain.'

And Harold answered her, 'You have not been idle either, by all accounts. What of Gospatric?'

'What of him?'

'You had him killed.'

'He tried to rape me!' The words she had repeated so often were hollow as little bells.

'What tale did you tell the King?'

'The tale he wanted to hear.'

'And Gamel Ormsson and Ulf Dolfinsson – did they try to rape you also?'

'I know nothing of them!'

'Tostig does though, I'll wager!'

At the mention of Tostig's name Aldwyth paled. 'You cannot prove a thing and the King will never believe a word you say!'

For a dish of scrabbed eggs, Hwita Clatter-Clogs the minstrel played at the King's festal-board at Candle-Mass. Ever watchful, Hwita saw the spite in King Edward's pale eyes as he stole glances at Harold, and how he hugged himself to see that mighty Earl so crestfallen, but

185

wondering too, like as not, if he could be so moon-mad as to ransom all he possessed for the sake of the hostages . . .

And harp on shoulder, Hwita Clatter-Clogs had turned up on the steps of the hall of Godwine in Southwark, knocking to be let in. The whole family was gathered, among them Menglad and Wendelwulf with their children, toddling twin daughters and a boy, a babe in arms. And Freawaru and Gondul, little maids no longer, but wearing head-wraps and girdle-hangers and playing fox-and-geese with two young hus-carls, brawny, good-looking lads, Aelfmod, thane of Wantage and Biarki a horse-thane of Leofwine's troop.

And it was as Harold sat among them, deep in thought, that Tostig said, 'Cat got your tongue?'

A fire burned on the hearth, mended of apple and hawthorn wood. Turning from it, Harold said, 'Nay. I was thinking of the Ploughing Ale and if you'd be going to your earldom for it.'

'I might.'

'Well, you'd best take the King's hearth-troop as well as your own. You'll need them.'

'I'm not afraid of that mob.'

'Aren't ye?'

'My reeves can handle trouble.'

'Like they did Ulf Dolfinsson and Gamel Ormsson?'

Tostig stared at him, his face blenching. The harping of Hwita Clatter-Clogs had prudently ceased. All eyes were upon them. Upon Tostig, and Harold rising up gradually to his full height – and the only sound was the crackle and hiss of the fire.

Tostig said in a voice choked with fury, 'God damn ye, Harold!' And struck him in the face with a balled fist. Harold's head went back and blood spurted from his mouth, but even Tostig's full strength behind the blow only staggered him. Then picking up his cloak, Harold took horse and rode from London.

At Worcester, Bishop Wulfstan said, 'So it was true!'

'Aye, Father, and Aldwyth his accomplice. She'd cut out her heart for Tostig. It's been thus since they were children.' Harold knelt before the Bishop. His mouth was still swollen and his shoulders were hunched. 'I'm afraid the north will rise against him for this.'

'You might be wrong.' But Wulfstan's voice was without conviction.

'There cannot be war, Father. There cannot!'

'War? Between the shires?'

186

Harold nodded bleakly. 'The King has let Tostig have his way for so long now.'

Wulfstan, ever-wise, ever-knowing, said quietly, 'And the other thing you fear? Tell me.'

Harold lifted his head. 'That the Bastard of Falaise has his sights set on England.'

'Ah! Naboth's Vineyard!' And Wulfstan reached out to touch Harold's bruised cheek.

Judith moaned aloud when she heard of it. Ragnhild told her where she sat stitching in her bower with the royal maids Margaret and Christina.

'O, Tostig! O, my foolish one!'

Christina whispered, 'Did Earl Harold strike him back?'

'Nay.' Ragnhild looked wan in a white headrail.

Margaret said, 'You mean he did nothing?'

Ragnhild twisted her rosary beads in long ringless fingers. 'Harold won't ever fight if he can walk away.'

The harvest fared badly that year and the crops were lean. In Northumbria there was not enough corn to pay the render and the fish yield was scarce. But Tostig's deputy Copsi sent out the reeves to levy the geld regardless, and stacked it in the coffers of York hall, right down to a brewing of malt and the last half-pound of pence.

Queen Aldwyth's foundation at Wilton was hallowed with all ceremony in the Weed-Month and all the noble folk and churchmen of England crowded into the tall stone-pillared confines, already sweet and cloudy with incense.

Her head-wrap, crucifix and holy beads cast off, Aldwyth moaned in ecstasy at Heardwin's love-making. Since the night of Gospatric's slaying she'd been wary of Njal the Icelander, having him in her bed but seldom. His eyes read her mind, looked down into her soul . . . But Heardwin was different. All he had was between his legs, and drenched in his sweat from the July heat, she whispered, 'Was it not fair, my church?'

Heardwin had attended her throughout the day, dumb, reverent, adoring. 'Indeed, my lady.'

'The King was ill pleased.'

'Why?'

187

'Because his church of St Peter will not be ready until Child-Mass day.'

'But I still don't see . . .'

Aldwyth laughed softly and pressed her lips to his throat. 'No, you wouldn't. Your heart is too pure, Heardwin.'

And it had been that last half-pound of pence which was the spark to the wood, and in October of the year Northumbria rebelled and declared for Morkere Aelfgarsson to be its new Earl.

News of the uprising came to the King's hunting lodge at Britford near Salisbury. The King himself and Tostig had been out hawking and they returned wet and mud-splashed from riding at all speed through the forest.

His voice high and thin with rage, King Edward demanded to know the whereabouts of the rebels.

'They are camped at Northampton.' It was Harold who answered. He'd been awaiting them in the ground-floor chamber. Tostig strode in, throwing off his cloak. He went straight to the fire without a word.

The King said, 'Why do you stand thus? You must stop them, Harold!'

'First it should go to the Witanagemot.'

Tostig swung round from the fire then. 'You're enjoying this, aren't you?' he said. 'You wanted this to happen!'

The Witenagemot was summoned. Men rode thither and King Edward chafed at the delay. When it was duly gathered, Harold proposed talks with the rebels.

'But it is treason!' the King had burst out.

However, the Witenagemot were in favour of negotiations, and Harold journeyed to Northampton to speak with the leaders. And with terms grudgingly agreed and surety given, Harold returned to the King's lodge, where the Witenagemot sat, and said, 'They demand Morkere Aelfgarsson to be made earl in the north. Even the families at feud with each other are willing to accept him. And Tostig to be exiled.'

'Exiled?' King Edward started up from his chair. 'Who are they to lay down the law to me?'

'Sire, 'tis either that or they hang him.'

Queen Aldwyth and Countess Judith were both there and together they cried out at this. King Edward slammed a be-ringed fist down on

188

the moot table. He said, 'I command you, Harold, to raise the southern fyrd and march against these rebels!'

Thus they faced each other, watched keenly by the men of the Witenagemot.

Harold answered him, 'Nay, Sire. I will not take an army of Englishmen to fight Englishmen.'

Edward stared at Harold as though he hadn't heard him rightly. His mouth was agape. Then he seemed to crumple and he sat down, wrapping himself round with his arms and began to sob harshly.

Tostig was filled with fear and disgust. He had expected more from his lord than this – what use blubbing when his life hung by a thread?

He turned on Harold. 'You two-faced scheming bastard!' He spewed the words.

And Harold shook his head sadly. 'Lad,' he said, 'O, lad!'

Tostig's eyes were dry and hard. 'Bastard!' he said again.

Judith put out her hands to him but he paid her no heed. Her face was a mask of misery. And even then the northern army was pushing down towards Oxford, splitting England at the Thames . . .

Harold met them at Oxford with the decision of the Witenagemot, and it was received with much rejoicing. War had been averted and Tostig would live on, though in banishment, to hate his guts.

And thus it was in the chamber of the lodge where the rush torches flickered and cast many shadows, that Tostig asked of Harold, 'How long have I got?'

'Yestereve's a sennight,' Harold answered.

No use to look to the King, for he sat staring into the fire, sunk in gloom. Tostig rose up then from where he'd been kneeling by Aldwyth's side, never taking his eyes from Harold's face. 'You worked it out well, didn't you? Sucking up to those northern swine!'

'You have ten days.' Tostig laughed. Harold said, 'Your men in York had no chance.'

'As if I care!'

'You have your life.'

'O, and I am grateful!' Tostig's smiling lips twisted and his voice curdled with bitterness. 'And you for your sodding pains have all England!'

Harold said simply, 'I have nothing.'

'You bloody liar!' Tostig snatched his bone-handled seax from his belt and lunged at Harold.

But moving swiftly, Wendelwulf the marshal grabbed his arm and twisted the weapon from his hand so that it struck the mortar floor, its blade shuddering. Stumbling against the table, Tostig beat his fists on it in an agony of rage, tears streaming down his face.

Aldwyth ran to him, clinging to him, her cheek pressed to his broad back. Then she said to Harold, 'O, get out, can you not? You have got what you wanted! Go on, for God's sake – leave us alone!'

From the Blood-Month to the Night of the Mothers

ount Baldwin of Flanders, Judith's father, offered refuge at his court in Bruges. Back at the Wardrobe Palace, King Edward said to Harold, 'How can you bear to be at silence with your thoughts?'

Tostig was to take his hearth-troop with him and they went willing for love of their lord. Copsi, his deputy, who had escaped the massacre in York, came in unto him with pledges of loyalty.

Thus Gyrth said to Harold, 'Tostig is swearing revenge on you. He swears to kill you.'

'Have you seen him?'

'Aye, haven't you?'

'And have the door slammed in my face?'

When Tostig had gone, King Edward moved from the Wardrobe Palace to the Palace of Westminster and was not seen to stir from his chamber from one day to the next. He hunted rarely and the sound of hawk-bells was painful to him, being so much like Tostig's laughter. 'I failed him!' he'd be wont to lament. 'When he needed me most I was a miserable weakling! Tostig! Tostig!'

And the only one he would have with him was Queen Aldwyth, spinning wool or stitching her altar-cloths. Aldwyth, who was as his daughter and who loved him as a father, he was sure. For had he not spared her the indignities of the marriage bed? The ordeal of having a great bulging pizzle thrusting within her night after night?

And the days grew short as the Blood-Month dwindled and grey mists begirt the Isle of Thorns, pierced only by the cry of the curlew and the swoop of a gull.

'Child,' the King would whisper, times, glancing up from the fire, 'child, we loved him – we loved Tostig, did we not – you and I both?'

And plying her needle, Aldwyth would answer softly, 'Aye, my lord.'

*   *   *

Gazing at the abbey-church of St Peter, Archbishop Stigand said, 'That is all that's keeping the King alive. And when it is finished . . .'

Cumbra crossed himself devoutly. 'You believe he is dying?'

Stigand picked up a heap of documents brought thither by Cumbra. He made no answer to the young monk's question. 'Someone must have been working the night long to sign these.'

'Earl Harold,' said Cumbra. 'I saw the light burning in his chamber betwixt Compline and Matins and Lauds.'

Harold Dux was written across the parchments in a large, careful hand. Stigand fingered the bold daub of wax bearing the stamp of the Great Seal. 'I don't know why he doesn't sign Anglosaxorum Rex Dei Gratia. For he might as well be King already!'

And that was the gist of the talk on the mead-benches, among the hus-carls and thanes. And Njal the Icelander said to Queen Aldwyth, 'Will you not be glad for your brother to be chosen?'

After hours spent watching through the Litany by King Edward's side she drank of the wine-cup her bower-thane offered. 'I care for nothing,' she replied. 'He took Tostig from me.'

'Ah, that is not true and you know it!' Aldwyth hid her face in the big gold bowl of the cup. Njal said bluntly, 'If it hadn't been for Harold your beloved Tostig would have swung from a tree like the rest of his men. He begged them – no easy thing when men are blood-hot from injustice and drunk with loot. And he put up as surety not just his lands in Wessex, but all he owned in England – the ransom he was to give for Wulfnoth – to win Tostig those ten days!'

Countess Godgyfu journeyed to Westminster with Eahlswith and lodged in a bower there. From every shire men began arriving for the Christmas festival. The clergy – the highest in the land – had come for the consecration of St Peter's Minster. And with its weather-vane turned from bronze to crystal by the first snow-falls of winter, it stood on its isle of ice reeds to await them.

Archbishops Stigand and Ealdred thawed frozen fingers before the blazing fires. 'And it was at Jerusalem the feast of the dedication and it was winter,' quoth Ealdred. To which Stigand replied tartly, 'And you can see who ordered the fires to be lit. See all the logs! Ah, well, at least we'll be warm in this bog hole!'

The royal maid Margaret, along with Christina and Edgar, was summoned often to her great uncle's presence. There would be nothing to do but sit hour after hour whilst the King dozed on his day-bed.

Margaret hated the smoke-reasty chamber strewn with Yule-straw, ever seeking to escape.

It was Christmas Eve, the ancient Night of the Mothers, and the candle lit to guide the Christ Child through the darkness. Ah, but then was that not Harold Godwinesson in the doorway? It was. For how could you mistake him for any other? He seldom came in unto the King in those days, for the chamber usually had its compliment of mostly Norman retainers. And she had missed him so! Her cheek grew warm and her heart quickened as through her lashes she noted his braceleted, muscle-heavy arms, the cloak of sheepskin spanning the awesome breadth from shoulder to shoulder, fastened with silver brooches like twin moons.

Women watched him, Margaret knew, even as she did, and she blushed guiltily to think that it was the more so in the summer months when, as men were wont, he wore no trousers under his tunic. Earl Leofwine laughed and called it 'cock-watching' and Earl Harold just smiled and seemed not to care. But even when he did wear trousers, the huge bulk of his manhood was outlined plain to see.

Margaret had overheard Countess Godgyfu say to her granddaughter, 'Never seen anything to match the Earl of Wessex, have you, my dear?'

And Eahlswith answered, 'The others are malkins compared to him!'

Why, hadn't Margaret once seen Eahlswith offer the Earl a flower? A flower with a stiff red spike and a pale creamy opening, the likeness of male and female genitals? Lords and Ladies, she had called it. Will you play Lords and Ladies?

And how Margaret had longed to cast away her crippling shyness and to be a jade and play Lords and Ladies with Harold Godwinesson in a dark and lonely wood.

193

The Lay of Twelfth tide

nce, finding Harold in the passageway, Bishop Wulfstan said, 'When did you last sleep?' And Harold shrugged. 'The world can still go on while you sleep, my son.'

Prime. Sext. Nones. Vespers . . . The chapel bell chiming through the ever deepening winter-light . . .

And it was after Compline that Eadwine Aelfgarsson sought to waylay Harold with a call of, 'My lord!'

Harold swung round. Eadwine carried a torch and in its flare Harold loomed gigantic, looking the age of all his winters. Eadwine put on a bold voice to hide the fact that he quaked in his boots. 'The King is going to die, is he not?'

Harold answered, 'Maybe. Maybe not. I'm no leech, lad.'

The snow drove thinly between them, Harold keeping most of it off with his shoulders. Eadwine said, 'Men will be calling for you. Ah, do not try to deny it. Ye know 'tis true. And we'll be loyal to ye, Morkere and I, bringing the allegiance of our shires. And our sister Eahlswith – she'd lief be more than your friend. She loves ye, Harold, and has done ever since that first night at Blickling. Wed her and join our two houses. As brothers-in-law we'll hold all England.'

Cocky little bleeder, thought Harold, looking down at him, his eyes narrowed. Eadwine's tongue forbade him and he thrust out his jaw. Harold said, 'You seem to forget I am already married.'

'Only after the Danish way.'

'She is my wife. I can love no other.'

Countess Gytha said, 'Are you sure?'

Harold had gone to his mother's house and he stood half-turned to the silent loom.

'I have been faithful these eighteen years. She is the beat of my heart.'

194

Gytha sighed. 'Have they threatened to withhold their voice at the Witenagemot?'

'Nay.'

'Then gloze them. They are but boys, novices at the game, though well schooled by Godgyfu, I've no doubt. Go to Eadgyth – tell her all. Bring me back her answer.'

Thus in her bower at Nazeing Eadgyth drew the tidings from Harold, while the apple wood smoked on the hearth. 'I knew it,' she whispered, 'that the lure of the crown would come betwixt us!'

'The blame is mine.'

'You cannot help it.'

'I look to be a selfish bugger!'

'Nay – O, Harold,' Eadgyth drew him against her, all the might and weight of him, 'I always told you that I would never stand in your way.'

'I cannot lose you!'

'You won't!'

Harold looked up at Eadgyth. 'What of our boys? And our little Gytha? Nay, I'll not do it. Let them keep their bloody throne!' And he pulled away from her, getting to his feet, blocking out the rush light, leaving Eadgyth crouched by the fire in a warm well of darkness.

'What of England, Harold?'

'England can go to hell! I've had a gutful!'

Later, stroking his head lain in her lap, she whispered, 'Tell them you will marry her. Just let them think it.'

'Eadgyth. O, Eadgyth . . .'

'Appease them.'

'Those two little sods!'

'They think they are being men, and as I mind once you said the maid was fair.'

'So she is but she's only a little lass.'

'Do you think the promise of a betrothal would give you the support of Northumbria and Mercia?'

'I don't know. There's no telling.'

And upon hearing this from Harold, Countess Gytha said, 'Eadgyth is right. A promise can do no harm.'

King Edward presided over the Yule Feast, but next morning he rose not at the break of day as was his habit, nor yet for Matins and Lauds, and Fitz-Baldwin, the physician, was summoned to his bedside.

Simples and salves had he by the score, so when the King complained of head pains, a syrup of mandrake apples was administered and he slept.

Child-Mass day dawned snow-blinded. 'The Feast of the Holy Innocents!' whispered many. 'The unluckiest day of the year!'

But thus upon it was the abbey church of St Peter's hallowed, with Harold taking the King's place, leading the way down the long timber-roofed nave to where the lantern tower vaulted, borne aloft by mighty arches above the altar. The whole was as a huge geode; cave-like, hewn of raw crystal. A vast sparkling web of candles and gold and shadows. And while the church grims nattered in the belfry and the wind sighed among the ropes, one by one the members of the procession knelt to genuflect before the Cross. But no matter the splendour of the tapestries and curtains and the tall stained-glass windows showering rainbows in the gloom, it was a dour, charnel-smelling place.

The Benedictine monks of the old church and those of the monastery at Aldgate, led by the abbot of Westminster, sang its praises and sprinkled holy water, and the burning of gum frankincense made sweet blue clouds in the rafters.

On his return from the minster, Harold went in unto the King where he lay a-bed beneath a canopy of crimson velvet. Christmas evergreens hung upon the walls, holly and ivy and the branches of pine, and rosemary and lavender. Braziers burned damson-wood and elm in a sullen slow fire to ward off ague and the shot of elves.

And told of the ceremony, King Edward said, 'Was it good? Was it fine?'

Taking off his black bearskin, glistening with snow, Harold answered him, ''Twas a rare sight, Sire!'

So the King gave a sigh and closed his eyes and by candle-light a fever was upon him. He woke and slept by fits and starts, often calling for Harold in the witching hour and as he broke fast in the hall.

'He's lucky to get away for a piss,' observed Eadnoth the staller.

And Aelhhunn the mass-priest, bringing Harold a cup of warmed ale, said, 'Ragnhild sends why not come to the Countess's bower and rest?' Harold was sitting dozing on a hard bench in the King's chamber and it was midnight. 'You can do no good here, lord.'

News of the King's illness had spread through London Town by then to the villages down-river, and folk in their dozens began to gather in the hall-yard.

By Jesus Day King Edward had received the Extreme Unction and

196

been shriven. And upon the Eve of the Feast of the Epiphany he had grown weaker still. In earlier, clear-headed moments he had asked that the dishes of food he would have eaten be given to the poor. That they might be bathed and sheltered in his name and that money be distributed. He wished to be buried before the altar of his abbey church.

Also his life-long companions William, bishop of London, and Ralf the staller, had caused much wrath among the watching thanes as they had bent to their lord to whisper remembrance of Normandy and of his cousin, the Duke, begging that his claim should be favoured.

'My veins shall be dry of blood ere that comes to pass!' said one.

Others muttered loudly, 'O'er God's forebode! Never the Norman!'

Thus when the King roused at last, Harold was fallen asleep and it was Archbishop Stigand who wakened him. Harold knuckled his eyes open, heaving himself up straight.

'Say masses for me. Pray for me,' King Edward was saying. 'Harold . . . Are you there?'

'I am here, Sire.'

And so suddenly was everyone else. Even Edgar the Aetheling had been bundled from his bed and stood wan-faced and yawning. He had not been groomed to succeed his royal kinsman. He had been promised nothing – save a hawk which he'd had for Christmas and a horse that was to be his at Candle-Mass . . .

The King was bidding Harold Godwinesson to take care of Queen Aldwyth and of all his kinfolk and vassals and friends who were far from their native lands.

And Harold answered, 'It shall be as ye wish, Sire. Trust me!'

'Come nearer!'

To Harold, bending close, nothing but a ramble came from the King's lips. He couldn't make head nor tail of it. Something about danger and fiends and horror. Fire and slaughter. And King Edward, realising that Harold hadn't understood the words slurring from his tongue, began to pluck at his jerkin straps. So long had he savoured playing men off against each other. Now it was too late to undo what had been done. He could have wept. He could have shouted. But he had no strength and little voice.

He begged Harold to sit him up and Harold did so, easily supporting him with one arm. He shivered, seeing dozens of watchers surrounding the bed, and all was hazy with fruit-wood smoke and starred with crucifixes and icons and amber glass prayer-beads.

'Harold!'

'Yes, Sire?'

'It grows dark – and cold!'

'Hush now!'

'Listen!'

Harold did but could hear nothing. He loomed over the King, his own crucifix dangling between them.

'The Kingdom . . . The Kingdom, Harold!' he said, mustering a last great effort to make himself heard and heeded.

Harold's heart was in his mouth. He looked down at the man in his arms and saw the life ebbing fast. The feeble beat of the pulse, the glazing eyes. Then they came, those last, few, stumbling laboured words, 'Take it, Harold! I bequeath it to you!'

The King's head fell back and blood ran from out of his nose and mouth. Fitz-Baldwin brought cloths to staunch it. Aldwyth began to sob. And thus as they knelt, those watchers in the chamber and in the passage-way yonder, was Harold Godwinesson seen to cross himself with deep reverence, and to say, 'The King is dead.'

And the runes, cut and coloured, were told.

Harold's Eve

'efore they'd even closed the old King's eyes men were asking Harold what they should do. For see, there isn't any other!' said Dagobert the Marshal to Eadgyth. He had ridden full pelt beneath the stars to Nazeing.

Eadgyth, a robe over her night-rail, hair the colour of barley flowers, loose over her shoulders, said, 'He has been waiting a long time.'

'He's a patient man.'

'Dagobert!'

'I must get back, my lady! O, do not ask me how I feel or my heart'll burst else!'

The great hall of Westminster was lit by rush torches and the body of King Edward, washed and anointed with oil and spices, brought to lie in state on a candle-ringed bier draped with the black grave-cloth of the Saxon Kings. His face was uncovered, his hands pressed together as though in prayer, an ivory and silver crucifix between them, and on the forefinger of his right hand was the sapphire ring of the Pilgrim.

Many a thane took it in turn to kneel in vigil that night while the monks chanted the Psalms for the Dead. Queen Aldwyth was at the King's head and Bishop William and Ralf the staller at his feet.

The doors were propped open wide into the bitter darkness, and hour by hour the crowds from London Town grew, filling the hall-yard, while the melancholy tolling of the bell of St Stephen's chapel was echoed by the bells of St Peter's, across the ice-blocked Thames and the frozen Fleet – and picked up by the churches from Wapping to the little village of Stepney, and from St Erkonwald's abbey at Barking to St Giles at Camberwell.

Harold stood in the doorway and watched the people come. He wore a cloak of raw sheep-wool and few noticed him. They filed by the

199

bier, be-shawled, hooded, their plain homespun snow-covered, gazing down on the dead white face, crossing themselves, curious, wondering, shedding tears . . .

Men went to prepare the burial place by the altar, and for the first time light streamed from the brilliant, gaunt windows of the abbey church.

'An omen!' whispered Cumbra the monk. 'To be sure, a lucky one for Earl Harold!'

Archbishop Stigand answered, 'Keep your mind on your prayers, my lad. You have just missed a paternoster!'

During the night lyke-wake candles had burned in houses and churches along the river, in villages and the walled town. And it was scarcely half-light, the Hour of Matins and Lauds on the Feast of the Epiphany, when the funeral procession left the Palace . . .

The King's body, packed with aromatics and resins, was wrapped in woollen binding and shrouded with a rich pall, his face still un-covered, but his head bound with a coif. Following behind came Harold and Gyrth and Leofwine, then Eadwine and Morkere, flanked by the marshals and thanes and priests vested for requiem and the black-robed monks. The bells continued to toll and the snow to drift, and afterwards crowds were to flock to the first of the royal shrines in the abbey-church. Miracles were to be rumoured. Money was given to the poor and needy for their prayers, and masses offered for King Edward's soul for three hundred days.

Gytha, Countess of the West Saxons, looked up with eyes lustrous as a girl's. She wore a head-wrap of white linen and garnet beads at her breast. Harold was back from the funeral, cold and chary of words. His hair was wind-blown and there was much grey in the flaxen.

'The Witanagemot are meeting,' the Countess said.

'What chance the Aetheling?'

'None. His youth is against him.'

Harold sat down on the settle. Suddenly, unbidden, the shadow of Wulfnoth, captive in Normandy, was between them. What of his freedom now? What of his safety? Harold wondered if his mother blamed him, held him responsible. He had seen little of her or indeed any of his kinfolk since Tostig's outlawing. He knew they grieved for him, especially the Countess. That her third-born should not have come to say farewell . . .

*   *   *

200

Tostig. King Edward. Who could have foreseen the losing of both of them within months? Not Aldwyth. Her position, her counsel-power – what would become of them? She said to Njal Uggarsson, 'When Harold is King you'll swear fealty to him?'

'Aye, my lady.'

Her heart forbade her. It would be thus with Heardwin. All men of the same mind.

Bleakly Aldwyth went in unto Princess Agatha. 'I hold much land in Wessex. Winchester was my dower. I shall be returning there ere long. Would it please you to come?'

The Princess said, 'What of my son?'

'It will be Harold who'll hold sway.'

And to Princess Agatha it seemed all had been said.

To be deprived of a kingdom mattered little then to the Aetheling, set against the earthy pleasures he had shared with Harold. Ah, but yes, had he not taught him to ride, to hunt, to fly that new hawk? And had Edgar not revelled in Harold's smell of straw and sweat and leather? 'I have no wish to leave Westminster, my lady,' said Edgar to Queen Aldwyth.

'Nor I,' said Margaret.

Aldwyth looked at her slantwise. 'It will avail you naught to stay. There will be no place for any of us.'

'But he promised the King that he would care for the foreign folk and dependents in his keeping.'

'What is it you seek, pretty maid? A place in Harold's bed?' And Aldwyth was rewarded with seeing Margaret's cheeks flush scarlet. 'I have seen you look at him, casting eyes at him. But have you not heard of his plans to marry Eahlswith, sister of Eadwine and Morkere?'

The Songster's Tale

o hear Hwita Clatter-Clogs tell of the crowning of Harold Godwinesson was to be there. And at Little-Bethlehem-of-the-Rushes they listened spellbound. He had the hall in his pocket that night.

'The abbesses carried his cloak and rushes were laid at his feet so that he might walk dry-shod over the snow. And the women kissed him! Eh, dear hearts! What a sight it was! And all the people – past counting!' Hwita paused then to drain his mug and it was gladly filled again.

'What was the like of his robes?' whispered Darryl.

'Purple, lad, and of the most wondrous seen! The length and span of them foursquare and double their breadth and fastened with ouches and rings of gold!'

'What was the crown like?' said Wynter.

'You couldn't see it for the gems!'

'Who put it on his head?' This from Young Leofsi.

'Ealdred of York.'

'What did he promise?' said Rudgang Wolf-Cloak, stirred by it all, though loth to admit it.

Hwita Clatter-Clogs scratched his ear and took a deep breath: 'He bound himself by oath to preserve peace. Peace for the church and for the people he ruled. To forbid harm and greed and hurt to folk of every rank . . .'

And Lilla the chaplain spoke up then from the other side of the hearth: 'Do they love him, d'you think?'

'Aye,' said Hwita Clatter-Clogs, thinking back on the abbey and the hundreds who'd thronged it, whether in velvet or goat-skin, silk or tattered coats, while without the bells had pealed to the bright winter sky. 'Aye, they love him, right enough!'

202

From the Month of the Bear to the Passion-Tide

he news from England had been quick to reach Normandy and William the Duke had felt a loss of face keenly before his court.

His half-brother, Odo, Bishop of Bayeux, stroked his favourite peregrine's hooded and plumed head. 'Well, what is it that you propose to do?' He was secretly enjoying his kinsman's discomfort.

But William paid him no heed. For fourteen years he had expected England as his inheritance. His right. His neighbours knew of his expectations also, and all the people of his own duchy. How could he endure the taunts of Anjou, Ponthieu, Aquitaine – the new King of France? The contempt of his barons? The gossip of the field workers by the Seine? The wagging tongues of Rouen?

Tostig received the news in Flanders and he said to Judith, 'Harold crowned! Perhaps he will find a way to restore my lands!'

Judith felt the colour drain from her face. 'O, do not fret for them, Tostig,' she said. 'They are lost. Can you not be satisfied with what we have? Our sons – and my father has offered you a good position – Marshal of St Omer . . .'

Tostig laughed. 'Marshal of a stinking fish port? That is a bloody lot of good to me!'

Whereat Judith whispered, 'And we used to be so happy together!' And despite herself tears trickled down her cheeks.

Tostig turned to look at her and his heart smote him. He dropped on his knees by her side. 'I'm sorry!' he said. 'Ah, Judith, forgive me!' He mopped at her tears. 'You think I am day-dreaming, do you not, when I plan to reclaim my earldom? O, I know full well Harold won't help me. I was mazed a moment to believe he would. He wanted to be rid of me. I understand that now . . .'

Back it came, the low, dark anger in his voice. Judith felt him suddenly grow tense. He was looking up at her with that queer glassing of his blue eyes she had noticed of late. He could see the peridot and gold cross winking at her breast on its thin, thread-like chain . . .

'Why do ye always wear that?' he said, dangerously low and soft. 'A paltry thing – and never the necklets I gave you. Because it was a gift from Harold?' And he broke the chain, tossing it among the rushes. 'Women!' he spat out the word. 'They're all alike!'

Within a month of his crowning, Harold made plans to ride to the north. It was Candle-Mass and Morkere heard of his decision with a sinking heart. 'It is your choice, my lord,' he said cautiously.

Harold shrugged. 'No man will blame you if they put a sword through my gut!'

Harold's wergeld was then inestimable. There would not be enough thrymsas in the whole of Northumbria to pay it. Morkere ventured, 'If there were to be a betrothal. A pledge to take my sister to wife. It might help matters.'

'I don't see how,' Harold replied. 'Is England's fate to hang by a lass's maidenhead? Nay. I must get it my own way.'

Later, Morkere said to Eahlswith, 'We ride for the north Thursday sennight.'

'Shall I be crowned in York Minster?'

'He is holding back. He is not keen.'

Eahlswith stared at her brother and said, 'But I thought it was agreed!'

'Not yet.'

Eahlswith had already chosen her gown, her care-cloth and bridal wreath. 'It is that slut,' she said. 'That whore of his. She has a witch's hold upon him!'

'The Swan-Neck would be no bar to him doing what he wanted.'

'Then why does he delay?'

About this time William the Norman bethought himself of a plan. He had brooded on it long enough. Had he not two daughters, Constance and Adela, legitimate issue and both comely maids? He was sure they had not been slow to notice Harold Godwinesson when he had been their guest, as was common with all females. He would offer one of them in marriage to Harold, with messages reminding him of King Edward's wish. Of his rightful claim to England.

Duchess Matilda, told of the plan, answered, 'But it would have to be at least two years hence. They are not ready for bedding. They do not even have breasts. And though I don't doubt the Godwinesson could get any woman pregnant in the blink of an eye, is it your grandchild or yourself you want to be King?'

At Nazeing, Harold's two eldest sons, Godwine and Edmund, had discovered what they thought to be the truth from Eadgyth. They had been dumb-struck, unbelieving, but in Harold's presence the fifteen-year-old Godwine found his voice: 'How could ye, father?'

And Edmund, a year the younger, 'Casting our mother aside!'

With the three of them in the bower there was hardly room to move. Harold said quietly, 'You do not understand.'

He was handling the reed used by Eadgyth for winding thread, and when it snapped under the pressure of his fingers, he stared at it, suddenly tired beyond words.

Eadgyth questioned him not, but when he loosed his sperm within her in the dark of the night, she wept slow, soft tears on his shoulder.

Accompanying him on the ride to York, apart from Morkere, was Bishop Wulfstan and a small band of hearth-troops led by Modred the marshal. As they progressed, the countryside grew wilder, more threatening, liken to the Glittering Plains in the Land of the Not Dead. The men sought comradeship from each other and courage from the sight of the wooden crosses by the wayside, raised in defiance of the Old Gods.

Harold rode first to Beverley where Archbishop Ealdred greeted him, relieved he had come thus far unharmed. There were crowds gathered from the Yorkshire Wolds and when Ealdred had pleaded for calm, it was for love of him that they obeyed. In the church Harold knelt before the great pulpit and crucifix, and prostrated himself on the steps of the shrine of gold and silver and precious stones, so beautiful as to make the heart catch in the throat.

And thence from Beverley Harold wended the way to York. In that city another throng awaited his arrival. They tracked him through the streets to the lofty, gilded, wide-gabled hall, brandishing torches, marking well his lack of armour, for though his hearth-troop were sword-girt, he was not.

And in that hall the moot was held and the old tribal tongues of the hidages met and mingled and words were winsome. Acclaim came loudly among the shields, and so it proved with the swearing of oaths.

In return Harold promised to uphold and upkeep their liberty, respect their freedom. To be as the Tree of the Wood where the sorrows of the folk are hung.

'It worked like a charm,' Morkere said. He and Eadwine faced each other in the hall at Chester. 'It was so easy.'
    'Did no one challenge him?'
    'Would you?'
    'But what of Eahlswith?'
    'He's befooled us.'

'There was no pledge given to the sons of Aelfgar,' said Ragnhild.
    'No plighting of a troth?' Eadgyth looked up from her stitch-work.
    Ragnhild shook her head. Lark-hearted, bearer of good tidings.
    Eadgyth said, 'And the north?'
    'His. As is all England.'
    'I am with child.'
    'Does he know?'
    'Not yet.'
    Ragnhild picked up the toddling Gytha, smoothing her fair curls. It was April and the woods of Nazeing were full of bursting, sticky green buds and bird-song. 'His joy will be great!'
    Eadgyth nodded and said, 'And I'd as lief be dead as share him with another.'

Upon Harold's return to Westminster the message from William of Normandy was waiting for him. And when the Witenagemot met again at Passion-tide on Thorney Isle there was very great wrath among them. They bade a reply be sent rejecting all demands and offers. Harold spoke then of his fears for England.

'Will the King call out the fyrd, my lord? Is there to be trouble as rumoured?' asked Cumbra the monk of Archbishop Stigand. They too were of the gathering on Thorney Isle.
    'We are supposed to be men of God,' Stigand said. 'Fill not your head with thoughts of bloodshed!' Chastised, Cumbra bent to his bone writing tablet, pen scratching in the wax. Meanwhile the Archbishop picked out a coin from the gipsire at his girdle and sat to contemplate it. Freshly minted, of a new design, hundreds were being issued from moneyers in every borough: coins by the tubful. Harold's image was life-like. The engraver, a skilled limner, hadn't spared that broken, belaboured profile. He wore the crown of England. Stigand had

crowned kings – he knew its jewels by heart. The great ruby for valour. Emeralds for justice, sapphires for chastity, amethysts for a king's love for his people and his duty towards them. Chrysolite for wisdom, chalcedony for fortitude. Sardonyx for lowliness, mercy and truth. Then he turned the coin over in his palm to read the reverse. There was but one word chipped there. Pax . . . Peace.

William of Normandy called his barons to him and talked of wondrous things. Of treasures and land beyond their wildest dreams. And when they asked how could such things be, he answered them, 'In England.'

Most of them were only a step away from the robber-barons of his boyhood, with a thirst for power and plunder. But though bound by feudal rights to the Duchy, they were doubtful. And as William spoke of sailing in force to England and challenging Harold Godwinesson in battle, they put up countless obstacles in the path of such a venture.

In the months of February and April two councils were held in the castle at Lillebonne. Both ended in uproar and chaos. William tried to impress upon them the fortune that lay in store for those willing to take the chance.

'After the slaughter of the men – what of their women?' he said. 'Wives and daughters and mothers and sisters. Heiresses in their own right!'

As some began to be won over so the lust for wealth spread. And it was at this time that Duke William besought the help of Prior Lanfranc the Lombard of Pavia. He had been useful to him before by persuading the Pope to recognise his marriage to Matilda.

Thus Lanfranc, summoned from the monastic college of Bec, came to confer with the Duke in a chamber at Rouen. He said, 'If only your royal kinsman had issued charters with oaths solemnly sworn and witnesses to prove your claim beyond doubt . . .'

'Does it matter?'

Lanfranc spread his bony hands. 'It might be overcome.'

'If Rome sanctions my cause, I would benefit the Holy See generously with my new-found fortune.'

'That of course would help.'

William nodded. 'I thought that might be the way of things,' he said.

Lanfranc looked up quickly. 'You realise that the Holy Church cannot become involved merely for gain?'

Duke William leaned closer. 'How does the favour tree shake, Father?'

207

'You wish me to make out a case for you at the Papal Court? Then it must be for the declaration of a Holy War.' Lanfranc put his hands both together, steepling his long thin brown fingers. 'I could bring many accusations against the English Church and have every church in Normandy to support my accusations. Also the Saxon men treat their women as equals. Exalt them – believing them to be endowed with the gift of prophesy – contrary to the teachings of St Paul. Women have great power there. The spindle not the spear holds sway in that land!'

The Duke said, 'A crusade, then?'

'Against a corrupt church,' agreed Lanfranc.

William smiled, indeed it was all he could do to stop himself laughing out loud, thinking of the appointments of many of his friends and relations to posts in the high-ranking clergy – got for a price. Most notable of all was the promotion of Odo with his brutality and his concubines, to the Bishopric of Bayeux.

But now he had an ally in this Lombard. Wily, foxy-minded. He said, 'You will drink on it?'

Whereupon Lanfranc accepted. The bargain struck, wine was brought.

The Harvest of the Quiet Eye

A t Emhain Abhlach there was little accounting of time. A twelve-month was two herring seasons. Summer's end a hang of apples. Boats came and went that way two or three times a year between La Lughnasa and La Bealtaine, but Hereward never wanted for their news.

Hogni Tricksleeve said, 'Don't you ever wonder what the world's doing?'

'No.' And with that Hereward would continue forking hay.

He'd grown broad as a door and Muirgheal had pierced one of his ears with a gold ring and sewn bells onto the hem of the tunic she'd woven for him all of the gipsy colours of hound's-tongue flowers.

'All your folk must think you're dead by now.'

And Hereward shrugged. 'Let them.'

So when Hogni cast the runes he did so in secret then, in the wood or behind the turf shed, for Hereward had threatened to clout his ear if he caught him. 'Bloody things!' he'd say. 'Always trouble!'

But Blathnad would climb on his knee and put her arms about him and call him 'Scealai'.

And Hereward would whisper, 'Ah, leanbh! My nabbity blossom!'

'What am I?'

'You are mine!'

'What shall I be?'

'The lady of Little-Bethlehem-of-the-Rushes!' What would they say – his mother and his kinfolk – if they could see this child, his child, so fair and with not a mark on her. Her bearing-cloth woven of sunbeams and dew-drops. Kept safe the caul she'd been born in. Had Wynter got such, he wondered, or Darryl or Young Leofsi?

'Scealai! That's for all the tales you tell her!' said Muirgheal.

'There's truth behind them.'

209

'About her being a great lady?' Hereward nodded. 'If you went back . . .'

'I'm not!'

Muirgheal looked down at the coarse cloth in her hands. She was stitching Blathnad a smock. 'She'd have silks . . .'

'Bugger the silks!'

'Cara! I sometimes wonder if we're not spoiling things for Blathnad – keeping her here when maybe there is the chance of something better.'

'Like what? I'm thinking that my mother would only try to make a nun out of her.'

It was after Imbolg that Hereward began to build a boat. A curragh it was, of wicker-work and hides.

'Will you sail away in it?' whispered Muirgheal, sitting down on a rock.

'How d'you mean?'

'Will you leave me and go venturing?'

Hereward looked up at her, narrowing his eyes against the sun. ''Tis only for fishing,' he said.

Muirgheal watched his big careful hands intent on their work. Nearby Blathnad played among the pools. She wore necklaces and bracelets and ankle-rings of shells that Hereward had made for her. Muirgheal said, 'If ever you wanted to go, you know I would not stop you.'

'Are you tired of me?' Hereward said, and gave her a look that cleft her bowels.

Muirgheal shook her head. 'Nay!'

'Then why should I go – when my life is here?'

'You are so young!'

'I am a man.'

Muirgheal drew her shawl about her. It was fastened with a brooch of garnets and gold, like a daub of fire on the shabby weave. 'You are content?'

'Aye, lass,' Hereward answered her. 'I am content.'

From the Feast of May to the Summer Solstice

eturning to Rouen after his successful mission in Rome, Prior Lanfranc said, 'They have yet to pronounce the Godwinesson Anathema. But it is only a matter of time.'

Duke William had been examining the Papal banner, emblazoned with the Vatican Bull, sent to him to carry into battle, spreading it against the sun. Also the ring for his finger that contained a thumbnail of St Peter himself.

Of course what had swayed the decision of the College of Cardinals had been the prospect of bringing those ancient seats of learning under their domination. That – and their wealth, as yet only to be guessed at. Lanfranc had pledged the gold rood of Waltham abbey as tribute when they conquered. Thus the invasion and subjection of England was given the Pope's blessing.

'And preparations go a-pace . . . But there is one condition.'

'What?' The Duke looked up quickly.

'His Holiness demands that you hold all England for him as his vassal.'

William's first retort was to tell the Pope to go to the Devil. A vassal! It was an effort to swallow. Lanfranc imagined the frantic workings of the Norman's brain. He waited, cowled in silence. Then William put the ring on his finger and gave a curt nod.

Thus with a Holy War declared against England, mercenaries came pouring into Normandy from every part of the Continent. From the Ushant to the Scheldt. Landless, tatterdemalion knights from Flanders and Aquitaine, Picardy and Poitou and Maine and France and Brittany, and hordes of brigands from Italy and the Alsace.

And it was after the full Paschal-moon and before the Kalends of May, that a strange star was sighted moving slowly from west to east across the night sky, trailing a tail of fire.

211

In England old men searched their memories to recall that such an omen was seen before Ashingdon, and even before that, so their grandfathers had told them, heralding the Danish invasions.

At Emhain Abhlach Hogni Tricksleeve saw it also. He'd been looking for a bucket in which to catch moon beams. He knew he could do it for he'd already hung his cap on one. When all at once the heavens seemed to shrink about that lone white-blazing star. And Hogni said, 'God's fingers and thumbs!' And hid his face for fear.

In Europe it was given many meanings, and in its wake Tostig came to the court of Rouen.

'How two brothers could be so different!' said Duchess Matilda.

'He will be a thorn in Harold Godwinesson's side,' William answered her.

'Do you let him in on your schemes?'

'That rash one?' The Duke shook his head. 'Ah, no!' He had seen the wild light in Tostig's blue eyes, recognised a recklessness akin to his own, yet unmastered.

Bitterest of all had been Tostig's meeting with his brother Wulfnoth. No love had been lost there.

'Harold has all he wants now,' Tostig had said to him. 'A fat lot he cares for you!'

And there in the hall at Rouen, before the whole court, Wulfnoth would have gone for his throat had not that altar-thane stopped him.

Thinking of it made Tostig seethe. To dote on Harold thus! Had Wulfnoth become half-witted? Did he live in a world of dreams? To still believe that there was a chance of rescue from his hostagedom!

So Tostig took himself back to Flanders and Judith's bower rang to his wrath. 'That Bastard of Falaise will give me no aid! He plots to hog all the glory for himself. Well, I'll see him in hell first!' He began to strap on his war-coat.

Judith gripped his hands, staying them. 'No more trouble,' she implored. 'O, Tostig, for my sake!'

'For your sake?' The expression in his eyes chilled her. Then he pushed her away. 'Do you fear to be a widow, eh? Or maybe not. You can always carry a tale of woe to Harold. He'd believe anything!' And Tostig laughed to see Judith's cheek redden, then grow pale.

He said, 'Your father keeps his ships from me as though keeping liquor from a drunken man. Do you think I don't know it? But he shan't shackle me! I'll find ships and crews of my own!'

And he did.

'The bloody fool!' said Harold when he heard the news from Dagobert the Marshal of Tostig's attack on the Isle of Wight and how he had been soundly beaten off and deserted by his followers.

Dagobert had other names for him. He stared out at the blossoming trees. 'Do you think it was planned betwixt him and Normandy?'

'I don't know,' Harold answered.

'What do we do?'

Harold gnawed at his huge rough knuckles. 'What would ye have me do?'

'Call out the fyrd.'

Put to the Witenagemot at the Mass of St Grimbald, it was agreed. By this time the corn was knee-high and the skeps buzzing and the orchards laden with fruit.

Aldwyth was at Winchester when Harold came to her one day. She was in her garden, apple picking, with Torquil her deaf-mute giant of a dish-thane in attendance.

Forestalling Harold's greeting, she said, 'I have no more men on my lands, if that is what you have come for. Even Njal and Heardwin have left me – and you cannot mean to take Torquil!'

Whereat Torquil moved nearer his lady. He was colossal, topping Harold by half a head. But there was no menace in the flax-flower-blue eyes, only the dumb strain of trying to understand what went on about him.

Harold said, 'Aldwyth, have you given aid to Tostig?'

'He has never sent to me for any, but if he had, I should.'

Harold said softly, 'Ah, lass, do not let your love of him blind ye!'

Aldwyth glanced down at the jewels on her wrists, the rings on her fingers. 'All of these he could have . . .'

'And use them to ruin England?'

'Why should I care for that?'

'You are still its Queen. Come back to London.'

'Why for? There would be no place for me side by side with your new wife's household.'

'I take no wife.'

'What of Aelfgar's daughter?'

'She's young enough to be one of my own. Do they really think I'd snatch from cradles?'

'You lead them to believe such.'

'My head was full of fear for want of courage. Like a dark storm. I thought that maybe the north would not acknowledge me. But they did. They accepted me as King before they got wind of any plans for an alliance. I have England firm in my grasp. I am strong.'

Yea, the men of the wealds and marsh, the fell and crag, were besotted with him. The thanes, the hus-carls, the tillers of the soil, the harrowers and hedge-menders, waggoners and woodcutters. His was a rough, sweet magic . . .

'The Aelfgarssons will take it ill that you tricked them.'

'' Twas no trick. They can push me only so far.'

'William the Bastard offers you one of his daughters, and 'tis said that Harald Sigurdsson the Haardrada has a daughter. I wonder he does not give her to you.'

Harold sighed and said slowly, 'Aldwyth, I know how much you thought of Tostig. But he's playing a sod's game. Raiding like any pirate. He cannot destroy all I have worked for. I won't let him!'

Dividing his time between Westminster and the south coast where the army and fleet lay in full strength, Harold rode the old way across the Downs. The grass, full of sow-bread and wild thyme and foxgloves, cloaked the rolling miles betwixt the Andreasweald and the cliffs. And Gyrth would ride at his brother's side.

Often they'd stop on a ridge within sight of St Mary's-in-the-Wood, famed for its twelve golden bells. And upon that ridge a hoar apple tree grew by itself and it was there that Harold would brood the while . . .

The Pope's ruling in Rome had shaken all England and the shock of it still lingered. For the Holy Father to have blessed the Norman cause in return for gain! Sanctioning the looting and despoiling of their churches, the bid to seize their country with carnage, the rape of the common land. Parcelled off like chattel to foreign mercenaries . . .

Harold rarely spoke of it, but it was there. From dawn to dusk, all through the eating, sleeping, waking hours. The task of watching and waiting and praying.

'Do not let it turn you from God,' Bishop Wulfstan had said. 'My son, be of faith.'

Eadgyth was at Harold's house at Bosham then with the children. And one night when she was drawing very near her time, Harold whispered,

'If anything happens to me, you must promise that you'll go with my mother – take Modred and little Gytha. Heed her counsel.'

And on hearing those words, the babe, boy-high in her belly, that had been kicking so hard, suddenly felt like a leaden weight within her.

Tears stood on Harold's lashes, not falling. 'Promise me, Eadgyth.'

He'd wept against her times without number, whether for joy, anger or very weariness – but there was something in those frozen tears that frightened her.

'Nothing can happen to you!' Eadgyth clutched his shaggy, flaxen hair. 'Every one of your hearth-troop would have to be dead!'

'Promise me.'

And to please him Eadgyth did. Thus three days later she was delivered of another son.

From the Mead-Month to Need-Fire Night

Morkere Aelgarsson came to Westminster to beg Harold for some of his hus-carls. Tostig had been raiding the Northumbrian coast, having a safe haven in Scottish waters and the protection of King Mael-Coluimb, his arms-fellow. Also it was certain that Tostig had been to the court of Harald Sigurdsson in Norway and gifts had been exchanged.

But Harold would spare none of his men. He feared attack from Normandy first.

'The Bastard! That is all he thinks of!' said Morkere to Eadwine when he returned down-cast to York.

Word had lately come that the Norsemen were amassing a fleet in Solundir fjord near Bergen and at Scapa Flow.

'What else did he say?' said Eadwine.

'That if we were attacked first he would bring the whole of the land force to our aid. He swore it.'

Morkere was wandering round his great hall. Yonder came the sound of the rush-bearers' hymn from the churches. It was the Feast of St Oswald. And the mead honey – the honey of the field bees – gathered.

'D'you think he means it?'

'I don't know.'

'He swore he'd wed with Eahlswith.'

'No, he didn't. He swore nothing. He was just stringing us along.'

'He's cunning.'

'Ah, he's been at it a long while.'

'Eadgyth of the Swan-Neck has borne him another baby. He'll never leave her. Never. She just gets pregnant again and he's butter-salve in her hands.'

Morkere flung himself down on a bench. 'There'll be no alliance.'

Eadwine shrugged. 'He doesn't need one. Not now.'

*   *   *

In the previous winter Freawaru had been betrothed to the thane Aelfmod of Wantage, and in the spring they had wed. Now three months later Freawaru was with child. Gondul watched her sister's happiness with no small pang in her heart, for she wished it could be so for her and Biarki. But Countess Gytha had said she was too young, not yet fourteen.

'But mother was my age when she wed father,' said Gondul to Eadgyth when she came to stay at Bosham.

'Perhaps it is because she doesn't want to lose you,' Eadgyth said.

'There are Menglad's children. They fill her days.' Gondul's blue eyes sparkled then with tears. 'And Biarki – he might find himself another!'

Hag Annis sat rocking the cradle wherein the new babe lay. Named Wulf, he was blond and red-cheeked. Strands of coral and bells protected him from all harm. She said to Gondul, 'He won't! Not if I give you a charm to keep him!' And with Hag Annis it was no idle boast. She had both scrying-mirror and spell-box. She could open locks with moonwort as her key, and collected puff balls, the fart of goblins, in her scrip.

'How?' whispered Gondul, gazing at the Wise Woman.

Hag Annis smiled. 'You'll see, my yeanling!' And she began to croon, 'Whistle, O, whistle, daffy-down-dilly, And you shall have a man . . .'

Meanwhile the princesses Agatha, Margaret and Christina had been invited to Queen Aldwyth's house at Winchester. Edgar the Aetheling also, though he chafed to be in the midst of the happenings further down the coast.

'He tires of being so much in a household of women,' Princess Agatha said to Aldwyth by way of explaining the boy's sulks.

Aldwyth smiled, stitching with a needle of bone, then turned her hazel eyes upon Christina. 'Why, you are nearly a woman grown! And you also!' Margaret looked up from her lace-making to find the Queen's gaze upon herself. 'You are a year the elder, are you not? How it would have pleased my lord if King Mael-Coluimb had wed you! But it might yet still come to pass. 'Tis rumoured that his wife has died of a fever . . .'

Christina said, 'Ah, Greta! You'd be Queen of Scotland!'

Margaret jabbed a needle into her finger, watching the blood spurt in a single ruby-drop. 'What, a widower with children?' she said.

'At least it bespeaks his manhood,' Aldwyth answered her.

'He gives shelter to Lord Tostig.'

'Loyalties shift. Who is a foe one moment is an ally the next.'

'I do not like him.'

Aldwyth stitched calmly. 'What has liking to do with it? You will have your own household. You will be crowned.'

'You should be thankful to the Queen,' said Princess Agatha. 'She has done more for us than anyone.'

Aldwyth said quietly, 'Would you burden your mother with worry? Be sensible. It is for the best.'

Margaret felt suddenly like the fly in a spider's web. And later, out of earshot, Aldwyth had gripped her arm, her nails catching in the hanging sleeve, and said in a low, sweet voice, 'If you think to save your mouth and breasts and belly for Harold, you'll die an old maid of the waiting!'

It was the Rye-Month and Mercia and Northumbria knew an uneasy peace. At the hall of Little-Bethlehem-of-the-Rushes, Morkere knelt by Countess Godgyfu's high-seat to beg for the men of her lands to join with his own and Eadwine's.

'The King will give us none of his hus-carls.'

'You have hus-carls.'

'Not the like of his.'

And it was the reputation of those hus-carls that was the fret of the large, ever-growing mercenary force where the ships rode anchor at Dives-sur-Mer.

Bishop Odo said, 'Remember those of the Godwinesson's troop at Rouen?' All the while watching Duke William out of the corner of his eye.

'They are men. Only men,' William answered him. And the lamps smoked and the barge *Mora*, a gift from Duchess Matilda, pulled at its moorings. It was richly decorated, and the figurehead on the prow was of a boy with one hand pointing across the sea, the other holding an ivory horn to his lips. It dominated the fleet, harbour-bound by the northerly winds . . .

Thus it was with King Harald Sigurdsson. Though he had long considered England to be his – a throwback to Knut's empire which had included Denmark and Sweden, the Isle of Man and Ireland and the Western Isles – he was still full of doubts. Listening to them, Tostig,

218

who had chafed the past month in his counsels, was stung to answer, 'If I did not know you to be the greatest warrior this side of Constantinople – you who have gouged out the eyes of a Byzantine Emperor – I'd say it was the age of your bones talking!'

Whereupon the Norse King, a mighty figure, his cloak cunningly stitched of many white wolf skins, had fixed Tostig with a level gaze and said, 'It is true that I am no longer young. I fought the sons of Ragnar Lodbrok while you sucked your mother's breast. But any man would be right to have caution for what you propose.'

'You have nothing to lose, O, Skull-Splitter!'

'I'd be staking my whole kingdom.'

'Think of all the treasure you have ever seen and imagine it a hundred times over in England!'

'But what of your brother Harold Godwinesson? By the balls of Ymir! Do you think he'll stand idly by and watch?'

'Wessex is his. They're soft-brained about him there. But Northumbria – he won't risk his precious army defending them!'

So it was that the war-arrow was quartered and the Viking ships had begun to gather.

Keeping St Hyacinth's Mass in Earl Leofric's hall at Coventry, Countess Godgyfu presided over the Wapentake. And times, reflecting on the crucifix at her breast, she wondered what Leofric would have made of it all. What would have been his counsel?

Eahlswith was spinning. Beautiful child. Godgyfu watched her, remembering her bitter, tearful words when she'd heard of Eadgyth the Swan-Neck's birthing, 'I hope her milk turns to curd!' And so saying she had dashed her amber-whorled spindle to the ground. She had grown quieter of late, though, and ever since that day she had spoken of Harold Godwinesson no more.

For at that same tithing of Coventry, one of the stallers was the thane Sebald Thoroldsson. His household duties were many but he was often to be found in the stables tending the horses. Quite young, he was, with scars on his arms from the Welsh wars. Eahslwith had watched him, night times, covertly in the hall, for he was cup-bearer at her grandmother's table.

And that day when she had discovered all that she had ever wanted was as a fruit sucked dry, Sebald Thoroldsson had been humping straw into the stalls. The warmth of the Dry Month was heavy and soft, and full of flower seeds and ripe, shiny, dropping berries.

Brain a-swim with the scents, Eahlswith lingered at the stable door.

219

Sebald wore only a shirt and the bulges of his muscles packed the sweat-stained cloth to breaking point. And when he bent over, baring his buttocks, Eahlswith marvelled that they were so hairy.

Softly, sliding past the door post, Eahlswith said, 'That is a job for stable boys.'

The young staller turned and smiled, showing fine white teeth in a bronzed face. 'Why, I do not mind, my lady,' he said.

Coming forward, dragging her bare feet, Eahlswith kept her hands behind her back so that her breasts stuck out under her saffron smock. 'You used to serve my father,' she said.

'Aye, that's so.'

Eahlswith smiled, beguiling. 'Your name is Sebald, is it not?'

'Aye, my lady.'

'Tell me, Sebald, you don't think I am a child, do you?' She chewed on a hay-stalk, gazing up at him through the sunbeams a-dance with dust motes.

'Why, no, my lady.'

'Do you think I am pretty?'

Sebald let his eyes wander openly over her body. He nodded, then said, 'But you are betrothed to King Harold himself!'

'Nay, I'm not. 'Twas all just – talk.'

She'd bitten her lips to make them redder. Sebald said, 'You don't know what it is that you do!'

Eahlswith moved closer to him and murmured plaintively, 'Do? Why, what any maid can do with a man. Don't you want it?'

And all of a sudden Sebald had an injured look and he drew breath quickly. 'Aye!' he whispered. 'I want it!'

Eahlswith almost jumped on him, straddling his hips, begging his mouth. Sebald, tasting her, stripped off her smock and carried her into a nearby stall, laying her among the fodder. With no trousers to hamper him, Sebald's penis was already roused up and swollen. Eahlswith stared at it in wonder. She had seen her brothers naked when they were young. Theirs had been like thin white worms – but this! A real man's cock – big and hard and rosy-red!

Sebald broke her maidenhead as gently as he could, hearing her muffled cries of pain and pleasure, feeling her tiny sharp nails scratching his back and shoulders, digging into his buttocks. Mindful that she had been a virgin, he tried to check his motion lest he swamp her, but when he climaxed, springing his sperm, he beheld her wet and clinging and eager for more.

'Am I as good as the others you've had, Sebald?'

220

'I've never had one like you, my lady!' he panted.

'How many have you had?'

'My share.'

'And I'm the best?'

'I could eat ye with a spoon!'

Eahlswith laughed softly, nuzzling against his hairy chest. 'Will you be here again tomorrow?'

'I am always around, my lady.'

'I'd lief see you.'

'You shall!'

With the thwarting of her plans for Eahlswith, it had been Countess Godgyfu's wish that she should be put in the keeping of the nuns at Croyland. For her to be under the protection of the lamp of St Aethelthryth and her blessed handmaidens. But in answer, Eahlswith had threatened to drown herself in the mere: 'And the child in my womb shall die also!'

'Child?' said Countess Godgyfu. She seized Eahlswith's wrists.

'Aye!' Eahlswith's face was pansy-brown among her tresses. 'I am with child by Sebald Thoroldsson!'

And fleeing the Countess's reproaches, Eahlswith went to Earl Eadwine's house at Chester.

Eadwine said, 'You had given your heart to Harold Godwinesson all those years ago at Blickling!'

'He doesn't want me!'

'He might have done.'

'While he still beds his slut?'

'How much gone are you?'

'Three months.'

Eahlswith looked across at Eadwine. 'I thought to make him jealous.'

'Who? Harold? What is it to him that you get yourself bedded by a staller? Could you not have waited?'

Eahlswith flung up her head, her eyes tear-bright. 'Why should I? Other maids younger than me have real betrothals. Bridal-ales. Morning-gifts. A man in their beds!'

Eahlswith, Eadwine thought; one day she would inherit all the estates at present held by their grandmother. Ely alone was one of the richest jewels bequeathed by the writ of the great Leofric. Ah, if they could but have been linked with the land-wealth of the Godwinessons!

221

Eadwine said then, 'Do you want to wed with Sebald Thoroldsson? Do you love him?'

Whereupon Eahlswith shook her head and shed tears.

As September drew near, Dagobert the marshal said, 'The men are restless.'

The ears of corn, a blaze of gold betwixt the earth and sky, were fit to burst, the orchards ankle-deep in fallen apples, the boughs crying out with their load. Harold watched the flies and gnats and midges feast on the sweet rottenness. Receiving no answer, Dagobert said, 'We'll have to let them go home.'

Harold nodded, the ache and fear closer in this quiet place than when he rode from camp to camp or lay out with the fleet. 'How much longer can we hang on?'

'Until the Birthday of Our Lady.'

'A week.'

'Aye.'

Harold picked up a worm-ridden fruit, squashing it to mush in his huge fist, flinging it against a gnarled tree-trunk.

Dagobert leaned down from his saddle. 'My lord, think you that the Norman Bastard must be having like troubles? His men want feeding. He's fart-arsed the summer away – with what to show?'

'Bugger all,' said Harold slowly, lifting his face.

Dagobert smiled. 'Let them get back to their fields, their bean-steads and haysel gathering. Let them lay with their wives. There is a glut everywhere. We can reprovision if we have to.'

Harold nodded, taking comfort from Dagobert's gut-sense. 'Aye,' he said, 'you're right.'

No church bells had been allowed to ring in England since the May of the year. The great Weald and forests of the south, from Selsey to Old Sarum, sounding to nothing louder than bird-song. And in York the bells too had been stilled. St Cuthbert's and St Wilfrid's and the Church of the Holy Wisdom. Even the seven bells of Croyland hung motionless in the gloom of the tower.

On the Eve of the Nativity of St Mary, Harold sat at his mother's feet while she embroidered the results of her summer's handiwork – a battle standard woven of blue and purple and scarlet – sewing agates and amethysts and carbuncles and topaz upon it in a design both laborious and wonderful.

As she stitched she plied Harold with gossip. His skin was tanned

222

to the colour of old leather, his hair turned palest gold by the sun. His hands rested on his knees and he was absorbed all into himself.

'A fine job that young loaf-eater has done! Clefting his new branch on the old Leofricsson wood!' And the Countess smiled and shook her head at the thought.

Harold shrugged his shoulders. 'She's not the first lass to conceive from a roll in the hay.'

'Never the less, a cruel blow to their ambitions!'

'They should not have tried to use her as a pawn.'

'She was a willing one!' Countess Gytha chose a gem stone. 'Tell me, would you have married the little Eahlswith if you'd had to? If the future of England had depended on it?'

And Harold gave her his answer thus: 'It didn't. So what matter now?'

He stood up then, straightening to his full height. He said, 'Tomorrow the fleet disbands. The men go back to their work.'

Countess Gytha paused, threading her needle afresh by the dying light. 'Will you stay behind and watch the shore by yourself alone?'

The gentle mockery was not lost on Harold. He smiled. 'Ah, no, I'm going back also.' The smile fled his mouth then. He lifted his head, watching a flight of moorhens cross the stars. 'But I know that as soon as I do the Bastard will come!'

Eadgyth was returned to Nazeing with the children, and Ragnhild and Gondul made her company also. And it was there that Harold came in unto her, bringing several of his men, and among them was Biarki the beloved. And braiding lavender in the chimney corner, Hag Annis watched to see the working of her charm.

After supper and the lighting of the rush candles, it was Gondul who played the harp before the company, her touch being the sweetest, and they sang of the old songs. The men asking:

> Can you make me a cambric shirt?
> Parsley, sage, rosemary and thyme,
> Without any seam or needlework,
> And you shall be a true lover of mine.

> Can you wash it in yonder well?
> Parsley, sage, rosemary and thyme,
> Where never sprung water nor rain ever fell,
> And you shall be a true lover of mine.

Can you dry it on yonder thorn?
Parsley, sage, rosemary and thyme,
Which never bore blossom since Adam was born,
And you shall be a true lover of mine.

And the women answering:

Now you've asked me questions three,
Parsley, sage, rosemary and thyme,
I hope you'll answer as many for me,
And you shall be a true lover of mine.

Can you find me an acre of land?
Parsley, sage, rosemary and thyme,
Between the salt water and the sea sand,
And you shall be a true lover of mine.

Can you plough it with a ram's horn?
Parsley, sage, rosemary and thyme,
And sow all over with one peppercorn,
And you shall be a true lover of mine.

Can you reap it with a sickle of leather?
Parsley, sage, rosemary and thyme,
And bind it up with a peacock's feather,
And you shall be a true lover of mine.

When you have done and finished your work,
Parsley, sage, rosemary and thyme,
Then come to me for your cambric shirt,
And you shall be a true lover of mine.

And the next day, before he was due to ride back with Harold, Biarki sought Gondul out where she picked blackberries. It was early, just after sunrise, when he came upon her. Kneeling, she wore no head-wrap and her hair was tumbling loose.

'Ah, lass!' said he to her. 'Do you still care for me?'

Startled at the sound of his voice, Gondul looked up and saw him standing against the sun. She set aside her trug of fruits and said, 'You ask me that?'

'There have been no tokens given.'

'Mother thinks I am too young.'

'And maybe I'm not rich enough?'

'Nay! 'Tis not so!'

Biarki shrugged his big shoulders. He was nowhere near the size of Harold, but his arms and legs were well-muscled, bare then, and sunburned to the brown of cobnuts. 'Others could give ye bracelets and rings, fit for a King's sister. I have only my few fields and my house.'

With a quick-beating heart, Gondul whispered, 'For my dower?'

'All the doves of my four cotes for thine and the fish of my pool and the grape that grows, and all my wheat and goat flocks.'

'O, Biarki!' Gondul answered him. 'I'd have you if you had but rags on your back!'

Whereat Biarki stooped and pulled her into his arms. The sudden joy of his embrace robbed Gondul of speech and Biarki began kissing her. Her eyes and mouth and throat. 'Gondul! Ah, my honey, my heart!'

'Biarki! Don't leave me a maid!'

'Do you bleed?'

'Aye, this past year or more.'

'What of the orchard? 'Tis not far.'

'I doubt I can walk . . .'

'I'll carry ye!'

And so he did, down into the green fastness of the ancient trees. Biarki stripped himself first, making a pillow of his shirt for her head, then he took off her kirtle and smock and lay upon her. 'Ye're trembling!' Biarki whispered. 'Are ye afraid?'

He smelt of hay-flowers and wood sorrel and the heavy warmth of his balls was comforting. 'No!' said Gondul.

'Don't be!' He cupped her breasts. 'You've lovely tits, lass. Like little white apples!' And he wet the nipple of each with his tongue. Then by the look in her eyes he knew she had felt the first hard pressure of his swelling cock. 'It's all right!' Biarki panted softly. 'He just wants thy cunt, love. He'll not hurt thee!'

And how sweet had been the taking of her. They'd both hungered for it and lain wet and weeping in each other's arms. But what of her morning-gift? Curtains for her bed? He needs must build her a bower of wicker and willow-wands and make a cradle for their baby! Thus

225

were the thoughts of Biarki the horse-thane as he rode back with Harold that day.

With each clop of the hooves his heart smote him and finally he plucked up the courage to say, 'I love Gondul, my lord! And she loves me!'

Harold turned in the saddle to look at him. 'I had noticed,' he answered, and smiled.

'You don't mind?'

Harold shook his head. 'Why should I?'

'I'd thought –'

'What, lad?'

'You are the King.'

'So I am, but my great-grandfather was a swine-herd.'

Biarki looked up then, meeting Harold's eyes squarely. 'I'll be a good husband to Gondul, my lord. She'll not want. I'll fend for her and cherish her!'

'Aye,' Harold said slowly. 'I reckon you will at that.'

'But what of the Countess?'

'My mother will give her blessing.'

At Nazeing only Ragnhild remained. She sat with Eadgyth in her bower watching her nurse Wulf.

'How broad he grows!'

'Aye,' said Eadgyth, 'and he's but two months!'

'The maid Eahlswith will bear before the spring.'

'Is she still at Chester?'

'Nay, Aldwyth has taken her under her wing at Winchester, and her lover Sebald Thoroldsson has gone to join Earl Morkere's men in York.'

'Poor lass!'

'You can say that?' Ragnhild beheld her brother's hand-fast wife with new eyes. Eadgyth's gaze strayed from the babe suckling at her breast to the gymmal-ring on her third finger, the heart-finger, a plain thing among the garnets and gold.

'I suppose the staller was handsome and she was weak for him. She's not yet fifteen.'

To which Ragnhild replied, 'I'll wager when she was on her back she shut her eyes and made believe it was Harold!'

'Ah, yes!' Eadgyth whispered. 'I thought once that I'd lose him. After all the years . . . That he would take another woman to his bed and give her babies – for the sake of the crown!'

226

And it was then that Ragnhild went on her knees to take Eadgyth's hands between her own. 'The crown was bestowed by the Witenagemot. Harold was chosen. The people want him. He has their hearts. And if he can steer the country safe, no man will ever question his right again!'

On September 8th the fleet left the Channel and headed for London. The custom was for the laying up of the ships to be between the feast days of St Bartholomew and St Cyprian before the autumn equinox. But the weather broke suddenly, bringing gales and rough seas, and a number of ships were lost before they could reach safe harbour in the Thames. The remainder limped into dock with much damage to their timbers and pride.

'That's buggered it!' said Leofwine, and spat into the water. 'How long to repair them?'

Many weeks was the opinion of the ship-wrights but they were cheered by the knowledge that William of Normandy's fleet had also suffered ruin when he'd moved it up-river to St Valery-sur-Somme in the Countship of Ponthieu. The Norwegian fleet, whose size, known only to the land-spirits and the fisher-folk and the birds, but rumoured to be nearly three hundred strong, besides store-ships and little skutas, was in the Solundir fjord. There were another hundred in Scapa Flow, and they had all ridden out the storm without much harm. Their rearing, serpent-necked, coiled, whorled, dragon-masked prows were turned towards England.

It had been Mischief Eve when Hogni Tricksleeve had scratched ten runes on a piece of whalebone and sent them away. And Need-Fire Night when they returned bringing terror and injury and woe.

227

A Full Moon Rising Red

efore Harald Sigurdsson left Widaros, he first went to the shrine of his brother St Olaf and opened it. He cut his hair and nails, then shutting the shrine, threw the keys into the river.

Thus putting out from the Solundir fjord, each rower sitting on his own personal sea-chest, the Norwegian fleet met up with the ships from Scapa Flow, and as one they sailed round the Northumbrian coast, striking at Tynemouth and down to Cleveland. Thence on they met bold resistance at Scarborough, so from the summit of a hill overlooking the town the Norsemen showered burning brands onto the thatched roofs of the houses, razing all to the ground.

Meanwhile the bells of the moorland churches had begun to ring. Across stream and hillside and heather and the meadows massed with wild orchids, the peal was picked up by the churches in the scattered villages and by King Alfred's horn at Ripon and fell on the ears of York city in the doom tones of the Holy Wisdom and St Wilfrid's and St Peter's and St Cuthbert's clanging bronze tongues . . .

Morkere had kept his few score hus-carls at the ready and the local fyrd on call for weeks. The Hall at York was crammed with chain-mail, scrimasaxes, spears and swords. His head full of the sound of the bells, Morkere shoved through the press of harnessing men to gain the stairs to the timbered gallery high up, from whose window holes he could see the horizon was as yet tranquil. Nothing untoward could yet be seen in the flat watery distances of quivering marshland, gleaned fields and emerald pasture. And the sharply coloured sails of his own fleet were way out on the river . . .

Waltheof Siwardsson was at his side then, sunlight glancing off his war-coat. 'You have sent to your brother?'

'Yea. He'll come swift, God willing!'

'And to the King?'

'By messenger last night.'

Morkere beat with his fists in soft threnody on the ledge. 'Ah! But if only he'd lent me some of his men – his hearth-troop! They would have been a backbone for my fyrd!'

Eadwine called upon every man in his earldom – upon Rudgang Wolf-Cloak and the hus-carls from Little-Bethlehem-of-the-Rushes. And Wynter went also, leaving his wife and child, and Darryl, a torque of gold at his throat, and even Young Leofsi, his burel robe hid beneath a coat of mail.

Lilla the chaplain had shriven them when they'd come to him, unshouldering axes and bill-hooks and scythes to kneel, and devoutly prayed, 'God go with you.'

And after they'd left him in his priest's-garden at the breaking of day, they had sought Old-Wor-Will-Be-So.

'What brings ye hithertowards?' Old Wor was frying elderflower pancakes and when they told him, he said, 'Ah! That I were a young man!' And from out of his box of herbs and bones and shrivelled blossoms, he gave them each an amulet sung over with charms powerful enough to fend off the shot of elves and demons and to blunt the blades of the Norsemen.

But by the time the Mercian fyrd reached York the Viking fleet had swept past Flamborough Head and Holderness, ravaging the coastal villages as they went, rounding Spurn Head and so into the mouth of the river Humber, and on to the river Ouse.

Within the city division ran deep amongst the chief men whether to wait for help from the south or to attack. Voices were raised for and against. From the tower at the hall of York they could see the broad arc of the river and catch a far-off glimpse of hundreds of Viking mast-heads and sails, so many painted snakes, writhing under a glaring, windless sun.

Further up the English fleet lay at anchor. It was then the day before the Eve of the Vigil of St Mathias and the outcome of the moot was that they would do battle with the enemy the next morning.

'O, they'll chew the fat for hours,' said Tostig to King Harald Sigurds-son. They stood together on the deck of the Norseman's ship. Its sails were as black and yellow as the shields that hung over the sides.

'Perhaps they are awaiting your brother. They could hold out for a month behind those walls,' said the Haardrada.

And Tostig turned to him, both fists clenched. 'My lord, I tell you, Harold will not come!'

But though the bells were still ringing the countryside was strangely quiet, and King Harald could not shake off the feeling of unease. The voyage to England had been dream-laden. Hag-ridden. One man had seen a witch-woman sitting astride a grey wolf feeding it human flesh. Another had told of the fylgiar – the caul-spirit all bloody, bringing violent death. He thought also of his wife Queen Elizabeth of Novgorod and his daughter Mary betrothed to his jarl-in-chief Einar Orre – left behind on the Isle of Orkney.

As Tostig Godwinesson had brought his sons Skyle and Ketil, so had Harald brought Olaf, the youngest of his sons, offspring of his concubine Thora. And the royal treasure-hoard was aboard also as was custom, with a huge block of unflawed gold needing twelve men to lift it – his victory omen. His banner, the Land-Waster, flew from the mast. But even with eighteen thousand men under his command, Harald Haardrada knew full well that it would be no simple task.

'They'll give hostages and seek peace,' said Tostig, breaking in on Harald's thoughts. 'They won't fight for fear we'll fire their hay-ricks and spoil their corn!'

But not for the last time was Tostig Godwinesson wrong, as when before the Hour of Prime, the Norse look-outs sighted an English army approaching and heard the skirl of the ancient pipes of Northumbria.

The Loom of Battle

t was a short march to Gate Fulford on the north bank of the river Ouse, a village two miles to the south of York. A large body of priests travelled with the army to defend St Wilfrid's seat, and Waltheof Siwardsson rode at the forefront alongside earls Eadwine and Morkere, bearing the banner of St Cuthbert.

The Norsemen, quitting their ships, well armed and ordered, took up their positions on a stretch of rising ground that on one side sloped to the river and on the other ended in marsh-lands. The right of their line was divided from the marsh by a deep ditch. The Haardrada's banner was set up by the river alongside Tostig's Lion of Northumbria, with a wall of stout linden shields drawn up, over-locking in Odin's battle square.

The messenger from York reached London Town in two days. It was September 14th, the Day of the Holy Rood. And upon hearing the news, Harold gave this answer: 'Tell them that we march on the Eve of St Mathias. Bid them to wait. To hold the gates until we come.'

Dagobert said slowly, 'The Eve of St Mathias. That is but six days.'

But in those six days the fyrd from the nearest shires were recalled, reprovisioned and mustered in London Town. When it became clear that Gyrth intended to lead his own hus-carls men wondered at it. It was different with Leofwine the strapping and bold, darling of the mead-benches – but Gyrth the Quiet-Counsel – what things were coming to pass? Cwichelm the Child-Master came hence from Worcester, his saddle bags packed with leechdoms. Harold accepted his help gladly. 'Though,' as Cwichelm said, 'what use my salves for cold weak livers and worms and the laxes will be, I know not!' Aelhhunn was to go also and all Ragnhild's pleas were in vain.

Leaving London Town before daybreak to the sound of lurs and trumpets, the whole army halted at Waltham by the Lea to hear Mass

231

sung by Abbot Aethelnoth. Harold knelt before the rood of gold and behind him, packing the minster-church and kneeling in the grounds outside, the men voiced the responses.

Then the march began in earnest. The speed was set not by the hus-carls who travelled as mounted infantry, but by the fyrd in their leather and goat-skin coats, shouldering their field tools; pitchforks honed to vicious spikes, scythes razor-sharp, long-handled slashers and bill-hooks, sledge-hammers and axes. They struck the Ermine Street, the ancient highway to York, singing and whistling, cheered always by the sight of Harold somewhere near them, times at their side, others before them, even rounding up the laggards in the rear. Men joined them from villages along the way, from field and farmstead, those who had been too far flung to answer Eadwine Aelfgarsson's call.

And it was on the third day, with the Danelagh and the Brunne-sweald and the Lincoln Wolds behind them, that the men began to tire. The road was stony and dusty and by mid-morning the sun was overhead in a cloudless blue sky. Sheep-shearing, dung-spreading, weed-clearing weather, and their throats were parched for a yard of ale. And wise to this, Harold was among them, riding in and out of the ranks constantly then.

To one brawny fellow carrying an axe fine as any the hus-carls bore he said, 'A mighty wind that'll make!'

'I forged the blade myself,' the man answered. 'I'm a blacksmith. Aethelmaer of Bambweare!'

Encouraging, joking, throwing their grumbling back on them: 'Would there were a lass awaiting me on the road-side tonight!' a man called.

'And what would you do with her?' Harold shouted back in answer.

'Ah, my lord, just give me the chance!'

Harold laughed, his jerkin flapping open, and chided the bronzed, flaxen-haired shiremen for a bunch of randy sods.

'And they love him for it,' said Modred the marshal, wiping his face with a sweat-drenched sleeve.

The Norse shields were blazoned with birds and biting-beasts and the yawning snouts of fire-drakes. King Harald's own shield bore the figure of a sky god, huge phallus erect, axe in hand. A wondrous, gaudy, gut-wrenching sight, with Tostig's golden lion rampant on a scarlet weave and the banner of the Land-Waster liken to a white winding sheet, a cobble of dragon skins, spanned by a monstrous raven like

232

that said to crouch at the northern edge of the sky, spreading out to hide the sun.

Eadwine Aelfgarsson drew rain, glancing this way and that. The hazy heat-prickled air swam with rank upon rank of grey-mailed, grim-bitten men, some wearing helmets with horns ending in eagle's beaks, the sign of Odin, thronging from the Ings to the Ridge. On the left lay the swamps of Tillmire, massed with the blue of water forget-me-nots.

'Bloody hell! There's thousands of them!' Beneath the banner of St Cuthbert Morkere's heart forbade him. 'Maybe we should have waited!'

'It is a bit late for that now!'

'Do we split forces or go forth as one?'

'As one!' said Eadwine, and drew his broad-sword

The Choosers of the Slain

hus the battle rune was unbound as the hastily gathered shire-fyrd of Mercia and Northumbria clashed with the Norse army after the Hour of Matins and Lauds on the Eve of the Vigil of St Mathias, and the slaughter was great.

Both sides fought on foot, the Norse chanting, 'Antan-antan-a-tan! Antan-antan-a-tan!' and the English drowning it with, 'Hosanna! God save us!' and 'God's strength! Rood of Christ!' cutting and hacking their way into the close drawn ranks, striving to break through the Viking shield-wall.

Tostig had control of the right wing of the battle square with Copsi hard by. Harald Sigurdsson dominated the centre and left with the help of the Earls of Orkney and for a time the fierce, white-hot rage of the English attack had them worried. The fyrd, led by the thanes and fronted by the axe wielding hus-carls, came at the shields in wave after wave, and the wall showed signs of weakening, of giving way.

Marshalling more men to bolster it up, filling in the gaps along the line, Tostig, his helmet flung off, sweating and panting, came upon his Norse lord. The Haardrada's axe dripped blood, butcher-bright. 'Is this how they sue for peace?' he yelled above the din of chanting and screaming.

Tostig's face was hewn of flint. 'They can't keep it up. Stupid young buggers! I'll make them crawl for this!'

But none could deny that the English Earls had led their men bravely that day, and as fate wove the web of carnage in cold mist across the field, Morkere stopped to gaze about him as one pole-axed. He'd seen dead men before, hanging men, but nothing like this. God Almighty, the blood was ankle deep. He leaned on his iron and be-gemmed sword hilt, feeling the world and his belly reel.

'Tomorrow is devil's nutting day!' said he out loud for no reason, his knuckles splashed suddenly with scalding tears.

234

And it was soon after that the English fury began to ebb, to crumble, the core eaten away. Waltheof Siwardsson, his shield black with blood, his armour rent, the links gaping, stumbled towards Eadwine in the eye of the fray. 'There's too many of them! They're too strong! Sod and damn them!'

'We can't surrender!' bawled Eadwine.

'What else, for Christ's sake!'

'Fight on!'

'Are you mazed? Do you want our own men to be carrion feed?'

It was past the Hour of Vespers. The Norse ranks were moving forward, shrithing, in full swine array, led by their King, slowly, unrelenting, their shields riven and brain-splattered, their chanting growing louder: 'Antan-antan-a-tan! Antan-antan-a-tan! Antan-antan-a-tan! Antan-antan-a-tan!'

In vain did Morkere strive to stop the Northumbrian retreat, likewise Eadwine with his Mercian fyrd.

Gospatric Snow, followed by the thanes Arkill and Karl of Risewood, came upon Morkere by the Ings. He'd shouted himself hoarse and hid his face from the stars that mocked him. 'Hence, man! Shift yourself! For the love of God!' urged Gospatric. 'To York! It's our only hope!'

York was two miles away with the Ouse to be forded. Many men were running, casting down their weapons, a war-hoard abandoned to wolves and corpse-strippers.

'Antan-antan-a-tan! Antan-antan-a-tan!' The raven screamed for victory on the shroud weave of the Land-Waster borne aloft. The field is ours! the drums said from a dozen leather throats. A blast of a bronze lur challenged the Northumbrian pipes as they sounded both a retreat and a lament. And the biting-beasts, writhing creatures, taloned and pop-eyed, danced on the linden wood shields.

Great numbers of the fyrd-men were drowned in the river, whilst hundreds more perished in the fen. So thick were the fallen that the Norsemen were able to pursue the beaten army, flying them in hopeless confusion, dry-shod across the corpse-packed ditches.

And that was where Wynter, son of Ceawlin, found Darryl the Offspring lying for dead with the half of his face hacked away . . .

Tostig, roaming the groan-ridden field by torchlight, counted at least a hundred priests slain, with ring-coats over their woollen robes. Eyeballs, genitals, bits of fingers were strewn among the rushes. Bog

235

orchids and yellow asphodel, sweet-grass and milk parsley were stiff with gouts of blood. Whinny Moor would be a crowded way that night. He gave orders for the Christian burial of as many as possible and consoled himself with the thought that it was Harold's fault. The slaughter of these men was on his head, not Tostig's own.

The Northumbrians were a proud people and it befitted them ill to bend the knee. But when Waltheof Siwardsson and a half score of hus-carls saw an army march into Tadcaster on the night of September 24th, they knelt, not believing the sight of their eyes. Rumour, like wind blown seeds, had told of the approach of a mighty war-gang, dust rising in clouds from the road, seen for miles.

Then a voice called Waltheof Siwardsson by name, and Harold Godwinesson, hot and sweaty like the rest of them, leaned down from the saddle, blocking the moon with his shoulders, 'What of York?'

Whereupon Waltheof stood up and answered, 'Surrendered.'

'You did battle?'

'And were defeated.'

'What losses?'

'Past counting.'

And cursing their balls, Harold slid stiffly from the saddle and went into the town's moot-house.

There had been no sacking or burning of York city. The Norsemen had advanced on it and surrounded it and the gates had been opened unto them. A hefty ransom had been levied, hostages given and pledges wrung from the chief men that were left that they would support the claim of Harald Sigurdsson. There was to be a meeting the next morning at Stamford Bridge where the roads crossed from the Vale of York, the Wolds and the Vale of Pickering.

'The Norsemen want horses and supplies,' said Waltheof.

'Sure of themselves, eh?' said Leofwine, draining a mug of ale and pouring another.

'They are.' This was from Gospatric Snow. Stung to the quick by defeat, they were surly, bitter and ashamed.

Gyrth, his blond hair grey with dust, said, 'How many will be there?'

'Almost all,' Waltheof replied, 'save for the guard on the ships anchored down-river at Riccall.'

'They left you free to come and go from the city?' said Harold, leaning against the lucky roof-tree, rubbing his aching back.

Gospatric gave a wry smile. 'We are but a score, lord, and well have we been put in our place. They do not feel threatened by us!'

Harold said, 'And they have no knowledge of my coming?'

To which all the northern thanes answered, 'None.'

Food was distributed among the men and five hours' sleep allotted. Thus before the Hour of Matins the next morning they were war-coat clad and fifteen thousand strong at the gates of York.

In dread wonder Eadwine and Morkere watched them enter by Jubber Gate and swell the ancient cobbled ways of Whip-ma-whop-ma Street and the Street of the Cup-Makers.

And drawing rein by the steps of the great timber hall, its gables rhinestone-glowing in the first light, 'Didn't think to see me, did you?' Harold said to the northern earls as they came to greet him. He was in full battle harness and an awesome sight.

Eadwine gave back defiance. 'We had no choice!'

And Morkere, avoiding the steady blue gaze of Harold's eyes, said, 'We could have crushed them. We were their match. But the day went against us.'

The Norsemen had left them their sword belts and arm-rings and festoon-beads, but taken all else. For sure the coffers gaped bare in the counting chamber.

Harold shrugged, then said, 'Have you men fit to fight?' When they answered yea, Harold ordered them to muster all able-bodied levies.

'Whither?' said Morkere.

'To Stamford Bridge,' Harold replied.

Gaudy Sunrise

he Norsemen were bathing in the shallows of the river Derwent that flowed through the village of Stamford Bridge, cutting it in two halves, and lying mother-naked on the grassy banks, the stream being summer-low and sluggish – the shallows the more so – when the flash of sunlight shimmering on steel roused the look-out.

On the furthest bank, seeing the very horizon take on the weft and warp of chain-mail and spears, Harald Sigurdsson growled, 'You swore he would never come!'

Tostig shook his head as one spellbound. 'My God!' he kept saying, 'O, my God! I cannot understand it! It's all wrong!'

The Norseman's rage was cold. Much of his towering bulk of muscle had run to fat. His hairy paps quivered. His belly was overhung and with his tree-trunk legs spaced apart, his scrotum dangled like a bull's. In that moment he itched to join his two hands round Tostig's throat and squeeze that sweetly-speaking, sweetly-misleading wind-pipe.

Dragging on his breeches, Copsi the deputy said, 'What orders, my lord?'

Tostig said, 'We must get back to camp – gather the whole of our force. We'll need every man jack of 'em! Harold has half the fyrd muster of the south!'

But the Haardrada, true to his creed, refused. 'And have it said I ran from battle?'

'My lord! For the love of God! Who talks of running away?'

Whereupon the Norse King said shrewdly, 'You are very much afraid of him, are you not?'

Harold bade the army halt on the west levels above the timber bridge while he rode down to the river-edge alone. The hus-carls, dismounting, tethered their horses. Full of misgivings they watched him go.

He called Tostig by name, his deep voice echoing across the lily-choked stream.

Tostig shouted back, 'What do you want with me?' He stood then in his war-gear among the waist-high reeds, one hand shielding his eyes, the other on the hilt of his sword.

There was little to separate Harold from the rest of the hus-carls save for the Dragon of Wessex on his helmet and the shield on his arm flashing gems. 'Ah, lad, let there be an end to this now! No more fighting! Swear allegiance to me and I'll see ye rich rewarded!'

'With what?'

'I'll give ye Wessex!'

For a moment the lure of England's richest shire was a blind of glory. Finding his tongue, Tostig said, 'Why should I trust you?'

Harold answered simply, 'I'm giving you a chance before more blood is shed!'

You had to be careful with Harold or he'd be after drawing the soul from your body. Tostig said, 'They are fair words, brother. But what of the King of Norway and all his men?'

'What of them?'

'Will you pay them for their trouble?'

'Buggered why I should!'

'No earldoms? No gold?'

Gnats and midges clustered on the mane of Harold's horse and he smote at them before replying slowly, 'All I'll give the King of Norway is seven foot of English earth for a grave. Aye, or since he's taller, twelve inches more!'

And when Tostig recounted this to Harald Sigurdsson as he put on his helmet with its staring eyes and beak as of a bird of prey, he spat lustily on the ground and was seen to laugh.

239

The Breaking of the Spears

For the Norsemen a stand on the west bank was impossible. A force would have to hold the bridge against the oncoming English while their comrades got across, mounted the slope and drew up in their ranks on the flat fields where the Land-Waster had been planted. The Norsemen left to the defence unslung their shields and waited attack . . .

To the chieftains looking down it seemed that the two sides were met in a blaze of light as the slaughtering blades of sword and axe rose and fell. And for a while the band of Norsemen held their own, and the blows exchanged had the ground a bloody mire in no time. But no defence could withstand the war-play of the English hus-carls for long, and lo, the Norse ranks gave and broke before them . . .

Harold, at the head of the hus-carls, got first footing on the bridge. It was wide enough for only two men to cross abreast and there were still remnants of the die-hard Norse defenders to block it. Modred the Marshal was at Harold's side. There was small room for axe wielding, but the broad sword wreaked its own havoc and the war-corslets sang a fearful song. That was until they confronted a huge warrior garbed only in a cloak and carrying a shield rimmed with the fangs of the white witch-bear. Harold took his measure to be near enough two ells, a good head taller than himself, and he was of great girth.

One by one the hus-carls went forth to attack, but were either cut down or beaten back. Spears and hand-axes were hurled, and buried themselves in the warrior's shield and he only laughed, flinging them away as a bull horning a pack of baiting dogs. Then he threw off his cloak and stood stark naked athwart the bridge.

'A Berserker!'

'Possessed of the One-Eyed!'

'A Shape-changer!'

Seeing the English stopped in their tracks the man laughed even more, biting his shield and howling like a wolf. Then he began to call for their King to show himself. Which one was he? Where did he skulk, hiding among his men? A puny fellow without balls! Let him fight naked thus – hand to hand!

As Harold started to unbuckle his sword belt, heavy with gold mounts, and unfasten the straps of his harness, Leofwine would have stayed him and Dagobert said, 'Nay, lad, let me!'

But Harold bade them keep their peace and finished stripping off the elf-links and his shirt and trousers beneath, so that he stood forth naked, feet planted in the gaps among the slain, broad-sword in hand, shield on arm.

Thus with eyes glinting through a mass of sweat-soggy hair, the Berserker bared his teeth in a wild beast's snarl and goaded the King of the Anglo-Saxons to venture hither. And in the full, glaring sun, to the shouts of 'Aoi! Aoi! Aoi!' from the Norse army, they hewed and hacked at each other, the bridge swaying to the fury of the fight. Once, managing to pound the Berserker to his knees, Harold raised his sword for the death-stroke, whereupon the warrior, uttering wolf-language, swung his fanged shield, knocking Harold sideways with the force, winding him.

Squatting on his haunches, panting and clinging to the ropes, Harold felt for his swollen, bleeding jaw, making sure he still had his teeth. 'How to beat this sod?' he gasped.

And it was then that a spear was seen to suddenly thrust up between the planks and stab the Norseman in the buttocks from the back, twisting, ripping out his bowels, so that he toppled screaming into the river below, already running scarlet in the shallows, paler in the broad stream, the reed banks boasting a cargo of corpses.

One of the fyrd-men had accomplished the task by floating under the bridge in a salting-tub. The Norse army, who had bawled encouragement to their champion throughout the struggle, were silenced and Harold, groping for his belt, drew forth a knife sheathed in turquoises and threw it as a boon into the fyrd-man's hands.

Thus, the resistance broken, the bridge was gained, and the English surged over. As it took a time to get them all across, Harold, lacerated on groin and chest and staunching the blood, strapped on his harness, and called to Tostig, 'I will spare your life and the lives of every Norseman, by my oath, if you will surrender! Go home in peace!'

Wendelwulf the marshal said low into Harold's ear, 'He'll tell you to piss off, man.'

And loud came back the answer he had expected.

241

To Norse eyes it seemed that the valley floor itself moved as the English began to sweep up towards them. The banners were unfurling, borne on high, Harold's at the forefront, those of the Red Dragon of Wessex and the Holy Rood sewn with topaz and beryls, and the White Horse of Kent, alongside the battle-rent, blood-spattered fabric of St Cuthbert's standard.

And as they reached the top of the slope, the Northumbrian pipes, silent on the march for the sake of surprise, blared forth, and the dazzle and blaze of the Norse shields massed under the Land-Waster and the Lion of the North, almost leaped at them. Leafwine spat on his axe and swore: 'These devices – they are alive!'

Their lines were three in number, wedged behind the shields, forming a triangle. From the front the wings curved round leaving the centre hollow. The spears of the first rank were set in the ground to bear the shock and to strike back at breast level. The spears of the second thrust in between, while the third stood to reinforce and to meet any breakthrough. Harald Sigurdsson flung a spear over the heads of the English from whom a shout went up: 'Holy Rood! Holy Rood! God Almighty!'

And with this battle-cry and the pipes at full blast, they hurled themselves on the Norsemen. The echo of the shield clash as the two armies met was said to have been heard in York city. The hus-carls were free to wield their prized axes – those of the ash and apple-wood shafts and the iron blades – and did so, splintering the spear defence in minutes, each drawing their man-price a dozen times over in Norse blood.

Where the hus-carls smashed a hole, the fyrd shoved in, their farm tools put to deadly use, braining with rakes and mattocks, gutting swiftly with shears and pig-killing knives. The Norse lines shuddered, shields locking, swaying under the weight.

Harold slid on a mass of entrails. It was hot as hell in the chain-mail, the metal rings biting deep through sweat-stiff shirt and into his flesh, the palms of his hands blood-wet. Then Haakon lurched against him in the hurl of battle and they gripped forearms, steadying each other.

Harold yelled above the clamour, 'All right?'

Haakon nodded, looking up into Harold's strong, seamed face. And he was filled with the sudden desire to cling to him, to bury his head into that massive, heaving chest, blotting out the shrieks of agony, the cursing and the stench. He fought it back, clenching his teeth, ashamed of such weakness.

Harold said loudly, 'Seen Tostig?'

Haakon shook his head, but Modred the marshal close by, shouted, 'I have! He's under the banner pole with that plot-hatcher Copsi!'

'Has he hurts?'

'Nay! He's in one piece, more's the pity!'

And Tostig looked for Harold. Through the slaughterous red haze, the accursed flies that stung, picking out one man from a multitude was nigh on impossible. Then he saw the Dragon of Wessex, its ruby-scaled wings rearing from the helm, the flashing cheek-guards, the jewelled shield gleaming under the blood, and wondered why he hadn't seen him all the time.

Swan-Song

he northern earls led their fyrd-men with reckless courage yet again. Their losses were heavy but jubilant came the shouts when the wall of shields was breached. On the left wing the Norse dead were heaped belly-high.

It was noonday. Far across the heath a church bell chimed for Sext. Morkere drank from a leather bottle. The ale was warm and blood-salty. He spat it out.

'I saw Dolfyn fall.'

'The sons of Maldred also,' said Eadwine.

Waltheof leaned on his axe shaft. 'And the grandsons of Sybilla, my kinsmen, and Rudgang Wolf-Cloak and his hearth-troop . . .'

But it had been on that day of saga fame and skald's ballad, long before King Harald Sigurdsson had witnessed the thinning of his ranks and the dread work of the English axes, that he had sent a messenger to summon the rest of his men from Riccall. Thus received, Einar Orre marshalled the troops and marched without delay. Weighted down with their weapons, they hurried over farmlands by way of Esrick, Wheldrake, Elvington and Kexby, crossing the Derwent and yet more reaped fields.

Whatever the sight they had imagined to await them, no brain-pictures could have equalled the horror of the slaughter that met their eyes, beggaring all description, after the sound had already deafened their ears three fields away from Stamford Bridge.

With Harold ever in the forefront, the English attacked again and again until the Norsemen, knowing no respite, sore-smitten with iron, could have wept for weariness.

The Haardrada was fending off a dozen hus-carls by the Hour of Nones. The sun was slipping, the shield-wall dwindling, most of his best warriors death-wrapt, so much wolf-fodder at his feet.

By Vespers the reinforcements had arrived and thrown themselves into the battle, stopping the gaps with their own bodies. The shield-wall had collapsed and the whole field was then a mass of hand to hand combat, no quarter asked and none given.

Harold's armour was so thick with blood there was no telling the links were precious metal. Blood was on the sun, the sky; the rising, southing moon, welkin-wanderer, was glimpsed through a wash of crimson . . .

Then a shout went up and another until the clamour formed speech. The Haardrada was fallen. A javelin through his neck. Harold couldn't see him for the mass of slain, the litter of axes, of shields, of toes and turd, crucifixes and cloven heads. But the hus-carls had broken through to the middle of the shield enclosure, felling Tostig's Lion of Northumbria, and were then hacking down the Land-Waster, and over the darkening heathland its terrible death-screech was heard.

Watching the banner topple, Harold crossed himself. 'God in heaven!' he whispered.

And it crumpled, the yards and yards of shroud-white stuff, swallowed up and sucked down in the blood and dirt, the raven croaking and flapping its mangled wings. It was Gyrth, head and breast armour riven, an unknown, hard-faced, hollow-eyed Gyrth, who stamped on it and ground it under the heel of his boot. 'No more shall it live! No more!'

'Victory!' the cry was echoing through the fast-coming twilight. 'God Almighty!' the hus-carls were shouting. 'Victory! Holy Rood! Holy Rood!'

Harold turned then and blundered through the chaos in search of Tostig. Amidst a knot of foe-men he saw him. He was fighting hand to hand, his helmet knocked off, his dark hair tangled in bloody elf-locks. Copsi his deputy was not with him. They'd striven together elbow to elbow the day long, but now he was alone.

The Trampled Field
of Sorcerers

ogni Tricksleeve had made himself a Book of Shadows, its covers of coarse-hewn leather. Hogni was not ignorant of letters, and in it was all manner of runic scripts, and riddles. Loved a riddle, did Hogni. And spells. Good at it as the master's white-handed woman. But maybe she'd the edge over him. He'd give her that. Strong magic she worked.

And on a day in September, when the bryony berries waxed yellow, Hogni meddled in magic so mickle, that he had elf-hiccups for two days after.

'Tostig!' A man's voice bellowed, 'Tostig!'

And Hogni Tricksleeve was become as the being in the broom bush. Good job he'd put his cap on, for a rain of blood was pouring and all the stars in creation were in the sky above a-birthing and a-dying and the old Corpse-Gate open wide.

'Tostig! Tostig!'

But a craze was on him and he heard not. Swearing, Harold shoved all from his path and grabbed Tostig by the hair, dragging him round and thus they faced each other. Tostig looked up at him as though his brain was goblin-robbed. Harold shook him. 'He's dead! Harald Sigurdsson is dead! For the love of Christ – give in! Let there be an end to this slaughter!'

'That's what Copsi wanted – the nithing! Scared for his own lousy skin! He's quit the field!' Tostig's blue eyes burned fever-bright in his blood-caked face. 'But the battle is not over yet!' And his voice was thick and furred with venom.

'Battle? 'Tis just sheer killing! Help me to stop it!'

Tostig laughed, flinging back his head, that laughter sweeter than hawk and harebells, while men hacked each other to death not two

246

foot away from him. 'And come crawling back?' he spat at Harold. 'You might have all those other weak-headed sods up your arse but not me!' And so saying he swung his axe, landing a blow across the side of Harold's helmet that knocked him onto his knees. He struck again, but the arc went wide and the axe buried itself helve-deep in the swampy ground.

Harold swayed like a drunken man, blood running from his nose, his ears banging. But for the thick padding between head and helmet, his skull would surely have been broken. Black fog filled the world and even as it cleared, he saw Tostig come at him again. A jolt to the gut made Harold bring up his own axe only just in time, taking the full impact of blade on blade, spark-showers flying. Insensate, Tostig aimed a third swipe, but Harold was on his feet by then, unsteady but towering, and once more did the blow miss its mark.

'Don't be such a pig headed bugger!' Harold besought him.

Tostig, though, kept on coming and laying about him with mighty strokes. Time and time again Harold warded them off.

'Afraid to strike?' Tostig jeered.

But Harold waited his chance and as Tostig stumbled, he brought up his enormous clenched fist and hit him on the jaw, knocking him flat on his back, and kicked the axe away from him, far out of his reach. Curses flowed like bile from Tostig's split, purpling mouth as he clawed in the mud, dragging himself up. He flung himself on Harold, their harnesses locking and grinding, rings torn from leather, but with Harold being so much the bigger, his strength waxed greatly over Tostig's.

'Give in! For Jesus' sake! Save yourself and all these others!'

But Tostig wrenched free and grabbing a broadsword, both hands locked about the rock-crystal hilt: 'Arm yourself!'

But Harold would not. All he took up was a dead man's shield to fend off the sword strokes, and they rained down upon it until the shield was broken in twain and the blade all but blunted.

'Fight me, God damn you!' screamed Tostig, and suddenly, slipping in the welter of flesh and slime, Harold lost his footing and went down hard amidst bog myrtle bushes cobbled with blood. Hogni was in the next clump, hiding among the whin pods and he felt the roots tremble. Tostig saw his chance . . .

And that was the last thing he did see, for seconds later he fell sprawled across Harold, an axe buried in his back, cleaving him from shoulder to buttock, the war-coat shredded like rotten silk. Dagobert, retrieving his axe, sweat pouring down his face, was trying to haul Harold to his feet. 'What ails ye, lad? Were you in a trance?'

Harold said, 'Tostig!' And then he was sick.

Dagobert said, 'Dead, aye, and thank Christ for it!' But he knelt down by Harold, putting both hands on his heaving shoulders. 'Ah, no,' he said. 'No, do not!'

Modred the Marshal was forcing his way through. 'They're butchered to a man – not without those who've fled the field!'

Then he saw Tostig and guessed the story, and looking to Harold, white in the face from retching, he gave a long low sigh and said, ''Twas either you or him, and no peace for any of us while he drew breath!'

And with the taste of vomit still sour in his mouth, Harold went to where the hus-carls were making matchwood of the banner shafts.

> Who reddens the blades?
> Who chops meat for the wolf?
> Harold reddens the blades.
> The host chops meat for the wolf!

And Hogni Tricksleeve like a man half-dead, limped and hobbled and crawled to the cow byre and swooned away in the straw.

Corpse-Strand

C wichelm the Child-Master wandered the torchlit field, the hem of his robe sodden and foul, his leechdoms and wort-cunning useless among the carnage. 'How can I knit smashed limbs and mend broken heads?'

But his salves brought some relief and his sleeping-draughts stilled at least a few of the ceaseless screams of pain.

Gyrth said to Leofwine, 'What of Harold?'

'On the field.'

Gyrth took off his helmet, the mess of blood on it, black under the moon, having no more power to revolt. He had been in the thick of battle the day long, earning the respect of his hard-bitten hearth-troop. He had killed many where once he had sorrowed for the breaking of a bird's wing.

Then Njal Uggarsson, with strips of cloth clumsily binding running wounds, came and said, 'Priests. They're crying for priests and most of them are dead!'

Gyrth felt in his belt for his crucifix. 'I know the absolution. The rites. I was trained for it. Come, show me where.' And Njal Uggarsson looked at him, relieved and tearful and bone-weary.

The constant ferrying of wounded to York city continued on Harold's orders. He had forbidden robbery of the dead. The fallen of both sides would have Christian burial. And though there was grumbling no one disobeyed him. Stretcher after stretcher, hides slung betwixt two poles, and any man still living was picked up and taken thither by the monks of St Wilfrid's Minster.

'Where is Harold?' said Modred to Wendelwulf. The marshal of the men of Kent was cleaning his sword. His hands were not steady and he cursed himself for it.

'Looking for Tostig,' he gave answer.

Thus Harold trod among it all with the wind-driven stars for guidance, mingling with the many searchers, mostly the women-folk of the villages come to look for husbands and sons and fathers and brothers and lovers. He met Aelhhunn the mass-priest where he strove among the dead and dying, and said, 'Have you seen aught of Tostig?'

And Aelhhunn, his handsome face gaunt, his hands all over blood, replied, 'Nay, my lord.'

Harold came then to the place where the bog myrtle grew, its leaves motionless in the caul of blood. And there he dropped on his knees and began shifting aside the piles of corpses until he found the one he sought. Eadnoth the staller loomed against the moon, carrying a tallow torch. With him were the thanes Aelfmod, husband of Freawaru, and Biarki the beloved of Gondul. And looking up Harold was dimly thankful that they were without hurts for the sake of his sisters. Then the light of the torch flickering over the slaughter heaps caught the blue of Tostig's wide open eyes and the congealed blood that had gushed from his mouth. Two monks brought a stretcher and Eadnoth bent as though to help Harold, but Harold would do it by himself. Tostig was stiffening then and heavy and cold, and it was with difficulty that Harold managed to lift him in his arms, the broad-sword still clenched in Tostig's rigid fist, and lay him on the stretcher, covering him from flung-back head to stubborn out-thrust toe with his own wolf-skin cloak.

'Not all of them?' Countess Godgyfu said when she heard of the slaying of Rudgang Wolf-Cloak and the hearth-troop.

She sat upon her high-seat surrounded by weeping bower-maids.

And there, Wulfric the Heron of Wrokesham, staring at his bony knees, nodded. Coming through unscathed the way he had was almost to his shame.

Lilla said, 'What of Wynter? And Darryl? And Young Leofsi?'

'The fair one – Wynter – may still be alive. I don't know.' Wulfric took out a kerchief and blew his nose. 'As for the other – I thought I saw him cut down at Fulford. And the priest . . .' He shrugged. 'But I remember Aethelmaer the blacksmith swinging his axe and the heads rolling like walnuts off a branch!'

Before Rudgang Wolf-Cloak had left for the north, he had polished the war-coat of Leofric, that wizard-wrought, wondrous mesh of gold elf-links, and lain it back in its chest, snapping shut the nine locks. 'Open for no man,' he'd besought it, 'save for him that's meant.'

How fare the Gods?
How fare the Elves?

nd he buried our father in York Minster,' said Skyle, 'and Archbishop Ealdred sang masses for his soul.'

'And the bells were tolled,' whispered Ketil, shedding tears.

Countess Judith looked down at the two heads bent then over her lap, her heart like a stone in her breast. On looking up she saw the eyes of her sister the Duchess Matilda fixed keenly upon her.

'So he killed your Tostig!' she said. She wore a gown of green flox-silk woven of fleurs-de-lys and her little hands with their many rings winked in the folds of the hanging sleeves. 'And the old Northern Bear! Who would have thought it?'

The Duchess knelt then by the side of her two sobbing nephews. 'What tribute did he take from you? Hostages? Oaths?'

Skyle lifted washed-out eyes. 'Nothing. He had us brought from the ships – Olaf, King Harald's son also – and gave us food and warm ale. Ketil went to sleep on his knee.'

'It was the ale that made me tired. We had been up since before daybreak,' said Ketil, lest he be thought childish.

Skyle's voice was wan. 'He let Olaf have his father's body – wrapped in purple and honourably treated – and as many ships as was needed for the Norsemen to sail home.'

'They had four hundred,' whispered Ketil, 'yet they needed then only eighteen.'

'Mary Mother of God!' said Judith.

Skyle trembled at the memory. 'And the King asked Olaf only one thing, that never again should their two lands and people fight each other. That there should be peace between them for all time. Olaf pledged that it would be so.'

And Judith began to weep, slow, cold tears.

251

Matilda said, 'What of his army? How many are left? Are there many hundred score wounded?'

Skyle shook his head. 'Aye – nay. I don't know. York was terrible that night. The house that was once father's was full of men. I've never seen so many men. English and Norse – past counting.' Skyle put his fingers to his ears as though to shut out the moans and curses of those warriors. 'But the King – he made sure that no man died without being shriven. There were but a handful of priests. My uncle Gyrth slept not for two days and nights hearing confession and giving the unction . . .'

'Is he whole?'

'The King?'

'The Usurper – has he wounds?'

'There was much blood on him, but it wasn't his.'

The news of the battle of Stamford Bridge, bits and pieces coming in hourly, like the fitting together of a puzzle, had come too late to reach the ears of any but a household of women, striplings and aged vassals, and of course the hostages, for Duke William had already sailed with his fleet from St Valery-sur-Somme the night before.

'My lord had no knowing which of the namesakes he would have to face. But now one is slain and God willing the other shall be also!' The Duchess gnawed at her lips yet her colour and her spirits were high. How long had they gazed at the weather-vane on the church tower of St Valery? Why, even the body of the saint himself had been brought out for solemn veneration and prayers offered for the wind to change. Then as if by a miracle it had. O, fortune! From northerly to south, and the call to raise anchor rang out – the lanterns ducking and bobbing in the night – and her own ship-gift bore her lord to his destiny.

Judith said, 'Talk no more of death, Mald!'

Matilda cried, 'But when my lord has crushed the English and is master there you will be restored to your title and wealth!'

Judith put aside her two sons and stood up. 'I do not want it.'

'Have you been speaking with Wulfnoth the Hostage,' Matilda demanded fiercely, 'or that Saxon priest?' Matilda had seen them lighting candles in the chapel not an hour past – doubtless for the soul of Tostig Godwinesson and the deliverance of the Usurper.

But when Judith shook her head, Matilda went to her and said in a voice deceiving-soft, 'Jugge! Jugge!' – her pet name for Judith made them girls again in Flanders – 'Ah, you are distraught. You grieve your loss. Forgive me!'

And in those moments Judith wished she was at her father's court,

252

a maid still. That she had never looked up to see Tostig Godwinesson that fateful night in the banquet hall, and come under the spell of his beautiful blue eyes. 'The killing and the misery – when will there be an end to it?'

The Duchess squeezed her arm. 'Soon, Jugge, very soon! You'll see, when my lord sits upon the throne!'

Whereat Judith turned to her sister and said, 'Ah, no, Mald! I fear it will be then only just beginning!'

With no men left at the Hall of Little-Bethlehem-of-the-Rushes, Old Wor-Will-Be-So begged a boon of Countess Godgyfu: the chest clasped over with nine locks. And Godgyfu granted it without knowing what she did.

Old Wor did not pry the locks nor disturb it in any way, for it would have been no use, as the locks defied iron and man-strength, held fast by the slain Rudgang Wolf-Cloak's word-charm.

So Old Wor drew a magic circle on the floor of his hut and stood the chest inside it and sang a magic song. He rubbed it over with mugwort, mother-of-herbs, and strewed it with the leaves of woodbine – not ragged, but like a man's heart. 'Do you wait?' he whispered. A question would do no harm.

And from within the chest, as though in answer, there came the faintest stirring.

'Have you waited long?'

Again the stirring.

'Is it for a man of the Leofric blood?'

Another stirring, louder.

'Is it Eadwine or Morkere?'

But all was suddenly still then, and Old Wor rubbed his chin, believing his ears to have played tricks on him.

'There is no one else,' he cried, 'all the others are dead! Aelfgar the first born, Hereward the Changeling . . .'

And as he uttered those last three words the stirring began once more and became movement within the chest until it rocked and the locks trembled with the force of it, like that of a living, breathing thing struggling to be freed.

The victory feast in York lasted a week and out on the battle field the monks still laboured to shift and bury the unclaimed dead.

Thus it was to Harold there that a messenger brought news of the Norman landing on the south coast. It was at Pevensey. The English fleet had sailed but had been too late to stop the crossing. In the space of a quarter-hour Harold gathered the chief men to him in the hall and said, 'We must march tomorrow.'

'I have barely two score hus-carls left,' said Eadwine.

'Nor I.' Morkere lifted a young ravaged face. Within a week his earldom had twice given the flower of its manhood.

'Much of our weaponry lies at the bottom of Tillmire,' Waltheof said. 'We'd never make it to London.'

Harold said, 'Then give me whatever you can and equip yourselves and follow after.'

The fyrd had been badly mauled but Harold's own hearth-troop and those of his brothers were still war-worthy though battered, and all able-bodied men joined the march, leaving York a city of the old, the maimed and the dead.

Harold drove them relentlessly southward, fast as he had marched them thither to York but a week before, covering thirty to forty miles a day, dawn till dusk, and they found it hard to joke or sing or think of anything save their swollen blistered feet. Half-healed wounds opened and bled afresh and as they tramped under a fine hot sun it seemed their weapon-fetters grew ever more burdensome. And thus like a tattered, limping beggar band the army reached London Town within six days.

There, amid rumour-rife and woe-ridden Westminster, Harold held moot in the hall so that all might bring him news. And the gist of it was this: the Norman host, after disembarking with their horses and supplies, had dug a fortified stronghold at Pevensey from whence they had plundered and devastated the countryside. Still clinging to the shoreline they had pushed east to capture the port of Hastings. There by the estuaries of the Brede and Asten they had built a wooden castle and laid waste the corn. The men of Romney had beaten off their raiding gangs but most of the land folk took refuge in the churches and the bells, silent for months, rang across the Weald and warning beacons flamed on the headlands. From the mouths of the men of the South Downs came tales of pillage and rape and killing.

That night, for the first time since Stamford Bridge, Harold faced his mother. Over her knees lay that wondrously worked banner in threads of silk and precious jewels.

'For you,' Countess Gytha said, and as she raised her eyes to Harold she saw his to be full of tears.

254

Then slowly he knelt, his huge fists knotted together, and began to weep. For himself, for the slain, for the ache in his back, the stiffness of his limbs, the enormity of something there was no comprehending. Gytha let him weep, and as the tears fell his tongue was loosed. 'Tostig – he did not die by my sword or my axe.'

'I know.' Gytha's voice was past sorrow.

'He's cost me dear, mother, and England brought to ruin and bleeding because of him.'

'How many?'

'Thousands.'

'And the Norse?'

Harold shook his head. 'The dear Lord knows,' he answered.

The figure of the warrior that the Countess had so patiently stitched wielded an axe of agates and golden beryls. Such was the war glamour, the myth of the saga-weavers! The truth was this immense, weeping, way-worn man, bowed down like a forest oak before her.

'O, that you two could have united against this Norman foe!' she said.

Harold looked up, wiping his nose on the back of his hand. There were deep lines etched on his face and shadows under his wet blue eyes. 'Had it not been for Tostig I would have been there awaiting them.'

From Winchester Margaret gave Ragnhild tidings of Queen Aldwyth, soul-crushed by Tostig's death, and of the many candles she burned for him and the masses said. 'And Eahlswith the Maid also has her grief. Sebald Thoroldsson fell at Gate Fulford fighting alongside Earl Eadwine.'

'Though why you mourn so,' Queen Aldwyth said to Eahlswith, 'you didn't love him – not like I loved my brother.'

The peach and apricot vines would not fruit again for another year. But Madonna lilies grew for the Queen and her window boxes were fragrant with wall-flowers and thyme.

Eahlswith felt the child stir within her and tried to picture Sebald's face. Had his hair been blonde or brown? She remembered hearing the talk of her father's hus-carls, of how the corpses of men left on a battle field rotted slowly, became carrion, the air and the sun bleaching their bones white . . . 'At least you know, my lady, that Lord Tostig had a Christian burial.'

'Aye, beside the tomb of St Cuthbert, and with him Harold buried his conscience.'

When the banner of the Fighting Man was spread across the moot table its jewels held the autumn sun and cloned fire. Edgar the Aetheling had slipped in among the men at the back of the hall, fingering war-coats and sword-hilts and shields. One of the hus-carls gave him a scrimasaxe to keep in his belt.

'How old King Harold looks,' said Edgar afterwards to Margaret. 'I've heard that he is past five-and-forty.'

'Of what did they talk?'

'Of a battle place.'

'Where?'

'A ridge where a tree grows. A hoar apple tree, not far from Hastings town. He knows those Downs like the back of his hand.' Edgar stroked the scrimasaxe, counting the ligures on the handle. 'Some of the men wanted to delay the march to the south. To wait for more levies . . .'

It was Gyrth who had counselled thus, wisely, soundly. He had found support for his words among the thanes. But Harold would only repeat the coronation oath he had sworn, 'To forbid violence and greed and robbery to folk of every rank. Will you have me break it?'

Having sent Hugues Maigrot, a monk from the Benedicite of Caen, on a mission to London, Duke William inspected the tribute gathered, wondering at the already considerable wealth of icons and precious vessels with which even the small churches were endowed.

'Caen will benefit well from this!' he had said to his serge-garbed messenger.

Unwilling was Maigrot, considering the task beneath him, more worthy of a lackey. In a low voice he had said, 'But beau Seigneur, what if they kill me?'

'They won't. They will respect your cloth.' Yea, brought by a churchman the warning would be as great a body-blow as if its bearer had been armed from head to foot and bristling with steel.

The Duke's seneschal was William Fitz-Osbern, and he favoured pushing on to Winchester to seize the royal treasure-hoard. This had been seconded by Bishop Odo, but Duke William hesitated. With scant knowledge of the countryside he was loath to venture too far.

Eustace, Count of Boulogne, still widely mistrusted as ever, though he had pledged his loyalty, said, 'Fitz-Baldwin, the old King's physician, sends that the Godwinesson is gathering a great army.' As he and William were old adversaries and uneasy allies, the Duke was wont to take most of his utterances with a pinch of salt. 'I also have my watching ears at Westminster, the good Bishop of London and the staller Ralf. They report that the hus-carls are thin in ranks and nurse many wounds,' he answered him.

'But they have destroyed the Norsemen. A task surely worthy of the gods themselves!' said a certain Hugh de Grandmesnil. 'What if he brings such an army against us?'

Whereupon, Robert, Count of Mortain, himself a half-brother to Duke William, made light of their fears. 'He hasn't got anywhere near the number he needs!'

'Spine of God! Let us hope you are right,' said Bishop Odo. He was hungry for women and gold, his thick fingers were crammed with rings and his cloak clasped with a great brooch, looted from a thane's house along the way. He fed a white rat to the crimson-jessed peregrine on his wrist.

'We have got the Godwinesson in his weak spot.' Duke William spoke almost dreamily. Far in the distance on all sides smoke from burning villages and fields darkened the skies. 'The screams of his peasants will bring him. For them he will come!'

Archbishop Stigand sat in his house and stared at the empty hearth. Young Cumbra had joined the bands of monks who were to march with the Great Fyrd. His home was in the South Weald and he was fretting for his kinfolk. Many was the churchman that would don chain-mail on the day, the bishop of Winchester and his abbots among them.

At Worcester Bishop Wulfstan neither encouraged nor forbade. But when Ealdfrith the mass-thane limped up to tell him of his decision to leave bearing the banner of St Mary under which all the men of the surrounding tithes would fight, Wulfstan felt an almost unbearable sorrow. It was one of the rare times his calm broke.

'Not you!' he had said, standing in the porchway, hatless, blinking his poor-sighted eyes.

Ealdfrith, who had so long been as a brother-cum-helpmeet and friend to the Bishop, although some years the younger, had set his lean strong shoulders and replied simply, 'I may be of some use.'

'Who else goes?'

And Ealdfrith named another half-dozen of the brethren. They waited then at the gate rather than bring weapons into the House of

257

the Lord. Cwichelm the Child-Master was still at Westminster. Thus apart from the sacrist and a few older monks and boys, Wulfstan would be left alone at Worcester.

So he set to scrub the altar and pavement of his church. And it was there that Harold beheld him, hands water reddened, lighting candles for Compline . . .

Fumbling with his strike-a-light, Wulfstan turned in the gloom. 'My son, is it you?'

'Aye, Father,' said Harold.

The chapel seemed to shrink as Harold came into it, bending the knee in reverence to the cross, his mantle trailing the floor rushes. Everywhere the smell was of incense and soap and wood-sage. He sat down then heavily in one of the stalls, weary from his hard riding, and put his head in his hands. Wulfstan waited for him to speak. 'Father, can a man under the threat of excommunication still pray?'

'What is this you are saying, my son?' Thus did Wulfstan draw the story. The monk of Caen had arrived at Westminster with demands from Duke William that Harold resign his throne.

'I told him that he must speak with the men of the Witenagemot.'

And Wulfstan could imagine that reception. Those hard, patient, immovable men, their world still reeling from the quake of battle, swords un-girt in the King's presence.

'Then he spoke of the excommunication – if I refused to surrender up my crown. And not just for myself but for all the men who follow me.'

For Wulfstan it was as if the corner stone of his faith had been shattered. When he tried to give priestly consolations the very words rang hollow in his ears. All men had looked to Rome for justice and protection and truth. And Harold felt sorry that it should be so. If possible the good Bishop suffered more than he.

Harold said quietly, 'So you see I had to come. To have you near me. If only for a little while.'

'I have always been near you, my son,' Wulfstan replied, a great weight pressing on his heart. 'Stay, hear Compline with me.'

'I cannot. Four days hence we march from London Town.'

'So soon?'

'My folk are being slaughtered. A Bastard bestrides my lands. What manner of King would I be if I didn't go to them? What manner of man?'

The plain, simple truth was there. How to refute it? Wulfstan spread out his hands, let them fall.

'Would you ride back with me?'

'I could set forth tomorrow.'

'Too late for me, Father.'

'With haste I may be in time.'

Harold stood up, heedful of the bell that chimed the hour. He said, 'I was shriven and absolved for Stamford Bridge by Archbishop Ealdred.'

'Absolution,' Wulfstan said. 'Ah, yes!'

'For battle sins. For Tostig. It was he that wanted the death revenge but it was me felt like the murderer.'

Wulfstan bowed his head. 'My son,' he said, 'O, my son!'

'But the worst thing is the change in Gyrth. You'd not know him any more. He's grown hard.'

Wulfstan followed Harold to the door and with each step the foreboding deepened. He was loath to let him go. How should he keep him here? Harold had the door open and was stooped beneath the lintel. Wulfstan said, 'Is there aught else I can do?'

Harold gave it a moment's thought, then answered, 'Pray for me, Father.'

At Westminster Harold looked to the welfare of his own kin and those of Edward the Aetheling. His two eldest sons, Godwine and Edmund, he had sent to the court of Dairmaid Mac Mael na mbo in Baile Atha Cliath. Aelhhunn the mass-priest was to be responsible for the womenfolk.

From the window of Eadgyth's bower at Nazeing the small cluster of cottages, the chapel and the ale-house and the handful of fields that made up Harold's park were dark in the wane of the moon.

Eadgyth unbraided her hair, her fingers usually so deft were clumsy and garnet pins scattered. 'Harold,' she said. And he turned from the window, bending his head under the low beams. 'Lintrude can take the children to London to be in the care of your mother, but I am not going.'

'Lass, did ye not promise me?'

'Aye, but now I'm breaking it. I am following after you, Harold. Hag Annis shall come with me.' The wise woman with Harold's life-token, his man's water in a thumb-bottle in her scrip.

Harold squatted, reaching out to plunge his hands into her hair. 'Nay, I won't let you!'

Eadgyth whispered, 'How shall you stop me?'

Then suddenly his head was in her lap and she was holding him

259

and he kept on saying, 'If only I'd had a bit longer . . .' and his mouth was muffled in her kirtle. 'Peace was all I wanted. To be left in peace. To govern in peace. 'Tis a fair sweet land. A good land. And I wanted to give it all I had. God knows, I've no quarrel with any man, but the buggers won't let me alone!'

Njal Uggarsson the Icelander rode to Winchester to offer to escort Queen Aldwyth to the safety of London Town. Admitting him to her chamber, she said, 'Who sent you?'

'The King.'

'Why for?'

'He's worried that harm may come to you.'

Aldwyth laughed. 'His concern is touching!' She sat on her high-seat, Queen of all she surveyed.

Njal said slowly, 'Aye, it is.'

Her ears pricking to the tone of his voice, Aldwyth left her high-seat and went to the fire that burned on the hearth, mended of pine and medlar. 'Does he think I cannot defend my own city?'

Njal shrugged. 'I am carrying out his orders, ma'am.'

Aldwyth stretched out slender, ring-clad fingers to the flames. 'Tell him I need not his help!'

Njal's handsome face was stony. 'As you will, ma'am.' And he turned to go.

'Njal!'

Her command was swift as ever. Njal swung round on his heel. She had never been able to make him eat out of her hand as Heardwin and so many of the others had done. He had never been humble and grateful in bed; he had taken her like a whore and she'd enjoyed it. His arrogance, passion and mastery . . .

'Njal.' Her voice quavered like a reed in the wind. 'You cannot expect me to forgive him the killing of Tostig. He was all I ever loved. No one understood him but me.'

Njal had big clotted wounds on his arms, those livid scars of Stamford Bridge. 'The King didn't kill him. Go hang your bleeding heart on Dagobert the marshal, my lady. He was the one that cut him down, as I would have done given the chance. Like treading on a spitting viper!'

Aldwyth looked at him, her eyes wide and glazed, then she turned back to the fire, shivering. Her head-rail was of purest silk held by a thin crown of beryls. 'Njal,' she said softly, 'Njal.'

'What?'

'You'll march with Harold to this place of the hoar apple tree, won't you?'

Njal nodded. 'And I'd cut out my guts for him.'

'But whether he wins or nay, what will be my future?'

'How can any of us tell that?'

Wrapping her arms about herself, rubbing her chin on her finger-rings, she whispered, 'I am afraid.'

On the night of October 10th Harold went for the last time to his church of the Holy Rood at Waltham. Gyrth and Leofwine let him go alone, not even one hus-carl rode with him, and when the lazy cawings of the rooks was stilled in the tall trees and the water grass whispered, there was an enchantment and a scattering of fern-seed stars in the sky. Harold had brought costly gifts and he knelt both in the minster doorway and before the wooden rood with its figure of the suffering Christ. All was wreathed in sweet incense; myrrh and spikenard and cinnamon. Harold lit a candle and placed it in the altar sconce. He let a callous-knuckled hand linger on the ivory carvings, the gem-encrusted book covers, and bent to kiss the lid of one cask of the many containing holy relics.

'To abandon my wordly occupation,' he said quietly, 'by day and by night to remain in my church and watch by alms-light, crying to God and imploring forgiveness with groaning spirit, kneeling on the sign of the Cross, to shed tears and bewail my sins . . .'

Just then there was a step on the threshold and Abbot Aethelnoth entered, followed by several canons. It was the Hour of Vespers.

When Duke William received Hugues Maigrot in his tent he questioned him closely. Armed guards were everywhere, spears pointing outwards into the night.

'So they would rather die to the last man, would they?' William drummed his fingers on the trencher-board at which he sat. 'Thus spake the Witenagemot!' Then he said, 'Did you see him?'

'The Godwinesson? Indeed, Seigneur!'

'What did he say when you told him of the Pope's ruling?'

'He paled but spoke no word.'

The Duke offered Maigrot a cup of malvoisie. 'Well,' he said, 'you had better rest yourself, master messenger, for tomorrow you ride for London again. But this time it will not be a poor garron that shall carry you, but a destrier with chamfron and silver stirrups!'

*   *   *

Thronged with the fyrd of many shires, London Town counted her force in thousands.

'Do you think those of York would have been here by now if King Harold had wed the sister of the northern Earls?' said Christina, as she stitched by candlelight.

Margaret answered, 'With more than half their men dead and wounded? 'Tis said they could scarce put one foot in front of the other.'

'Rumour has it that Eahlswith Aelfgarsson has fled again to Chester and to the safety of Earl Eadwine's house.'

'She will never be Queen,' said Margaret.

'Nor lay with the King!' said Christina.

The door opened then and Edgar the Aetheling came in and flung himself down on the rushes. His usually lazy pale blue eyes were a-dance with excitement. He had been out in the streets without his mother's knowing. He often found his way into the hus-carls' quarters and learned the way of things from them.

'That is old news!' said he. 'What will you give to hear the talk of the benches this very night?'

'A fig for a liar!' said Christina.

'A tuck for thy tongue!' said Margaret.

Whereupon Edgar smote his knees. 'William the Duke has sent King Harold a war horse offering to meet him, each with a company of their own men, in mounted combat.'

This was news indeed. Christina scoffed no more, but said, 'And what answer gave the King?'

'He refused, saying it was not the English way. But he offered his own challenge. Let the Duke of Normandy meet himself, Harold Godwinesson, on foot, man to man!'

'In single combat? You and he?' exclaimed Ralph of Tosny, lord of Conches. 'No, Seigneur! You cannot mean to accept such a challenge!'

'What would the men say if they knew? Alone against the Godwinesson!' This from Hugh de Montfort of Montfort-sur-Risle.

'It would be wrong! Madness!' said Alan Fergeant, called La Roux, Count of the Bretons. And the Sires of Longueville-la-Gifard and de Warenne and de Mandeville agreed.

But the challenge appealed to Duke William, fascinating him, stirring his vanity. He looked round on his barons and vavasours, and demanded, 'So you think I am not man enough, Despardieux?' At which his men broke into hasty denials. They praised their suzerain to the skies. All save Odo of Bayeux, who sat eating grapes and spitting out the pips onto the ground. 'He is too big,' he said.

William stood, hands on hips, looking all of his near six-foot. 'And I am a dwarf, I suppose?'

'A blow of one of his fists could drive a man's jaw into his brain,' said Odo.

'Does my being in mortal danger distress you so, kinsman?'

The Bishop of Bayeux gave back stare for stare. 'Most of us here have wagered all we own on your head,' he said, drawing himself upright, 'ransomed estates, beggared ourselves to get you this far. But we have not done it just for you to throw away! What if you are cut down by that Saxon giant? *Mort de ma vie!* Have you thought what would happen to the rest of us then?'

Thus it was by October 10th neither side had taken up the other's challenge. And the moon slipped into its last quarter.

At Little-Bethlehem-of-the-Rushes Lilla the chaplain upon opening his door beheld three men all ragged and filthy, and two of them were half-carrying the third. It was not an unusual sight, for many were the bands of stragglers still trying to find their way home from the battle-fields of the north, coming to beg for food and shelter. But in the lamp-glow Lilla saw that it was Wynter and Young Leofsi who stood there, and the other, his face all bloody, dark hair in elf-knots, he recognised only by the torque of gold at his throat to be Darryl the Offspring.

The Folk King

t was still dark when Harold bestirred himself, shifting his tremendous bulk from off Eadgyth's body.

'O, Harold,' she whispered, 'not yet!'

'I must.'

She clung to him and he kissed her, withdrawing himself, parting from her.

Eadgyth helped him wash as his shoulders and back were still stiff and wound-bitten. Green-salve soothed the lacerations on his groin and chest. Eadgyth kissed each welt and hurt and Harold said softly, 'I'm getting too old for all this.'

Then he clothed his nakedness in trousers and shirt and a sheepskin jerkin, and Eadgyth watched him, her heart cloven with pain, as he went to her store-chest and took out his other battle harness. A queen of war-coats this, for workmanship surpassing the one he'd worn at Stamford Bridge. With every ring golden as Draupnir, sewn on leather, its weight was a full fifteen pounds. Silently Eadgyth began to weep. She knew how much Harold had pinned his hopes on bringing William of Normandy to hand to hand combat, and so avert the coming battle and spare the lives of thousands of English shiremen. Even the cautious Witenagemot had approved, knowing that Harold in his might would win. And predictably the Normans had known it also.

Seeing her tears, Harold said, 'Ah, lass! Do not! You'll wake the babes.'

Gytha and Wulf slept in their cradles, pink fists bunched like may buds. Harold stooped and kissed them. Eadgyth wiped her eyes. Harold turned to her, blotting out the thin starlight and said softly, 'Be brave for me now as you have always been.' And he drew her up against him, holding her tight, so that his heart beat against her cheek, enclosing her with the one arm, the other full of his armour-hoard.

'Let me carry your love, Eadgyth, for without ye I'm but a snivelling coward!'

The King's gifts had enriched the church of the Holy Rood three-fold, but Abbot Aethelnoth and his canons scarce noticed the precious array bestrewing the high altar, as they knelt in dread. Their eyes were upon the figure of the Suffering Christ, whose head had until that night been upheld. Now the head was fallen forward, the chin sagging deep on its breast, and the black Lutegarsbury flint from which it was chipped was wet with salt tears.

It was the privilege of the Men of Kent to strike the first blow in battle for the King and for the London Men the right to bear his standards. Thus the White Horse on its purple background and the standards of the Holy Rood and the Red Dragon of Wessex and the Fighting Man were carried on high at the head of the army as it marched through the streets while the bells of the many churches were ringing for the Hour of Prime.

Harold rode slowly at the forefront, a simple cloak of combed wool over his shoulders, and Gyrth and Leofwine with the Marshals and their hearth-troops followed in the rear, many wounds and bandages hidden under byrnics and kept behind shields, and these backed by the thanes and fyrd-men. From the house of Tyburn Bridge Edgar the Aetheling looked out to see them go by. The lurs were sounding and the drums beating, and Princess Agatha, crossing herself at the terrible beauty of the sight, sought to pull Edgar away. But Margaret and Christina had joined him at the casement, waving and calling, and were overjoyed when Harold drew his broad-sword and kissed the hilt in salute to them.

At the Hall of Southwark the womenfolk of Godwine waited. With Countess Gytha there was Menglad, once her foster-lean, then mother to Wendelwulf the Marshal's four children, the youngest but a babe. And Freawaru, heavy with child and trembling in fear for her thane Aelfmod. Gondul's lot had been but a few moments alone with Biarki since his return from Stamford Bridge, and bitter to her it was that her courses ran regular, that she had not conceived by him, and her womb yawned within her. And Ragnhild – of whom Dagobert the Marshal had asked favour: would she take his ring for him? Keep it safe? – looked at it then, worked of silver and niello, in the palm of her hand. But there, the army was going by – passing – and she ran to the window with all the other women, crowding for one last glimpse of their kinsmen and lovers . . .

265

Thus the army left London Town, following the Old Kent Road to New Cross and thence to Dartford. The Surrey woods – hornbeam and oak and chestnut, crab-apple and elder and spindle – that stretched deep into the ancient hidages of the tribes of the Oht Gaga and the Hwicce and Nox Gaga, were in their final glory of gold and amber and scarlet. And marching there the feet of the men and the hooves of the horses were dulled by the thickly-fallen leaves and masses of dead bracken, the only sound, save for the charming of the birds, being the jingle of bridle-brass and the clank of iron.

At an old crossroads a man came out from under a hawthorn thicket, harp on shoulder. He wore a coat of jags and rags of all colours and on his head a cap of weasel skin.

'A minstrel!' some of the men called. 'Be welcome and give us a song!'

But Hwita Clatter-Clogs said, 'I'm puffed from walking far!'

'Then ride, minstrel!' said Harold, and hauled him up into the saddle at his back.

And thus did Hwita Clatter-Clogs sing and play . . .

On the Watling Street the going was good. They were joined on the way by men from the villages and farmsteads who had already suffered the brutality of the Normans, bringing with them sickles and spades, cudgels and shearing hooks, broad axes and hoof-cleaning knives, thirsty for revenge.

By Vespers on the first day Harold halted the army on a hill overlooking the Medway, resting them, letting them build fires among the gorse and cook their food and yarn away the night, while in the distance the Vale of Kent was a trough of stars.

The North Downs were split from the South by the Andreasweald, and it was through that mighty forest – decked as the woods of Surrey had been in the mantle of the fall – haunt of deer and hare and rook and raven and wolf – that Harold led the army next day and into the following, coming out to the Southern Weald on the Eve of the Feast of St Calixtus. Friday October 13th.

266

The Lone Hoar Apple Tree

he slopes covered with clover and lady's fingers and the last few poppies of the field were purpling in the gathering dusk and the will-o'-the-wisps were clinging to the lance tips, but the gaunt shape of the hoar apple tree was clear as ever, keeping lonely vigil on the ridge.

Gyrth pointed towards the coast where the reflected glow of watch-fires was to be seen. 'The Bastard has had news of us.'

Harold stood on the ridge alongside his brother, once again weighing the virtues of its defence; the soggy ground below, the steep gut-rupturing climb. Moonlight softened the scarred forehead and broken nose. He chewed a blade of grass. 'He'll move against us tomorrow, aye, surely. Stuck where he is there's no chance for him.'

The English army covered the upper reaches of the slope. Fires were kindled, sweetening the night with heather smoke. Hare and partridge sizzled on spits. Men prayed, confessed and were shriven. Rosary beads clicked, armour was burnished, both head and chest-cladding. Knives were sharpened and cudgels made more deadly with bear teeth and iron nails. Harold could do no more. Thrice he'd walked the length of the ridge, drawing up the battle plan in his mind's eye, but then his belly craved food. His wound-sores gnawed at him, his great muscles seeming to clutter his shoulders like a penance.

He sat down among the men beside one of the many fires and speared a chunk of meat from the cooking pan, sopping a corn cake in the gravy. A man offered him mead from a jug. It was sweet and strong.

'Humble-bee honey?' Harold asked the man, who replied, 'Aye, twice-brewed.' And when Harold went to return the jug, the man said, 'Nay, drink thy fill. You need it – and sleep.'

It was not long before Harold's head began to nod and his eyes to droop and he laid himself down. The ground was a hard bed but to

Harold it felt goodly-soft as a mattress of feathers. Men walked past him, stepped over him. He heard their good-natured grumbling and cursing, the rattle of the sheep's ankle-bones they used for dice.

And when he woke he found he had been covered up with a warm woollen blanket and that it was grey and misty and not yet dawn.

Modred the Marshal was leaning over him, prodding him gently. 'Harold,' he said, 'the Bastard has sent his messenger again. That monk of Caen.'

Harold muttered, 'O, bloody hell!'

And all at once the whole camp was bestirring and fires raked afresh. Harold fastened his jerkin, aware of his dew-damp shirt, the grass seeds in his hair.

It was Hugues Maigrot and with him he had brought the Papal gonfanon there to unfurl the Vatican Bull and by virtue of ring and relics proclaim a War of the Cross.

'And when I asked to be taken to his tent the Godwinesson himself came forward from the rest of the men, unkempt, half-dressed, and said that he had no tent and whatever I had to say could be said in front of them all.'

Duke William was in full armour among his weapons and alone in his tent, and save for the ministerings of a servant and a brief visit of his barons – 'I'm no man's company tonight,' he'd said – he had stayed alone. He was preoccupied, withdrawn. Even the triumph of robbing men of their God held little.

'I told them that the word had come from Rome – Ex Cathedra, from the mouth of the Holy Father – that the Godwinesson was excommunicate. The Anti-Christ. And any man who took up arms on his behalf would suffer damnation . . .'

'And they understood?'

'They understood very well, beau Seigneur,' Hugues Mairgrot replied. And he saw again the sea of faces and their expressions as he had spread the gonfanon and displayed the hair and fingers of the Saints. Disbelief, some shying away, others making the sign of the Cross, but for the most part sullen, a few ready to draw steel on him . . .

'They called me names in their tongue, berating me and from among the footmen there was stone throwing.' Maigrot showed a bloodying bruise on his jaw bone. The whole was distasteful to him. In his obedience he reproached his lord: 'Then the Godwinesson said many bold things. That he feared no man. That he was chosen King by his people, and was ready to do battle this day for the country that

268

had borne him. And he advised me for my own sake and safety that I would be best to take myself back whence I came.'

It was the Feast of St Calixtus, Saturday October 14th, and the Bishop of Winchester sang a High Mass for victory and the Eucharist was celebrated at the Hour of Matins and Lauds, as the first shafts of sunlight broke across the Weald.

Before the Hour of Prime the English army was in full battle array the length of the ridge, four to five ranks deep, the hus-carls fronting it behind their shields, the select-fyrd directly at the back of them. Yard upon yard of wood and steel, locked one upon the other, solid as a rock yet strangely beautiful to see like a wall be-hung with many jewels.

Leofwine had found a clump of childling pinks. He plucked a handful and said, 'Ah, and me with no lass to give 'em to!'

Gyrth tried to smile, buckling on his sword-belt. Strangely enough, in the midst of the battle against the Norsemen he had not felt afraid. It was beforehand when the priest-conscience smote him. He put on his helmet. He would not allow himself to think.

A wind was brewing, flapping the banners driven in about the hoar apple tree. A cheer went up from the densely packed shire-fyrd as the Fighting Man rose above them and the Dragon of Wessex reared, smiting the fetlocks of the White Horse and the Holy Rood, which was stitched on a fabric so fine it seemed to be no more than a cross of gold on the sky.

Harold was the last to armour himself. Garbed in the great war-coat of mail, covering shoulder to shoulder, throat to knee in a mass of shimmering rings, it was Dagobert who strove to fasten the straps for him, his fingers fumbling.

'If you'd only stay in one place,' he muttered, 'darting about like a may fly! Keep still, man!'

Thus harnessed and strapped, he girded on the sword-belt inlaid with huge silver studs betwixt amber and raw rubies. The hilt of his broad-sword was set with magic amethyst stones. Then lastly he put on his helmet, battered, dented, with the Red Dragon of Wessex rampant across it.

It was impossible to mistake him shoving through the ranks. He bade the fyrd stick to their positions no matter what, calling them the Flower of England, the hearth-troop Well-Loved Shieldsmen. He was pummelled and cheered, and times almost lifted off the ground by the sheer press of manpower. Gyrth and Leofwine and Haakon were

269

awaiting him in the hollow between the four standard poles. Eadnoth the staller put the two-headed axe in his grip and Wendelwulf the Marshal gave him the gem-crusted shield.

High above a lark song, its thin, liquid notes almost beyond hearing, and as Harold glanced up to see it, the first glint of metal caught his eye, no more than a pin-point, then followed by others, the dots growing bigger, spreading out, until it took on the form of an army breasting the rise of Telham Hill.

Dance of Limewood, Smile of Ash

 uke William, riding at the head of the main contingent of horsemen, felt the same atavistic awe as the rest of them on beholding the wall of shields.

Also in his division were Roger de Montgomeri and William Fitz-Osbern and Robert of Mortain with the forces of Picardy and the Countship of Boulogne and the French. Count Alan Fergeant led the second with the bulk from Brittany and Maine and Poitou, intermixed with Normans under their Norman chiefs. The Sires of Beaufort and de Ferrers and de Mohun tried to hold themselves aloof from the sprawling mongrel bands of mercenaries who outnumbered them on all sides. But their proudness in their war horses, black, bay or roan stallions, unprotected, trained to kick and bite in battle, their bright long stirrups and spurs, their crested, pear-shaped shields, seemed plunged into great unease as they halted all within sight of the Papal Bull and stared across the valley and upwards at the ridge.

'God's Belly!' said Bishop Odo, shouldering his mace. Men exchanged looks. The waiting shields had the sun in them. William felt himself grow dizzy with the glare. He sought the relics hung about his neck.

'Look at the ground,' said some of those in the Breton host. 'It is quagmire! We will flounder in it!' A general hubbub arose. Like weather-cocks their allegiance swung to change and change again. Stirred to anger by their jibbing, Duke William turned in his saddle and bawled oaths on their heads, calling them rascailles and dung-hills. 'Bones of Christ! You want to wrest their lands from them, do you not? Then to get them you are going to have to fight for them, fight harder than you have ever fought for anything in your lives!'

The English lines waited stock-still in an unbreathing hush that seemed like passing years, as the oncoming army split into three and began to deploy, crossing the treacherous ground below, fed by dozens of clean springs, quivering with marsh foxtail and misty with the blue of gentians. Here and there scores went ankle deep in mud. The archers came first, with footmen behind them bearing slings and spears, followed by the heavier armed soldiers and lastly the mounted knights.

Half-way up the slope the archers sent their first volley of arrows against the shield-wall. Iron tips thrummed on wood the length of the line. The English fyrd made answer with a rain of missiles, hand-axes, sling-stones and sharpened sticks. The archers fell back and the knights, lances couched and swords unsheathed, pushed on past them, taking the slope at full gallop. 'Ha Rou! Ha Rou! Notre Dame! Notre Dame et Dex aide!'

Dagobert spat on his hands to get a better grip on his axe-helve, and when the horses, necks clothed in thunder, driven on by spurs and goads, smashed against the shield-wall, the echo of it rang a thousand hollows from ridge to forest. And the very roots of the trees of the forest trembled with a howl. Bearing the stupendous weight of rider and beast, the shields held, and the men of Kent struck the first blows with the shout of, 'Holy Rood! Holy Rood! Out! Out! Out!'

Lances were thrown. Spears flashed. Javelins pelted swift death-bringing showers. Swords hacked down on the shields. Then, alternately protecting his fellow, the length of the ridge, one hus-carl of a pair unslung his shield so that the great axes might speak. Taking the enemy on the least protected right side, the terror was immediate. The horses, foaming, proud war-chargers, shrieked and fought madly to escape. The knights hurled from their saddles fell as dead men under the glittering blades. Blood was everywhere. A red harvest, the ground slaughter-furrowed and the battle scarce begun.

'Out! Out! Out! Hosanna! Hosanna!' The roar went up from the English ranks and the knights broke before the wall and fled back down the slope.

Duke William, urging his horse forward, rode into their blind retreat: 'Get back! Dogs! Swine! *Par le splendeur Dex!* Is this how you won your spurs?' Whereupon he sent thirty, forty, fifty more up with a half score hundred foot soldiers at their backs and prepared to follow with his clutch of barons, the Papal gonfanon carried on high.

The hus-carls wedged their shields, overlapping like winged serpents scales, and took the force of the assault head on. Lances flung into the centre press took their toll. The fyrd retaliated with more sling-stones, razor-honed flints and mattocks. Where they pulled the Normans over their horses' heads into their midst they beat out their brains with hammers and cudgels and spades. The shields moaned with the voices of many timbers, swords locking in battle-play, spears hurled by the select-fyrd finding their mark.

The scene was already carnage when Duke William plunged in among it. To witness the destruction wrought by those double-bladed axes at work stifled the oaths in his throat. A doom-wind they loosed. He laid on furiously, hacking and slashing at the unyielding shield-wall. Within minutes his horse was killed beneath him and he looked about in vain for another mount. One was forthcoming from Roger d'Ivry the Butler.

'Take it, beau Seigneur!' he yelled, thrusting the reins into William's hands. Its former rider lay split to the chine, fast being covered by the falling dead. But even as the Duke strove to reach the shield-wall once more was he swept back by the panic of retreat. In the raging chaos the knights, many with blood pouring from mortal wounds, arms hanging from a single tendon, legs severed like lumps of butcher's meat, let their half-crazed horses stampede into the valley, carrying them where they would.

Men of Aquitaine, Flanders, Poitou and Anjou, their bold colours and devices torn from their hauberks, sprawled in the saddle, blood covering them from helm to stirrup. They dropped and lay in the streams and lo, the water soon ran red. The mass of foot soldiers joined in the flight, scattering in wild confusion, trampling on the human litter that by then strewed the breadth of the slope.

Duke William braked his horse to a standstill, panting, sweat stinging his eyes, the stump of a broken lance in his fist. Odo came up, his wooden mace bloody with brains and hair.

'God in heaven!' he shouted. 'What now?'

William's gaze was suddenly rooted in fascination on a man who only by pressing forth on his saddle pommel kept the two sides of his belly together. Odo followed his gaze. All guts looked alike. He repeated, 'What now?'

'Round up the draff! We take the slope again! Body of Christ! They call themselves knights!'

One blow of an axe with its five-foot shaft and double-head, each blade a foot long, could cleave through rider and saddle and horse's back, splitting bone to the hoof, and time and time again that day, those proud animals fell maimed and screaming, as the knights, having ripped their flanks to bloody-raw ribbons with spurs, rode them onto the English shields.

Staunching a deep wound in his shoulder, Aelfmod, thane of

273

Wantage, answered Harold's 'How do they hold?' with 'Strong, my lord!' It was by then the Hour of Sext. The sun was bright and shone direct in the eyes of the English from a cloudless blue sky. But the mellow air of the Weald was tainted with a fetid charnel smell and hordes of flies were already buzzing on the slaughter heaps.

The hearth-troops, given respite by a lull in the fighting, let their shoulders sag, tended their hurts, scratched, made water. Leofwine opened his trousers. 'My cock's fit to bust!' and he sighed with relief, splashing vigorously.

Sharing an ale horn with Gyrth, Wendelwulf said, 'Twice that Bastard has come within my reach!'

Gyrth squatted, his head down between his knees. Crouching beside them, Haakon said, 'And three times he's been unhorsed!'

'God send him near me again!' Wendelwulf gulped ale. 'That's all I ask!' He looked at Gyrth then. 'D'you feel sick?'

Whereupon Gyrth raised his violet eyes like smudged shadows. 'I've drunk that ale on an empty belly.'

'Well, spew it out!'

Modred the Marshal found them then and said, 'They're coming! Make haste!'

Cursing, grabbing his axe, Wendelwulf stumbled to the front rank, followed by Leofwine and Haakon, where they joined Harold once more beneath the banners. Gyrth came slower, trying to get a firm grip on his sword-hilt slippery with blood.

Repulsed yet again from the shield-wall, the Bretons were loath to be mustered. Brian of Penthievre and Iudhael the Marshal strove for control of them when Bishop Odo rode among them landing all and sundry blows with his mace. 'Get those sons of bitches up there,' he yelled, 'or I'll flay the hides off you!'

Thus driven up the slope they made a feeble attempt to breach the left flank and bolted under the axe blows, the weald-wild poppies, scarlet, poisonous, like laughing faces bobbing and dancing to mock their flight. There, the English, though dug in hard, were weakening ever so slightly. Discipline had been the more difficult to keep among the shire-fyrd, many feeling they had personal scores to settle for their ravaged fields and homes, though they had stuck it, obeying orders, never flinching. But the sight of the Bretons fleeing with their tails between their legs proved too much for a lot of them and they broke ranks and rushed down the slope in pursuit.

Harold saw it, bawled at them to close the wall. It shut in moments,

274

shield cleft to shield. 'Stupid sods!' Harold rasped a bloody-knuckled hand over his face. Powerless to do anything, he watched as the routed knights turned suddenly and rode at the levies, killing them to a man.

The Bloody Noon Past:
A Poem of the Shields, Shrill the Arrow Song

By the Hour of Nones the hus-carls showed the signs of strain. For what felt an eternity they had withstood the unceasing attacks, the living ever moving forward to take the place of the dead, the hard wood talking, gory, gaudy bucklers answering the shaft.

But to the Norman host and those of Brittany and Picardy and the motley mercenary hordes regrouping in the valley, it seemed that not dart nor spear nor sword could shift them. Made without fear, they were wrought of iron. Closing eyes that had looked on a nightmare, a knight cried, 'They'll never break! Never! We are dead men every one!'

He was Richard de Clare, Gilbert of Brionne's son, and so thickly covered in blood that William Fitz-Osbern knew him only by the shredded colours of his helm. 'Shut your mouth you cain-livered fool! Do you want that scum to hear?' Fitz-Osbern cocked a thumb at the brigand bands from Italy. 'Scullions promised lordships! Whole towns and villages flung to the rabble like chickpeas! Rich pickings! Fair dames for raping! Bowels of God, did they think to find it handed to them on a platter?'

Twice the rumour that Duke William had been killed had nearly caused mutiny. Odo of Bayeux and Fitz-Osbern and Hugh de Montford of Montfort-sur-Risle had quelled the outbursts and the Duke had ridden among them, his helmet off, to show that he was whole and unharmed.

Bishop Odo had two vassals, Wadard and Vitalis, who were without bold hearts, and they besought their lord to release them from their fief. Whereupon Odo said, 'By the spine of God – if you go now, you go as paupers!'

As the losses mounted the strongest of the fighting men were fit to stumble for weariness, the firmest of the levies fallen to the earth. The shield-wall tightened unto itself, shut as with a close seal.

Njal Uggarsson found himself face to face with Harold in the crush. He brought tidings of the grave wounding of Eadnoth the staller and many deaths, the Bishop of Winchester among them. Blood was oozing through the links of Harold's mail. Old hurts opening and new thrusts found. 'You have wounds, lord?'

Harold shook his head, blue eyes straying from one wing of the ridge to the other, across axe blades blunted and clotted crimson, the still unbroken bulwark of shields.

'I'm all right, lad,' he said.

During the repeated lulls Harold was up and down the ranks helping to carry the dead and wounded. To the shiremen the sight of him stooping, squatting in the mud, giving comfort and offering drink from his own beer-skin, worked like an old, old charm. He was as a tree with many branches and room enough beneath them for all. He saw Aelfweard the thane, husband of Mahault the bower-dame, dead. And there he saw a young monk borne hither, his breast stoved in, and recognised him as Archbishop Stigand's novice Cumbra. Men were dropping from grievous wounds and exhaustion, most all but dead on their feet, crowding the already hard-pressed hus-carls.

Biarki slid to his knees by Harold. The cheek guards of his helmet were sundered. A great gash laid bare his cheek from ear to jaw-bone. 'Haakon is slain!' he said.

Harold stared at him numbly. 'How?'

'Cut down. He fell bravely. I did for the sod that slew him!'

Thus Harold carried on his task wordlessly and it was with a man slung over each shoulder that he staggered to the rear of the lines. It was a bed of slaughter, awful to behold, the piles of dead were six deep and heaping higher by the minute. Monks in bloodied robes and torn war-coats strove to bring succour to the wounded and dying. On all sides came the cries of, 'Shrive me, Father!'

'Father, hear me!'

'Water – for the love of God!'

There were only soiled, reeking rags for bandages, wounds were washed with apple-wine for want of water, and there was barely a space to put a foot betwixt the slain. Unseeing eyes were closed.

O, clement, O, loving, O, sweet Virgin Mary!

And one of the monks was lame.

'Ealdfrith!'

'My lord!'

Harold unshouldered his lifeless burdens, then Ealdfrith showed him Haakon the foster-lean lying among the dead. Harold looked in silence, his heart wrung dry. Then he said, 'There is another load of wounded to be moved or they'll be smothered else.'

'What of your Marshals?' Ealdfrith leaned on a rake, suddenly too tired to lift his head. 'Won't they wonder where you're at?'

Rubbing the sweat from his face, his fingers stiff with blood, Harold blinked back hot tears and answered, 'These poor buggers are dying for me. 'Tis the least I can do.'

Duke William looked at his once proud gonfanon and the Pope's ring on his mailed fist. Tears of rage glittered in his eyes. How ends the dream? he thought. By the Heart of Christ!

Robert of Mortain who had commanded groups from his Countships of Vitre and Laval and Toulouse the day-long, sat his horse like a bull-beggar in the coldly fading light. The shouts and moans and weeping, the squelching of hooves in blood made its own weird threnody.

'And what have we got to show?' His greed was momentarily overcome by black despair. 'Where is the glory? For the love of Jesus!'

How many were the corpses of man and beast? Who was there to count them? To dig among the severed heads and eye-balls and steaming entrails . . .

'Turn on me, would you, brother?' William snarled. 'You'll go to hell with me for what we do this day! It was your will as much as mine! Your damnation!' And he spurred his horse on savagely to begin to round up the wayward, exhausted forces. When the men of Picardy refused, Odo slew their captain and for fear of the mace-wielding Bishop they fell in line with Flanders and Aquitaine. Of the knights no more than a hundred could get to horse. Across the shivering scarlet streams William saw their pathetic array. The foot soldiers were more plentiful, their arrow-quivers half full, but they were shying from the task despite the threats of Odo and Fitz-Osbern, more ready to go to the mouth of purgatory than to that dwindling wall of shields. Thus approaching the Hour of Vespers the English still held the ridge.

A star appeared, then another, dogging the moon, the shadows lengthening. From the forest came the loud churring of a night-jar and the sweeter sound of the nightingale – piu, piu, piu – venturing forth from its dense thicket. There was relief in the sunset, ease from the hot, sticky, chafing leather of the war-coats, the biting metal armour-rings. From under the standard Harold watched the enemy host reforming and regrouping in the valley.

'Looks like the sods are coming back for more,' said Dagobert.

Slipping and toiling up the slope came the archer-footmen. The English fyrd hurled the last of their sling-stones and mattocks and hand-axes. Bill-hooks, long-handled slashers, thatching knives and scythes had they left. The hearth-troops stiffened, waiting, their eyes on the knights who were moving like mounted phantoms in the wake of the soldiers. The archers stopped short of the English lines and fired high into the air. To meet the storm-gust of arrows, string-driven, the hus-carls raised their shields. The thwacking of iron tips on wood sounded as one clap. And with Duke William, having beforehand regaled them with a mocking, '*Faites vos devoirs, preux chevaliers!*' and Odo of Bayeux and Fitz-Osbern the seneschal and the other barons pointing drawn swords at their backs, the knights were ordered to charge.

Told all in Tongues of Iron

One minute Harold was there and the next he'd gone down. Gyrth scrambled over the thickly-packed bodies with scarce a patch of earth to put his foot. The hus-carls were reeling under the hail of arrows, shields bristled with them, striking down onto the piles of those already dead, thick as flies on dung.

'Harold! Harold!' Gyrth dropped on his knees where Harold was lying between the banner poles at the root of the hoar apple tree, half turned on his side, his head hanging down. If nothing else his helmet emblazoned with the Wessex Dragon marked him among the thronging slain.

'Lad! Harold, lad!' Gyrth struggled to turn him over, his colossal weight made the more so by the leather and gold rings. An arrow was in his forehead, above the right eye. He'd snapped the shaft and it was still clutched in his hand. Throwing back his head, heedless of the still falling arrows, Gyrth screamed above the din, 'For the love of God! Help me! The King is hit!' Hus-carls crawled over their dead whilst others filled their places, shields held high over their backs, over their heads.

A big shireman was at Gyrth's side. Someone yelled to him through the crush, 'What's with him, Aethelmaer?'

And Aethelmaer the blacksmith cried, 'Sweet Jesus! He's bad!'

'I can't shift him!' Gyrth was taking off Harold's helmet, loosing down his hair.

Then Harold broke the word-hoard in his throat: 'Nay! Let me be. Let me lie here.' He gritted his teeth and groaned aloud. 'Sod it! I can't see! I can't see a bloody thing! O, Mary Mother of God! The pain . . .' And his head slumped onto Gyrth's shoulder.

Leofwine was there and Modred and Wendelwulf and a half score of the hus-carls, cramming into that hollow between the banner poles, at the very roots of the hoar apple tree, impotent in their sweating strength.

Dagobert fell on his knees. 'Harold! O, Harold!' And tears started bright as crystal to his eyes.

With difficulty Ealdfrith struggled through the press, dragging his weak leg. 'The wound,' he said, 'how bad? Let me see!'

And Gyrth gave him to look. Harold's face was a mass of blood down one side – to touch him was to be covered in it, sweet, wet and hot – and the cruel iron tip of the arrow was buried deep. All the wort-cunning in the world Ealdfrith knew would be useless. He crossed himself. 'Mary, Mother of Mercy,' mouthing the words, lips stiff and numb. It was soul-blood. Harold was bleeding to death and his soul was passing out with his blood.

Heardwin, son of Eadnoth the staller, crawling through the mud, saw Harold's head fallen sideways in Gyrth's lap. 'O, Christ that died on the Rood!' he sobbed.

Leofwine ripped off his shirt from beneath his war-coat, the others doing the same, tearing the cloth into strips, trying to soak up that precious red soul-blood. A queer-looking fellow took off his jaggedy, tattery coat and thrust it into Gyrth's arms.

'We've got to move him! Get him to the back!' shouted Modred. He was weeping, the tears streaming down his leathery tanned cheek.

'There's nowhere left!' Wendelwulf cried in answer, shedding tears likewise. 'The buggers are coming at us from all sides!'

'He's down!' yelled Fitz-Osbern the seneschal.

'The Godwinesson is down!'

'Dead?' called the Bishop of Bayeux.

'I pray not!' breathed Duke William through a burning, dry throat. 'I want him to be alive to feel it!'

Gyrth stroked the muddied mass of Harold's flaxen hair, cradling his head, pillowed on the sordid gay cloth of Hwita Clatter-Clogs' coat, wiping the blood and spit from his mouth. 'My God,' he whispered, 'my God, why hast thou forsaken us?'

The fyrd knew within minutes of Harold's wounding. They cried as on a roar and it was as if the ridge spoke beneath their feet. Those that could laid on with what weapons they had, and great still was the havoc wreaked on horse and rider with bill-hooks and felling-axes and shears, while the scant hearth-troop made an as yet unbroken backbone along two thirds of the ridge.

281

The band by the hoar apple tree knelt, faces ravaged by fatigue and grief, crossing themselves, voicing the Lord's Prayer, and some began to sing the battle hymn of Maldon, while Hwita Clatter-Clogs, then clad only in his shirt, played for them, his beloved harp having suffered much, the soul within it – just a little mouse-white soul – crying softly among the battered strings.

The banners of the Kentish Horse and the Red Dragon of Wessex flew with those of the Holy Rood, blowing, spreading out across the darkening sky, the gems of the Fighting Man tracing legends in the dusk.

Horsemen were breaking through the ranks where the overpowered shire-fyrd fought them with their bare hands. Hus-carls hurried to aid them, wielding the dread axes, and the shield-wall shrank to less than a quarter of the size it had been that morn.

Crouching by Harold, Ealdfrith rummaged through his scrip, and lo, there was but a drop of holy oil left, and the bottle broken to shards. Dipping his thumb in it, Ealdfrith anointed Harold's eyelids, ears and nostrils, his mouth and hands in the form of the Cross. His grey-blonde hair matted about his haggard face, the mass-thane of Worcester lifted up his voice: '*Kyrie, eleison, Christe, eleison. Kyrie eleison. Pater noster* . . .' Njal Uggarsson and Biarki stood guard. '*Domine, exaudi, meam. Et clamor meus, ad te veniat!* Jesus! Jesus! Jesus!'

Yellow Sunset

Hogni Tricksleeve is sitting on the shore. He is making himself a pipe of clay from a stream bed on which moonlight has shone, his eyes now and then searching the horizon for his long lost childhood. When suddenly, towards him, many men on horseback are riding. He's meddled in no magic this time. This is unbidden, unwanted, and Hogni Tricksleeve is mortal afraid.

The hooves pound the sand while a bloody mist, raging and shrieking, shrouds earth and sky. 'Sacred Heart of Jesus!' cries Hogni, cowering, grovelling, looking to the left and the right of him to escape. But from all sides they're coming. They're riding into him, over him, through him, like an icy tide. His bones shake within his skin. He's pissed himself with fright and he's weeping.

He hears the swords humming. The sound of the sun falling. He sees the terrible shining of the world's end. He sees . . .

Four, five, six riders smashing through the front line of hus-carls before the standards. Dagobert the Marshal hurls himself forward. The shields take the brunt of the charge. There are the flailing hooves, the glint of teeth. The hoarse cries of, '*Hola! Hola! Ha Rou! Ha Rou! Notre Dame! Notre Dame et Dex aide!*'

The chain-mailed backs of the hus-carls are making a human barrier between the knights and the banner shafts. Dagobert goes down and Aelfmod the thane, and two, three hus-carls, the swords of the horsemen stabbing and slashing. Njal the Icelander hews into them, bringing a roan stallion screaming to its knees, and gutting the rider with a single blow before being cut down and trampled.

Harold moves in Gyrth's arms, a ripple of his old, matchless strength. Leofwine and Modred bestride the slain, blocking the path of the horsemen, holding them off, until outnumbered, they fall under

283

a storm of sword-strokes. Now Wendelwulf and Heardwin and with them, Aethelmaer, wielding his elf-forged axe, bar the oncomers for precious moments from gaining the place of the banners, before they too are felled and those same banners brought crashing down about them.

Hwita Clatter-Clogs' harp is shattered and trodden in the mud.

Ealdfrith is killed where he prays and Gyrth flings himself on top of Harold, so does Biarki. Amidst splintering banner poles and yards of rending cloth, sword blows rain on Gyrth's back. Lances run Biarki through. Two more hus-carls, managing to crawl, also throw their bodies over the King, war-coats and harnesses making his shield. And only when those hus-carls, a dozen all told, and lastly Gyrth – they have to chop his hands off before he'll let go – are hewn aside, do the horsemen reach Harold.

Under a black sky robbed of the moon and stars, Hogni Tricksleeve lies stunned-stupid. In his ears the anguished clamour has swollen, dwindled and died. He lies there the night long.

On waking to grey drizzle, he whispers, 'How is it with you, ye ravens? Whence are ye come with bloody beak at the dawning of day?'

The Dogs of the Evil Norns

E adnoth the staller lived for four months after the battle. He had been carried back to London Town on an ox wain, tumbled in with a mass of others, so that blood oozed in gobbets from out between the planks, leaving trails across the Weald crimson-bright. Hundreds had fled the field after midnight, many to what little – if anything – was left of their homes. There were those who relished the thought of the deep, bracken-filled hollow behind the ridge to the westerly end, where in the half-darkness, the triumphant knights had lost their bearings and plunged in head first, man and beast, to be slaughtered by the shire-fyrd. And one of them, a tall lean man with a leaping-pole and bill, tracked through the forest on heron's legs, bound for Wrokesham.

Already the cobbled lanes of London swarmed with maimed, ragged, dirty men, seeking to be shriven, calling for succour. What monks remained from the monastery of Aldgate, of St Erkonwald's abbey and St Mary Overy rallied to Bishop Wulfstan and Cwichelm the Child-Master, and worked tirelessly among the survivors, washing wounds, giving the last rites, burying the dead.

Countess Gytha threw open her house at Southwark and sat in her bower beside the empty loom. But more terrible than that or the sobs of Menglad and Freawaru and the bower-maids, was Gondul, who did not weep, but sat on the floor in the corner with her face turned inward to the wall and spoke no word. And Ragnhild, wearing Dagobert's ring on the chain with her crucifix, begged Eadnoth the staller to tell her the fate of her kinsmen.

Cwichelm the Child-Master, hobbling up, his crippled back bent the more so, was bemoaning the lack of fox-fat and strawberry stalk, the marrow of roe. Called for in a dozen places at once, he stooped to Ragnhild and said, 'He needs rest, my child!'

And answering Ragnhild's anguished pleas, Eadnoth would only repeat that they were dead and all the hearth-troop, to a man, his own son among them, and that all was lost.

But as bone-salve and holy-salve drew on his many wounds, he said to Aelhhunn, 'I saw him die! Hacked to collops he was! Didn't have a chance!'

Bells tolled from every church in the town, echoing down-river to the fishing villages. The chapel of St Stephen at Westminster was more full of burning candles than at Advent. Day and night the psalms were chanted, the masses sung.

'Tell me!' Aelhhunn said, so low as to be a whisper. 'I have to know!'

And as Eadnoth gasped out his eye-truth, Aelhhunn was there, squatting in the mud, watching.

He saw Harold flat on his back among the sundered banner poles, drenched with the blood of his hearth-troop, those fabled, iron-cast men.

As Gyrth had been dragged from him, fending off the blows with mutilated arms, he'd screamed, 'Holy Mary Mother of God! He's blind!'

A knight rode over Gyrth. He was Ralph of Tosny. 'Hola! The Godwinesson breathes!' he exulted, urging on those at his flank. One of them was Duke William himself. And as he strove to break through the press with many oaths, others, crazy with blood-lust, were already doing the job. Eustace of Boulogne and Urse d'Abetot and Roger Bigod and Count Robert of Eu among them, slashed at Harold's war-coat, tearing it wide open, retrieving the wondrous great belt of amber and rubies, to be grabbed at by a dozen greedy hands, fighting for the jewel-rich sword and shield. They ripped his shirt and trousers to shreds, pulling him this way and that until he was stark naked and bleeding from countless fresh wounds.

Then with a cry of, 'For Normandy!' Ralph of Tosny drove his sword deep into Harold's chest, going through bone and muscle with such force that the blade snapped.

'To kill the bear before the sport is begun!' Duke William, cheated of the glory, raged at the panting knights. And thus saying, he hacked at Harold's head, smiting it off at the third blow.

The riders, joined then by the Sires of Montgomeri and de Bohun and Ferrers, fearing to be outdone, chopped at Harold's legs and arms. Eustace of Boulogne cleaved open his belly, disembowelling him. Count Robert of Eu hewed at his genitals, severing penis and scrotum, and bearing the bloody mangle on the tip of his sword.

Bishop Odo, thrusting in with Fitz-Osbern and Geoffrey de Mandeville, to witness this last, had swung his butchering mace heaven-ward
and laughed. 'You'll love a woman no more, Harold Godwinesson!'

Aethelnoth, Abbot of Waltham, head bent over his crucifix, said, 'She
killed herself.'
    'The Swan-Neck?'
    'In the Norman's tent.'
    Then the rumours besetting Winchester were founded. Mahault,
dame-of-the-robes, had already fled the chamber weeping, as though
by some foretokening she knew that her thane Aelfweard was dead.
Soon the tatters of the fyrd would be streaming in.
    Aldwyth felt the blood drain from her temples, leaving a queer
singing sound in her ears. She sat down. The bangles of moonstones
on her wrists were a mockery of tears. How long before the enemy host
moved against her city? She said, 'What with?'
    'Poison – doubtless got from the Wise Hag's leech-box.'
    'And the Wise Hag?'
    'Vanished without trace!'

Aethelnoth had ridden down from Waltham Minster to accompany
Eadgyth and Hag Annis to London Town, thence to the battle site,
where they'd arrived past the Hour of Compline, when though the
fighting was all but over, the real horror had only just begun.
    Eadgyth was in a gown of silk with two rich-woven tunics over it,
girdled with gemstones and a mantle fastened with gold brooches, the
hood sewn with tiny beads. Strings of blue and brown and pink topazes
were at her neck and wrists. The Wise Hag was garbed from head to
foot in a heavy dark hooded cloak and bore a chanting-wand.
    Abbot Aethelnoth had besought them to come away from the place.
Wolves from the forest were already prowling, drawn by the smell of
fresh-killed flesh, and gangs of foreign-spoken mercenaries busy looting
the English dead of their armour, slitting the throats of those still living,
seizing their weapons, axes and treasure-loaded swords, stamping on
mouths that begged for a priest, to be shriven, for water, prizing gems
from their shields.
    'Do you think I would leave him here?' Eadgyth had said.
'Alone?'
    And after walking but a few yards across the slope that seemed to
weep for its own self, her gown had been blood-sodden to the knee.
    'My lady! there'll be no finding him! No knowing him!' Eadgyth,

twisting the gymmal-ring on her finger, had answered, 'I shall know him, good Aethelnoth.'

Christina sat with idle hands, no needle to stitch with, no thread to spin. ''Tis said that the Swan-Neck searched through the bodies till nearly dawn. That they were piled so high as to be taller than the height of a man!'

Margaret gave her no heed. She had been as one elf-shot since news had come of the defeat.

Princess Agatha had begun to pack belongings into a chest in frantic haste, then all at once she'd had her doubts of venturing into that dark, cruel, hostile world yonder. So the house doors were kept bolted and the Princess and her faithful Magyar servants knelt to offer up prayers to God for safe deliverance.

He was unrecognisable. Even the Swan-Neck could not have been sure if it hadn't been for his ring.' Christina's voice was hushed. 'You'll never guess what they had done to him . . .'

'Owl-like, Edgar the Aetheling sat wrapped in sable skins before a coldling hearth. He said, 'They chopped off his manhood. 'Tis said he'd balls the size of apples! Then bore it aloft round the camp fire. And the knight who did it is to be given lordship of Hastings town and one of the five rapes of Sussex by Duke William.'

'O, but there is more!' said Christina, leaning forward, and Edgar pricked up his ears. 'Where his body had lain they say a spring now gushes from the earth!'

'But there are many such springs.'

'This is a spring of blood!'

Gilbert de Heugleville, a kinsman of Duke William, had been in the ducal tent, pitched amidst the place of slaughter, when a woman accompanied by a priest and another – an eldritch beldame – had been brought thither by men-at-arms. They had come upon them toiling among the slain, they said, and knowing by the woman's raiments that she must be a dame of rank, they had stopped them from taking parts of a man's body from the field. The men-at-arms were white-faced and babbling. And their story was that where the butchered corpse had lain – from the very spot – a fountain of blood had spouted!

The woman had blood up to her elbows and the hem of her gown was so heavy with it that she walked slowly. All the men gathered in the tent, de Heugleville included, had put down their wine cups and stared at the appalling yet exquisite sight of she who had to be Eadgyth of the Swan-Neck.

The contents of the bundles that she and the priest and the beldame carried were emptied onto the floor by Duke William's command. And de Heugleville, who had thought never to be shocked or sickened again after that day, felt his gorge rise as he looked at the mangled remains lying there. That she should want them. Bear them so lovingly in her arms . . .

Eadgyth stripped off her necklace and bracelets, her brooches and jewelled girdle and held them outstretched. 'Take these,' she said, 'and give the King to me.'

De Heugleville saw Bishop Odo's eyes gloat on the precious stones. Saw him put out a hand to William which was quickly shrugged off.

'What does she say? What does she want?'

A certain William Malet of Graville-Saint-Honorine translated ponderously from English into Norman-French. The Duke answered, 'There is no King. Tell her I am Normandy!' Whether he would or nay, William found his gaze drawn towards Eadgyth. He expected to see passionate hate, anger, tears, even fear. Her eyes were the colour of those blue water flowers he'd noticed by chance in the valley that morning. But she wasn't seeing him. She was looking through him and past him, as if he, William, the man, did not exist. Just a shape in battle harness. And Malet was saying, 'She says she knows who you are.'

To William's morbid fancy it was as though acknowledging that a post held up the tent or a cloak was coarse, unfit for a lady's skin.

Eadgyth spoke again. Malet repeated, 'She wants to bury the King.'

Eh, Bowels of God, she does, does she? thought William, irked by those blue eyes that saw him not. Gripping the relics round his neck with both hands to still their sudden tremor, he answered, 'No. He was excommunicate. Anathema. He died a heathen. There can be no Christian burial!'

Malet was too stunned for the moment to translate. He faltered, 'Beau Seigneur . . .'

But Eadgyth, guessing the meaning of what was said, went down on her knees and picked up Harold's head, holding the weight of it on her breast, cradling it, kissing it, stroking the blooded, shaggy mane.

Odo gave a low chuckle. 'The most important bit to her is missing anyway! What am I give for a pudenda?'

Thus, Gilbert de Heugleville found himself beseeching, 'Have compassion, kinsman! Has there not been enough suffering this day?'

289

The Duke turned on him a white face with a pulse throbbing on the jaw. A look which said, Be warned! Cross me not!

And de Heugleville had known that to allow that one thing would have been an admission that he was wrong. Not just then, but for all time.

Humfrey of Tilleul had watched the mercenaries and even the knights themselves fight like dogs for the plunder of the slaughter field. Every thane and hus-carl stripped, every link of armour, every ounce of gold.

Women came from the outlying places of the forest and Weald to recover their menfolk and to plunge their hands and faces into that crimson spring which still gushed on the ridge. And there was the bitter agony of weeping when they had found what they sought. Mud had been flung at the Duke's tent, the gonfanon spat on and defiled, and when the men-at-arms threatened them with swords they had backed away slowly. Times three of them would be carrying a grisly burden. Lovely, fair-skinned, large-boned women, blonde hair hidden by shawls. Pale eyes – wondrous shades of blue and green and grey and lavender – full of loathing and hatred. 'The King will come again,' they had said in their strange, ancient tongue.

After Eadgyth the Swan-Neck had died by her own hand, Harold Godwinesson's remains had been pitched over the cliff on the night following the Great Battle for the rocks to smash further, the sea to claim. The next morning they were gone.

'The tide,' said Robert of Mortain.

'More likely those superstitious peasants!' replied Odo. 'A pity about the Godwinesson's whore. I could have fancied her for my guerdon with or without her jewels!'

And Duke William had slammed down his fists. 'By the Bones of Christ, have done!' he said. And no man dared mention such again.

And when at last the time came to move camp and hundreds of mercenaries had crossed from Normandy, Humfrey of Tilleul was to stay behind to command the garrison at Hastings. William Fitz-Osbern's loud voice proclaimed, 'The Duke desires vengeance on Romney! Then it's on to Dover! She'll yield well!'

And Humfrey turned to Hugh de Grandmesnil and said, 'God in heaven, what have we done? To think of them and all that scum who will follow – unleashed on this country!'

And Hugh de Grandmesnil had shrugged, content to let his gaze

290

wander to the pleasant slopes further off. Anything rather than look at what surrounded them where the wolf and raven had done their work. 'They're not our lands. Not our worry. The Duke has got what he wanted. Why should we care?'

The Lay of Sod-Apples and of the Lamps without Oil

ogni Tricksleeve shrank from his Book of Shadows. He dug a hole and buried it behind the cowshed, and coming on him there, Hereward said, 'What've you been up to?'

But Hogni only shook his head and betook himself off. Next he'd have to get rid of the runes. So he took those restless carvings and flung them into the sea. But they returned. Hogni Tricksleeve went widdershins on Nut Crack Night, but he could not break the spell.

On Christmas Day the moon turned black.

'Something is amiss,' said Muirgheal to Hereward. 'I can feel it.'

'What?'

'Enchantments left undone. Bad spells.'

'It'll be that damn fool Hogni. He's a half-troll anyway!'

And when Hereward saw him again he grabbed him by the ear. Hogni looked so white and scared that though Hereward was tempted to clout him, he didn't. Instead he said, 'Out with it!'

It was a great relief for Hogni to tell someone, no matter that Hereward believed him or not.

Meantime, he'd clambered up a tree and sat athwart a branch, there to tell his tale. Apples were heavy upon it. Sod apples, quoddling-soft.

Hereward already knew of the Norwegian host of Haardrada sailing in great numbers to England, and after two battles which had shaken the earth having but a few left to sail out again. That had been the talk of the boats.

'Give you a fright, did it?' said Hereward.

'They couldn't see me!' said Hogni.

'How d'you know, ye daft bugger?'

'Because I was in a bush and no bigger'n a damsel-fly!'

But that other battle – fought against the forces of the Bastard of Normandy and the English defeated with great slaughter – there was only Hogni's word for that. Yet Hereward was in half a mind to believe

292

him. He'd got the wind up, right enough. And when he told of the crash of the standards and the blood and the stars, his skinny knees were knocking together . . .

'Said as how those runes would only bring trouble, didn't I?'

'They have to be!' said Hogni.

Hereward whacked him on the shin with a wrestling-pole. 'If I see 'em I'll burn 'em!'

Whereupon Hogni Tricksleeve yowled and rubbed his shin-bone, then looked sly. 'Like Harold Godwinesson did?' He narrowed his eyes. 'That great big bloke! Even he could not escape their power!'

Hereward felt a cold hand suddenly on his spine. He flung down the pole and said, 'Ah, shut up about it now, will ye?'

But fishing and gutting and salting, Hereward began to think . . .

He thought. O, how he thought. Mending and planting and clod-turning. I'm never going back. But what of the fen fields clothed in Lent lilies? I'm never leaving here. But what of his cot up under the eaves-thatch – that had been his father's long before his – and that great, white flummoxing moon?

What of it? It's gone. It's not yours any more. But who sat then upon the high-seat?

With a scythe Hereward went at the weeds and briars with a will. He cleared the lot, working himself into a sweat. He knew without telling that his father was dead. He had to be. But what of the others? His mother had fled from the Hall, doubtless. But his kinsmen – did they lie somewhere rotting among the countless slain? Who dipped their dirty fingers into the honey of Wyntering? Who stole the peace of the elves?

Muirgheal noticed the difference in Hereward quickly enough. True, in the straw he was strong and hungry as ever and she enjoyed him as she'd never thought to go on enjoying any man. But there were times – even when he thrust deep in her womb – that she felt he wasn't with her. And often he'd have a listening look about him and she knew that she wasn't the only thing on his mind.

'Ah, jewel, what is it?'

'Thought I heard the wind in the knot-hole.'

'*Musha!* There's no wind, darling!'

And after, as they dressed, though the hawthorn scent of his loosed sperm still clung about her, Muirgheal knew for certain that something stood between herself and Hereward's heart.

'Blathnad asked me if I liked you because your cock is so big and red.'

Hereward was pulling on his shirt. He said, 'And do you?'

Muirgheal nodded, watching his eyes. 'And for so much more. Now will you not tell me what is wrong?'

And when Hereward did, Muirgheal drew her shawl about her and said, 'How do you know that one is telling the truth?' She had never taken to Hogni Tricksleeve, not even after all those years. That one, she called him, or Lean-Trot or Wolf-Shins.

'Yon bugger knows better than to tell such a lie. Knows I'd throttle him!'

'You said you were foredone with your home.'

'And so I am.'

'Cara! Cara!'

'You are sure it was Harold?' said Morkere. 'That he could not be alive still – somewhere?'

The northern men had arrived in London Town by this time; the march-weary fyrd and their strength-shorn hearth-troops. What power was left in the land, what hope of leadership, of salvation, was cornered in despair in the moot chamber. Archbishop Stigand, already weaving his plans, listened and shook his head pityingly. It was ever thus. From out of the hoard of rumour and speculation they still chose to believe in a fairy tale. That by the waving of a magic wand those butchered limbs might be made whole again, that huge figure risen to its full height come striding back out of the shadows, to take the burden from off their shoulders. The only reality was the Norman advance. An advance they were powerless to stop. The burning and plundering of Dover. The fall of Canterbury, with oaths sworn and hostages given. And every village, beanstead and farmstead inbetween and surrounding for many miles burned to the ground. Whole tithes had been set alight, livestock slaughtered, granaries looted. Next they pushed forth on London, going by way of the North Downs and not the old Canterbury road, razing vast tracts of the Weald, whole settlements and churches. At the shrine of St Mary-in-the-Wood the row of solid gold bells for which it was famed was cut down, and when Gilbert de Heugleville remonstrated with the soldiers, Bishop Odo said, 'I should hold your peace. There's not one of them that wouldn't slit your throat for your purse-chain!'

Camberwell was burned by a detachment of soldiers sent by Duke William to test the town's defences, but they met fierce opposition at

Southwark and retreated, firing the houses, and fled back to the Duke's army under a cover of smoke.

At Winchester Queen Aldwyth surrendered her city, fearful lest they should burn it down about her ears. But as she watched the great detachment of mercenaries swarm through the streets and saw William Fitz-Osbern the seneschal treating her house as though he'd bought it, fingering the beautiful tapestries, opening her ivory work-box, looking over at her with an insolent smile, she said, 'How dare you come into my bower? Handle my things? Get out!' Aldwyth spoke Norman-French with tongue-lashing fluency.

Whereupon Fitz-Osbern had feigned fear. 'Can it be that you are the old King's wife?'

Aldwyth wore a head-rail crowned with heliotrope jaspers. Her cheek flamed red as those stones. 'I am the Queen,' she said. 'This is my house and this is my city!'

From the upper storey came the sounds of breaking glass; blades splintering wood, the babble of foreign voices. Aldwyth rushed to the stairway but was held back by the crossed lances of the men-at-arms. With half an eye Fitz-Osbern regarded her hedged about in her pride. All these Saxon women were proud, brought up to think themselves a man's equal. Swiftly he calculated his new-found wealth, the dues from this royal treasure-house of Kings – for the Duke had promised him all the lands of Harold Godwinesson, as well as estates in the middle country.

Aldwyth's anger had almost robbed her of her tongue, but when she saw Fitz-Osbern smiling while he counted the hides and pigs and fisheries, she found it again: 'I order you to leave!' It was a command that no man would have ever dreamed of disobeying.

Fitz-Osbern looked at her narrowly and said, 'Madam, you order no more!'

And with that one of the men-at-arms had fastened a swarthy hand on Aldwyth and tried to snatch the collar of gems from her throat. She cried out and Fitz-Osbern laughed, but his laughter was short-lived as the bold man-at-arms was suddenly flung like a heap of rags to the ground, his skull split, felled by a single blow, and Torquil the dish-thane was before them.

'I would never have believed a man could be that size! He was bigger even than the Godwinesson!' So said Fitz-Osbern to Duke William at camp afterwards. The seneschal, though no coward, had felt his blood run cold at the sight of the monstrous Saxon.

295

Having neither benefit of hearing or speech, gauging hours by the sky-candle, making his thoughts known by hand-pictures, Torquil had watched from the orchard where he worked – for there were no men left to do the husbandry – and seen the ranks of soldiers, strange hordes at the gates, and his first thought was for his Queen. His wood cleaver he used on the pack of land-thieves he overcame in the hall. And Fitz-Osbern had first beheld him bursting through the iron-hinged bower doors.

'He slaughtered a dozen with his bare hands. Bowels of God! Never have I witnessed the like! He broke their necks and their backs. One he hugged to death like a bear.' Fitz-Osbern made his point by tearing both legs from a roast fowl and snapping the bones.

Duke William watched him moodily. He was drawn and pale, having fallen grievous sick of the bloody flux.

Fitz-Osbern reached for the wine jug. 'It took a score to hold the brute. The fiend's strength was in him. Though I'll wager he kept his lady warm at night!' And Fitz-Osbern smiled, licking his greasy fingers, to think that it would be so no more. For it had been a sobbing, retching Aldwyth who had been forced to watch her dish-thane hang . . .

Duke William said, 'I sometimes wonder if I have not promised away too much land. Land I have yet to gain.'

Feeling the wine warm his belly, Fitz-Osbern said, 'But most of the thanes are dead – slain on the field. Every peasant who fought for the Godwinesson will lose his goods and freedom. Kept down thus they won't dare show their teeth. Besides, you would have had no army to flock to your banner without rich rewards!' He leaned forward. 'And this country is rich. Ah, beau Seigneur, you told us that it was so – but I never dreamed how much. Just this southern part boasts more than all our other conquests put together. Eh, more than in the whole of Gaul! The taxes that can be levied in the year could pay a dozen King's ransoms.'

From the Month of the Dead to the After-Yule

rchbishop Stigand, after much thought, decided that he owed nothing to any man, and so he went in unto the Norman camp at Wallingford on the Thames and did homage.

Meanwhile, the Witenagemot in London Town had chosen Edgar the Aetheling to be their King.

Aelhhunn counselled, 'We must leave.'

'Whither?' said Ragnhild.

'To Exeter. There's safety there – for a short time, anyway.'

Outside it was snowing and folk came in daily from the countryside about, clutching their scant belongings, seeking refuge from the marauding mercenary bands bent on pillage and rape.

Ragnhild said, 'It is hopeless, isn't it?'

Aelhhunn looked at the faces of his Ring-Giver's women-folk. They were rich in lands. Exeter city had been Countess Gytha's morning-gift. Even Freawaru and Gondul, who sat so still and spoke no word, had been made wealthy by gifts from Harold. Menglad, widow of Wendelwulf the Marshal already owned much in her own right. A bequest of ruin and want and bitterness and sorrow and ashes and horror and despair.

Blathnad had brought a basket of wild strawberries and said, 'Weave me a bracelet!'

Hereward had looked down to see his child and answered, 'You can do it for yourself. I taught you how.'

Thus the summertime had passed in bewilderment for Blathnad. That the blond head which stored all the fireside tales should turn away from her towards the sea. That the huge shoulders she loved to ride upon should be hunched as if shutting her out.

'What's he looking at?' she'd asked Hogni Tricksleeve.

'Why, yonder lies his old home.'

Blathnad could not imagine Hereward anywhere but Emhain Abhlach. She'd squatted on the ground and tugged at a clump of thin grass. 'He won't make me any bracelets!'

Hogni had been carving a doll with his knife, having the spirit of the wood still trapped inside it. 'He's got a lot on his mind. Thinking, like.'

'What of?'

'Of times before you were born.'

And now it was winter. La Bealtaine passed, the Yule-tide over, and Hereward took to polishing his war-gear daily. The animal heads and bird-masks of the belt of the Fiann shone. By the fitful glow of the turf fire the emblems of the swine of battle took life on sword Brain-Biter's ancient blade.

And Muirgheal guessed in all sadness what the outcome would be. 'You want to go, do you not?'

'I've no plans.'

'You're not priest-bound. Nothing to stop you.'

'There's you.'

'I've lived alone near all my life, cara!'

'What of the little one?'

'She'll be with me.'

'Hogni shall stay. He'll do your bidding.'

'Nay – not him!'

'Why do you not like him?'

'He's got sly, prying ways.'

'Ye misjudge him. Hogni's not so bad.'

Muirgheal put her hand on Hereward's arm. 'Where will you go?'

'Only to King Dairmaid's court.'

'At Baile Atha Cliath?'

'Aye.'

'Not across the water?'

Hereward shook his head. 'I'll be back before the ploughing.'

'I can do that.'

'Nay. 'Tis too heavy for ye!'

'Hereward – Hereward!'

Hereward took her hands and kissed them. Kissed the long leech finger. 'I'm a bugger, am I not?'

'If it settles your mind.'

'Maybe 'tis better not to know.'

'You already know too much!'

The Earls Eadwine and Morkere who had previously pledged their support for Edgar the Aetheling withdrew it. Standing before a sad fire while the bells rang and the wind drove across the river, Eadwine said, 'He's but a stripling. Still tied to his mother's apron strings. Christ! Can you see an army with him at its head?'

Waltheof Siwardsson groaned. 'What is there left for us?'

'I don't know,' Eadwine answered.

Waltheof was full of the frustration of idle muscles, of the inexorable power of the Wyrd. 'God Almighty! There has to be something!'

'That old fox Stigand,' said Morkere, 'he took a chance.' He was listening to the bell-song.

Eadwine shrugged. 'He is no loss.'

Bishop Wulfstan came then and said, 'The Abbot of Chertsey has surrendered, and his brother the thane Oswald.'

And thus the submissions began. The fear of losing life and property outweighed all else. The Norman army then marched from Wallingford to the north-east of London, across the Icknield Way, devastating and plundering, growing stronger with mercenary reinforcements whilst the shire folk grew weaker.

Other detachments were sent to Cambridge and St Neots and Stony Stratford. In December they were at Hertford. Queen Aldwyth had since fled from Winchester to her Church of the Nuns at Wilton and Ealhswith to the court of her kinsman by marriage, Bleddyn of North Wales.

Through the frozen panes of honey-glass Margaret watched the small party that set out one bleak morning before the Hour of Prime; Archbishop Ealdred and Bishop Wulfstan of Worcester, with her brother Edgar on a mount between them, the Earls Eadwine and Morkere following.

'He is not to be King?' Princess Agatha had stared in bewilderment when Edgar was taken from her.

'Your Highness, we are taking him to the Norman camp at Berkenhempsted. He will be safe with us,' Archbishop Ealdred had said.

Princess Agatha had looked from one man's face to another. They sought to placate her. To soothe her fears. What promises they had made. What shining dreams they had hung before her eyes. That her child should be restored to the throne of his forefathers. Now after they had bestowed it first on that beguiling, deep-spoken Saxon giant, they

299

were to surrender it to a barbarous Bastard. A tanner's grandson, already soaked in the blood of many thousands . . . 'But they will gouge out his eyes. Or poison him. No, you shall not have him!'

It was Bishop Wulfstan who had persuaded her, but she sobbed bitterly at Edgar's going, sure that she would never see him alive again.

Now Margaret turned from the window and saw Christina come carrying the golden treasure that Harold Godwinesson had brought back from Rome. 'What are you doing with that?'

Christina said, 'Do you want the Norman dogs to take it?'

'They would not dare!'

Christina shook her head. 'That's what Queen Aldwyth thought but they looted her house at Winchester, aye, and put to the gallows her dish-thane who tried to stop them.' She set the treasure down on the table. 'How brightly the light shines!' And her fingers lingered on the golden figures of the king and queen and their courtiers and guards. 'I wish it was mine!' And she made as though to take one of the golden knives.

Margaret sprang forward. 'No!' she cried.

But it was done and as they watched spell-bound, the figure of the boy with the bent bow shot an arrow at the carbuncle and for a moment all was darkness and full of yells as of demons. The colour of the figures had turned leaden, the light extinguished, the treasure a pool of dust. Margaret fell on her knees on the rushes and Christina looked down on what she'd wrought with a white, frightened face. It was as if the seal had been set upon the Dooms.

The Corpse-Feeders

T he lot of Ivo Tallebois was a goodly hall and tithes in Spalding and Kesteven in the Middle Land, and he thought himself lucky to get them. Such had been the crazed, cut-throat scramble for lands in those first months, that Norman baron had clashed with Flemish mercenary and Poitou knight with Ushant brigand for every field, every farm and village, every mill and fish-pond and pan of salt.

Rich they were, those holdings that he had, though smaller than he had hoped for; some, which had belonged to men who had fought at the Battle of the Norsemen, were empty and ready for the taking, but for a few old dotards and boys and some women – luscious creatures they were, with their milk-white skins and hair like hanks of corn. Nothing like them had come his way in Anjou. No wonder their men had fought so hard! But once he'd had his fill of them he hungered for more. Their fear was to his taste as were their broad fertile acres and the taxes to be levied from them. And why shouldn't he? Hadn't he and his Angevin rutters striven gut-deep every step of the way to aid the Duke of the Normans to his kingdom? Hadn't he been one of those who'd witnessed the hacking to death of the Godwinesson – seen his genitals borne aloft, tossed from spear tip to sword point? Hadn't he looked on as one of many as the white-throated, gem-decked woman had come seeking the iron-rent corpse?

He will come again.

Bowels of God! How many men had he, Ivo Tallebois, in the space from Candle-Mass to Eastertide, and from his lands alone, hanged for saying that? A score – two score? Almost as many as he'd hanged for taking the fowl of the woods and the fish of the meres that he now owned. Sullen, brawny clod-hoppers with plenty of breeding years left in them – he'd strung them on high and there they'd blackened and rotted, carrion-feed, with ever more to join them when a second gibbet

301

had been built and yet a third and a fourth, until the accursed place was filled with charnel birds' wings and the skittle of bones.

'Hang them and who is to do the work?' Urse d'Abetot was fond of saying. For his part in the butchery of Hastings Field he had the Sheriffdom of Worcester, and with the aid of his men-at-arms, his name was become a dread by-word.

The Pack was gathered in London, casting wolf's eyes at each other, wary lest they should lose out on something, be robbed of their blood-gains. Two castles were in the building in that town, both of wood, one nameless by the river to the south-east, the other known as Baignard to the south-west.

'And who will reap the fields and draw the water and cut the wood and pay the taxes? Do you, *haute seigneurs*, wish to labour in the corn as their chief men always did? Mingling sweat with all and sundry, and have callouses on your hands?'

Ivo Tallebois listened from his lesser seat while the Land-Fatted Ones held court. A handful these, already hoarding lands which had belonged to many hundreds, and yet more were coming up for the taking every day, it seemed. The mercenaries recruited from Continental duchies, freebooters and felons, arrived to swell the ranks of the marauding armies swarming unchecked across the country like a plague of locusts, with the blessings of the Land-Fatted Ones as long as they brought back most of the plunder-spoils to their feet.

Heart of Christ! Ivo Tallebois was moved to wonder at the glorious possibilities of it all. To drown in such wealth. Beyond the dreams of avarice. It was enough to make a man mad.

And thus thought William at Rouen: he had left it a doubt-ridden Duke and returned in triumph, a King. True to his word, Waltham church had been despoiled and the cross of gold sent to the Pope as tribute, along with the promise to raise an abbey on the field of the Great Battle.

And then, dropping a string of precious gems into his Duchess's hands, he'd said, 'There is much more where they came from, Mald!'

Half-crooning, Matilda held the stones – they were sapphires – to match against the mantle she wore – another of her lord's gifts – rich blue threaded in gold and of incomparable English work, got from some Saxon dame's tow-chest. And again she begged William to tell her of his coronation, of the treasures of the great Abbey of Westminster, and of the marvel of the robes and of the gorgeous crown. And he did so to please her – avid, clamorous Mald – but there was no pleasure

302

in that memory for him. What should have been the greatest day of any man's life had been witnessed only by a few and celebrated behind barred doors, with fire and slaughter in the streets its climax.

'When shall I be crowned, my lord?'

Matilda's voice brought William back to her in the upper chamber at Rouen.

'When, my lord, O, when?'

'Soon, Mald. But I have yet to crush the south! I want you in no danger!'

'Next year?'

'Eh, what cupboard love is this?'

'Tease me not!'

And William, relenting, said, 'In the spring – perhaps.'

And Matilda laughed and kissed his thunder-brown cheek.

Aye, there was the south! Wessex, the Godwinesson's shire, had yielded plenty. Had it not been some of its choicest spoils that he had paraded through the streets of Rouen? And not forgetting Edgar the Aetheling, Eadwine and his brother Morkere and Waltheof Siwards-son, landless then, and as far as he knew the last scions of the ancient stock – brought thither under guard and shown off before the curious, admiring crowds.

Northumbria had gone to Copsi, Tostig Godwinesson's deputy, and had already been contested by Oswulf of the House of the Bear. And snapping around like curs for the kill, scullions and grooms and outlaws from Alsace to the Schelt – promised villages and ploughteams and orchards and vineyards – all held in tenancy from he, William, their suzerain. All allegiance due to him.

But was it?

Odo and Fitz-Osbern William had left behind with Hugh de Montfort – this last seigneur grown mighty haughty in the office of Constable – to rule England in his stead. They had assured him with messages that all was under control. Yet rumours had come of outbreaks of revolt – that God-damned turn-coat Eustace of Boulogne stirring up trouble for his own ends. And Odo the Concubine-Keeper – was there really any trusting him? Admittedly the first Great Tax had been levied with success and had brought most of the southern shires to their knees. Many castles were built and the barons were loose on the land and the purge was begun of the men from thane to cottager who had fought for Harold Godwinesson. And their land was taken, from fine halls and farmsteads to the mere strip of field tilled by the humblest member of the Great Fyrd.

303

But whither was it going, that stream of riches? Into his own coffers, or those of his half-brother? Is Odo gorging himself to satiation on England's carcass in my absence? thought William. All that should be mine bloating his purse . . .

Eh, Splendour of God! If I do not return soon it may be too late!

The cupidity of Ivo Tallebois had often dwelt upon Little-Bethlehem-of-the-Rushes in the neighbouring hidages. Now there was a place to his fancy. Seat of the Saxon Leofric, and still held by his widow Godgyfu, though where she might be was any man's guess. No one had been granted those lands yet but he'd heard that a raiding party had already been there and after looting the great hall and hacking the wondrous mass of pearls from the chapel walls, there had been a lesser hall nearby and the prize of a thane's wife to rape.

Six or more in that raiding party had taken their turns on her body, but never lived to tell of the pleasure, for her husband had come in upon them with a reaping-hook and axe from the fields and brained and gutted the lot. His wife had died from the rough handling and rape-wounds, and the thane had fired his own hall and his orchards and crops, and with his one male child had taken off into the deep of the Fens. A price was on his head, one of hundreds, and if caught the penalty was castration, mutilation or death.

A kinsman of Leofric he had been. Wynter of Wyntering Hall.

A sigh upon the Harp

At the court of Baile Atha Cliath a warm welcome awaited Hereward from King Dairmaid Mac Mael na mbo and Padraig O'Connor. They could not believe their eyes that it should be him. After all those years! And to think they had sorrowed for his loss!

He was made much of. He was turned around and yet around again and slapped and pummelled and praised.

'By the Stone of Fal – ye've grown. A strapping lad you were before – but now!' And King Dairmaid hugged Hereward for the dozenth time.

'Will ye look at his plaids! *Musha!* And bells! A ring in his ear too. Ah, cara, you're a sight to pleasure my old heart!'

'And we mourned you so,' said Padraig. There were a few flecks of grey in the red glory of his hair.

King Dairmaid laughed. 'But we should have known that it would not be that easy to get the better of a man of the Feinnidh!'

Hereward and Padraig held each other at arm's length.

'How have the years treated ye?' said Padraig.

And Hereward told him of Muirgheal and Blathnad. 'You're a lucky man!'

'And you?'

'I was to have married – but there was fever and she died.'

And as Hereward saw the light go out of Padraig's blue eyes like picked gromwell, his heart smote him. But King Dairmaid came between them then with ale-cups and Padraig turned away to the fire.

'The evil tidings have doubtless brought you to us?' the King said to Hereward.

And Hereward nodded. 'They're true?'

'Aye, they're true! God's pity upon us!'

So Hogni Tricksleeve had told no lie.

305

And during the days that Hereward was in Baile Atha Cliath fugitives were coming in all the time.

'The sons of Harold were here,' said Padraig.

'Now they have gone to Denmark to their uncle the King.'

At which Dairmaid Mac Mael na mbo snorted. 'Yerrah! Svein Estrithsson is never quick to help any one – whether kin or not. Too fond of playing with his gold chessmen!'

So Hereward went back to Emhain Abhlach, then returned yet again to the court of King Dairmaid. And there in the hall a group of travel-weary folk sat by the hearthside. One of them, a woman in a mantle that had once been finest crimson velvet and a gown with rich embroidery at neck and sleeve and hem, now frayed and threadbare, looked up then and said south-country-wise, yet with more than a trace of Danish, 'You are!' Her eyes fell upon the pledge-ring of ravens rampant.

'Hereward, ma'am.'

'The son of Leofric and Godgyfu?'

'Aye.'

'And all the world thought you were dead! I am Gytha, once Countess of the West Saxons. Ah, Hereward Leofricsson, will you bide a while to hear a tale of weal and woe?'

Hereward did. He knelt at her feet. And after he had heard all there was to tell and found it to be much worse than he had ever imagined, he said, 'My mother?'

'God knows what has become of her!' the Countess answered him.

So she fared among wolves. Would she still shy from his brawn or disown him for a changeling? He said, 'But what can I do?'

'Go home.'

'Ma'am, you forget I was made a Wolf's-Head. The folk of my father's shire both hated and feared me. Like as not still do.'

'When the lands that should be yours are torn up between Flemish scullions and grooms from Angers you think those folk.would not welcome you back?' said Countess Gytha. 'What's past is past. There are no more grudges borne in England now – only sorrows!'

Hereward was reluctant, all without confidence and difficult to beguile. That he should jeopardise his peace, the peace of Muirgheal – for what? He had no experience. No knowledge of armies or warfare. He'd never even killed a man.

'You are young and strong,' Gytha said, 'Leofric's son. That alone would win you favour from the Humber to the Thames!'

And King Dairmaid was ready with the offer of a ship and crew. 'You cannot mean not to go to your mother. Think how great will be her joy when she finds you alive!'

Hereward was in over his head and he knew it. He journeyed back to Emhain Abhlach once more.

Muirgheal stood by the well, a shawl about her shoulders. 'You have not come back to stay?'

Hereward felt his soul to be glass and himself foresworn in courage. 'They've got half England.'

'Your home?'

'Like as not. They're fair, those hidages.'

'Fairer than this?'

''Tisn't the same.'

'You are lord of them?'

'By rights.'

'Yet these thieves have what's yours.'

'Aye.'

Muirgheal was determined she would not gainsay him or attempt to keep him. He had to make up his own mind.

'I'll bide till Imbolg to think on it.'

Hogni Tricksleeve had done the rough work though he couldn't begin to match Hereward's strength at wood-chopping and the like. Gladly he gave up the axe. 'Take me with ye when ye go!'

'Who said I was going?'

Hogni looked sage. He said, 'You will!'

Hereward could have wrung his neck for a thought-reader. So he took up the plough and tilled the earth. He set the crop and sowed both vegetables and herbs. But when Imbolg drew near, he said to Muirgheal, 'I go tomorrow.'

She had been singing that morning whilst milking the red-eared cow, sweet as the birds on Lough Swilly. She set the pail down. Hereward drank in the looks of her, the dark flowers and honey of her hair and mouth.

'So be it,' she whispered.

'I keep to thinking of all the years before we met. Seems funny, but I cannot bring to mind life without ye.'

'Hereward!' Muirgheal said softly. 'Cara!'

'We have been happy together, have we not?'

Muirgheal nodded. 'There has neither been mine nor thine and I've lain as a silver branch in your arms.'

307

'And will do again,' Hereward said. 'Would you ever marry me, Muirgheal?'

She gave the same reply as always: 'Nay, I would not.'

Blathnad wept that he should go again and Hogni Tricksleeve took it ill that he should not follow. But Hereward would be burdened with no company other than his own.

At Baile Atha Cliath a ship was waiting. King Dairmaid asked Hereward of his plan to which he replied that he had none.

'Padraig tells me that you have a wife and a child – a daughter. Padraig's a lonely man since his sweetheart died before their wedding day. He envies ye!'

Hereward sighed and said, 'And I'm wondering if I'm being all sorts of a fool to leave them.'

Whereupon King Dairmaid clasped Hereward's forearms and said, 'By the Oak of Mughna! If you're the man I think ye to be – what else could ye have done? *Go dtéir slán abhaile!*'

A Glut of Crows

hen Countess Godgyfu sought sanctuary at Croyland Abbey, brought there from the fall of Coventry by Lilla with a single sumpter-mule bearing all their worldly goods, she found Wynter already there.

But the Wynter she knew of the fair and open face, the gentle-hearted, was no more. And Darryl, who came in shortly after, his face a puckered up mass of bad scars, cared no longer that his shirt should lack silk or his wrist a gold clasp.

Hwita Clatter-Clogs came also, from whence no man knew, missing an ear and a hand, but with a cap of rushes on his head and a new harp of magic blackthorn wood on his shoulder.

Wynter had an axe, a small axe, ivory bound, which he was wont to talk to and pat as a living thing. With it he had killed five of the rapists on that fateful day and he kept it ever by him, stuffed in his belt or under his straw bolster, ever at the ready.

With his son Pery given into the keeping of the monks, he became quiet and took to going off by himself and bringing back news and tales and occasionally blood on his axe blade, which he never cleaned save to christen it again. 'Little-Bethlehem-of-the-Rushes is given to a Flemish kitchen hand – a favour of the Bastard himself for a well-cooked dish of eel-pout!'

'This will be next,' said Abbot Ulfketyl of Croyland. And Countess Godgyfu, her bed Leofric's grave-slab, heard him in dread.

Thus England had been half-subjected when William saw fit to send for Matilda and have her crowned in Winchester.

Greedy for the sight of her new kingdom, Matilda leaned from her litter, seeing fields and villages and orchards by the score – and gibbets. 'That is the tenth we have passed! Eh, the stink!'

And the captain of the men-at-arms answered 'Ma'am, they steal the game from the woods and the fish from the streams and say that they were always there to be taken by any man!'

'Then the lands must be closed off!'

'They say the lands are theirs – held from God and the sun!'

'Theirs?' Matilda said behind her handkerchief. 'All the land belongs to my lord the King!'

Vast areas had already been confiscated for the hunting chases of the King and his barons. He had the right of all hare hunting, the wild honey of the woods, the fowl of the forests, hawk, falcons, herons and eagles. Venison – the deer, roebuck and boar; all these were then the privilege of the King. And with the crippling fines and taxes and the constant seizure of lands, money was pouring into the treasury at Winchester . . .

'Is it not wonderful, Mald? Look at it – feel it!'

Matilda, crowned and anointed, clung to William's arm in the chamber and gazed on the plunder-store. The door was shut behind them, axe-shaft thick.

'It will grow, Mald! Like the tree my mother dreamt sprang from her womb before I was born.'

And strange it was, after Matilda had feasted her eyes and her senses, the very mass of it all seemed somehow weird and oppressive. Glancing up she saw William watching her.

'Are the mercenaries to be paid from this?' she said. 'Your knights and vavasours?'

'No. There's enough from the taxes as yet to keep them satisfied, as well as what they get for themselves.'

'Have your seigneurs seen this place?'

'No!'

'Not even Odo?'

'*Mort de ma vie!*' said William. 'Never Odo.'

'He must be curious – yes? They all must.'

'A plague of God on their curiosity! No man has leave to come here save me. This key,' and he fingered the iron tool, 'is fettered to my belt always. All this is mine!'

'Ours?' whispered Matilda.

Whereat William, whose dark brows had begun to beetle together and to glower, laughed. Thus riding high on his good humour, Matilda plucked up a carved box and, opening it, found strings of blue and brown topazes and grass-green emeralds.

310

'They were got from Nazeing,' said William. 'The estate yielded rich. They belonged to the Godwinesson's Swan-Neck.'

Matilda could not but gasp at the size of some of the stones. She wanted them and William gave them to her.

Later, in bed, the curtains drawn, Matilda said, 'Those sons of Aelfgar and Waltheof, son of Siward – you should not let them be alone together so much lest they plot treachery.'

'What do you suggest?' William looked down into her face. 'That I keep them in a cage?'

'Isn't that what you are planning to do with Wulfnoth Godwinesson?'

'Perhaps.'

'Or find them wives?'

'Now who plots?'

Matilda smiled. 'You have a niece – your sister's daughter. Bedworthy soon. And what of our daughters?'

'I'd thought of Alan la Roux for one.'

'Then what of the others?'

What of them? Another three – and their sons Robert and Richard and William, tagged the Rufus. Thrusting, ever wanting, their voices were growing raucous-loud. He had settled much land on his own bastard son and made provision for Matilda's daughter – marriage to a wealthy noble.

But Matilda was chuckling against his shoulder then and when William demanded to know the jest, she said, 'I was just thinking of Roger de Montgomeri and those haute sires of Bigod and Ferrers and de Clare and that Ralph of Tosny who boils the heads of Infidels – when they find one of those mettlesome young Saxons your son-in-law and neighbour!'

William wanted to laugh also at those dread, rapacious barons stopped in their tracks – yet he could not. For though he would admit it to no living soul he had begun to fear them. True, Gilbert de Heugleville had refused the estates offered him belonging of many dead thanes and sokemen, and sore-smitten by conscience, returned home. Hugh de Grandmesnil and Humfrey of Tilleul looked set to follow his example, sickening of the endless horror. But they were but a few. The rest would slaver and swallow their leavings as dogs with fresh-cast vomit. Drenched with blood and drunk with pillage, they had already smashed down the very civilisation they had envied and lusted to covet. More and more land was required to please them, more taxes, more gold . . .

311

But he, William, had to have them or else he could not survive. As he had to have castles ever a-building and guards and mercenaries, no matter what the cost. Yards of steel between himself and the darkness, else there would be no sleep of nights . . .

The Warrior of the Elves

wita Clatter-Clogs tapped at the low hidden door of the hut on Hart's-Booze. And upon opening it, Old Wor-Will-Be-So said, 'What's to do?'

'There's a man abroad this night.'

'A man?'

'Aye, I've followed him – though he's on horseback he's riding slow – across fen and through thicket.' Hwita held his clogs in his one hand. 'The stink of the gibbets draw him. He stopped at each one from Holbeach to Bourne-by-Holy-Brook. And after the fifth he spewed up in a hedge.'

'How does he look?'

'Green now, I'll wager! But there's no moon and he's wearing a hood. I couldn't tell ye – yet 'twas strange, for he knew how to cross the Witch's Ladder. And he's been to Bambweare – to Aethelmaer the blacksmith's old place.'

'I'll be buggered!'

'What d'you think of it?'

'Where is he?'

'At Wyntering.'

'But there's nowt there!'

'I last saw him sitting among the broken timbers and weeds – and he was weeping.'

And so they sat and waited with but a stub of a grease candle, until there was a movement outside and a tap on the door. Then Old Wor-Will-Be-So heard himself called by name.

'Who are ye that knows me?'

'I am Hereward,' came the reply, 'Leofric's son!'

Hwita Clatter-Clogs crossed himself. Old Wor said, 'Be gone, liar! Bog-fiend! Hereward is dead!'

''Tis me, I tell ye!' the voice from without pleaded. 'Didn't I always

313

want ye to make me handsome? Didn't I eat pluck-pie and listen to your tales? O, whistle me the battle song of Ashingdon!'

Thus it was with a shaky hand that Old Wor-Will-Be-So pulled open the door, and saw a man stoop low, taking down his hood.

'Laws-a-massy-me!' said Hwita Clatter-Clogs.

'Thunder and giblets!' said Old Wor.

And as Hereward came into the hut, wedging his shoulders between the posts, the two of them backed away into the corner. Then Old Wor, always a one with his wits about him, said with a flash of cunning, 'If you be him – and not a bogy out the water – let us see you open these!' And Old Wor pointed to the chest guarded with nine locks. 'If you be him they'll open in your hands sweet like the seed pods of Broken Hearts!'

Hereward saw the chest and went to it. 'Father!' he said softly, 'O, father! 'Tis me! Me that's your son! Hereward!'

And as he spoke those words a stirring began within the chest, rising to a great sighing, wailing clamour. Thus he unfastened the locks easily until all nine of them lay upon the ground. And both Old Wor and Hwita took cover as Hereward raised the lid, and saw his face and arms to be glowing with the rainbow radiance of the golden work of the elves that twisted and coiled and cried and reached for him. Then suddenly the radiance dulled and the wailing quieted to a whisper, and Hereward lifted the war-coat out, holding it in his arms. It lay meek and wondrous beautiful. It knew him.

Old Wor-Will-Be-So whispered, 'O, Hereward! Are ye risen and come back, dear heart?'

Whereupon Hereward clapped the old spell-working hands on the muscles of his arm: 'I'm alive, bor!' he said. 'Feel me!'

Old Wor was like to drop then and had to sit down on his log stool, leaving Hwita Clatter-Clogs to tell Hereward of all that had happened. Of Wynter and his young wife, of Aethelmaer – 'I saw him fall by the King! I was there!' And tears poured down Hwita's cheek.

And Hereward, squatting, burning up and stunned and sick, saw Hwita's hand go to the hole at the side of his head. His other arm ended in but a red stump.

'Mary, Mother of God!' said Hereward.

Old Wor reached out a gnarled hand and touched Hereward's face wonderingly. 'Ah lad, lad – how we have longed for ye!'

Mopping his tears, Hwita said, 'Why for have ye come?'

'To rid my house of a pestilence!'

'There's too many,' said Hwita. 'Let me come!'

314

'Nay,' said Hereward. 'I go alone.'

'He thinks we'd be useless buggers dragging on him,' said Old Wor.

'Then let us put the coat on ye!' cried Hwita Clatter-Clogs. 'Let it cover your back. Let us buckle it!'

And so Hereward did. And it clothed him, clinging to him, hugging him, cleaving to shoulder and armpit and chest.

''Tis a close fit. You're bigger than your father, more like your grandfather,' said Old Wor.

And where it lacked inches it began to drop more rings, dozens of them, pure gold, broadening, lengthening, until it reached his knees, the metal warm and supple and murmurous, and the hands of Old Wor and Hwita were a-tingle to the fingertips where they touched its rainbow fire.

Thus did the power of the elves come upon Hereward from that time on. The rest would be legend . . .

Wynter's little axe was growing thirsty. It told him so, moving restlessly in his grip. So he left the monks of Croyland at their labours and slipped off into the Fens. As usual his wanderings brought him to the lands about the Hall of Little-Bethlehem-of-the-Rushes. And there among the purple willows he'd crouch and watch and wait.

And that night whilst on his lonely vigil, his keen ears picked up the sound of footfalls crossing the causeway. Some Norman lost his bearings? It had to be. Like as not one of those belonging to Tallebois the Bloody-Hand at Spalding. No Englishman was allowed out after dark. Wynter hastily shoved his little axe in his jerkin lest by shrieking for her supper she spoiled the surprise . . .

The causeway was still as Hereward remembered it, spanning Witch-Water, the vast reed-ronds whispering softly, the stars filling the sky without end. Then, suddenly, a movement was behind him and an arm round his throat, squeezing the breath from him. Hereward jabbed his elbows back into his attacker's belly, but the man had him fast. Hereward then strove to break the hold by sheer strength, and doing so, he hauled the man over his shoulder and fell on him. He saw the wicked winking of an axe blade and they fought for it, Hereward getting the upper hand, overpowering, forcing submission. Then he saw the face of the man beneath him.

'Wynter! Christ Almighty! Don't ye know me?' Hereward's cloak was off and his golden armour aflame. Panting, the spittle running down his chin, he watched the grasp of truth come into his kinsman's eyes.

'It can't be,' Wynter kept saying, 'I was going to kill you!'

'Ah, and bloody well nearly did!'

Then, just as suddenly, Wynter began to cry, and Hereward flung his arms round him and they clung tightly together like two boys.

Afterwards Wynter told a broken tale, most of which Hereward already knew. 'We sang masses for your soul!' said Wynter, drying his eyes on a dirty sleeve.

And Hereward was obliged to do his own bit of explaining. Wynter heard him in silence, unquestioning. But not once did he let go of Hereward's hand.

'You've a mind to do something, bor?'

Hereward jerked his head. 'How many are there in my father's Hall?'

'A score, maybe.'

'If there was ten score of 'em, would ye be willing?'

And Wynter was on his feet, axe in hand, a smile on his mouth. 'You ask me that?' he said.

Hogni's Lay

Not all the elves have fled the Hall at the coming of the foreign strangers!' said Hogni Tricksleeve to Blathnad.

'How do you know?' asked Blathnad.

Whereat Hogni winked and rubbed his nose. 'I can see! Haven't I always told 'ee Hogni Tricksleeve sees everything!'

Blathnad plaited the fringe of her smock, looking up at Hogni and wondering. 'And what have they done?' she said.

Hogni grinned. 'Why, they've told the rain elves who tap on the window-panes how their home has been taken. How the beautiful tapestries have been torn down and the house-place looted and despoiled.

'And to the water elves who sail in eggshells across the mere and to the flying elves who venture through key-holes how a fat black-bearded cook sits in the high-seat of Leofric! How the so-called knights, sweepings of the Flemish and Norman kennels, wine running from their noses and mouths, carouse on the benches with their camp-followers, dirty snaggle-toothed whores be-decked in shabby, reeking finery, where once Rudgang Wolf-Cloak and the hus-carls whiled away the night a-telling of the old sagas . . .' Hogni nodded and sighed. ''Tis a sad time for Elf-Folk, for they needs must steal or go hungry, for there are no crumbs left to 'em nor a knob of butter, nor yet even a sup of sweet mead!'

Later, Hogni gathered thorn-apples. Already grown giddy from smelling the flowers, he burnt the lot and mixed them with myrtle, henbane and rue and deadly nightshade.

And it seemed to him that he saw the Hall of Little-Bethlehem-of-the-Rushes and the foreign strangers within, lying sprawled in their cups, when suddenly the door was kicked open wide and sent clanging back on its iron hinges, and a man — nay, two — but the first over the threshold was a wondrous sight in a coat of gold rings that blazed as

317

the noonday sun as he stood a moment, outlined against the dark of the sky.

Now Hogni was apt to be a bit hazy as to what happened next, but he heard the first man – whose jib and brawn there was no mistaking – yell, 'Awake! Awake!' until the timbers rattled and the harlots in their gaudery rags ran screaming.

And Hereward, slamming the door shut behind the fleeing women, stood with his back against it. Black bile rose in his throat at what he saw until it almost choked him and the rage sang in his ears.

'Awake!' he yelled again, throwing back his head as on a howl. Wynter was beside him. He laughed and spat on his axe-blade.

The men were stumbling this way and that, most of them too drunk to stand. In terror they sought to smash glass goblets to use as weapons, fumbling among greasy table leavings for knives, groping in search of armour with foul oaths and curses.

Then, with both hands on the hilt, Hereward swung sword Brain-Biter and brought it down on the head of the nearest man, splitting him open from brain-pan to breast-bone. A blow which Hwita Clatter-Clogs, having followed to peer through the crack in the door, his knees gone to jelly, grubby fingers stuffed in his mouth, was to sing of for ever after.

Beholding his first kill, Hereward was shaking from head to toe but the great rush of blood steadied him. He tasted it as it splashed upon him, smelt it, was near blinded by it. The debt was being repaid. It felt good. And the wounding-wand, with joyous shuddering, leapt to do his will.

Wynter, with axe and knife, slew swiftly, throat-slitting with ease, and soon the walls and the floor-rushes were dewed thick with gore.

With a sweet, rancid smoke in his nostrils and mouth, Hogni Tricksleeve gazed in wonder through a clearing fog as Hereward, hewing like a berserker, teeth clenched, laid low the Flemish cook who sought to contest him.

And keep quiet Hogni could not. 'Look 'ee!' he cried, throwing down his cap and dancing on it. 'There goes the bugger's head! Both arms gone! O, lordy me! O, Hereward, lad! Ye've come home! Ah, dear to goodness!' And he fell flat on his face on the ground.

Those few candles still burning gave a soft glow to the place of slaughter. Hereward and Wynter looked at each other, both pale, outwardly calm, but with furious hammering pulses and racing hearts.

'What now?' Wynter spoke first.

'Wash our blades,' Hereward answered him.

And it was kneeling by mere Witch-Water that the remembrance of the dream came to him. The old dream. The dream of a boy long ago in a summer of bean-flowers and water-lilies. His dream. And now he was that man grown. The man who scrubbed gouts of blood from iron with his hands. He was the Lord of Little-Bethlehem-of-the-Rushes.

Wynter bent close to him then and said, 'All my skeps are bare, but there's a swarm of bees in the old wych-elm yonder. I must make haste now, lad, to tell them that the Master is come!'

The Water Awakens

I f these lands are in revolt as you say, why do you stand whole before me? Why have you no wounds?' Thus said William the Norman to his birds of prey gathered before him. They wore dead men's armour and carried dead men's swords. They lived in dead men's houses and ate dead men's food. They were by name Drogo de Beuviere and Ivo Tallebois of Spalding and Sir Robert of Deeping and Raoul de Dol and Sir Ascelin, whilom of St Valery, a nephew of Abbot Torauld of Malmesbury. They thought their suzerain to deal harshly with them in their plight.

'We had our wives to think of, lord King. For their sake we were forced to flee!'

Ivo Tallebois had no wife, but when his henchmen had deserted him on hearing the news of the English rising, he had thrown in his lot with Sir Robert of Deeping, not without cramming his saddle-bags and wagon-wain with all he could lay his hands on, and headed for London Town, there to seek help of the King.

William had noticed the amount and quality of the bag and baggage they had managed to escape with. 'You did not leave much behind you, I see!'

They protested in answer that they needs must be clothed and have gold to buy food.

He scorns us for grave-robbers and bone-pickers, thought Ivo Tallebois, casting greedy eyes about the hall wherein they stood. But what is that velvet cloak he wears, clasped with brooches such as I'd give my soul for, but gotten off a corpse's back? Those enormous gold bracelets, and that one of balas-rubies – had not Harold Godwinesson worn them? He is no better than I!

Robert of Deeping was saying, 'They call him Hereward, son of Leofric. They say he has returned from the dead!'

The conflicting rumours whirled in William's brain. God's Heart and Bowels! Did they now believe in ghosts? Fifteen bloody grinning heads stuck on the gables of the hall of Little-Bethlehem-of-the-Rushes! 'Where is he gone, this spirit man?' he demanded.

'He walked into thin air, beau Sire!' said Sir Ascelin.

'They're hiding him!' growled Raoul de Dol. 'He's in some hut or priest house!'

'He was outlawed by them once – now he is their darling!' said Drogo de Beuviere.

Ivo Tallebois girded up his sword belt, gorgeous with silver-work, another acquisition of the battle field, and said with a swagger, 'An army of men, lord King, and we will crush the swine!'

'You had men before. Your own men – each one of you! Where in God's name are they to?'

'They had milk-water for guts, Sire. They ran!'

Drumming brown, heavily-ringed fingers on the arm of his chair, William felt himself to be beset on all sides. His shadow was spat on, the flesh-chewers followed everywhere like blow-flies round a rotting carcass.

'Some men, lord King,' said Ivo Tallebois, 'so we can regain our lands!'

Whereupon William turned on him with sudden anger. 'Confound your lands!' he said. 'Belly of Christ! Cannot you settle your own troubles? Do you expect me to abandon all to chase a will-o'-the-wisp?'

'I tell you that hall of Leofric the Saxon is bewitched!' Robert of Deeping had said to Ivo Tallebois ere they had fled the Fens. 'Men have heard and seen things there!'

'Ah, you are crazy!' Tallebois had scoffed. Yet he thought with no comfort upon the Hall of Little-Bethlehem-of-the-Rushes. There had been talk, stupid talk; elf-haunted, they'd called it. Bunch of half-wits. By the Heart of Christ!

'Would you go there alone – and at night?' Sir Robert had said.

To which Tallebois had answered, 'I'd go nowhere in this accursed land alone, day or night. But I fear not a pack of hobgoblins!'

'Then why not take a stout band of men and lay claim to the hall?' Sir Robert had watched Tallebois narrowly. 'It was always to your taste.'

And so Tallebois had, but was forced to turn back with all his company, when a sudden storm broke over their heads. A storm so mickle that men said it was the work of enchantment.

Shortly after, word came that the North was in uproar and that all

321

the Normans there had been slaughtered and Edgar the Aetheling proclaimed King . . .

And so again, William looked at his birds of prey and said, 'There is war to be waged in the north. You could recover your losses and more in gold from York's coffers.' He needed their kind to quell rebellion. They were already donning helmets with nose-pieces like vultures' beaks, and would not hesitate to hamstring each other's horses in the bid to grab the largest share. 'And then perhaps we will deal with this fen-devil of yours!'

From Croyland to Holbeach where a boat waited, from Baile Atha Cliath to Emhain Abhlach . . .
  And so it was at the doorway of the mud hut that Hereward unstrapped sword Brain-Biter. The same warrior's light was about his head that the monks had beheld at St Guthlac's Minster, and the Irish crewmen also, and King Dairmaid Mael na mbo himself.
  'Like Conn of the Hundred Battles!' said Muirgheal, gazing full upon him in his glowing elf-coat.
  But Hereward only threw himself down in the straw to sleep and said no word for three days.
  Then he rose and bade Hogni Tricksleeve to load their possessions up onto Mare Swallow, and to Muirgheal he turned and said, 'Will ye leave all this for my sake?'
  The herb garden – the sacred woods – the protection of the folk of the Sidhe. 'What of Morrighan and Badbh?' Grey in the muzzle and long of tooth they were then.
  'In a basket they'll be safe enough on Swallow's saddle-bow.'
  To Muirgheal the light about his head had not dimmed. 'You saw your mother?' Hereward nodded.

At Croyland, in the dark chancel, they had faced each other, and the beauty so beloved of Leofric had been wan and wasted, and she staring at him, not able to believe her eyes. 'You?'
  'Aye.'
  'Tell me you are not a dream!'
  'I'm no dream.'
  'But how?'
  'Does it matter? I've cleared the hall this night and Wynter has told the bees.'
  'Hereward! O, Hereward!'

322

And the chancel had echoed with her voice and all the church grims, dark-skinned and misshapen, had scuttled down from their perches to spy . . .

Hereward said to Muirgheal, 'But I could not let her touch me at first, see, for my hands were wet and all over blood!'

Hereward had watched through that night in the chapel with Lilla and young Leofsi and heard Mass celebrated by Abbot Ulfketyl for the first time in many years. And he had sat beneath the bells.

'Guthlac and Bartholomew and Bettelm are the biggest, Turketil and Tatwine in the middle, and there Bega and Pega the little ones!' Wynter had said, sitting athwart the cross-beam, gazing up at the giants of bronze and brass. 'But doubtless you'll remember!' Hereward did.

None of it had changed. But the people – they had changed, every one.

'You must be to them a very great hero,' said Muirgheal.

Hereward had not thought of it that way. But his deed had caused the war-arrow to be split and the bells to ring and the war-horn to sound from dyke to dyke and a stirring to be felt in the ancient barrows of the Tomsaetan.

He was not wearing his war-coat then. It rested in a saddle bag mending its own broken links.

And thus they took the cauldron and the flesh-fork, and with Muirgheal up before him and Blathnad behind and Hogni Tricksleeve trotting alongside, they journeyed forth to the court of King Dairmaid Mac Mael na mbo.

And in that strange place, full of comings and goings, the wood-child Blathnad was shy. She kept close to Muirgheal and smiled at no one, save for the night when she first saw Padraig O'Connor.

323

The Dragon in the Wood

T he Normans, led by their King, marched on York. Driven out, the chief thanes fell back on Durham. Edgar the Aetheling retreated to Scotland. After the plunder of York and the execution of whatever rebels were to be had and the building of a castle on the banks of the Ouse, the army pressed on across the moors towards Durham where a great fog of darkness suddenly fell upon them and they heard Wear roaring in his gorge.

'It is the wrath of St Cuthbert!' cried those bold knights. 'Whoever invades his holy soil does not go unpunished!'

'Palsy, plague and madness! God save us!'

'Ha Rou! Ha Rou! Cowards of dogs!' Odo, then nicknamed the Butcher, yelled after them as by the score they turned and fled.

William sat his horse. He did not give chase. To where and into what? It was impossible to see a hand before the face.

'To be afraid of a Saxon saint dead these three centuries!' scoffed Urse d'Abetot.

William forebore to mention of d'Abetot's own retreat from the gates of Worcester Abbey, where as sheriff he had had the idea of rounding up the Englishmen it harboured behind its sanctuary ropes and sampling for himself the rumoured glory of its chapels – only to be confronted by Bishop Wulfstan on the steps with staff and cow bell.

Ah, yes! But Wulfstan was one of the few then. The Pastor of Souls. And the memory of those steady, hooded eyes was an uncomfortable one. Did he now know he lived on borrowed time? That he lived at all because as King, he, William, was pleased to be merciful? The truth was that the man Wulfstan fascinated him. Why, there was no telling. He wanted to destroy him and so the links with Harold Godwinesson. Yet at the same time he wanted to look at him, to watch him and to listen to the queer, richly-vowelled speech whose words he could not be bothered to learn. William smote his hands then, cursing the cold and the darkness of that wild moor. Eh, he thought, let the Saxons keep their hedge-priest a little longer. Bowels of God, the last thing they had need of was martyrs!

The Lay of the Cunning of the Elves

hen Hereward returned to Little-Bethlehem-of-the-Rushes the Lent lilies were waving in the grass of the field. And within the hall he fancied he saw the handiwork of the elves. Was not the floor swept cleaner? Did not the window panes shine? And on the stairs flowers were strewn – their own flowers; bluebells, clover, primroses and forget-me-nots. And the house-place was full of company though there was not a soul to be seen.

Hereward had brought the war-coat, a mesh of dripping gold, begotten upon itself and healed good as new. The chest with the nine locks had been restored and it stood open and waiting then.

Aware of a hundred pairs of eyes on his back, Hereward laid the coat inside, feeling it sigh to leave him, and shut the lid, snapping the locks. 'Guard it!' he said to the listening rafters, the breathing timber. 'O, keep it for me! Smite down them from my door that would steal it!'

And for a moment – no more than a heartbeat – the ancient black crucks of wood were radiant, living, blossoming magic trees and the hall-space filled with the whirring wings of a host of tiny green fairy birds.

With the fenlands rid of the Normans, for that while at least, men began to come in from the surrounding hidages and beyond, bringing weapons and all of what little they possessed.

And at Croyland Abbot Ulfketyl watched them arrive, sometimes a score in one day, brought hither by Wynter or Darryl, often finding the way by themselves. One specially had won his renown. Wulfric Raher, Wulfric the Heron of Wrokeshame.

And when Hereward saw him, he said, 'I know you!' There was no mistaking the raw bones and long legs.

Wulfric pushed back his cap. 'Sure ye do! The wrestling match in Bragi's Meadow!'

'You spoke for me. Why?' It seemed a thousand moons ago.

'Because I liked the looks of ye!'

Wulfric had saved four brothers from the gibbet on Wrokesham Bridge and slain six Norman guards, hangman and all. But he stroked his long brown bill, the slaying tool, and said, 'Ah, but what's a half dozen of the buggers to your fifteen?' And he smiled till the corners of his wide mouth reached the sides of his long nose.

There were men who had fought in the battles against Haardrada and others who had fought in the Great Battle; sometimes, rarely, in both. Men who had led and been led, who had seen hard fighting and hard discipline. Hereward had them all to him, to listen and learn from them. How things were in Coventry, beyond Charnwood and Ely, Nottingham and Derby.

'The Normans have all the lands – lands that were belonging to your kinsmen Eadwine and Morkere but in truth belong to you!'

'And castles – a swarm of them in Norfolk and Suffolk. In Lincoln and Bedford and Cambridge . . .'

'All over the bloody place!' said Wulfric the Heron, and spat.

''Tis said that the Danes are to bring an army. To seize them the throne for Svein Estrithsson,' said Hwita Clatter-Clogs, recounting news learned as he wandered, lucky to get a mess of water-rats or a bowl of cabbage-water in those days. 'But where they are to is any man's guess!'

Hereward went to and fro between Baile Atha Cliath and Croyland often before ever he brought Muirgheal and Blathnad back with him for good. And when he did it was along with many a man from King Dairmaid's court, chiefest among them being Padraig O'Connor.

It was a wild journey across the sea with a wind sharp as knives and lashing rain. Plentiful were the omens to be read in such weather, but the most dread was sighted off the ship's bow before they were a quarter-way out.

'Mer-women!'

'Come for a life!'

'Lord have mercy on us!'

Hereward could see nothing but the boiling green waves. The sail whipped and smacked on high, while two men wrestled with the massive rudder.

Muirgheal gazed out and said, 'They are there!' Then turning to Hereward, 'Put me over the side that I might deal with them!'

'Buggered you will!' Hereward gripped her wrists. 'What's the matter with all of ye?' he demanded of the men.

But by this time the whole crew was clamouring that they could both see and hear the mer-women.

'They're hanging on the oars!'

'They want their due!'

'Or we're done for!'

Hereward drew sword Brain-Biter, but an old sailor said, 'You'll not be rid of them that way! They'll follow and drown the lot of us if they don't get a man!'

Sitting under an upturned creel, Hogni Tricksleeve said, 'Draw lots!'

And so they did, and Padraig O'Connor was chosen. At this Blathnad sprang up with such a cry that it was agreed to give him a second chance. Thus he was chosen again, and yet a third time – and all aboard were loath to lose his strength and skill and the good nature of him.

Blathnad was become wild with fear and despair and no one had ever seen her thus before. Her shyness gone, she clung to Padraig O'Connor, her cheek crushed against his beating heart.

'Wisha!' he said. 'Wisha, my dove!' And he felt the savage, sweet joy of being able to hold her wet, shaking body in his arms, and to press his mouth to her honeyed hair.

Stunned a moment by the woman he'd glimpsed in his little daughter, Hereward yelled at the others, 'Enough of this! 'Twas a fool's idea to start with! Heathen doings!' And he kicked Hogni so hard that he rolled over, upended in his creel. 'Bloody stupid!'

'Will you sacrifice the lot of us – for one?' the men gave him back in answer.

Padraig O'Connor said, 'I'm willing. But first a boon I ask of ye.' His boon granted, Padraig gave the weeping Blathnad up to Muirgheal and went to the ship's bow. There he began to sing. He had a fine, deep voice and the song was of his ancestors in the ancient Gaelic tongue, the words rich and sad and so old as to be beyond memory. And as he sang it seemed that the wind kept it, not throwing it away, and all on a sudden the men felt the oars to be freed and the ship to shake off a great burden.

Men said that the mer-women must have been well pleased with the looks and sound of Padraig O'Connor. Even the waves were spellbound. And ahead, though a long ways off, the sky was clearing.

'God be praised!' the cry went up.

And so they sailed the rest of the journey in safety.

A Litany of Blood

Why don't you ride against these marsh outlaws with your armies, my lord? Crush them like you have crushed those rebels in the north!' So said Matilda to William in Winchester. In that past year she had conceived and been delivered of another son whom they had called Henry. She had him upon her knee wrapped in swaddling bands, a lenten babe.

William grunted in answer. It was all very well for Mald to talk when venom dripped from the very leaves and hate beat like a hot sun from the sky. Fifteen rotten stinking heads, eyes mortal staring. Only a Flemish cook and his canaille. But their cloven white bones were seen as symbols of defiance. The doings of this one they called Wake. For a Norman to hear that shout was surely to die! By the Holy Face! William paced the floor. At Croyland he was, this son of Leofric, or was he? A cancer to wax upon a wound. Rumour had him here, there and everywhere. All manner of ruffians claimed kinship with him. All manner of deeds were attributed to him. But at Croyland he would be provided with grain and flesh-meat by the monks, the fish of five rivers to be taken by rod or net. He knew the country like the palm of his hand. Some strange kind of charm was spun about him.

'They say he has a sorceress for his mate. A witch with two black fiends in the shape of cats. And a female child – also a witch like her mother.' Matilda had much such gossip to tell. But William had no time for hearsay. Nor did he intend to lead his men into those wild fens where half of them would be swallowed in bogs. He couldn't afford to gamble with their numbers – draff though they were, they cost money to arm and feed. Grab, grab, grabbing. Whining and complaining, no whit different to the churchmen and barons who swelled his councils.

So with his dog-keepers and falconers he went hunting in the Forest of Dean. And news came to him there that a Danish army had landed in Humber mouth, and thus all England north of the Watling Street was in rebellion.

William Malet of Graville-Saint-Honorine, given the Honour of Constable, had been entrusted with the castle at York. In the knowledge that the armies of the Northumbrians and the Norsemen were coming, he had sent his own message to his suzerain.

It was answered in bald terms by a King of not even half a kingdom, telling Malet to hold out in York until the last. Malet was aware of trepidation on the part of his lord and so he made his rejoinder a blithe one.

'He can hold out in York for a year?' growled Odo on hearing the reply. 'God's Heart and Belly! He might as well be sat within walls of paper! If that army numbers great, as reported, they will batter them down ere the week's done!'

Revolts flared from Cornwall to Dorset. Everywhere the Normans were packing as much plunder as they could on wain and sumpter-mules and quitting the country. Many jewels were dropped in their haste, much gold abandoned in the scramble.

'Let them flee!' William shouted at Odo when he brought him news of the flitting. 'Rats! Cullions! Curs! Craven cowards! Their names have been marked well! I will see that they never prosper again!'

But he had the pack. The birds of prey – a hundred of the kidney of Ivo Tallebois. Mercenaries were flocking yet again from the piss-holes and dung hills of the Continent, eager for the double payment promised and unlimited plunder.

In the knowledge that Geoffrey de Mowbray, Bishop of Coutances, had gone to deal with the uprisings in the west country, stripping the south-east of troops to subject Devon and Cornwall, William marched his army north.

Though the Danes, under the leadership of Ashbjorn the Jarl, brother to Svein Estrithsson, had captured York – set ablaze by the routed Normans and all but half-destroyed – they had failed to follow up their victory and hold the city strong. Instead they had gone back to their ships moored off the Island of Axholme in Lindsey, and it was there that William came upon them.

Across the sullen water vulture looked at wolf, and wolf at vulture. The vast dark menace of those Viking ships riding at anchor, serpent-prowed, crimson-sailed, the challenge clear to all who beheld them – William felt it creep into his bones, as a shaft of autumn sunlight struck the brazen masts and the awesome wrought monsters of the night reared and flung back their heads and breathed fire. What would they

331

do? Where would they strike? Bowels of God, how came they into the scheme of things? How much of the plunder-hoard would he have to share with them again and again ere they'd cease to hound him?

Thus, ridden with these woes, William the Norman left men to watch the doom fleet while he moved west to where the Mercians under Eadwine and Morkere, who had fled from Westminster, and aided by the Welsh, had rebelled. There, in hard fighting, he defeated them.

And it was to the hall nearby, strife-torn and loud with weapons, that William Malet, whilom of York, came in unto his lord. The tale he told of York's surrender and capture brought a response that Malet, who thought he knew well his suzerain, upon whose mercy he had thrown himself, could never have foreseen.

Rooted to the spot he felt the full, unbridled fury of William's wrath. He railed, he beat upon table and wall, he swore by God and all the saints in heaven. 'Traitors!' he yelled, striding the breadth of the hall and back. 'Vile dogs of traitors! What bargain did you strike with the Danes to save your miserable skin, eh?'

In vain did Malet protest, pleading the safety of his wife and children, but William was deaf to all but the sound of the kingdom for which he'd sold his soul and slain many countless thousands crashing about his ears.

York lost.

But he had Malet and his wretched band of miscreants. Captains, they called themselves. By the Heart of Christ, they would rue the day their mothers bore them! So as an example to all men he had their hands cut off and their eyes thrust out, and Malet he stripped of honours and flung into prison in irons.

'They must understand,' William said afterwards to Fitz-Baldwin, once the royal physician, grown even fatter then in his land-holdings, and who travelled with the army to administer the religious rites, 'that there is no place for those who fail me.'

And it was in that same week that news came that the Danes were preparing to move once more on York.

The Lay of the Speech of the Runes

ome here! See!' says Hogni Tricksleeve to Hereward. Hogni is excited. Queer, wild-eyed. In the hedge tapers' light his hair is in pull tow-knots and he is trembling.

'What've you been up to?' are Hereward's first words.

'Hush! I've been far!' Hogni is sitting among a clump of many-trunked yews and Hereward squats by him but a bit apart. The yews are greenish-black and darker than the night.

Hereward takes a wheat cake out of his pocket and bites into it. Then he notices Hogni's hands. They are crooked and crabbed and something is moving within their grasp. 'What the bloody hell?' he whispers.

'I've been there!' says Hogni Tricksleeve.

'Where?'

'Hell.'

'How?'

Hogni gives a mirthless grin in answer. Hereward spits out the mouthful he's chewing and shivers. 'You been at those runes again?'

Hogni looks sly. 'They cost me! I won't tell you how much! But I've seen it! O, I know! And I wasn't alone! All the shining chivalry of Normandy was with me! D'you want to see it?'

'Nay!'

And Hogni opens his hands. They are blistered raw, the skin of the palms burnt and peeling. He has the runes. Red and smoking hot, they cry to be told. Cast, they conjure pictures and begin to speak.

It is the Nativity of Christ. The regalia of Kingship has been sent north from Winchester and William wears the royal robes and the crown of England. Where the Danes had boasted to keep their Yule-Tide, he sits in armed and uneasy splendour.

'Eat! Feast yourselves!' he urges his knights and vassals and cuts great slices of roast ox to keep his board. And thus commanded, the

333

liegemen hack at meat and break bread on their platters. The hall of York, though badly charred without by the fires that have raged all about it for the space of days and nights, is miraculously untouched within. And even though its walls are stripped bare of the tapestries, the glory of Saxon weaving and needle-skill, there is still a grandeur in it: rafters set like spear shafts, the high-seat between the twin pillars of monstrous living oak, the carved galleries and the gilded windows.

And blood laps at its doors . . .

'I don't want to see any more!'

And Hereward goes to pull away, but Hogni Tricksleeve holds him fast by the arm, spindly, tough fingers gripping: 'You have to!'

They are afraid, those knights, behind their goblets, stooping to their platters. For they have wrought fearful carnage, the horror of which they will carry to their graves.

'And the angels have locked the gates of hell behind them and the veil of the temple is rent in twain from the top to the bottom!' says Hogni Tricksleeve in Hereward's ear.

There then are the scorched remains of the beautiful church of St Wilfrid – pillaged bare before it burned – and only three walls and half a roof of that holy place are left.

'Look!' says Hogni Tricksleeve.

And Hereward beholds the coming of the knights into that blackened tabernacle, many of them, in chainmail and hauberks, and they throw themselves on the granite flags where once the fabled silver rood had risen over the desecrated altar – and merciful Jesus! Do not those very flagstones beneath their hands and feet begin to bleed?

And when the few who do not flee the place in terror beg the Eucharist is not the bread on the paten suddenly devoured by maggots and the wine become reeking piss?

Now it is snowing.

Death is putting on white weeds. And where a havoc moon mops and mows among the splintered branches of a rotting oak, the incalculable litter of frozen bodies is hid, save for the odd hand or foot upon which perches the carrion crow feasting the Epiphany, and the grey wolf grown bold in his slaughter-search.

'Holy Mary Mother of God!' And Hereward crosses himself.

'No God there!' says Hogni Tricksleeve. And taking up the runes in both hands, and screaming, he falls back . . .

The Plaint of the Jewel

Τhe ice in the streets was frozen blood.

Hugh of Evermue watched his King ride upon it and thought of how on his orders every man and boy of the Saxon race had been slain on the march to York. The mass slaughter continued long after the city had surrendered. And hundreds of villages and farmsteads had been razed to the ground, and all killed within, while without the horses had been houghed, the cattle driven off, the crops trampled and all provender and provisions and ploughs and tools heaped in great piles and burned.

And about him he heard the talk of the knights: 'It is said those of the English left alive dig for roots or eat mice and rats, and I'll wager in time even each other's corpses!'

'The King plans to march on Durham when the year is new. The men grow restless. There is room in their sacks for more plunder yet!'

'Eh, by the Face of Christ! We do not want to spread it about, though! Much of the stuff is too precious for the likes of those swine!'

And January had seen the army split into bands and the same wholesale slaughter begun from York onwards . . .

If he lived to be ninety, Hugh of Evermue thought he would never rid his mouth and nose of the taste and stench of blood. 'Does it not make your gorge rise? Make you afraid?' he said to Sir Ascelin of St Valery.

'Why should it?' came the reply. 'They have only themselves to blame. They defied the King.' His saddle bags and bolsters were crammed with loot. Hugh of Evermue was envious and shamed, angry at his weak stomach. Sir Ascelin looked at him askance. 'You are not going to turn monk, are you?' he said.

There had been reports of knights who had. A spate of vision-seeing. Others crying at their prayers, 'Father, we have sinned against heaven and against thee! And are no more worthy to be called thy sons!'

335

Only the hard glare of gold kept the rest of them sane.

And of the Danes?

They had, they believed, done their task. The venture had brought them little glory and heavy losses – and still the English had been stubborn in their preference for that lack-witted child of the House of the South Saxons. So they had retreated to their ships at the Norman advance and William had bargained with them. A great geld would be theirs if they agreed to go back whence they came.

Watching the transfer of the ransom, Odo said, 'I suppose you know that they will be back. That you haven't seen the last of them.'

It was bitterly cold and a driving sleet blotted out water and sky. But the rampant red of the Danish sails glowed as fire beacons. The witch colour of nightmare.

That had been before Christmas.

Thus by Candle-Mass Day, and in the wake of further devastation, the north had all but surrendered . . .

'They are lying by the roadsides – many are women and they carry dead children in their arms! Surely, Sire, they can do us no harm!' So said a knight come in unto his suzerain in the smoke-filled tent.

Whereupon William gave him answer: 'Spare no one! D'you hear me? Kill them all!'

And later, grown lax with unaccustomed wine – for every man drank his way through those nights to drown out the wind and their own thoughts – William said to any who had half an ear to hear him, 'Did I not intend to rule them fairly? And what chance have they given me? None!' And he ground his teeth against the golden goblet when he thought of how they had thrown open their gates and their hearts and done homage to Harold Godwinesson.

They'd chosen him. That winsome-tongued enchanter – who had tricked them into believing that he, William of Normandy, was their enemy. Harold Godwinesson, whom they still persisted in calling Lord and King.

'Well, Sire, they have shed the last of their blood!' said Urse d'Abetot, standing at his suzerain's side in the bleak light of dawn. 'There are no more males of begetting age left!'

And as William surveyed the vast, thunderous desolation from the keep of Durham castle, the last fugitives were being hunted down. As a people they had been obliterated. Wiped clean from the face of the earth.

*   *   *

336

Then, with his army, William turned south-west, crossing the Pennines in the freezing teeth of the month of February. Chester was his goal, where rebel bands still defied him under the leadership of both Eadwine Aelfgarsson and the Welsh Kings.

The sheer hell of the march had many of the mercenaries – even the hardiest and greediest – praying to be dismissed, to go home. Slaying an almost unarmed land-folk they could face. But the snow that had turned to ice-rain, swelling the rivers to torrents and turning the lower peat slopes into bogs, the huge wind-haunted forests and the black gorges they could not stomach. They could not go on. They would not. William swore at them, spat on them, abandoned them. Though they had so thoroughly massacred the population of the shires they had overrun, here they were breaking new ground and came under attack from hill and wood dwellers who set on them with axes and bill-hooks and rolled great boulders down upon their heads from the limestone crags.

Thus, William left scores to their fate. He at last engaged the mixed English and Welsh forces in a string of battles about Chester, and finally overcame them, putting an end to them. But half of his army died there also from wounds and exhaustion, and unable to capture and hang the rebel leaders, who had fled back over the Welsh border through the Pass of Mold, William strengthened the walls of the city and burned the surrounding villages for many miles.

And with the choicest loot, chief among it the shrine of gold and precious jewels from the smoking ruins of the church of Beverley and the gospel book of St Wilfrid in its box of gold, and accompanied by a pack of barons, William made for Salisbury and thence to Winchester, there to hold Easter and in a fit of magnanimity to invest Aubrey de Courcy with the lands of Northumbria.

Northumbria, thought de Courcy. Bowels of God! A graveyard. A place heaped with rotting carcasses. What can I get from it? What will it yield me? 'I marked you well,' the King had said, and de Courcy had shown the expected gratitude.

But to that vile glutton Hugh the Fat, Vicomte d'Avaranche, father-in-law to Robert of Mortain and newly arrived in England, had gone the rich barony of Chester. And the rebels Gospatric and Waltheof Siwardsson, a berserker in battle yet wanting of counsel when he had no axe to hand, had done homage in return for rewards.

Upon the heels of the butchery throughout the north came famine and pestilence. Nothing lived. Nothing moved.

What de Courcy would have given, as he ventured there a year later, just to hear a bird sing. The land, once good, giving land, was black and useless, the pools and streams fouled by decaying bodies. The highways and hollows, the fertile places, were acres of sour soil and mouldering humanity, piled with bones and skeletons and rags.

Only the outlines were left of what were once large prospering settlements and farms and cornfields. Whole villages and churches had disappeared without trace. And the shires from the Trent to the Tyne and beyond were one Godforsaken, barren, stinking wilderness. 'Reduced to desert by the malice, slaughter and harryings of evil men,' wrote the chronicler, quoting Job. 'From generation to generation it shall lie waste. None shall pass through it for ever and ever.'

The Subjection of the Dove

ooden staff, wooden staff, I am old, thought Bishop Wulfstan at five and sixty, clutching his gnarled wand of lime. The inner fire was all but burned out of him, leaving his face pale and drawn, his dim-sighted eyes failed to near blindness. Though he had Cwichelm the Child-Master – much loved and needed – Wulfstan missed Ealdfrith, his mass-thane, sorely still. It had been as the losing of his right hand.

And when I die or am removed from here as well I may be, what will become of my sheep?

William the Norman had requested his presence in London Town twice since his coronation and both those times the monks of Worcester had watched their beloved Bishop leave in dread, sure they would never see him again. But he had returned. Though how long it would continue to be thus was any man's guess.

Lighting candles for Harold Godwinesson in the chapel shrine, Wulfstan dwelt in an amber past. But without in the cold light of day the future was as a shapeless monster in the womb of time.

The worldling Stigand had been deposed and Lanfranc the Pavian lately brought over to be consecrated Archbishop of Canterbury. And between them, he and William were ridding the churches of their English bishops and abbots and priors and monks, and replacing them with Normans. And one by one the ancient foundations were being looted, then pulled down or razed by fire. The books suffered. The chronicles and the lunar almanacs, the gospels and the flower-painted bibles and the collections of poems and the passions, and the psalters and the gorgeous illuminated manuscripts as whole libraries were burned. As religious overlord Lanfranc sanctioned and supervised the wholesale destruction. The magnificent altar goods he kept confiscate, but not their writings – the continuance of hand and brain and will. He let the wind blow their words away.

O, how Lanfranc hated dealing with the English clergy. They would not speak Norman-French and the intricacies of the Saxon language were beyond him. He besought the King. He besought the Holy Father in Rome who had caused him to be promoted to the illustrious See. They wished the fruits but could give no help to communicate with these taciturn, hostile, blue-eyed men.

In many communities the Norman masters were already making their presence felt with a vengeance. And Lanfranc himself, bewildered and frustrated by the ancient and varied observances of the English churches, had seen to it personally that dozens of their native saints with their unpronounceable names were struck from the calendar.

At Glastonbury, richest of all the houses, the Abbot of Caen had been defied by the monks when he tried to change the old ceremonies to those of Normandy and replace the Gregorian Chant with that of Dijon. They had armed themselves with church furniture and taken refuge before the altar where they had been shot down by Norman men-at-arms from the gallery. The Abbot had been hastily returned to Caen forthwith.

Everywhere new foundations were springing up, ruled and run by aliens, their only aim being to drain wealth from England and send it back to Normandy. The barons had made merry with their vast stolen estates, giving away great chunks of land to Continental houses.

But the great fenland Minsters of Ely and Croyland remained free, though French clergy were within Peterborough, and news came to them there of the ruin of the north and the failure of the Danes to take York for Svein Estrithsson. Hundreds of fugitives arrived broken and spent, with only the rags they stood up in. Many had wives and children, a few had money and weapons which they had risked life and limb to bring hither, and each had their own tale of horror to tell.

One of them was Morkere Aelfgarsson.

By this time Croyland was bursting at the seams with a gathering of men greater than any in England. 'An army!' said Morkere as he beheld them.

'Aye, we're all of us soldiers of God here, bor!' Wynter answered him, reverently stroking his little chuckling axe.

Morkere had not believed in the tales of such a place and yet there he was. Then all that he had heard was true. Of the night raids, of the heads spiked on gables, of the hoards of grain and salted meat distributed among the local people where they hungered. Of how these raiders with seax and hand-axe in their belts seemed to rise up out of the water or drop from the clouds, falling upon the enemy, slaughtering swiftly.

And the net of fear was spreading wider until no Norman felt his life to be safe. And so the fenmen said that when the birds – gull and sea-mew, swan and wild duck and heron, and swallow-kite and starling – rose from the meres to fill the boundless skies at sunrise and sunset, they gave forth with one voice the cry of A Wake! A Wake!

'You are taking me to my kinsman?' said Morkere to Wynter.

'Who else?'

And passing through the Stranger's Hall and thence to Abbot Ulfketyl's lodging, Morkere beheld a heavy shouldered, rough-featured, blond-bearded man turn round from the peat fire.

'You don't know me, but I am your brother's son.' And thus saying, Morkere knelt and put his hands between Hereward's own.

A Joy of Wild Asses

Beyond the fruiting apple and pear trees the birds of prey waited. Beyond the yard-lands of corn they prowled and circled, chief among them Urse d'Abetot, returned from the harrying of the north bloody and lustful for the fair soke of Worcester. And as ever only the presence of Bishop Wulfstan held him back. The monks took strength from this and were filled with fear if their Bishop were to hint that one day it might not always be so.

And to King William at Old Sarum, where he was paying off the mercenaries or rewarding them with the glut of forfeited lands, Urse d'Abetot said, 'Your leave, beau Sire, to clean out the Saxon wasp-nest at Worcester. They plot treason and now give shelter to northern rebels!'

Suddenly a bold, rude voice broke in: 'You talk of a wasp-nest? Eh, Bones of Christ! A paltry abbey when the east country is fallen to this Wake!' It was Ivo Tallebois who spoke. A desperate man, grim with weapons. 'Never will you be able to call yourself King, Sire. Not while he lives!'

'God's Belly!' William smote his knee with a ringed fist. 'What does he know of warfare? The arts of fighting? Nothing! How many campaigns has he led? How many battles has he won? None!'

'He is learning, Sire – and quick! He has gut-cunning and the strength of three men. Hundreds are flocking to him!'

'Where?'

'Cruland,' said Ivo Tallebois.

'Croyland,' amended Abbot Torauld of Fecamp, whilom of Malmesbury, who lusted for the gold of Peterborough. Tallebois threw that sleek priest a look of fire, then said, 'And so many there that it is said even those fat lands cannot support them and they cast about for another place!'

342

William listened and gave thought. Perhaps it was not so bad as he had feared after all – not for the time being. For was there not a saying that a bird in the hand was worth two in the bush? Well, he had two such birds – fine feathered cock-birds in his hand and the biggest and most splendid of them would surely prove to be the undoing of the rest.

And it was the bishop of Durham, Aethelwine by name, who came in sad case to Croyland with the news of just how great the undoing would be. He had fled from the city as it had yielded to the Normans, bearing the Lindisfarne Gospels. He said, 'Gospatric Snow and Waltheof Siwardsson have gone over to the Norman. And Waltheof Lack-Counsel – may God's judgement be upon him! – has married with the kinswoman of William Bastard and been granted not only his own lands but those of Cambridge and Lincoln – here – this very earth on which we stand!'

'These lands are mine,' said Hereward, 'as they were my father's before me!'

And Morkere, joined then by Eadwine, lost and woebegone, made no protest.

Wrapped in pole-cat skins amidst heavy bed curtains, Abbot Brand wrung together his frail hands and said, 'The Norman's aim is to set you against each other! An old trick! The men of Northumbria will stick to Waltheof as will those of York and Lindsey.'

Hereward had ridden by the ancient causeway to Peterborough. With him was Young Leofsi, his monk's habit trussed up past his knees and a leather coat over all. Time was of the essence then for the days and nights were taken up in moving weapons and men from Croyland to Ely, which had been mooted as the new camp of refuge. Hereward said, 'And here?'

'Who knows?' whispered the Abbot.

'Uncle, O, uncle . . .'

There was a movement and Prior Herluin came in. 'Ever haunting the passages, he slipped betwixt door and jamb like a hooded crow. Hereward swung round and was on his feet. 'A pretty scene!' said the churchman softly. 'The outlaw and his harbourer! When Abbot Torauld comes here to take his rightful place things will be different!'

Hereward looked long and hard on the taut, clever French face of Herluin. He said, 'He shall not enter these gates!'

'And who is to stop him?'

'Me!'

'You would not dare!'

'Would I not?' And Hereward laid a grip on sword Brain-Biter, heedless of Abbot Brand's hand on his arm, weakly restraining. 'I'll burn it over his bloody head and the heads of all his bloody Frenchmen!'

Bishop Odo sat and listened to the woes of Tallebois and his like. In his malice it pleased him that it should be so. But William was grown swollen-headed of late with his success, trapping Waltheof, ousting the sons of Aelfgar, flattening the north so that it would lie cannibalised and destitute for five score years hence. Luck had been on his side. But Odo had heard a rumour, a whisper: 'You have thought of everything, it seems. But had you planned on the Danes as well?'

Whereupon William turned, narrowing his eyes, and said, 'They are gone!'

'Are they?' said Odo the Concubine-Keeper. 'I wonder!'

Thus when Abbot Brand died in that winter and Torauld the Norman set forth to take Peterborough, Hereward sent him warning of what would befall him if he tried.

Odo, safe in his Kentish fortunes, could afford to laugh. 'The Englishman threatens that if our revered Abbot rides a mile from Lincoln town he shall walk back to it barefoot and in his shirt!'

So Torauld stayed in Lincoln, a thwarted and unforgiving man. Then came the news that set the Whitsuntide court by the ears. The Danes were returning. To raid the coast. To pillage. 'To get them your throne!' said Robert of Mortain to William. 'Svein Estrithsson is at their head and calls himself King of England already!'

Ely, the Sacred Isle, sanctuary of St Aethelthryth, sometimes also called the Isle of Poppies or the Isle of the Flowers of the Moon, was the place where the waters of three rivers met the Great White Lake – the Way of Angels – and the ships that rode the Ouse and the Nene and the Cam to converge there were past counting.

Svein Estrithsson had come to redeem, and, if needs be, to conquer – but what had he found? His brother Ashbjorn the Jarl moored off the east coast after allowing an upstart Bastard to buy him off with baubles.

'Why did you not take and hold York while you had the chance?' he had railed. 'Selling my kingdom for sod pottage!' And what was there left of York except black ruins? Or indeed of anything from the

344

Humber to the Tees – all was reeking and destitute. He had hoped to raise an army but all the men he had seen were dead.

Whereat Ashbjorn had answered him sullenly that the English were not to be trusted.

And Svein Estrithsson wondered if it would be so of the man who rode out to meet his ships on an ugly lean grey mare, with a gathering of land-folk behind him.

The King of Denmark faced Hereward across the cabin table. Sun streamed through the walrus-hide ship-ropes, latticing the boards. 'Would you have been for me, Hereward Leofricsson, if things had been different?'

Hereward answered, 'But they were not. So what matter now?'

King Svein sighed, thinking of the enormous cost of this venture, of how he had bragged of what he would accomplish. 'My men are in a dangerous mood. They expected much fighting – much gold to fall to their lot. Now we do not even have enough food to go round!'

'There is no gold left,' said Hereward.

'How am I to tell them that? They think to plunder Croyland!'

The blood drained from Hereward's face and his eyes flashed. 'Nay – not Croyland!' Muirgheal was there, Blathnad, his mother, Abbot Ulfketyl, and the monks who had given all to them, succour and shelter, throughout those bleak, desperate months. Hereward got up and paced the floor, then turning, he said, 'Croyland can supply you with food, my lord – you'll not want. But the wrath of St Guthlac will be on the first man who breaks his peace!'

'Wrath?' said Svein uneasily, and began to trace patterns with his knife. But looking up he saw that Hereward was smiling. 'A jest comes to you at such a time?'

'I am thinking of Peterborough.'

Abbot Brand the good shepherd was there no longer – but Herluin was. The Hoody One. Sitting on the fabled Borough of Riches awaiting Torauld like a hound awaiting his master, with his ever-increasing band of French monks in support. Hereward said, 'My father endowed Peterborough and as Earl of Mercia I surrender it up. Tell your men, my lord, that they shall have their gold. Their just reward!'

'The Minster sacked? Burned?' said Countess Godgyfu. 'And Hereward a party to it?'

Ywar the Churchwarden said, 'He was one of the leaders, ma'am!' And the events that befell on the fourth day of the Nones of June were

345

related, to the Countess's horror. Of the great fleet that had descended on Peterborough by way of Ramsay and Ugg and Whittlesey, surging across Trundle Mere and through Cotinglade by the Great West Water in a blaze of gaudy diamond-patterned sails and a thunder of drums. Of the looting and despoiling of the church. Of the loading of St Peter's golden pence onto the Danish ships. Of the shrines and crosses of silver and gems. The candelabra and images of the saints. Of altar-cloths, croziers, dorsals and bells . . .

'And the monks?'

'No harm was done them.'

'God be praised!'

'But Herluin the Frenchman was in a rare taking!'

Ywar's ordeal had not been so bad, for Hereward the elf-begotten had made sure that the brethren were safe, though true, the huge Jarl Ashbjorn and his marshals – men of Jomsburg and Orkney and Viking Waterford – had been hard-pressed to control the sheepskin-clad Jutlanders and heathen Letts and Finns who made up the bulk of the crews. Ywar could afford to be thankful that he was alive and in one piece.

He and most of the remaining English brothers had gathered up what gospels, mass-robes and cassocks they could carry and escaped on rush-rafts. Ah but the war-song of the Danes – the Yuch-hey-saa-saa! – was something he would never forget!

And Herluin, bringing out the gold box containing the filings of St Peter's own chains and many more relics besides – after he had hidden what treasures he could in the steeple – called for the Hand of the Lord to strike down the ungodly and a curse of Heaven upon Hereward Leofricsson, the Robber of Saints!

So the Abbey had burned and when Torauld of Fecamp came thither to lay claim to what was left, upon beholding the gaping, smoke-blackened walls and broken tabernacle-work, he demanded the excommunication of all those who had committed the foul and Satanic deed.

Meanwhile, the Danes, shorn of their hopes of conquest, but with ships well-laden, had since quit Ely, leaving England for once and all. But on the eve before they sailed there was a feast held in the great hall of St Aethelthryth.

Padraig O'Connor sat among the company, here and there being able to grasp the meaning of the words. Hereward always spoke with him in Gaelige. But folk had been kind, making him and his fellow

Irishmen welcome. And Blathnad – speaking both English and Gaelige – had helped him much.

The Little Flower. Did she know how precious she was to him? He looked for her, the old yearning in heart and belly. And suddenly she was there beside him, smelling of honey, like a forest-elf, and slipping her hands into his.

Nearby, both Wynter and Darryl – Darryl, who so often braided Blathnad's hair, his fingers skilful and deft as any woman's – saw the look that passed betwixt man and maid.

Nor was that look lost upon Muirgheal.

By the hearth King Svein was saying, 'You are to stay here?'

And Hereward nodded. 'Ely was my mother's morning-gift.' Aye, Countess Godgyfu, whom Hereward had not been to see, knowing full well how she would berate him. She would never try to understand the reason for what he'd done, but recount his sins betwixt the Litany, and judge him by the yard stick of his father.

'This Isle – it is half of it a garden,' said Svein, 'a rich place. And you think to hold it against the Norman?'

'Buggered if I don't see why not!' was Hereward's answer.

'Then you would not consider coming back to Denmark with us, Hereward Leofricsson? Bring what followers you will. We would be glad to have you!'

'What of your own men?' Hereward said. 'Dogs don't share bones. They'd think we were after their lands. There'd only be trouble.'

'But man, what is there here for you?'

'It is my home. My land. Where I was born.'

'With cold heart and bloody hand now ruling it?'

Hereward looked across at Svein Estrithsson in the rush-light and said, ''Twould only be running away.'

How Muirgheal wished they could! The ships of Padraig O'Connor and his followers would bear them back to Baile Atha Cliath and thence to Emhain Abhlach in a twinkling.

Sometimes she'd say to Hereward, 'O, that you had left me behind!'

'Why?'

'I bring you no fortune!'

At that Hereward would grow afraid and hold her tight, fit to crush her, breathing in her scent of herbs and flowers. 'What the hell's that got to do with it?'

347

'My charms – they fail! My spells are wanting!'
'Sod them! Has it not always been mine and thine?'

And so men continued to arrive, pouring into Croyland, only to find that their stronghold now lay in Ely.

Ely. The misty, swamp-ringed isle, clad in its queer, crystal warp of time and of water and poppies and sky. Its protection was the Lake of Angels, lying as ever just beyond the far horizon. And all those who came brought oil for its lamps.

The Isle of the Flowers of the Moon

he Danes are gone!' said Ivo Tallebois. 'The fen-devil is on his own! Eh, beau Sire, let us take Ely!'

William the King was in his court, the splendour of which, comparable to that of Byzantium, was already rupturing the coffers. William wanted more money, Tallebois money and revenge. Ely was blessed with all the world's goods, one of the last places as yet unplundered. Its treasures multiplied in the telling. Thus with the plan a-foot many begged to join the venture, mostly those who had fled or been driven from their stolen lands by the terror of the Wake.

At first sight the taking of Ely appeared to be simple. From miles away the tower of the great cathedral minster of St Aethelthryth looked near enough to touch, its fields of poppies scarlet in the sun. Sitting back in the saddle William fancied he could hide it with his hand. 'How now?' he said to his followers in blood.

But all was not as it appeared. Where the old bridle-way and the horse-fen and goose-fen met the forests of alder and sallow and willow and sedge lay the real Fen. The bottomless black peat of Haddenham Fen and Smithy Fen. A mile at least from one stretch of dry land to another. And there was the boundless shining of the Holy White Lake.

'They say there is a way into it, a place to cross, but a man could search the rest of his life and never find it!' said Drogo de Beuviere, the Fleming.

'What do they call that place?' said William, pointing yonder to a long green hump.

De Beuviere knew not, but Ralf de Gael said, 'Cherry Hill.'

'And there?'

'Monk's Wood.'

'And here?'

'Wil-lin-g-ham.'

'What of the west? What of the approaches there?'

349

None. Wicken Fen. Grunty Fen. Mose Water. The Clotten. Torow-Fare. Their very names were older than speech, older than time.

'And the east?'

Barraway and Thetford-in-the-Isle. Dry land neared Ely closer there than anywhere. But the rivers of the Cam and the Ouse made a wash of deep restless waters massed with the waxen yellow of lilies, their leaves surely big enough to walk upon.

Heart of Christ, William thought, to take this wilderness will need many hundreds.

He got them. Mercenaries in boat-loads from Normandy and France. They would advance by the bridle-way, it was decided, and attempt Haddenham Fen by use of timber and faggots cut from the trees and wagon-loads of brushwood and cattle hides that stunk to high heaven in the heat of the August day and which were to be blown up by bellows in the hopes of floating the cumbersome bridge and somehow spanning that black swampy mile.

Hogni Tricksleeve saw them first from where he sat in the Minster bell tower.

For days men had reported on the movements of an army, tracking their course. Thus it was at Stutney, the narrowest point between banks and the only likely place of attack, that a turf rampart of huge proportions had been thrown up and countless hands employed in building scaffolding of willow wands and overhanging hoardings of wattle with openings through which missiles could be hurled down onto the heads of the attackers beneath. Eadwine and Morkere, however, starved of action since their ill-fated northern uprising, were in favour of sallying forth to get the first blow in before the Normans gained a foothold. Hereward was not.

Resentful, Eadwine demanded, 'Do you intend us to sit here on our arses until we're overrun?'

'We must watch for the tide,' was all Hereward would say.

He went up to the bell tower. The Norman army was still toiling to build its causeway. Time and again they got so far, only to have the whole thing sink into the yawning depths of slime. Hereward ordered the bowmen of Ely to open fire. This they did with a will. Shower after shower of arrows hurtled over, maiming and killing by the dozen.

Witnessing these blundering preparations, King William grew wrath. It was the Hour of Sext and a molten sun blazed overhead. 'Bowels of God!' he let fly at them. 'Is this the best you can do?'

Another sheet of arrows took its toll. Piles were driven in, they held

350

not. Stouter ones fared no better. Hollowed beams were brought, then supported by the mass of bloated cattle hides. And with rope and plank and more poles they strove to bridge that dread mile.

Wynter stroked his axe. 'What plans, bor?' he said.

'Let the bleeders come!' Hereward answered him.

And come they did, for by the hour of Nones on the fourth day the causeway was ready for crossing.

Thurstan, Abbot of Ely, a timorous man, watched from the chapter-house window. 'What can he be thinking of? O, that we have put ourselves in his hands!'

At first there was order, the ranks of men in leather coats and armour rings. Knight and soldier and brigand, a mish-mash motley of them, hungry for plunder. Scaling ladders and grappling irons had they and full quivers of arrows and bows and slings. But as more and more surged onto the causeway – scores, nay, hundreds with hundreds following at their back – those who had stolen the forefront for themselves were pitched head-long, stumbling over each other, to be knocked flat by the men coming behind. Many were toppling into the black water and bottomless peat, yelling and struggling, weighed down with mail and weapons. Greedily the bogs swallowed them. The causeway gave a lurch, and where the ropes snapped countless more men plunged on top of their comrades. Meanwhile the rest of the army pushed forward heedlessly.

'Spine of God!' William the Norman sat his steed in impotent fury. They were as so many insects to him, like multitudes of ants, an inhuman shapeless mass suspended only a hand's breadth from disaster.

The gold of Ely dwelt within the walls. It was laid upon the altars and in the high places.

But the tide was on the ebb, going out with a singing sound, leaving a black quaking morass into which the bloated cattle-hides were rapidly sinking.

He knew! The Wake knew this would happen! Christ confound him, seethed Ivo Tallebois.

Men were taking to sows – cattle-hide boats – and rafts to cross the last quarter-mile. They clawed and fought each other for space, twenty trying to board rafts made to hold but a half-score, and where the rafts sank under the weight of numbers, the men clung to the sides of the other sows, thick with them as flies on a midden, trying to clamber aboard. And all the time the army was still pressing on across

351

the causeway and the screams and exhortations to stop fell on deaf ears.

More sows set out heavily laden, ankle-deep in sluggish waters. Those that could hurled grapnels at the turf and wattle ramparts and loosed arrows to pierce its stout length. Men floundered, wallowing waist deep, to be sucked down, and those behind climbed over their shoulders, on their heads. As a few struggled through the reeds, trying to gain the bank, the air a maddened din of war cries and screams, barrels of razor-sharp flints and stones were upended and emptied upon them, glaives were well-aimed and gusts of arrows shot, killing and wounding, and over their corpses crawled more to meet the same fate. The bodies formed perilous stepping stones. Floating mail-clad backs crammed the streams. Efforts were made to throw up scaling ladders but came to naught. If the grapnels held a moment they were flung down, if a ladder chanced to stand, even for the blinking of an eye, hoards of soldiers swarmed up it, only to be hacked back by the axes of Hereward's men. The ladders were hurled down into the mire.

Then while they wasted themselves against the unyielding rampart a great roar, louder than any screams, was heard and the causeway, burdened beyond endurance, broke in half and was quickly gobbled up by water and rotten brown bogs and mud.

'Drowned like shippen-rats! Dear knows how many of 'em!' Hereward swung Muirgheal into his arms. The sound of cheering and singing below was joined then by the clamour of bells as the brethren of Ely, hurrying thither to the tower, rang such a peal as was to echo the breadth of the Fens.

'The spirits were with you,' Muirgheal said. 'They walked at your side!' She had that look about her like when she was hearing sweet music from the Otherworld.

'O, Wise Woman!' said Hereward in awe.

'The arts of the Black Fiend!' Abbot Thurstan cried, and crossed himself.

But many was the head of forest boar that was roasted that night to give thanks for the deliverance of the Sacred Isle. Thus ended the first battle of Stutney.

A Court for Owls

W hat now?' said Matilda to William. Her head covered by a cyprus veil and circlet, she stitched by candlelight and cast sly glances at his glowering face.

'Heart of Christ, Mald!' he muttered. 'A quarter league of water!'

'Will you move against him?'

'Him?'

'The Wake.'

'Ply me not with questions!'

A plague of troubles had he. Firstly Mael-Coluimb of Scots had begun ravaging in Lothian. Then news was of the broken peace of northern France as Maine – the battleground of Norman interests – had been laid claim to by Fulk le Rechin of Anjou. And in Flanders William's brother-in-law had died leaving his widow Richildis to defend her lands and the inheritance of her son Arnoul against her kinsman Robert of Frisia. And desperate were the pleas from Richildis to William where he sat in all pomp at Westminster.

'She pledges marriage to the man who aids her.'

The pack heard him and licked their lips, thinking of wealthy Flanders for a guerdon. Most of them, however, were married and chafed at their ill luck. Alan la Roux of Brittany had lately wed with one of William's daughters and thus could afford to look well pleased.

William noted Odo, vain and carnal, hamstrung in his greed. Then Fitz-Osbern, widowered a year before, stood to take the offer. And so it was that he crossed to help Richildis and to claim her for his wife, and was killed in battle at Baunchove near Cassel. Arnoul, Richildis' son, was also slain and the lady herself captured.

William's mind was in turmoil, Normandy ringed by foes once more.

Odo sought him out. Peregrine on fist, he said, 'Fitz-Osbern's estates go a-begging. I would rule them!'

353

William was in Normandy that winter, but he returned before the following Easter, and was preparing to march north to quell the King of Scots. The family of Edward the Aetheling, finding refuge at the court in Perth, had stayed under the protection of Mael-Coluimb.

And there Princess Agatha had counselled Margaret to make herself more agreeable to the King. 'We owe him for the bread in our mouths. The clothes on our backs.'

But dreading his rough wooing, Margaret had said, 'Am I to pay for your keep with my body?' Her mother had answered sharply, 'You would have gladly given it to Harold Godwinesson for nothing!'

So it was that Margaret had been taken in marriage by Mael-Coluimb and by the spring was with child.

Outlaws came and went from the court during this time, chiefest among them her brother the Aetheling. Grown tall and fair he was in his eighteenth year, and already it seemed he had a lifetime of wandering behind him. 'Men!' he said. 'O, that I had an army!'

Mael-Coluimb stared moodily into the fire and said, 'You had an army in York. You and Gospatric and the Aelfgarssons – and were beaten!'

But the Scottish fortunes were to fare no better. A Norman army with William the King at its head marched north, going by way of Northumbria and Lothian and, crossing the Forth, penetrated the valley of the Tay. Thereat Mael-Coluimb did not offer battle but rather did homage to William at Abernethy. And thus when the time came that Margaret was delivered of a son, the heart of Scotland lay under the Norman heel, and his inheritance was bartered away.

Inheritances: the question possessed the mind of Matilda. Truly she felt herself to be Queen then as Aldwyth, widow of the sainted Edward, had lately died. It was not in Matilda's nature to be second. And there were her sons to consider. Robert and Richard and William and Henry – what of their father's conquests would fall to their lot? His bastards were well provided for. And her own daughter was the wife of Earl Warenne.

'Robert would prove himself,' said Matilda to William.

'How so?' he grunted in reply.

'Some lands. An office.'

'He is barely into his nineteenth year.'

'You were not half his age when you became Count of Normandy.'

So Mald was bargaining for their brood. Dabbling in dangerous waters. William knew his sons – Mald saw only what she wished to. 'The time is not yet,' he answered her.

Among the letters which arrived at the court was one from the newly appointed Pope Gregory VII, and what William heard when he bade a scribe read it to him was this:

> I believe it is known to you, most excellent son, how great was the love I bore you even before I gained the Papal Throne, and how I laboured for your advancement to royal rank. But in consequence I suffered dire calumny by the brethren saying that I gave sanction to great slaughter . . .

'So that is his game!' said Odo and chuckled. 'Ha! Wily old goat! I wonder what he wants?'

The See of Rome had been enriched beyond its wildest dreams by the treasures looted from England. 'That plaguey Tuscan monk!' William's rage was cold. 'I'll see him in hell before I pay lip-service to his conscience!'

How Many Miles to Babylon?

Ely, though a world unto itself, with fleece of sheep and skins of deer and feathers of fowl for covering and clothing, was cut off then by land and water, for the men of Ralf de Gael and Ivo Tallebois, and Robert of Deeping and Raoul de Dol and Sir Ascelin of St Valery held the river below the Isle.

'What does he look like, this Wake? Has any seen him?' said Sir Ascelin.

'What do his looks matter?' growled de Dol.

'So that we might know the fiend!' quoth the knight of St Valery.

Ivo Tallebois said, 'You will know him. The English once called him cursed of God before he became their darling. He bears a mark on his face and has the power of the Eye.'

William had long been in Normandy again. This time to combat the challenge of Fulk le Rechin. Maine was then as always the bone of contention between them, and in Fulk's absence it had been reduced to ashes. Knowing only too well that Philip of France's ambition was to break the Norman hold on England and thus bring William into line with his other vassals, he brooded but was cheered by his victory.

'You could never be a vassal to any man, O, lord!' said Ivo Tallebois to his suzerain when he came fenward once again to see the building of one of his castles. Weeting Castle would command the rivers Wissey and Little Ouse. There were over four hundred castles already built across England and hundreds more to come, to subdue and to cow and to dominate . . .

And William looked at Tallebois and said, 'What of the Wake?'

Ivo ate, slept and drank the Wake. He suffered the almost physical agony of his longing to possess and hoard the estates of Little-Bethlehem-of-the-Rushes and its Hall, which he feared to enter, and the rich fiefs of Ely. But close by sat another. Picot, sheriff of Cambridge,

356

called the Hog. He too lusted for the wealth of the Sacred Isle. 'Let us attack with all we have, beau Sire! No half measures! Let us smash them, rout them, kill them, every one!'

Muirgheal had made a scrying mirror of crystal. 'What do you see?' Hereward whispered.

'Men.'

'Where?'

'Coming.'

'How many?'

'Past counting!'

And as no man doubted Muirgheal's powers, none were surprised when what she saw came to pass. The spies who roved the lands for miles about brought word that a great army lay at Cambridge. Then two days later that same army was deployed in Willingham Fields. This time they had come equipped with entrenching tools and much timber and yet more cattle hides for the building of a new causeway and had commandeered the fishing boats of the Ouse to ferry the materials across. But never did they have a minute when they were not harassed by darts and stones and fire arrows from the ramparts of Ely. So much so that many downed tools and fled. At night the fen devils swam silently through the reeds to hack away the supports and slit the throats of the guards.

'Bones of Christ!' William railed as he beheld the destruction wrought. 'Treble the watch! And don't dare to hand me excuses!'

It was the time of the waxing of the moon and Muirgheal felt her powers grow even stronger. She was one with the ancient goddesses. She uttered prophesies of calamity to befall the enemy. She sat entranced, and men came to her and begged her to cast their nativities.

Thus when Abbot Thurstan tackled Hereward over Muirgheal's spell-working he got the answer, 'You want the French in here?' Thurstan did not.

'Then we must fight them with all the weapons we have!'

Throwing himself at Muirgheal's feet, Hereward said, 'How to keep them from crossing the water? Even as we shoot them down, more come!'

And Muirgheal, fingering her slumber pin, stooped and whispered against his ear, 'The reeds are dry, are they not, cara?'

'Aye, like bones. There's been no rain for weeks.'

357

'They'll burn.'

'Bloody right they will!'

And on the eighth day, though the causeway, resting on piles of wood and poles and then on cattle-skins and huge timber supports, was still far from satisfactory, William could stomach no more delay. Barges full of foreign mercenaries had come up from Cotinglade and the West Water, and lurked by the score in the vast reed-ronds. Rafts and sows were at the ready and the stretch of water, admittedly, did not seem so wide. As an example of faith in the causeway William trusted himself to ride its length on horseback, drawing cheers from his army. Below, pike circled lazily in the high clear waters, beguilingly blue, and there like a dream were the floating beds of meadowsweet and the yellow lilies and carpets of fen violets.

But something was wrong. Not with any of his preparations. He'd caused a four-towered wooden fortress to be erected on the land-side bank, and giant catapults and balisters were trundled into position and loaded. Hundreds of mailed, armed men, with battering rams and wall-borers and scaling ladders, chafed at the bit. The causeway should surely stand long enough to bear their weight – they were only ten foot short of their goal – the shores of Ely.

What then?

'How quiet it is!' William said to Fitz-Baldric the sheriff of Nottingham. 'Had you noticed?'

He had. Turning a brown, lean face to his suzerain, Fitz-Baldric said, 'And it was thus yesterday.'

There were no arrows, no darts – even the causeway builders had ceased to be plagued and killed. There was no sign of human life or movement the breadth of the Isle, and William suddenly felt afraid; a fear such as he'd never known before or during any battle. It got him in the gut, a foolish, senseless, superstitious fear that he would have laughed to scorn in others. But rather the clang of iron on iron, the chants and yells and curses of men, the flaming arrows and stones than this utter and unbroken silence.

It was a relief that the wind blew, rustling the miles of parched brown reeds, and that birds wheeled and cried.

Ivo Tallebois cared not for anything. All he thought of was the famous twelve altars, each more gorgeously arrayed than the last, and in the main chapel amid all the countless glories, hanging baskets of silver and emeralds bearing the Candles of Eternity, unquenchable as the lampads before the Throne of God.

Then there came the thin notes of an elder-wood pipe carrying across the water:

> How many miles to Babylon?
> Three score miles and ten.

Nerves jarred, William said, 'Spine of God! What's that?'

'Up there, Sire! In the bell tower!' said Fitz-Baldric.

And in the shadow of the bells Hogni Tricksleeve sniggered to see the fine warriors jump.

Babylon, by the Bowels of Christ! That's what Ely was, thought Tallebois. Splendid, fantastic, without equal. And his hands itched.

'Shoot the coystril down!' urged Ralf de Gael.

'Hola, men, take aim!'

'Damn you, no!' yelled William. 'Have you no sense? He's too far off!'

> Can I get there by candlelight?
> Aye, and back again.
> If your heels are nimble in flight,
> You may get there by candlelight.

A chill went down William's backbone and he could not but wonder just how many of them would get home by candlelight.

Thus to the weird accompaniment of the elder-wood pipe the army surged forth, clattering, pushing, jostling, clawing for a foothold.

'Go easy there! God Almighty! Have you dung and feathers for brains?' The captains echoed William's shout, cudgelling and swearing at those who would stampede the rest. Ivo felt his mouth water. Though he clung at his suzerain's side he ached to be out there ahead of the yowling mob, to be the first man to smash his way into Ely and bring the accursed Wake to hand-to-hand combat.

But had he known it, Hereward was nearer than he thought. Stripped naked, he swam soundlessly and unhampered beneath the chill water, watching as their greed stole what wit or reason they had.

In minutes the causeway was packed to suffocation and where it ended boats and sows and hollowed logs were sent out, dozens of them, groaning and sinking under the weight of men.

And still there was no retaliation from the Isle. It was uncanny, unnatural. William rode upon the causeway expecting any minute – what? He had no idea.

Then a shout went up. William turned in the saddle and saw smoke. Smoke on water? In the reeds? An orange-yellow belch of flame shot from one clump to another, whipped by the fen wind, and soon every rond the length of the shore was blazing, sparks flying across the water, catching the great middle banks alight, roaring, crackling, billowing out . . .

The army trapped on the causeway was roasted whole in a frenzied, screaming, fighting mass. The stench of burning flesh and hair was sickly-sweet and hundreds leaped like human torches into the black bogs. Barges and rafts were caught amid streams by the sheets of fire and men saw each other devoured by flames. And then as if by some signal all the ramparts and hoardings of Ely opened up with great showers of missiles, darts, spears, stones and the bowmen let loose their arrows in gusts.

In the terrible panic William was almost unhorsed. God's Belly! Smoke blinded him, choked him. He felt the chain mail frizzle on his back and his shield, arrow pierced, was smouldering. He urged his mount round and beat and lashed a path through the crazed throng, seeing nothing, ears deafened by the noise, until he dropped from his saddle on the far bank, gasping for breath and retching.

'Beau Sire!'

William looked up, wiping the vomit from his mouth and saw a fire-blackened face above him. It was Ivo Tallebois. His hair was scorched, his eyes bloodshot.

'What devil is loosed?' William's voice was a hoarse whisper.

'The Wake!'

And still the arrows pelted down on the heads of the dying multitudes and onto the glut of charred corpses that clogged every pool like drowned flies in foul honey, and the whole Isle swam through a shimmering haze of heat.

'There!' bellowed Ivo Tallebois. 'By all the Saints! Look!'

And William did and saw a naked man wade from the water further down-stream and shake himself like an otter, and there squat in the mud among the burnt-out reed beds, and watch the death throes of the Norman army in that second and last battle of Stutney.

'He smiled!' said William to Matilda. 'That Wake! And it cost me sixteen hundred men!'

'What will you do?'

'Heart of Christ! What would you have me do?'

'What of the monks of Ely?'

'Saxons all.'

'And afraid?'

William turned and looked at Matilda in the glow of the tallow keech candle. 'And now, my foxship?'

'They harbour a witch.'

'Eh, God's Death, Mald – what is a spell-caster to me?'

'Your means of getting Ely. Of slaying this Wake!'

The Wake. And William, balding then and beginning to grow corpulent, remembered that even as he'd beheld the Saxon across the boiling waters, he had felt a twinge of admiration despite himself, for the flat belly and the tawny-moor's tan and hard muscle – ah, he'd envied the man his fine body!

'Tell me!'

'Send to those monks of this Moon Flower Isle. Say you will allow them to remain in their church unmolested. That they may keep all they have for themselves – if they will deliver up the witch.'

'You believe the Wake would suffer that to be?'

'The rebel Bishop Aethelwine is there, Abbot Thurstan – all of them by defying you are defying Rome. Their alternative is excommunication.'

The Godwinesson had been excommunicate but candles were still lit for him and masses sung. 'They are full of craft!' said William.

'Then match craft with craft!' Matilda answered him.

361

The Elf-Kind and Goblins that go by Night

he repulse of the Normans gave great heart in Ely. Their camp of refuge was safe. But after the jubilation came the question – for how much longer?

'The Bastard will be back,' men said. 'He has possession of the iron fields of Surrey and Sussex and charcoal fires burn there day and night.'

Hereward knew there was reputed to be a supply of ore in the Lincoln Wolds – though it was scant and nothing like the amount they needed. There was many a good smith among the fugitives with skill going to waste. After the two attacks on Ely there had been a huge haul of weapons left by the fleeing French. But as the days passed iron was to become more precious than bread.

And so Eadwine and Morkere, tiring of life at Ely, betook themselves off. Hereward watched them go and shrugged. Yet at heart he was sore afraid. If others followed them then the whole resistance would crumble, and blinding, castration, mutilation and the gallows would be their lot. 'We'd be playing right into the hands of the Norman,' Hereward would say.

And the men, huddled round the smoking peat fires in the hall where the wind raged without, listening to the harp-song of Hwita Clatter-Clogs, and drinking deeply of mead and strong ale to ward off the water-elf disease and the shakes, pledged with oaths to stand or fall together.

But Eadwine and Morkere fared no better for leaving. Eadwine wandered for some months, doing good for no man, least of all himself. And so it came to pass while he was on his way to join the forces of the Kings of Wales, that he and his hus-carls were ambushed by the men of Hugh the Fat of Chester, and Eadwine slain.

'One less!' said Hugh, Vicomte d'Avranches, waddling into William's presence well pleased.

And William looked at the head of Eadwine Aelfgarsson that had been brought to him, and thought of his brother Morkere who had come in unto him only a few days before begging mercy. There was no putting faith in any of them. They would not hesitate to plot behind his back and stir rebellion. So he had showed no mercy to Morkere, but rather the inside of a newly-built dungeon.

And thus was the offspring of the branch of Aelfgar humbled.

Meanwhile at Ely men relied more and more upon Muirgheal's leechdoms and premonitions, and in those days Hereward never set one foot before the other without consulting her.

'What is she, Lilla?' Countess Godgyfu had said to her chaplain.

'I've seen her heal men by the laying on of hands.'

'With the shot of witches?'

'With goodness, my lady.'

And those she healed – tending their hurts, brewing wound-drinks and bringing succour to their wives and children who were ailing – called her Hereward's lady or his wife, with her skirt hemmed with tiny bells and her bright-coloured plaids.

Muirgheal could speak enough of the English tongue to make herself understood, but together she and Hereward spoke a mixture of English and Gaelige, a give-and-take language liken to nothing else.

He'd whisper, 'I'm scared!'

'Of what?'

'Losing ye!'

'Usha!' And Muirgheal would touch the marked side of his face. *'Slan mo chomhartha!* Ah, jewel, you won't!'

'Muirgheal – *mo bhean!*'

Theirs was a loft-space beneath sloping starry eaves, which Muirgheal had made comfortable, strewing sweet flowers among the rushes and heaping furs and shorn pelts for their bed.

Sometimes Hereward would fall asleep in her arms fully clothed, then others there would be the feel of his powerful, naked body against her own, and Muirgheal would wonder at herself grown wet for him, her nipples hardening even before he'd begun to suck on them.

'I've been desperate for ye a long while!'

'Why didn't you say?'

Hereward was sweating as if in the heat of a summer day. 'I never know whether you're wanting me or not.'

Muirgheal dragged his head down to her, pushing one of her nipples in his mouth, holding him there while he sucked. 'Have I ever turned from you?'

363

'Nay!'

Hereward's strong, warm tongue had brought her nipple up proud, the colour of dark wine. What Muirgheal felt for the man was almost pain.

'But I wish you'd come to me like you used to when I worked in the field.'

'Things are different now!'

'Not for us!'

Hereward shifted and Muirgheal felt the bulk of his cock between her knees. She rubbed its bristly underside gently, feeling it quiver and stiffen. Muirgheal felt for his balls, heavy and hairy and warm, and as she caressed them, gently squeezing them, Hereward moaned softly through clenched teeth, 'Muirgheal!'

'Usha! My love!' Muirgheal tasted his sweat on her tongue. 'But he's fine!'

Hereward sobbed aloud, '*A bhean!* Want me!'

'I do!' Muirgheal opened her legs wide, knees pressing his thighs, and Hereward shoved himself in as carefully as he could.

'*Acushla!*'

'Can ye feel him?'

Muirgheal could. Hot and hugely distended, his cock was pushing all the way up inside her, throbbing and growing even bigger in her womb.

'You fuck so sweet, lass!' Hereward panted, heaving over her, trapping her in the crook of one brawny arm. Then he began to lunge and to thrust, pulling at her bowels, and Muirgheal hung about his neck, searching with her mouth for the apple of his throat, knotting her fingers in his hair, gripping him tight while he laboured on her. He worked her up to a climax whether she would or nay; sweaty, shameless, painfully sweet; till she had no control over her limbs or her brain, till she came round to the reality of the half-rigid cock shuddering within her and the warm wetness of sperm dribbling between her legs.

His bearded cheek rasped hers. ''Twas good, was it not?' He licked the salt tears from her eyes. 'D'you love me?'

'*A mhic!* You know I do!'

'Let me hear you say it!'

'I love you!'

Hereward hadn't freed his cock, and Muirgheal felt the soft pulse of his blood. The deep beat of his heart.

'I'd lief stay in you!'

'There's nothing to stop you.'

'All night?'

'If you want! *Ni miste liom!*'

'Muirgheal . . .'

'What, cara?'

'You know ye're everything to me?'

'Am I?'

'I'd be a poor lummox without ye!'

While the land was in the grip of winter, and later when the waters rose with much crying, Ely stayed as a natural fortress, its strength the vast White Holy Lake and the rivers and the shining grey floods.

And during those long dark nights Abbot Thurstan had much time to consider his own position. Messages had lately come to him there sent by William the King, and which he believed to have been received in secret. It was plain that what had been done to others would be done to him. Only Wulfstan of Worcester and Aethelwige of Evesham still held out in defiance of the Norman swords and the curfew bell, token of servitude.

Surrender up the witch was the Bastard's demand. Open your doors unto us and you shall remain as Abbot thereafter. A fair exchange. Was she not be-belled and arrayed as the Mother of Harlots? Did she not commit fornication with that Changeling of Leofric? Surely it was right that she should be made to atone for her sins.

But Hogni the ever-watchful was wise to the traffick in messages, though when Hereward confronted the Abbot, shorn and shrewd, the churchman denied all knowledge.

'He's lying,' said Hereward to Muirgheal.

Whereupon Muirgheal's eyes grew dark in her pale face. 'If I'm captured their priests will burn me!'

'They shall not touch you!'

'They call me a witch!'

Abbot Thurstan had tried to reason with his monks in the chapter-house so that they should see things his way. But they dragged their feet and spoke of betrayal, and many of them were besotted and besmitten with the Sorceress, fetching and carrying for her, praising her skill, defending her use of star-craft and magic.

No – the brethren of Ely would never obey his orders to guide the Normans across to the Isle by the secret fen path, rather they would lead them into the quagmires and black swamps that quivered and sogged and stank. So Abbot Thurstan determined to go himself.

'Can he be trusted, Sire?' said Ivo Tallebois.

'If he breaks faith he loses all,' William answered. 'I'll wager the man's no fool!'

'Can we burn her?'

'Who?'

'The Saxon's hag.'

'Do what you will with her!'

'And him? The Wake?' Ivo spoke on an indrawn breath.

'I'm sure you'll think of something!' said William, and he smiled. 'But Spine of God, let us catch him first!'

Abbot Thurstan, burdened with what treasures he could carry, met the great troop of soldiers and showed them the hidden way – a path at low tide through the shallows of the Holy Lake. Ivo Tallebois could see no path. In the fast-fading light it looked to be just an endless expanse of pale water edged by forests of willow and accursed nicker-pools haunted by demons. On Abbot Thurstan's say so he had fitted wooden shoes to the horses' hooves.

Ivo Tallebois spoke to the Abbot through an interpreter: 'Tell him that if this is a trick, there'll be the King to answer to!'

It was bleak dusk and already the will o' the wisps clung to their lance-tips, while moths fluttered on the stars and the frogs were to be heard croaking for miles.

'If you stay on the path you'll not come to grief,' the Abbot gave back in answer.

Ivo turned again to the interpreter. 'Ask if the Wake is within.'

And Abbot Thurstan, being asked, vouchsafed, 'I know not.'

'Splendour of God, he had better be! Or it will go the worse for you, master foxy priest!'

With the going down of the spring floods Hereward and many of the men were out on raiding parties or else Thurstan would never have dared venture forth. But the crude swart Tallebois was not to know that.

Thus did the Normans cross the Way of Angels and enter the Sacred Isle and were met there with the bitterest opposition since the Great Battle. The army marched upon it from Cambridge and the fleet sailed from Southrey. William camped at Witchford-down-water and Tallebois came to him there bloody and awed. 'Ely is ours – but at a

366

price. Hundreds are dead. They turned berserk – they fought us like wolves!'

There had been boat-loads of women and children hidden in the rushes for safety, but as many again had been captured. Englishwomen were much prized for their fairness of skin and hair, guerdons to be fought for and shared out among the rabble. But what had astounded Ivo Tallebois was that they had often been killed by their own men to prevent them falling into Norman hands.

'The Wake?'

'Nowhere to be found, Sire!' Ivo lashed at his boot, tears of rage in his eyes.

'Heart of Christ! What bungling is this?'

'Many escaped, Sire. Some gone to Haddenham to muster help.'

'Are there prisoners?'

'They would not be taken alive, Sire!' said Sir Ascclin, who had entered the tent, his armour rent and blood-boltered.

'They were mad,' said Ivo Tallebois. 'But those who fled – we shall hunt them down, fear not!'

'The monks?' said William.

'They are on their way now to submit to your Majesty. And we took the rebel churchman Aethelwine.'

'What of the Wake's woman? The witch? Do they have her?'

'No, Sire,' said Ivo Tallebois. ''Tis said she turned herself into a toad and escaped.'

'A toad? And I suppose the Wake turned into a toad as well, eh? You credulous fool! Bowels of God! What tale would you not believe?'

Padraig O'Connor had brought Muirgheal and Blathnad out of Ely, and Mare Swallow bore the three of them with Hogni Tricksleeve running at her heels.

It was between Cherry Hill and the goose fen that they met with Hereward and a sizeable body of men, Wynter and Darryl and Young Leofsi among them, returning from a raid. They had rowed thence by barge and raft and were hurrying the last few miles on foot with well-laden pad-nags. And there under a clamorous, star-lit sky, while even then the roofs of Ely were being fired, the story was poured forth.

'Mary Mother of Mercy!' It came from Hereward's lips in a sob. For a space of moments he stood stunned, his fists clenched, brain reeling. Muirgheal slid from the saddle and flung her arms about his neck.

'This was not writ in your stars, Muirgheal!'

'I should have known!' she cried.

'You could not!'

'There had been warnings!'

'Aye, but we thought we were safe!'

'The secret path!' said Wynter's son Pery, a man grown then. 'It had to be. There's no other way!'

'And who to show them?' said Darryl softly. 'The loyal Abbot!'

And suddenly all their spoils – cloth and spice and wine and candles and oil and glass – mattered no whit then.

Hereward said, 'Give me Swallow!'

Seeing the queer light in his eyes, Padraig O'Connor stood to stop him. '*Nar lige Dia san!*' he implored. 'You cannot mean to go back. 'Twould be madness!'

'Let me by!' Hereward said warningly.

'Nay! What's the use of throwing your life away?'

'But they were only there on account of me. They came for refuge. O, Christ! I cannot just stand here and watch it!'

'You can do nothing.'

'Can't I? I'll have Thurstan to swing from his own bell rope or die in attempting it.' Hereward said to the men, 'Are you with me?'

And their assent rang to the stars. Padraig said, 'The Abbot has gone – fled – the monks surrendered.'

'Sod the Abbot! Sod them all! We'll have our man-price in French blood!'

Muirgheal stood back a pace from Hereward and Blathnad was at her side, and she holding the girl close to her. 'Nay,' she pleaded, 'if you go I'll be captured. They'll burn me! O, cara, do not! For my sake!'

'You'll be all right,' said Hereward. 'Padraig shall take you and Blathnad to my mother at Croyland.'

'Blathnad, yes,' said Muirgheal, 'but not me. If you go back I go with you. Force me to aught else and I will kill myself!' Muirgheal's black hair was blowing wild about her and she was shaking from head to foot. All the men beheld her dumb-struck.

Then Wynter's was the voice of command. 'Back to the boats,' he urged. 'The lands'll be lousy with Frenchers. And make less noise or we'll be heard.' And so they went, and putting Mare Swallow aboard the main barge, pushed off into the broad reedy stream that bore them through the dense willow forests and quaking sedge, nearing Ely by the west where the Clotton met Grunty Fen. The town was ablaze then and all about it rained cinders, and thick black smoke from the fields of smiling corn lay like fog upon the water. And the surrounding marsh sent up its own wild litany. Otters whistled and reeler birds sang their thin reeling song, and pole-cats and water rats, fire in their eyes, scuttled among the tall rushes and the bitterns boomed way out on the Wide Mere. Soon they were met with other boats escaping from the slaughter and many was the fugitive they found on the way who'd swum for it, bringing nothing with them but their lives and all with a tale of fury and treachery to tell.

The burning of Ely could be seen for a score of miles across the Fen, and the great Minster of St Aethelthryth stood up dark and ghastly, bathed in the yellow light.

William rode thither to watch it. 'Belly and Heart of God!' he said, fancying to see faces in the fire as it danced in the black sky. Even from afar off the tumult of noise was loud across the water.

'All of value is within the Minster, Sire,' cried Picot of Cambridge. 'All is safe.'

And it was later, much later when William ventured into the great chapel of Ely Cathedral and stood speechless, looking upon that wonder of wonders. The glorious play of colour of the patterned window glass was bright through the pall of smoke. There were tapestries and religious hangings of cloth of gold and wool and silk; the translucent enamels and gold of the crosses; the crucifixion scenes set with blood-red jade and rose moonstones and mother-of-pearl; bells encrusted with blue chrysoprase and sacred vessels; carvings of amethystine quartz and the twelve altars and the twelve roods of gold surmounted each one by a crown of ruby thorns; and the hanging baskets bearing the Candles of Eternity . . .

'I have never seen the like!' he said to Matilda. 'Jewels big as bulaces! How many miles to Babylon? Eh, by the Bones of Christ, Mald!'

But the glories of Ely did not go far, as William wished most of them for himself. Discontent sprang up among the barony. Their coffers were emptying fast. Though they imposed crippling services on the estates they then owned, seizing all common land and plough-teams, it was not enough, and they looked about for more. It irked Ralf de Gael who had braved the arrows of Ely, to see the King hoard it all as he hoarded all the land, and gave it out in dribs and drabs as the whim took him. And so de Gael plotted with others both Breton and Norman, and one who joined them in their folly was Waltheof Lack-Counsel. Hatched at a Bridal-Ale, their rebellion, when begun in Cambridge, took but a few days to quash by the forces of Odo the Butcher and Geoffrey of Mowbray, Bishop of Coutances.

Whereupon de Gael and his fellow conspirators fled the country rather than face William's wrath, and Waltheof Siwardsson, accused of complicity by his Norman wife, was beheaded.

It was a relief to be rid of Waltheof, the last remaining English Earl. 'Though those Saxon knaves have buried him at Croyland and now venerate him as a martyr,' said Ivo Tallebois. The last events had pleased him: the haughty de Gael riding for a fall. Eh, he'd enjoyed seeing him brought low. He'd enjoy his lands too, if he could get any of them: the fat tithes of East Anglia.

Queen Matilda said, 'What of the Wake?'

'He is crushed,' said William.

'But alive?'

'Not for long.' William thought of the hundreds who had been hanged as rebels after the fall of Ely, and the hundreds more mutilated to join the other wretched bands of the crippled and the castrated then roaming England. Both Abbot Thurstan and Bishop Aethelwine were dead. The former – no man knew why. The latter – starved to death at Abingdon.

He looked down at the fabulous sapphire ring of the pilgrim hacked from the hand of Harold Godwinesson, and the huge bracelet of gold and balas-rubies, arm-fetter of Wessex. Ten years. Thousands of men had stood then to bar his path – now there was only one.

The Lay of the Bees that Swarm on Dead Wood

ulfric Raher the Heron of Wrokeshame and Hwita Clatter-Clogs escaped from Ely, and with countless others, came in unto Hereward at Well. They had crossed the Wide Mere where the rivers of the Old Nene and the Welney met.

'All's lost!' said Wulfric.

But Hereward would not have it so.

At Croyland Lilla had urged him to stay. What of when the Fenland winter came again? 'What chance will you have out there?' he argued.

'What chance is there anywhere if I don't make one?' Hereward gave him back in answer. 'I do this as much for Blathnad's sake as any. She's my heiress. I would see her upon the high-seat of Little-Bethlehem-of-the-Rushes!'

The high-seat! The child of Hereward and that black-haired wood-woman, thought Godgyfu. Who would have believed it could have come to pass? But with both Eadwine and Morkere lost to her and Eahlswith as good as lost, 'Cannot I keep her with me?' said the Countess. 'I would teach her.'

But Blathnad had been loath to go to the great lady, and so they left Croyland and struck out for the wide trackless fen and the forest where a thousand men could lose themselves and never be seen again.

Thus fugitives – desperate, homeless, kinless men, dreaming desperate dreams – came and went from the camp in the months that followed, whether it was in turf huts on a marsh island or wands and daub in the wood's heart.

And in the summer, full of green rushes and stars and hopefulness, there was a grim pleasure in terrorising the Norman-French, burning their stolen halls over their heads, looting their granaries and waylaying and killing any foolish enough to ride through the countryside in a party of less than twenty.

And how they bewailed themselves, those proud, strutting conquerors!

371

The price of Hereward Leofricsson's head was doubled and yet doubled again. Rumour was that it was a man's weight in gold. But though many eyes were thrust out and tongues cut out likewise by Ivo Tallebois and his men in their search for the Wake, they came no closer to finding him.

'They won't tell!' stormed Tallebois. 'By the belly of Christ, I'll make them tell!'

'Perhaps they do not know,' said Sir Ascelin.

'Of course they know. Food and the shirt off their back is on offer to him in even the meanest hovel!'

Sir Ascelin mused on his mailed fist. 'Have you ever thought who would do that for us? No one. They only wait to slit our throats and dance on our graves.'

But in the winter when the sky was loud with birds and their old music smote the ear, in the crippling cold of snow and frost and grey seeping fog, to hoodwink and to bait the Norman was no longer such a jest to the out-of-law men, and they grew sullen and despairing and talked of death.

And Blathnad cleft close to Padraig O'Connor in those days, seeking to be with him, and Padraig, his heart torn all ways, vowed to himself not to touch her. But broke that vow with a kiss. And having had the taste of his mouth, Blathnad whispered, 'When shall I lie with you?'

But Padraig would take of her no more than the kiss. For how should he tell Hereward — her father and his friend? To ask another man for his daughter was not easy and Padraig would choose his words carefully.

'Blathnad has my heart,' he said at last, simply, to Hereward. '*Tá grá agam di*. I love her.'

They sat by the fire in the main hut and Hereward stared at Padraig as though he wasn't hearing right. 'Blathnad?' he said.

'It has been so these many months past.'

'You and Blathnad?'

And Padraig felt the look in Hereward's eyes was fit to slay him. And he knew then why they called him Elf-Begotten. Why some feared him. Hereward got up and went out without another word. And from the shadows Wynter said softly, 'Give him time, bor. He's not good at sharing.'

A week of days passed before Padraig tackled Hereward again. 'I would make her my wife. Take her back to Baile Atha Cliath.'

'No!' Hereward set his jaw, leathered hard, scored with cuts and scars. 'She is Lady of Mercia by rights!'

372

'What do these Normans care for rights?' said Padraig. 'They have most of your country. What hope is there?'

'We must fight!'

'We have fought, cara, and are faint for lack of blood. There is only so much that men can do. The Bastard draws his forces from abroad, and even English mercenaries – thousands against our few hundred!'

Padraig O'Connor had been a good friend, true and brave, in a struggle that was not yet his own. But where Blathnad was concerned Hereward would see no reason. 'What can you give her?' he demanded of the Irishman.

'Safety. A home. Children. I'm worthy of her. My mother was a princess of Tara.' Padraig stood his ground squarely. 'Why do you not come with us?'

Hereward had Blathnad brought to him and jerking his head towards Padraig, said, 'Do you love him?'

And Blathnad nodded. Hereward felt his heart would snap within him. 'As much as you love me?'

'It is not the same!' Blathnad whispered.

'I would have dragged down the moon and stars for ye, lass. Anything! As I am my father's son so you are my daughter. My world is in you – all I have!'

'Let her go,' said Muirgheal. The love between Padraig and Blathnad was well known to all, save maybe to Hereward. 'What else is there for her but marriage with an outlaw?'

Hereward thought of the high-seat between the god-pillars. Of the elf-ridden rafters. Were they still there, those elves, or had they forsaken the Hall?

'She's only a child.'

'Two years younger than you when you first became my lover.'

And Hereward looked up to see Muirgheal across the turf fire. The winter cold was savage and the days so dark as to be hardly any different to the night. Straw and rags and leaves and mud were used to fill the holes, and skins covered the walls of their crude shelter.

'But we got her – you and me.'

'You cannot keep her forever.'

The wind soughed through the icy trees and the fire smoked. Muirgheal was mending one of Blathnad's smocks, her hands stiff and red and chapped.

Hereward watched her and said, 'They're spoilt. Your lovely white hands!'

'Aye, and there's grey in my hair and my body's thinning to scrawny. If you make Blathnad live this life she will be as I am!'

'You think me a selfish sod?' Hereward crawled to Muirgheal's side and squatted by her.

'No,' she answered him. 'I know you only want what's best. 'Tis no blame.'

'I thought I did – and look at us,' Hereward said. 'Living worse than a pack of shacky beggars!' His voice was bitter and harsh and he took Muirgheal's roughened hands and kissed them.

'Ah, Hereward!'

'What are we to – you and me?'

And Muirgheal said, 'Let us go, Hereward – back to Emhain Abhlach.'

Hereward stopped and looked down at her. 'You want that?'

'O, cara, cara! It has been almost seven years. I've never said such before because of all it meant to you – your home, your land . . .'

Hereward said, 'You go back with Blathnad and Padraig O'Connor. Wait for me.'

'No, Hereward.'

'Why not?'

'I cannot be without the knowing of you.'

'You did not always have the knowing of me.'

'Did I not?' And she said it so hushed and strange that Hereward sat back on his heels and was awed.

Abbot Ulfketyl the Good, though a very old man then, was still spiritual father of Croyland, and when he saw Hereward come hither a year later, shaggy and unkempt, his only glory the brooches which fastened his bearskin cloak, he said, 'Lad, won't you bide with us? There's room here for you all!'

But Hereward would not. And he paid less and less heed to Muirgheal's counsels.

Old Wor-Will-Be-So in his hut by the water sat wizened as a chaff husk with his cowslip key. 'There's sense in it, lad. Croyland – you could raise another army there!' He gazed on Leofric's son in the half-light. It was summer again and a swath of flowers hid the door from mortal eyes.

'My place is here,' Hereward said.

'Here?' Old Wor laid a gnarled hand on Hereward's arm. 'What are you saying, bor?'

374

'My place is at Little-Bethlehem-of-the-Rushes. The Hall's been too long without its master.'

After Padraig O'Connor had claimed Blathnad for his bride, and the loss of her, which was how Hereward felt it to be, Muirgheal watched him grow apart from herself, and it grieved her heart to see him change in so many ways.

O, how different he had become to that muscle-bound, tongue-tied, fecund boy she'd found first upon the fairy shore. Emhain Abhlach. She thought of it with a great longing. Where I was myself and he was himself and we were together!

And as the numbers of the men at the camp dwindled and the raids got more daring, more foolhardy, Muirgheal would sit over her pan covered with rushes and weep.

Then one day she said to Young Leofsi, 'Will you take me to Croyland?'

'You, lady?'

Muirgheal with her healing hands, her wound-drinks and crystal-gazing, how should they fare if she left them? But Young Leofsi with leaden heart obeyed. And thus did Abbot Ulfketyl and Countess Godgyfu behold her walking barefoot into the Stranger's Hall.

When Hereward found Muirgheal gone, he sat down in silence, looking at his ragged coat and the dirty torn nails of his fingers. And the men sat down also. Then Hereward said to Young Leofsi, 'Why for did you take her?'

And Young Leofsi answered, 'She asked me to.'

Hereward bundled up the white bearskin and sent Hogni Tricksleeve to Croyland with it. Hogni came back wearing strings of St Cuthbert's beads and fallen angel's bones.

'They're for you,' he said. 'From her.'

'What did she say?'

'She thought you'd follow. See sense. I told her 'twasn't a bit of use.' Hogni held out the beads but Hereward would not touch them. 'Think they're covered in spells?' and he gave a piskie laugh.

'Then it's all up with us,' said Darryl.

'Will you leave me also?' Hereward demanded of them.

'But bor, at Croyland there is more chance for us. We can begin again,' said Young Leofsi.

'With what?'

'The monks are willing to help. Others will join us!'

Hereward was tired, bone-tired. He yearned to go to Muirgheal, to throw himself at her feet, to find sanctuary among her flowers and herbs and little tinkling bells. But in the end he would be cornered on that lonely isle and all would be flames and death and ruin.

That night he said, 'We must each make our own choice.'

And every one of the men chose to return to Croyland, save Wynter. Thus when Muirgheal saw the boats come next day, cleaving a path through the vast water-lily beds, oars flashing in the autumn sun, she hurried down to the mere's edge.

'He's not here, lady,' called Young Leofsi.

'He's gone back to Little-Bethlehem-of-the-Rushes,' said Darryl.

'Why did you not stop him?' said she to them.

'He's the Master,' answered Young Leofsi simply.

'He chose it, lady,' said Darryl, pushing back his sheep-wool cap, 'and when we argued with him he drew sword Brain-Biter upon us and told us to get hence!'

And so they left her by the mere and Muirgheal closed her eyes and smiled bitterly to herself. You were sinful proud in your love! You thought that he could not live without you!

There was a tug at her skirt and she looked down then to see Pery Wyntersson kneeling at her feet. With his man's hulking shoulders and arms and his boy's belief, he whispered, 'O, lady, can you not cast a binding spell?'

And Muirgheal answered, 'I fear my powers are all gone!'

Like the lilies, the brazen, buttery lilies that within days would be wilting on the mere.

Wolf's-Bane

In London Town William was watching the building proper of his tower castle with its massive rubble walls.

More soldiers had been brought in, bowmen and some with hounds, to control the surly, half-stripped workforce by fear and the lash.

A man had already been hanged that morning for striking down a guard. William could see his body dangling from one of the dozens of makeshift gallows from where he stood.

The Bishop of Coutances was saying, 'It is fitting that these English pigs should be made to labour on it.'

'Perhaps,' said Walter Gifard with a low chuckle. 'But let not your lemans nor your wife near them. For by the Holy Face our women fancy the brutes mightily!'

'Let us go down, make some sport with them,' said Odo from behind William's shoulder. 'Amuse ourselves. The day is a dull one.'

But William shook his head, knowing only too well the sport Odo had in mind. The Concubine-Keeper had a hawk upon each gloved fist, belled and hooded and jessed, iron talons and beak flashing.

'Ha, you do not fear those Saxon hogs, do you, brother?'

'Only fools have no fear,' William answered him. Odo and Robert, whilom of Mortain and lately made Earl of Cornwall, were the greatest landowners in the country after himself, and he was constantly on his guard with them in those days.

'I am surrounded by jackals and scavengers!' William was wont to lament to Matilda, who shrugged and said, 'It is to them and their like that you owe the getting of this kingdom!'

But in Winchester once more and in his treasure house to which he alone had the keys, his fears subsided and his temper sweetened. Here he had amassed a fortune that was beyond price and his half-brother and any other man he would see dead before they touched one gem.

Thus it was that Ivo Tallebois found him. 'The Wake, beau Sire!'

'What of him?'

'They say he is returned to his Hall. That he is at Little-Bethlehem-of-the-Rushes.'

William, half risen from his chair, said, 'Are you sure?'

Kneeling, Tallebois nodded.

'Beware lest it's a trap!'

'I have your leave, Sire?'

A roaring sound was in William's ears. He saw that Tallebois's hand trembled on the hilt of his sword. After all the months – the years . . . 'Waste no quiddits on me. Take it!' said William. 'Go!'

The Hall of the Flowers of the Elves

She thought you'd come about,' said Hogni Tricksleeve, perching on a beam. 'Fat chance of that!'

They had been at the Hall of Little-Bethlehem-of-the-Rushes for a week. In that time no one had ventured near. They were three unto themselves – Hereward and Wynter and Hogni Tricksleeve.

Hereward sat in the high-seat between the god-pillars that were carved all over poppies. Sat there for hours, he did, as if trying to absorb the spirit of his father.

Presently he said to Hogni, 'If you're so bloody clever why didn't you go also?'

'I told you I'd never leave you!'

'I don't want you!' and Hereward threw a boot at him.

But Hogni only dodged it and whickered and played a few notes on his pipe: 'I see the moon and the moon sees me!'

But it was on the ninth day, a night of brewing storm, as they sat at the trestle and broke bread and listened that there came the sound of hoof-beats echoing afar off on the causeway.

As Wynter stood up, hand on axe, Hogni Tricksleeve slipped to the space beneath the eaves and called from the stair, 'Normans!'

'Bolt and bar the door,' said Wynter.

'Nay – leave it!' said Hereward.

'Are your wits gone, man? You know what they're here for.'

'To drink a wassail-bowl with the Lord of Little-Bethlehem-of-the-Rushes.'

'Bugger that! They've come to kill us.'

'Are you afraid?'

'No.'

Hereward went to the chest with the nine locks and those locks opened unto him. Within lay the elf-armour, and as he gathered it up into his arms, the house-place seemed to be filled with a great unseen clamouring.

'Will you help me to put it on, lad?'

And Wynter did. The shimmering links allowing him to fasten them, where they fitted Hereward's shoulders sweetly, hugging his back and buttocks and thighs. He strapped on his belt of the Fiann and the hilt of sword Brain-Biter cleft to his hand.

Now Wynter had a coat of stout reindeer hide that could turn a blow as well as any mail, and both his little chuckling axe and a sword and shield. 'Shall we go out and bid them welcome?' said Wynter.

'Nay,' said Hereward and smiled. 'We'll welcome them from the floor of the Hall.'

Flames were upon the face of Witch-Water and the causeway was clung about with will-o'-the-wisps, glowing like a rainbow bridge of fire.

Hugh of Evermue had come with Ivo Tallebois and the pack, among them Raoul de Dol and Drogo de Beuverie and Robert of Deeping and Sir Ascelin of St Valery and their men-at-arms. It was not for gain or revenge that he rode thither, but for curiosity – at last to come face to face with the Wake.

And he got his wish and more besides, for as the door was burst in by a hammering rain of lance butts, and the low, cavernous, candlelit hall opened before them, one man of the two who waited within came forth. Short in stature he may have been compared to the rest of his race, but Hugh of Evermue knew without telling that it was he whom they sought.

And in that moment the glare of the gold armour was blinding. Even Tallebois halted, sword drawn, with a score of swords and lances at his back, to stare his fill.

Then suddenly everywhere was blood.

Hogni Tricksleeve came running, knife at the ready. 'Clear off, you daft sod!' Hereward yelled at him. 'Save yourself!'

But Hogni would budge no inch, so Hereward grabbed him by the scruff of his neck and flung him in a cupboard beneath the stairs and shot the bolt. Whereupon Hogni hurled himself against the door, beating on it with his two fists until they were red-raw and wailing to be loosed. But without the fight was raging so fiercely and such was the noise that all Hogni's wails went for naught.

And when at long last he ceased to beat and lay swooned and

crumpled at the crack, there came the voices – cursing, groaning, and the grunts and thuds and pants as of wild beasts.

'Splendour of God!' Ivo Tallebois gulped air, surveying the shambles. Sweat was running down his face.

Wiping his sword, Robert of Deeping cried, 'The dogs died hard. There'll be honours for us.'

'Eh, Bones of Christ,' whispered Drogo de Beuverie from a cracked throat. 'See there!' And pointing at that which lay on the floor, he crossed himself and stepped back quickly.

Hugh of Evermue looked and saw. The golden armour of the Wake. Truly that coat of rings was ensorcelled! It had defied and blunted their swords as had the rune-encrusted blade of Brain-Biter, and only when Wynter was fallen and Hereward beset on all sides and Brain-Biter's wounding-wand snapped at the hilt had they been able to overpower him – taking ten men to hold him down - stripping the charm-stiff armour from his back that had stung and hissed and scalded their hands and smiting off his head. But not before he had yelled out the barbarous name of his Hag, which had wakened a hundred queer echoes among the ancient black rafters.

And there, tossed of a heap, the elf-links that had been torn and riven apart had begun to move, to coil and crawl and to mend themselves, ring by precious gold ring before their eyes.

The men-at-arms turned and ran at the sight, leaving their dead – six in number – behind, having had all they could stomach of the Hall of Little-Bethlehem-of-the-Rushes.

'Hola!' yelled Robert of Deeping. 'Come back here! Cain-livered rogues.'

'Let the scum flee,' cried Tallebois. 'We don't need them now.'

Then suddenly the storm broke with a mighty clap of thunder and lightning struck the roof tree of the Hall, down to the high-seat, splitting it asunder. The timber walls shook and the window-glass shattered. And those left in possession of the house-place either stood rooted to the spot or else knelt shivering and moaning with fear.

It was something Tallebois never wished to be reminded of. To his shame he'd cowered before the charred seething hulk of the high-seat, his arms over his head.

But being the first to recover himself and look about him, to seize the belt of the Fiann with its wondrous masks of beast and bird, though letting the elf-coat well alone, he saw Raoul de Dol dead, guts ripped

381

out by the Wake's wizard-wrought sword, and the others crouching like men in a trance.

The pain of his wounds gave Tallebois fresh voice, and he shouted, 'The heads. On the gables with them!' He grabbed Hereward's by the hair. 'And his on the highest. A rare feast for the crows. To let those English swine see that their Wake – their darling – is dead!'

And it was three nights later, three nights which had been haunted without end by the howling of a hound, that to the door of the Hall of Little-Bethlehem-of-the-Rushes came a hobgoblinish creature, its teeth broken like a rat gnawed free of its cage, with a bundle under each arm, and who scratched to be let in.

Robert of Deeping, his courage strengthened by wine, looked out but recoiled at the sight of Hogni Tricksleeve carrying two severed heads. 'Sancta Maria!'

Hogni giggled, looking past into the hall, to the stairs, ankle-deep in flowers, and upwards as if to follow movements in the shadowy rafters. Then he said, 'Hast heard yon shuck a-yowling for souls? You'll be dead within a year! I see it!'

Robert of Deeping cried out, 'What babblest of, crazy fool?'

Ivo Tallebois and Drogo de Beuverie stood up from the table, swords in hand. 'God's Belly – what goes on?'

'Some Saxon cullion has stolen the heads!'

Whereat Tallebois and de Beuverie came forth with oaths and iron. But Hogni Tricksleeve only laughed to see them so, and at the sound of his laughter they were abashed.

'I curse you! And your ends will be thus.' Hogni pointed to Robert of Deeping with a bony finger. 'You of the bloody flux!' And to Drogo de Beuverie: 'Testicle-rot!' And finally to Ivo Tallebois: 'You'll end your days childless, raving, a deaf and dumb and blind man!'

They stood in thrall for the space of half a minute before Ivo shouted, 'Heart of Christ! One of you cut the scoundrel down!'

But no move was made and Hogni wiped his nose and with a cackling ran off into the night.

Inside of the twelvemonth both Robert of Deeping and Drogo de Beuverie were dead as Hogni foretold. Ivo Tallebois lived on to commit deeds which earned him the names of Slaughterer and Black Heart and Godless. But die he did without issue, lingering for weeks in a palsied fit unable to see or hear or speak. While from out of his open mouth ran toads and snakes and spiders.

*　　*　　*

382

With the help of Darryl and Young Leofsi, Wor-Will-Be-So dragged the corpses out of the reeds of Witch-Water whence they'd been flung.

'Ah, Hereward, Wynter, my lads!' said the old cunning-man, shedding tears and covering them with his own bell-wether fleece.

And so united with the heads, they bore them back by boat to Croyland.

Ivo Tallebois continued to urge William the King to give money and men for an attack on Croyland, but William hung back. He had since seen the death agonies of Robert of Deeping and Drogo de Beuverie, and Tallebois himself bore the mark of the damned.

'God's Heart and Bowels, you have great lands and halls! Is that not enough?'

And Ivo's dark brown face had flushed and his black eyes glittered. It was on the tip of his tongue to say, Look at what you have, but even then you are not satisfied. Eh, and still you lust for more! Instead he said no word and flung out of the court.

At Croyland almost daily they awaited the attack of the Normans but it never came.

In time Countess Godgyfu died and was buried with Earl Leofric, and Darryl took the robe of black burel worn by Lilla and Young Leofsi.

Muirgheal lived for a long time after Hereward and was remembered by men many years hence as the Spell-Spinner or the Old Woman of the Hands.

It was said that Hwita Clatter-Clogs set off in the search for another soul for his harp, and whether he found it or not was never told, but they never saw him again.

And of Hogni Tricksleeve and Wor-Will-Be-So? Of Wulfric the Heron or the fleet-hoofed Mare Swallow? Maybe they are there still. Like the Thickmost Shoe and the Buttercup Fields of the Moon.

Maybe . . .

Who knows?

The Stones of Darkness

en years have passed and it is the Christmas court held at Gloucester. William the King, vast of girth and ageing, sits in gloomy and bitter state. Queen Matilda is dead and Odo the Concubine-Keeper, for his base treachery, imprisoned in Normandy.

One by one in bloody succession William has warred against Maine and Brittany and Anjou and the cost of maintaining the mercenary troops for his endless continental ventures is so enormous that even the Great Geld levied twice-yearly from the whole of England cannot begin to pay for it.

His sheriffs have told him that there is no more money to be got. That there has been a winter of pestilence and storms and famine.

'Belly of God,' William roars at them. 'What care I for that? I need gold and gold I shall have!'

And so a Great Book is to be commissioned in order that the King may claim his dues from every garden and fishpond, on every plough and pig from every corner of the country. Nothing must be allowed to slip through his fingers.

And the English, reduced to mass serfdom and excluded for ever from having any share in Church or State, call the Great Book Domesday. End of the World.

Through smoking, rancid tallow-keech William looks round on his barons gathered for that Christmastide. By now there are eleven hundred and fifteen castles built in England. Wise, yes, to subjugate that Saxon creaturehood, but in some of these castles the lords are growing mighty bold and even tilting at his own power.

Take Hugh of Avranches, his chief vassal and Earl of Chester, so grossly fat now he can hardly crawl. Or the scheming Bigods of Norfolk. The violent de Warennes of Surrey and Sussex. Then there are the de

384

Montgomeris of Shrewsbury and Arundel, feared by all for the blood lust and madness that runs rampant in them.

Try their hand against me, would they? And William watches them and they in their turn watch him. He trusts no one, least of all his own kin. Had not Odo plotted against him and the plot been discovered? Nay – not even his sons born in wedlock can he be sure of. The eldest, Robert, called the Curt-Hose, weak-brained and impatient for power, has rebelled and led armies against him, ravaging to and fro across Normandy. But he has made his peace with Robert – for the time being. His second son Richard is dead. This leaves his namesake the Rufus of unnatural vice, amusing himself with his catamites. And the sly, greedy Henry, the youngest. Eh, such a brood for a man to beget! Mald, truly your womb has brought forth the very Devil!

And so it is now early in the following year – one and twenty since the Great Battle – as the Book of Domesday begins to be compiled and the villages to be torn to shreds by the Norman clerks – that William prepares to go on a new campaign to take advantage of a change of fortune in the French Vexin, where the country of Meulan had passed by marriage to his ally, Robert of Beaumont.

When his adversary, Philip of France, marches on the Duchy, William retaliates by taking and sacking Mantes on the Seine – capital of the French Vexin – and thus it is while riding through the smoking ruins that he is thrown against the pommel of his saddle and suffers a ruptured gut.

In agony he is forced to retire to Rouen and there, finding the injury worsened, he is borne to the Priory of St Gervase overlooking the city.

It does not take the vultures long to gather, foremost among them William's son Henry. On finding that his lot is five thousand pounds of silver, he immediately sets to weigh it out lest he be cheated, oblivious of his father who lies dying.

It is clear to all who watch through the long hours – and they are many – that the death of their suzerain is not to be an easy one.

They hear he has repented and agreed that Odo his half-brother should be released. But not Wulfnoth Godwincsson nor Morkere Aelfgarsson.

'Mercy, O, Sire!' whispers Guntard, Abbot of Jumieges. 'For the good of your soul!' But to no avail. Wulfnoth and Morkere are to stay prisoners.

By the time Robert and William Rufus come to their father's

bedside, Henry has already made off with his hoard of silver. And when they learn of their portions – Robert's being Normandy and William Rufus's being England – they rush to secure their inheritances without so much as a backward glance.

As the night comes William grows afraid and begs for candles to be lit. And he begins to talk of things long past and of people long dead. Sometimes he rambles feverishly, others his speech is clear. He confesses and is given absolution, but still he cannot find peace.

A scribe is sent for, got from his bed with much muttering and ill-grace, and thus with pen and parchment, as the King's tortured words pour forth, he writes them down.

'But I couldn't get them all,' the scribe says to his fellows afterwards, 'for he tossed and raved so, twice knocking over the candles. Crying and pleading for God's mercy, he was – bewailing the countless thousands who he'd killed by sword and fire in England . . .' The scribe smiles sourly, secretly to himself, thinking of the costly ring in his belt, removed with care from the hand of his suzerain in one of the rare moments he'd slept. 'Would you believe that the tears were rolling down his face? I am stained by the rivers of blood I have shed – those were his very words. Eh, truly he feared to meet his Maker!'

It is early the next day when William dies and the chamber is straightaway looted, and his body, not yet cold, left lying naked on the floor.

A great funeral is held at Caen amidst a town fire, and his youngest son Henry attends the service in the Abbey of St Etienne.

Just then a man comes forward to complain that he has been robbed of the burial plot and demands payment. And as they haggle, the stone coffin is found to be too small. Thus with much struggling, the heavy, unwieldy body is jammed into the coffin, whereupon it bursts open, filling the place with a terrible stench. And mourners and clergy alike flee from the Abbey, the latter tossing holy water as they go.

The Perishing of the Kindred Tree

ow the Tapestry is almost complete and the beautiful colours of crimson and green and gold and violet and blue are all used up. Left are those of black and of brown and grey that are the threads of the Web of Wyrd and they must be spun and told.

Nine and sixty years have passed since the Great Battle, and all the people whose tale has been woven are dead. And it is now the time of the War of the Barons in England.

There is dire famine and pestilence, misery and oppression. And in the hidage of the Tomsaetan, as across the rest of the country, you might go a whole day's journey and never find anyone occupying a village or the land tilled.

Thus two seigneurs, bound from Bourne-by-Holy-Brook, are riding with their company, and happen to pass by way of Strawberry Wood. There are some peasants, filthy, stunted, verminous creatures, most of them, digging for roots to eat. When they see the approaching horsemen they flee into the forest in terror.

One seigneur, a Norman, says, 'My grandfather told me that they had once been a race of giants. Scarce a man under six foot tall. Now look at what is left of them.'

And wrinkling his nose with distaste, his Breton companion answers, 'But still they survive!'

Then the Norman's eye is caught by one man who has not run and hidden. He is bigger than the others usually to be seen, a throwback of his accursed race. He has been gathering wood. Peasants are allowed only one small bundle of dead twigs and are forbidden on pain of castration to cut wood. He has cut both wood and twigs – enough for six faggots.

The Norman hails him, but the ignorant hog can understand no word. Three men-at-arms are sent to drag the Englishman to where the seigneurs sit their horses. Close to they see he is a strapping brute, blond, and if pock-fretton, handsome enough under the grime, and wide-shouldered.

Proud too. Eh, by the Heart of Christ! He has the nerve to hold up his head in their presence.

'Filthy pig of a Saxon!' says the Norman. 'Stealing wood! My wood!' And he strikes the man full hard in the face. For a moment fierce anger and hatred flares in the blue eyes and the fists clench to retaliate, muscles flexing under the rags, and he makes utterances in his queer and ancient tongue.

After they have hanged him, the Breton asks of his Norman friend, 'What did he say?'

'How should I know? I cannot speak their language!'

But another in the company enlightens them. 'Why, he said all this land once belonged to his great-grandfather – some Saxon knave of Wyntering!' And they shrug and ride on.

Of the Hall of Little-Bethlehem-of-the-Rushes only the black bog oak walls remain. The crucks and the backbone of the roof, the great beams, elf-forsaken, are fallen in.

Fool's cap and bindweed and hen-bells have the house-place, while goblin plants clamber over the broken pillars of the high-seat, and the cornfields are strangled by beggary.

The Book of Domesday records it not.

But it is at sunset or perhaps in the morning times, early, before the dawn, when the wind blows, rippling the slad all lashy, that the birds still come flocking by way of Powt Hole and Whaplode Fleet as they have always done. Returning to Leofric Country, in the hidages of the ancient tribes, scattered now, that were the lands of their ancestors. And there to circle and to wheel and to cry for it all, and to gather upon the waters of Swan Mere that was once the Place of Gulls.

GLOSSARY OF TERMS

alder-liefest   the dearest of all things
amber   a measure of weight
baggage-wain   a laden wagon
balas-ruby   a red spinel; a semi-precious gem
balister   a machine used in siege warfare
bandy-match   a precursor of field hockey
bee skep   a beehive
besom   a broom made of twigs
black ice   hard-packed ice
boggart   having to do with goblins
bogle-shotten   cursed, e.g., by hobgoblins
bonka   very good, very fine
boon-work   overtime at the harvest
bor   a term of friendship; a pal
bower-thane   a household official
bulace   a large, plum-like fruit
burel   a kind of cloth
byre   an animal pen
cailleach   a hag, witch
canaille   rabble, riffraff
cara   a friend
chair-bodger   a chair mender
chamfron   a horse's trappings; a protective cloth
clogger   a shoemaker
coystril   a rogue, scoundrel
cruck   a support beam in a roof
cucking-stool   old punishment—like the ducking stool
cullion   a good-for-nothing
destrier   a war-horse
docky   a snack

drink-hael   a toast to health

dumpsie-dearie   a strong apple wine

ealdorman   an old title for an earl; a district officer

eel-pout   a dish of cooked eels

ensorcelled   bewitched

Fafnir's hoàrd   the treasure of the legendary Norse dragon slain
    by Sigurd

fen-slodgers   inhabitants of the fenlands; fishers and fowlers

fetch   a doppelganger, ghost

fidchell   an old Irish board game

Fimbul-Winter   the legendary winter beginning three years before
    the end of the world

flittermice   bats

folk-moot   a local tribunal for small cases

foster-lean   an adopted child

frilla   a concubine

fyrd   the army of England

Garm of the Underworld   the Norse hound guarding road to the
    Realm of the Dead

garron   a workhorse

gipsire   a pouch

glaive   a spear used in eel catching

gleemen   minstrels, jongleurs

gongweafre   a spider

gouts   lumps

grapnels   irons used to scale walls during a siege

grigs   eel-baskets

guerdon   a reward

ha-and-hacker   a stammer

hackle-weirs   fisheries

haysel shed   a shed for storing dried hay

hearth-troops   bodyguards

hidage   an area of land belonging to a particular tribe

Holy Rood   the Cross

hot-pot   mulled ale

humming-beer   a honey-sweetened beer

hus-carls   bodyguards to a king or earl

infangenetheof   catching a thief red-handed

karum pie   blackbird pie

kirtle   a woman's skirt

knorr   a ship of Scandinavian design

Lammas   Harvest Festival for bread taking place on August 1st

lampads   lamps

lashy watery
Laws-a-massy-me! Lord have mercy on me!
levies armies of the English shires
liriconfancy lily-of-the-valley
lur a trumpet-like instrument
lyke-wake a deathwatch
malvoisie a sweet wine
mancus a measure of worth
mass-thane a priest
mattler an equal, match
mavoureen an Old Irish term of affection
mere a lake, pond
mickle much, deep
midden a dungheap
molly a foolish one
morning-gift a husband's gift to his wife the morning after their
    wedding
mouze to mope around
muckle a good quantity
mulct punishment
musha! "go on with you!"
nithing a term of contempt; worthless one
nixies water fairies
Nut Crack Night Halloween
Old Skrat the Devil (whence "Mr. Scratch")
ouche a jeweled brooch
ousel a blackbird
paigles cowslips
paten a dish for holding bread for mass
perche a measurement of length
piskie laugh a goblin-laugh
Plough Stots a country dance celebrating the New Year
rascailles rabble
reeve a local administrator, sheriff
sak and soke a landowner's rights
scalder scattering, shimmering
scrimasaxe a battle-axe
scrips a pouch or purse
scrowge a jammed, jostling crowd
scrying mirror a crystal mirror used for fortune-telling
seax a short-handled sword
select-fyrd a militia
sempects over a hundred years old

391

sennight   seven days
sestier   a measure of weight
shanny   a fool, simpleton
Shire-Moot   a court of law held every six months
Shuck   the Black Shuck; spectral hound; Odin's dog
shywanicking   boisterous play
skald   a bard, poet
skerrie   a flat-bottomed boat
slad   marshy ground
sprang-work   a crotchet-like handicraft
staller   a household office
sumpter-mule   a beast of burden
tatterdemalion   rags, patchwork
teazle   a thistle-like plant used in woolmaking
thane   a man of rank
theow   a slave
Thrithings   the three ancient divisions of land in north of England
thrymsas   the coinage of Northumbria
thursehole   a hole where goblins lived
Tiddy Ones   Spirits of the Flowers
trug   a basket
tumbril   a cart
unhouseled   not shriven; unconfessed
vair   a squirrel-like animal
vavasour   a vassal, feudal tenant
wapentake   literally, "grasping weapons"; division of shires according to the Danish system
wattle-weave   fence-making
weal   sorrow
Wear   river of Northern England
Web of Wyrd   Web of Fate
wer-geld   a monetary estimate of a man's worth based on rank
whimbrel   a marsh bird; curlew
Whinny Moor   the Bridge of the Dead in Northern England
widdershins   backwards, unlucky
wind-egg   an empty egg
wisha!   "well!"
Witenagemot   Great Council of England
word-hoard   speech, vocabulary
Yeth-Hounds   ghost dogs

GLOSSARY OF NAMES

Of the House of Leofric and of the Fen Country and   Emhain Abhlach

Earl Leofric, 'Shelterer of Men'   *Dear Ruler*
Countess Godgyfu, 'the Seelie'   *Gift of God*
Aelfgar, son of Leofric   *Elf-Spear*
Hereward, son of Leofric, 'the   *Guardian of the Army*
   Changeling'

Wynter, son of Ceawlin   *Friend-of-the-Ashwood*
Darryl, the Offspring   *Beloved*
Young Leofsi   *Dear One*

Rudgang Wolf-Cloak the   *Battle-Icicle*
   Marshal
Lilla the Chaplain   *Lily-of-the-Valley*
Old Wor-Will-Be-So of Hart's   *Cunning-Man and Blood-Charmer*
   Booze
Aethelmaer the Blacksmith   *Noble-Famous*

Hogni Tricksleeve   *Holy*

Muirgheal   *Sea-Sheen*

Of the House of Godwine

Countess Gytha, widow of   *War-Harp*
   Godwine the Land-Father
Queen Aldwyth, Lady of the   *Old Prophecy*
   English

Harold, son of Godwine, 'the Ruthful'	*Army-Power*
Tostig, son of Godwine, 'Whitsun-Born'	*Battle-Tusk*
Gyrth, son of Godwine	*Much-Loved*
Leofwine, son of Godwine	*Dear-Friend*
Ragnhild, daughter of Godwine	*Counsel-Maid*
Wulfnoth, son of Godwine, 'the Hostage'	*Wolf-Bold*
Gondul, daughter of Godwine	*Rainbow*
Freawaru, daughter of Godwine	*Angel-Peace*
Menglad the foster-lean	*Necklace-Glad*
Haakon Sweynsson the foster-lean	*High-Race*

Of the Hearth-Troop and Thanes

Modred, Marshal of the Hearth-Troop	*Brave Counsel*
Dagobert, Marshal of the Men of London	*Day-Bright*
Wendelwulf, Marshal of the Men of Kent	*Wandering-Wolf*
Njal Uggarsson the Bower-Thane	*Champion*
Biarki the Horse-Thane	*Little Bear*
Heardwin the Cup-Thane	*Intrepid-Friend*
Torquil the Dish-Thane	*Thor's Cauldron*
Eadnoth the Staller	*Rich-Bold*

Of Nazeing and the Holy Mother Church

Eadgyth of the Swan-Neck	*Precious Gift of Gems*
Wulfstan, Bishop of Worcester	*Wolf-Stone*
Ealdfrith the Mass-Thane	*Old Peace*
Aelhhunn the Priest	*All-Honey*
Cwichelm Crook-Back the Child-Master	*Divine Helmet*

394

Cumbra the Monk   *Dove*
Ecgwynn the Altar-Thane   *Sword-Friend*

Of Mercia and the North

Eadwine, son of Aelfgar   *Rich-Friend*
Morkere, son of Aelfgar   *Fair Child*
Eahlswith, daughter of Aelfgar   *White-Blessed*

Waltheof, son of Siward Digre   *Forest-Thief*

The Months
and Feasts of the Year

JANUARY... *The Month of the Wolf*
FEBRUARY ....*The Month of the Bear*
MARCH ....*The Month of the Goddess of Storm*
APRIL .... *The Month of Earth*
MAY.. *The Milk Month*
JUNE...*The Meadow Month or Dry Month*
JULY ....*The Mead Month or Month of Weeds*
AUGUST..*The Rye Month or Month of Barley*
SEPTEMBER ....*The Month of Harvest or Holy Month*
OCTOBER.. *The Wine Month*
NOVEMBER..*The Blood Month*
DECEMBER ....*The Month of Cakes*

THE NIGHT OF THE MOTHERS ....*Christmas Eve*
THE FEAST OF FOOLS...*April 1st*
THE FEAST OF ALL SOULS..*November 2nd*
THE EMBER DAYS ....*Lent, Whitsun and Holy Rood Day*
THE FEAST OF ELDMASS...*October 11th*